Praise for Elizabeth Engstrom

About *The Northwoods Chronicles*:
"*The Northwoods Chronicles* conjured up in me the same excitement and wonder I felt when I read Ray Bradbury's *The Martian Chronicles*. I was taken far away...inside my own heart, my fears, my hopes. I set it down to tend to life; forgot where I put it; got anxious just like Recon John when the monkey jawbone went missing. I finished it, but it's not over: I've been gifted with a life in a strange new world, not without its shadows, and the glimmer of weird on the water. This one is a keeper, and I'm one of its kept. Brava, Elizabeth Engstrom."
—Nancy Holder, author of *Son of the Shadows*

"To read Elizabeth Engstrom is to be guided by the sure hand of an accomplished writer whose stories have the power to transfer readers to places both real and surreal. We believe in the unbelievable, marvel at worlds created between dream and reality, and reach for all that transcends the limits of our imagination."
—Gail Tsukiyama, author of *The Street of a Thousand Blossoms*

"From the ominous opening to the soaring conclusion, these braided stories—subtle and spooky and smart—will keep the reader spellbound.. The Northwoods is a scary place to live, but in Ms. Engstom's hands, it's a fabulous visit."
—Karen Joy Fowler, author of *The Jane Austen Book Club*

"Were he still alive, Rod Serling would like Engstrom's book. Presented separately, each of her narratives would make a great segment of the classic "Twilight Zone" television program so popular in the 1960s. Taken together—and given Serling's absence among us—they give us another way to hold a book in our hands that gives our spines a tingle and makes us wonder if Serling is really so far away after all."
—Eugene Register Guard

About *Baggage Check:*
"The author is so deft at creating interesting, 3D characters that I was instantly hooked into Sweetann's plight (yes, Sweetann). Even the bad guys have depth and lives beyond the story. This is not a typical thriller which makes it much more interesting than the average shoot 'em up, and Sweetann is not a typical heroine. A guaranteed fun time."

– Christina Lay, author of *Death is a Star,* editor at Shadow Spinners Books

About *Black Leather:*
...a darkly seductive page-turner by a writer who knows how to put the erotic thrill into a thriller.

—*DarkEcho*

...an artfully written and highly recommended erotic and psychological suspense from first page to last.

—*Midwest Book Review*

About *Suspicions:*
"This is where she's at her best."

—*Locus*

"A spooky collection of tales."

—*Publishers Weekly*

"A hefty, genre-crossing pie spiced with images capable of snagging the imagination."

—*Booklist*

"Elizabeth Engstrom has selected twenty-five (four original to the collection) stories from the past twenty years of writing that reveal her as a suspicious sort. But then, aren't we all? We all suspect the unknown, death, sex, and "friends, family, love, work, technology, the government, and everything else." It's just that Elizabeth Engstrom can take her lack of trust and craft fine fiction from it. Like many fine writers, Engstrom's stories are across all genres. Some can be termed sf, others as mystery or fantasy or horror, still others are simply "fiction." A few are light and humorous. Most are quietly dark, slightly skewed, angled toward that indescribable place just at the edge of shadow. All are worth reading. Many are worth pondering. By the end, at least one suspicion will definitely be confirmed: Elizabeth Engstrom is one of the best. No doubts."

—*Cemetery Dance*

About *York's Moon*:
"York's Moon is so absorbing and unusual that you'll almost miss how beautifully written it is—almost. Elizabeth Engstrom's mesmerizing and unique style will draw you into a world of mystery, violence and heroic struggle. Ultimately, this story celebrates the uplifting power of the human spirit. Do not miss it."

—Susan Wiggs, bestselling author of *Marrying Daisy Bellamy*

"With quirky, engaging characters, York's Moon is as much about understanding the human condition as solving a murder mystery. I cannot imagine anyone but Liz Engstrom writing this fine novel."

—Terry Brooks, author of the Shannara series

About *Lizzie Borden*:
"Marvelous stuff. The pressures on Lizzie were vivid and completely real. You know, I think I'd have killed him myself..."

—Mercedes Lackey, author of the Heralds of Valdemar series

"Every door in the Borden house is metaphorically locked, and each room holds the terrible secrets of the occupant... Engstrom moves the reader inexorably toward the anticipated savage denouement."

—*Publishers Weekly*

"Elizabeth Engstrom has woven a fascinating tale of a lonely, tormented and frustrated young woman."

—*Rocky Mountain News*

About *Lizard Wine*:

"*Lizard Wine* is the book your mother warned you about, sleek, nasty, perfectly focused, smart as hell, absolutely convincing, and utterly single-minded. This novel wants to buy you a drink, whisper in your ear, coax you into a dark room and there seriously mess you up. Because Elizabeth Engstrom is a magnificently talented writer, her novel not only actually does these things, it leaves you grateful for the experience. *Lizard Wine* is the kind of book which enlarges and enriches the genre of the thriller."

—Peter Straub, author of *Ghost Story*

"...*Lizard Wine* is a book that will make your skin crawl."

—John Saul, author of *The Blackstone Chronicles*

"...hard! Should carry a health warning: Just reading this could leave you bruised..."

—Brian Lumley, author of the Necroscope series

"Excruciating suspense!"

—Bryce Courtenay, author of *The Power of One*

"*Lizard Wine* is a disturbing vintage... With a true literary voice, Elizabeth Engstrom details the madness of human relationships... It is as if Franz Kafka, Tom Robbins and Shirley Jackson collaborated on a story which only Engstrom could write. A brilliant, page-turning read."

—Douglas Clegg, author of *The Children's Hour*

"Supertaut storytelling..."

—*Kirkus Reviews*

"I often stopped with a low mental whistle of awe at Engstrom's seamless style..."

—*DarkEcho*

"...*Deliverance* meets *Misery*..."

—*The Fiction Addiction*

"...Don't read this book alone at night."

—Eugene *Register Guard*

"...The message of Lizard Wine is clear. This could be anybody. This could be you."

—*AmericaOnline*

About *When Darkness Loves Us*:
"Finding the light when swamped in darkness is never an easy thing. *When Darkness Loves Us* is a collection of two novellas from Elizabeth Engstrom. One story follows a young farm girl as she is engulfed by an underworld and yearns to escape, and an old woman who is facing the monsters of her past. Two engaging stories make *When Darkness Loves Us* quite a pick."

—*Midwest Book Review*

"Fresh, inventive, stylish and captivating."

—Dean Koontz

"A moving story of redemption and love."

—*West Coast Review of Books*

"A masterpiece, and one of the finest tragedies I've read in years."

—*Horror Show*

"Behind that soft-voiced style is power, is surprise, is... ferocity."

—Theodore Sturgeon

Books by Elizabeth Engstrom

When Darkness Loves Us
Black Ambrosia
Nightmare Flower
Lizzie Borden
Lizard Wine
The Alchemy of Love
Suspicions
Black Leather
Candyland
The Northwoods Chronicles
York's Moon
Something Happened to Grandma
Baggage Check
How to Write a Sizzling Sex Scene
Benediction Denied
Guys Named Bob

Word by Word (editor, with John Tullius)
Imagination Fully Dilated (co-editor)
Imagination Fully Dilated vol. II (editor)
Dead on Demand (editor)
Pronto! Writings from Rome (editor, with John Tullius)
Ship's Log: Writings at Sea (editor, with John Tullius)
Lies and Limericks (editor, with John Tullius)
Mota 9: Addiction (editor)

Guys Named Bob

a novel by

Elizabeth Engstrom

IFD Publishing
P.O. Box 40776
Eugene, Oregon 97404 U.S.A.
www.ifdpublishing.com

Cover art copyright © 2018 Alan M. Clark
ISBN 978-0-9996656-3-3

Printed in the United States

Guys Named Bob

a novel by

Elizabeth Engstrom

Dedicated to Maggie

MONDAY

It happened at the stop sign, right in front of the Springfield post office on a lovely June day. The passenger door of Darlene Martin's red Ford opened without warning and a skinny young blonde girl with tangled hair and ravenous eyes jumped in.

"Drive," she said.

"What?" Darlene was certain the girl had mistaken her for someone else.

Then the barrel of a gun appeared out of the girl's baggy and torn denim jacket. "*Drive*," she said again.

Darlene's mind emptied of all but the survival basics as her heart pumped down to her foot, which stomped on the gas. Then she let up, which jerked both of them back, and she hit the brakes, which chirped.

"Jesus," the girl said. "Drive normal."

Darlene took a deep breath, tried to collect herself. She looked over again at the gun. And at the girl. The scared, skinny little girl who had a hard time holding the heavy gun in her frail little hand. She was more afraid of Darlene than Darlene was of her. Maybe. Darlene was pretty scared.

She put her hand on her throat for a moment, took another deep breath and made herself relax. She had always wondered how she'd react if confronted with violent crime. She decided she would never give up her money to a creep at an ATM machine. She decided she'd bite somebody's pecker off if they tried to rape her. She decided she wouldn't stand for it, not any of it. Darlene Martin was no victim, and that was a fact.

She eased onto the gas and took another look at the pale girl sitting next to her.

Darlene had kids older than this, kids who had put her through worse than a carjacking, for God's sake. She could handle this. Her heartbeat slowed. She took a comfortable, competent grip on the steering wheel. "Okay," she said. "Where to?"

"Roseburg."

Darlene looked down at the gas gauge. "Not enough gas to get to Roseburg," she said.

"Then get some."

"You have money?"

"No," the girl said, her eyes wider, her nerves tauter, her skin tighter around her eyes and mouth. The cords in her wrist stood out where she gripped the pistol too tightly. "Don't you?" Darlene heard the faint sound of hysteria in her voice.

"Okay, okay, relax," Darlene said, feeling like the adult in charge and therefore oddly in control of the situation. "I just bought stamps, but I think I've got ten bucks."

"Get the gas somewhere else," the girl said, looking behind them. "Out of town somewheres."

"Okay." Darlene turned left and left again toward the I-5 on-ramp. "Did you just rob somebody or something?"

"Just drive," the girl said, her movements jerky, her eyes frantic.

Once on the freeway, the girl seemed to settle down a little bit, letting the gun fall to her knee, but her face was still tight. So young, Darlene thought. So hard.

"Hungry?" Darlene asked as she reached into the back seat.

The gun came up immediately. "What are you doing?"

Darlene grabbed a bag of pretzels from the grocery sack in the back seat. "I'm hungry," she said, and popped the bag open. She set it between the seats. "Help yourself."

"No, thanks."

Darlene munched while she thought.

Who could have imagined this? Who on earth could have predicted that she'd be carjacked on such a beautiful day? Just this morning she had soaked in a long, steamy bath scented with perfumed oils that had dissolved out of little opalescent pearls. She lay in the tub, late morning light coming through the small bathroom window, a candle burning on the lowered toilet lid. Carolyn told her that candle flames have special properties, and every time she thought to light one, she should. She had dripped warm slippery water over her breasts with the sponge while she thought about the long afternoon and evening before her.

Just this morning she had wondered what it would be like to know the future. If she knew with absolute certainty that she was just going to go the post office, buy stamps, come home and watch television, would she even bother to bathe, shave, shampoo? Maybe not. Maybe it was that tiny element of uncertainty—those tiny little surprises that life came up with that kept her grooming herself.

She'd watched her nipples shrivel as the bathroom door opened and cold air swept over them. Little toenails clicked along the bathroom floor, then a tiny white poodle face poked up over the edge of the tub.

"Hi, sweetie," Darlene said. Ashes wagged his little bobbed tail. "I'll be out in a minute."

He got down and clicked away.

But though the house was empty, the bathroom door was now open and her privacy and reverie disturbed. She sloshed more water over herself, liking the feel of her ample body. Would she be ashamed to show this to a new lover?

Perhaps. If she knew she was going to meet a new lover, she wouldn't have eaten that pasta and ice cream the night before. She would exercise more. She would take better care of herself.

Catch 22, she thought. Perhaps if I took better care of myself, then I would find a new lover.

Her fingers toyed with the hair below her belly that waved gently in the bath water. It was not as thick as the pubic hair on some women she'd seen, enviable, dark, thick glossy pubic hair. No, hers was sparse, and, she noticed with dismay, turning gray.

The familiar longing gnawed at her. Pleasure hunger. She could use a lover. All this sweetness going to waste. She wished she knew how to masturbate. She'd tried, but while it had always been moderately pleasurable, it was quite predictable, ultimately boring, and never satisfying.

She ran her hands over her legs, massaging in the hot oil. Then she pulled the plug, stood under the cool shower water and shampooed her hair.

No lover today, she thought. What a shame. What a waste.

As they passed a huge motorhome on the freeway, she pulled

another pretzel from the bag and remembered her morning bath. No lover today, she thought again. Just a carjacking. Maybe she should have masturbated instead of going to the post office.

"What's in Roseburg?"

"Huh?"

"I said, what's in Roseburg? Why are we going there?"

"*Listen*, just don't talk to me, okay?"

"You hijack my car and then you want to be rude to me too?"

The girl rolled her eyes. "Just fucking drive," she said.

Darlene grabbed another handful of pretzels. She didn't think this would be a good time to lecture the girl on her language. "I'm going to get a Diet Coke," she said, and reached to the back seat again. "Want one?"

"No. Yeah. No."

Darlene handed her one and she took it. They popped the tops and drank in silence. "I'm Darlene Martin. Who are you?"

"Don't talk to me."

"You hijack my car, you drink my Diet Coke and we have to drive all the way to Roseburg together, and you won't tell me your name?"

"Call me... call me Ice."

"Ice. Cool name." Darlene smiled at her joke, but the girl just scowled. Darlene remembered, when she was younger, how she wanted people to call her Jet. "How old are you, Ice?"

"Shut up. Just shut the fuck up." The girl waved the gun around. "I don't want to talk to you, and I don't want you talking to me. Just drive. Just drive. Just—"

"Okay. Sorry. I didn't want to upset you. It's just that... Well, I've got kids that are probably your age, and—"

The girl pushed the barrel of the gun up under the folds of one of Darlene's chins. "Shut the fuck up," she said.

Darlene knew the girl wouldn't shoot her while they were doing sixty-five on the freeway. "That means I'm the same age as your mom," she said.

The girl flounced back into her seat. "Of all the cars in Oregon..." she said.

"Yeah, you got lucky." Darlene munched some more pretzels, finished her Diet Coke, threw the empty onto the floor of the back

16

seat.

"Here!" the girl said, and pointed to the Curtin freeway exit. "Pull off here and get gas."

Darlene eased into the right lane, put her turn signal on and glided off the freeway into Curtin. She had the attendant put ten dollars in, then reached for her purse.

She had a vial of pepper spray, but it wasn't in her purse. It was in the coat she wore when she went out at night. Who'd have thought she'd need it going to the Springfield post office at noon?

"Ice" apparently never thought Darlene could have a defensive approach stashed in her purse, because she never gave it a second look when Darlene opened it and extracted her wallet. Nor did she give a thought as to any signal Darlene could give the service station attendant. This kid was a definite amateur.

But Darlene didn't do anything in front of the attendant. She just figured the kid needed a ride to Roseburg, and that would be the end of it.

She was wrong.

She slipped the ten dollar bill out of the window and started the car.

"Go west from here."

"Roseburg is south."

"I know where Roseburg is," the girl said. "And I told you to go west."

"If we do some sightseeing," Darlene said, "that ten dollars isn't going to get us very far, and unless you robbed a bank back there..."

"Go west."

"You da boss," Darlene said, and they started on the winding road toward Reedsport.

Desperate acts, Darlene thought as she munched those good pretzels. What would cause someone so young to be so desperate? She thought of her own children, fat they were, not in the same fleshy way as she, but fat with security, with sense of pride, sense of self, blessings and about as far from desperation as young people get. True, young adulthood is sometimes a moist breeding ground for desperation—uncertain young adulthood and emotionally-charged midlife—but Darlene's two kids were smiling, well-adjusted contributors to society.

She looked over at the pale profile of the young woman who wanted to be known as hard and cold. The stringy, unwashed blonde hair with the darker roots, the dark brown eyes, the nose with the turned up end, the lips that would be pert and sweet with a touch of pink lipstick. She could be beautiful, this girl. This could be Darlene's daughter, with a nice summer dress on, her hair back in a ponytail, bangs cut neatly above the brows and curled slightly, dangling earrings, prattling on about boys and school and such.

It could be. It should be. Life shouldn't be this hard or this burdensome on a child this age. Twenty? Eighteen?

A man. Darlene would bet her life that this girl was being driven to this desperation by some guy. Guys did that to women. Phil had done it to her. But Darlene had been older, and able to resist gun-toting desperation, although it had crossed her mind more than once.

"Okay, okay, okay," the girl said. "Slow down."

"Slow down?" They were only doing forty.

"See that old car?"

The rusted white rear end of some kind of small foreign car protruded from the underbrush at the side of the road.

"Yeah."

"Turn there."

"There? I thought we were going to Roseburg. Or Reedsport."

"Just turn in there."

Darlene didn't like the looks of this at all. Her security and superiority as pilot of the vehicle was about to be jeopardized. She didn't know what was back in that hollow in the woods, and didn't care to find out. She turned the corner, got off the main road and stopped the car.

"Keep going."

"I'm not driving you in there."

"Keep going," the girl said, and brought the muzzle of the gun back up.

Looking down the barrel of a gun was every bit as unsettling as she had always heard it was. "No," Darlene said. "You needed a ride and you got one."

"I didn't need a ride, you stupid cow," the girl said. "I need a car. Now drive on back there or I swear to God I'll shoot you and leave you to die in the weeds."

Darlene looked deep into the brown of this girl's eyes. That unfathomable desperation. No telling where it came from, no telling what it would do. She decided she could believe that this girl would do that very thing. Men can make women do unimaginable things.

She stepped on the gas and drove the car slowly down the rutted road, though a thick tangle of brush, across a rickety wooden bridge that spanned a wide, slow-moving creek, and on up a weed-choked path that hadn't seen the tires of a vehicle in years. Giant drops fell from the overhead trees to smat on the windshield. Farther along, ferns and bushes brushed both sides of her car as she drove slowly along, afraid for the paint job, afraid she would have to back up all the way back down, afraid she would get stuck, afraid of what was at the end of this godforsaken road.

The brush opened out and they kept driving through a stretch of graveled road, across a wide open field. The road ascended again, into the hills, and Darlene could see that it led directly to another wooded area.

She drove slowly and carefully. She didn't like this, she didn't like this at all.

The girl sat forward on the edge of the seat, gun in her lap, one hand on the dashboard. She was excited. Darlene drove slowly and steadily. The sun disappeared as they entered the woods. Weeds scratched again at the sides of her car. They closed in, and the road became less of a road and more of a rutted path.

Then she drove through a hole in a thick blackberry bramble and there it was. A cabin. A light curl of smoke slipped out of the chimney, but that was the only nice thing about it. It was a shack, now that she looked at it, its exterior half-shingled, and half tar-papered. Old rusted hulks of vehicles, some cars, some trucks, some machinery, all overgrown with ivy, blackberry brambles, and weeds littered the area. A bathtub and a toilet were set out under one tree, what seemed like hundreds of wooden boxes filled to overflowing with silver and rust-colored parts of things were stacked everywhere. Four television sets, one atop the other had been targets for some instrument of destruction, probably the pistol the girl had in her hand, wood was piled haphazardly in a half dozen spots, the moss-covered roof sagged in the middle and a portion of a rusty gutter funneled water from one sagging corner down and away from what must be the front door.

A yellow dog came wandering out from somewhere, and looked at Darlene with tired brown eyes and white muzzle. An old dog.

"Park over there," the girl said, and Darlene obeyed, pulling the car between a rusted truck body and an enormous stash of beer bottles whose cardboard cases had rotted in the rain and slumped over. She put the car in park and the girl snatched the keys from the ignition. "Wait here."

Darlene sat for a moment, listening to the sounds of the Oregon forest. She turned and watched the girl walk through the wet knee-high weeds in her dirty white tennis shoes.

The best defense is a good offense, Darlene thought, and opened the car door, heaved her bulk out and dusted off the pretzel crumbs. She walked slowly toward the door that had closed crookedly behind the girl.

Water seeped in to her little black slippers and she wondered how long she'd have to be with wet feet. Maybe they didn't really need a car. Maybe she'd just get her keys back and go home. She wanted to go home. She didn't want to stay here.

The dog came up to her and wagged its long tail slowly. Darlene patted its head, then scratched it between the ears. He closed his eyes and relished the attention. But he was dirty, and smelled like dog, and Darlene was sorry she had touched him, because now she needed to wash her hands.

The steps up to the porch were round slices of tree, and they were slippery with moss. A Grateful Dead bumper sticker held the ripped screen to its frame in the door, which didn't close by at least five inches. Darlene looked through it and saw the girl talking with a young man. He was backed up against the kitchen counter, she was leaning against him.

I knew it, Darlene thought. A man made her do this. And here he is in the flesh.

"I got us a car, Patrick, I got us a car. We can go now, right? C'mon, babe, let's go."

Patrick had a beer bottle in one hand and the other on the girl's shoulder. He looked up as the sagging porch creaked under Darlene's weight.

"Who is that?"

Darlene considered that an invitation. "Darlene Martin," she said, opened the door and stepped in.

Patrick looked at the girl. "You brought a *stranger* here?"

The girl looked at the floor. Shrugged. "You know I don't drive."

Patrick looked confused.

"She stole my car," Darlene said. "And I came with it."

"I thought I told you to stay in the car," the girl said.

Patrick pushed her away from him. He looked at her, then shook his head in speechless amazement. He held his hands up for quiet, then looked at Darlene, then looked back at the girl. "You stole her and her car?" he finally said.

"At gunpoint," Darlene added.

"At *gunpoint*?"

The girl began to back up, away from him. "You said we could leave here if we had a car, babe. I was only thinking about you, about us, you know."

Darlene relaxed as soon as she realized the girl had acted of her own miserable accord. This wasn't any kind of a band of merry thieves, it was just a couple of poor trashy kids eking out an existence, a bad existence, in the Oregon woods.

The kitchen was a mess. Dirty dishes were piled up everywhere, the floor hadn't been mopped in ages. An old wooden cookstove was perking along, and Darlene enjoyed the meager heat coming from it, although it wasn't a cold day. This cabin was cold, probably was always cold except maybe in the August heat.

Darlene wanted to sit down, but she didn't trust the rickety chairs, and besides that, they were filthy. The whole place was filthy. All it needed were a couple of chickens nesting on the couch and a baby trailing a messy diaper and it could be a real cartoon. It smelled sickly sweet, a smell she couldn't quite define, but probably had to do with the rotting floorboards.

And there was some kind of buzzing noise coming from the somewhere else in the place.

Patrick set his beer bottle down on the edge of the kitchen table. He spoke slowly and carefully to the girl, almost as if he were talking to a child. "I want you to go into the bedroom and wait for me there. Do not come out. I'll come in when I'm ready."

She obeyed without a word. She walked through a doorway on

21

the far side of the room and went around the corner.

Patrick, she saw, was only a little bit older than the girl, perhaps twenty-five. He was tall and lean, his hair short and neat. He had dark blue eyes and thin, almost feminine eyebrows that arched gracefully over each eye. His jeans were torn, but not dirty, his shirt, while not ironed, was not wrinkled and he wore it neatly tucked in, buttoned all the way to the collar, long sleeves buttoned at the cuff, looking modestly and incongruously formal. He was clean shaven and his eyes were clear and bright. When he smiled, he showed big, beautiful, straight teeth, the kind of teeth that had seen expensive care while he was growing up.

He leaned back against the sink, then ran his hands over his head. He crossed his arms over his chest and looked up at Darlene, gave her that dazzling smile. "I'm so sorry," he said.

"Then just give me my keys and I'll be on my way," Darlene said, "and I'll just think of it as giving her a ride home."

"Well, you know, that's the worst part of it," he said. "I surely do appreciate your generous offer there, I surely do, but now that you're here..." he shrugged. "Molly and me, we need that car."

"Come on, Patrick," Darlene said. "Don't make this into a lot of trouble for yourselves—for all of us. There are other ways to get a car without kidnapping at gunpoint and grand theft auto."

Patrick picked the beer up off the table and took its last swallow. "Beer?" he offered her as he turned to the fridge for a refill.

"No, thanks."

He unscrewed the cap on the fresh one and threw it in the general direction of the overflowing trash. "What if we gave you a ride back home and then kept your car? You could phone it in as stolen—give us a couple of days until we could get out of the state—and we would have us a nice car and you could collect on the insurance."

Darlene was unprepared for this brash proposal. She had to be careful here, she didn't want to antagonize these people, but she didn't want to damage herself, either.

"Well," she said, "first of all, that makes me an accessory. It would be an incredible inconvenience, and my insurance rates would go up. I can't see any reason why I would want to do that."

Patrick looked down into his beer bottle and nodded. "Yeah," he said. "I see your point. Why don't you wait here for a while and we'll go talk about it."

Darlene nodded.

"Sit down or something," he said, then he walked into the back room.

The buzzing stopped. Darlene heard voices. She could hear the girl's voice, she could hear Patrick's voice, and she heard another voice, a lower voice. Another man was here. Her heart pumped. An unknown quantity, yet to be reckoned with. She wished she had a big sloppy jelly donut.

But she didn't.

She looked around. This place was awful. There was no place she wanted to sit. She didn't want to stand. Her hands still smelled like dog, but she didn't want to wash them in that sink full of moldy dishes.

She was nervous, and she didn't know what to do with herself.

A brand new yellow sponge drew her attention like a beacon. It was still wrapped in plastic, leaning up against a grimy bottle of blue Dawn dishwashing soap.

She walked over to it, pushing up her sleeves. Before she knew it, she had a sink full of sudsy water, and was washing all those nasty dishes, cleaning up the table and wiping down the counters and surfaces.

Voices still murmured in the back room. Once, she thought she felt eyes on her back, and she was certain that someone had come to the doorway to see what she was doing, but she didn't stop. She just kept washing and cleaning. Let them look.

It was a tremendous task. It took four sinks of sudsy water. Took what seemed like hours. But when she was finished, all the dishes were washed and dried and stacked on a clean kitchen table. All the rotten, torn and curling Formica countertops were wiped down, as was the stove and the front of the refrigerator. Perspiration stuck a few wild gray hairs to her forehead, and her middle was wet in a horizontal line that matched the height of the countertop.

She dried her hands on the last clean dishtowel, hung it over the back of a chair, then opened the refrigerator and helped herself to a beer.

She thought the clean kitchen would make the place look better, but it didn't. It just made the rest of the house look rattier. The filthy kitchen somehow fit right in with the ambience of the place; the clean kitchen made her want to clean up the rest. The floor was crusty with food and mud and nastiness. It would take a dozen moppings and some work with a putty knife to get it clean. The windows were covered with cobwebs and spiderwebs and dust and dirt and who-knows-what that had been splashed on, sprayed over and wiped on over the years. The sills were deep in detritus. And the garbage.

Patrick came around the corner and stopped, stunned.

Darlene leaned back against the refrigerator so he could get a good view of the whole area. Her fingers were pruny and she had soaked off most of her fresh nail polish. She wished she had some hand lotion.

"Clean up that garbage, Patrick," she said.

"Yes ma'am." He pulled a box of plastic trash bags from under the sink, shook out a couple and began putting the trash into them.

While he was doing that, the girl came around the corner, and stopped with much the same kind of stunned look on her face.

"How come you can't keep the kitchen like this?" Patrick asked her. "Look what a trash heap this place has turned out to be. It wasn't this way before you came along."

"Not my job," she said. "You all just thought that because I was a woman, I ought to be cleaning up after you. I do my share."

"You don't do shit." Patrick hefted two black plastic sacks and slammed out the cabin door with them, leaving one more in the corner.

"You take that one out," Darlene said.

"So you're giving the orders around here?"

"I'm giving that order."

The girl gave her a look that was so familiar to Darlene that it made her want to backhand the little smartmouth. That look of defiance had seemed to be permanently etched on the face of Darlene's teenage daughter during those years of raging hormones and puberty out of control.

But the girl picked up the bag and carried it outside. She set it on the porch, then came back inside.

"Now put these here dishes away," Darlene said.

"Kiss my ass," the girl said.

"Come on, now. I washed them and dried them and stacked

them all nice. I'd put them away except that nobody would be able to find anything afterwards. Come on." Darlene picked up a stack of dinner plates. "Where do these go?"

With that same, typical, burdened teenage posture, the girl slumped over to the cupboard and opened it.

Darlene held her tongue. Within a couple of minutes, all the dishes were put away.

Patrick pulled out a chair, turned it around and straddled it. "This is more like it," he said, looking around. He put his hands on the clean kitchen table. "This is how it's supposed to be, Molly."

"Molly?" Darlene said with a smile. "That's a nice name. Much better than Ice."

"Shut up," Molly said.

"I hate it when you get your attitude in an uproar like this," Patrick said. "I do enough around here, you know that."

Molly hung her head.

"You could do a few things now and then."

Molly looked down at her hands, then pulled out a chair and sat down, too.

Darlene ached to sit in a chair, her knees hurt, her back hurt from standing so long doing the dishes, but she still didn't trust those rickety chairs.

"Sit down," Patrick invited.

"I don't like the looks of those chairs," she said.

Patrick jumped up and went into the other room, and when he returned he was carrying a sturdy captain's chair, with a round back, arms, and a little pad on the seat. He set it down, then bounced it a couple of times. "Sturdy."

She smiled and squeezed herself into it. Her legs and feet were grateful.

She finished her beer, then looked at her watch. "You know, it's time I got on home."

Patrick frowned, looked down at his hands again. "Well now," he said, "we've got a problem in that area."

Oh boy. Here we go again. "What's the problem?"

"Leathers," Patrick said. "Leathers says we keep the car."

"Who's Leathers?"

"He's..." Patrick nodded toward the open doorway that led to

25

the back room. "He's back there."

"Well, what business is it of his?"

"We owe him," Patrick said.

"I don't owe him," Darlene said. "Why do you think you need to pay him with my car?"

"Because we have it."

"Just give me the keys and I'll be out of your hair," Darlene said. "Find another way to pay whatshisname."

"Leathers."

"Leathers. What kind of a name is that, anyway?"

"I don't know," Patrick said. "I think it's because of what he does."

"What does he do?"

The buzzing in the back room stopped. Darlene had become so accustomed to it that she hadn't noticed it until it stopped.

Patrick and Molly both looked at their hands like naughty children.

Molly reached over and grabbed the sleeve of Patrick's shirt. He pulled away from her grip, smoothed his shirt, then leaned over to hear what she had to say. "Let's get out of here, Patrick," she whispered. "Let's go now."

Fear, real fear flushed through Darlene. This guy had a hold on these kids, and he was the fuel for Molly's desperation, not this Patrick kid. Whoever was in the back room, whatever he was, Darlene didn't want to deal with him at all. She wanted to go home. "Take me with you," Darlene whispered.

"Patrick?" Molly whined.

"Come *on*," Darlene said, conspiratorially. "Let's go now."

"Wouldn't be right," Patrick said.

Molly hit him hard on the arm. "Pussy," she said.

"It's not right to steal my car, Patrick," Darlene said.

"There are levels of right and not right," Patrick said, looking directly at Darlene. "Taking your car is not as bad as running out on Leathers. Not after all he's done for me."

"Yeah?" Molly said. "What?"

"You have no idea."

"That's right, Patrick," she said. "I have no idea. I have seen what he's done *to* you, but I haven't seen a thing that he's done *for* you."

"That's enough," Patrick said.

"I have no idea whatsofuckingever as to why you're so loyal to him. None. Seems to me there are other things you ought to be concerning yourself with, rather than that kind of weird loyalty. It's weird is what it is, Patrick, it's weird."

"Enough," Patrick said again, but Molly had already said her piece.

Silence descended on the table like a blanket. Darlene could feel Leathers' presence as clearly as if he had been sitting at the table with them. Was he listening to them?

Molly chewed a fingernail. Patrick thumbed perspiration from his beer bottle. Darlene cleared her throat. "All I know is that I've got a dog and a cat at home that need to be let out and fed. They're overdue."

"Can you call someone?" Patrick said.

"Call someone? No. I want to go home. Don't keep me here. Listen, Patrick, you're a smart boy. I'm telling you that if you give me my keys, I'll just go on home and chalk this day up to adventure. I gave Molly here a ride home, cleaned up your kitchen a little bit, visited with you and then went on home. If you keep me here, boy, you're asking for a heap of trouble that I don't think you want."

Patrick kept wiping the water off his beer.

"Let's have her take us to the freeway, babe," Molly said. "We can catch a ride. It's a good time for Arizona, you know? It won't be too hot yet. It's still June, isn't it? We can go to Arizona, remember, like we talked about? Patrick?"

A chair groaned and creaked in the back room. Tense silence grew in the kitchen. Darlene heard footsteps and shufflings back there, and then a voice.

"Patrick."

A deep voice, a dry voice.

Patrick jumped up so fast he almost spilled his beer. Without making eye contact with either Darlene or Molly, he went into the back room.

Darlene heard voices.

"What's the deal?" she whispered to Molly.

Molly just shook her head. Shrugged her shoulders and then shook her head again.

In a moment, Patrick was back, jangling like a puppet. "C'mon, Molly," he said. "We're going to the store." He tore the box top off the corn flakes and rooted around in a drawer for the stub of a pencil. "Here," he said as he handed it to Darlene. "Write down the number of who you want us to call to tend to your animals."

"You're leaving me here alone?"

"Just write it down," Patrick said. "Please. Don't cause no trouble now, and let's get them animals cared for." He pushed the box top and pencil toward her. "Please."

She wrote down her ex-husband's name and phone number. He had a key to her house. "Just tell him to take the dog and cat home with him," she said. "I can't be worried about them. Tell him I'll call him when I can."

Patrick grabbed up the paper. "Thanks. Uh... What was your name again?"

"Darlene."

"Darlene." He wrote that under Phil's phone number, and Darlene saw that he had that architect's way of writing. This boy had draftsman training. He was no dummy.

"C'mon," he said to Molly, and they went out the door.

Darlene stood up, and when she did, she found she brought the chair up with her. It took her a moment to free herself. "Don't leave me here alone," she said.

"You're not alone," Leathers said.

Darlene whipped around at the sound of his voice. His bulk filled the doorway. He was a big man, but more than that, he was flat-out astonishing. She'd never seen anything like him before. She stared and stared, even though she knew she was being rude. Eventually, her eyes found his and she slowly started to smile.

Phil began running up the back steps on the phone's third ring. Angela was letting it go to voicemail; she must be with the baby. The door slammed behind him and he grabbed for the kitchen extension.

"Hello? Hello?"

"Is this Phil?"

"Yes." He grabbed at the knot in his tie and loosened it.

"Darlene asked me to call you."

"Darlene? Yes?"

"She won't be home tonight and wanted you to pick up the animals so they can go out and be fed and stuff."

"Her animals? Darlene won't be home tonight? Who is this?"

"Um, this is just a friend."

"Friend? What kind of a friend? What's your name?"

"Patrick."

"Where is Darlene?" Phil felt an irritation begin to grow. An irritation that felt like fear.

Pause. "Camping."

"Camping? Where? With who?"

"With us. We're down in, um, Roseburg. Camping. I just came up to the store for some more food and she remembered she forgot to ask you to care for her animals while she was gone."

"How long is she going to be... camping?" Phil unbuttoned the top button of his dress shirt. Something wasn't right.

"Hard to say."

"Patrick what? What did you say your last name was?"

"Will you feed her animals?"

"Yes, of course."

The line clicked and a dial tone came on.

Phil stood for a moment, phone in hand. This was not right. *This was not right.*

"Who was it, hon?" Angela called from the living room.

"It was about Darlene," Phil yelled back.

"Darlene?"

"Yes."

"What did she want?"

"No, it was *about* Darlene."

"Darlene?"

"Yes."

"What did she want?"

"Just shut up," Phil said softly, and put the phone down. He hung up his suit coat in the hall closet and grabbed his jacket. He walked into the living room, where Angela, looking pert and perfect as always, was folding towels. Peaches gave him a gap—toothed grin and toddled over to him, her hands in the air. Phil lifted her high, heard her giggle and squeal, kissed her loudly and noisily on the cheek, then set her down again. She hugged his knee.

"Hi," Angela said.

"Hi." He kissed her on her proffered cheek. "I'm going to run over to Darlene's for a minute," he said. "Need anything?"

"Nope," she said, and he admired her slim firm butt as she bent over to pick up the stack of towels from the sofa.

"Back in a few," he said, and went to fetch Darlene's animals.

When Phil and Darlene divorced, they sold the family home in Springfield. Darlene bought the little two-bedroom house she lived in with her dog and her cat, and Phil and Angela bought a house east of Springfield, just far enough away from Darlene that they wouldn't likely be running into each other all the time, although it would be fine with Phil if they did. Phil felt only sadness when he thought about Darlene. He'd hurt her, hurt her badly, but she was a trooper, and it wasn't long before they were back on friendly terms. Phil and Darlene maintained a fine relationship, but Angela didn't share the affection.

Angela was never rude to Darlene, and Angela understood that Phil and Darlene had the two kids that would bind them together forever, but Angela was very young and literally the new kid on the block. She was like the little dog who put her hair up to seem bigger.

Hell, Phil wouldn't want to be in Angela's position. Angela was only a year older than Lari, his daughter. For Angela to inherit those two stepkids under these circumstances, well... she was doing all right with it, Phil had to hand it to her.

Darlene was no prize, Phil thought. She wasn't very nice looking and she had become terribly heavy, but she was a good woman with a good heart. Angela couldn't see beyond the fact that Darlene held a certain part of Phil's past, so in self-defense, she always focused on Darlene's cellulite.

Phil drove into Darlene's driveway just as dusk was beginning to settle.

Ashes, the poodle, dashed out between Phil's feet as soon as the door was open far enough for him to squeeze through. His poor bladder was probably fit to burst. Tina, the fat gray cat followed him out, although not quite so obviously in trouble. She began to dig in the rose bed.

Phil waited on the front porch until the animals had finished, then he called them back inside. They both came in, and greeted him with the enthusiasm of a long lost friend. He missed these guys. They used to be his pets, too.

Phil took a leisurely walk through Darlene's small house. Breakfast dishes were in the sink. Her bed was unmade. A note on the refrigerator said "BUY STAMPS!"

Her cell phone was on the nightstand, plugged in to the charger.

He walked into the garage. The camping stuff was untouched, as he knew it would be. Darlene was no camper. She didn't like roughing it. She wasn't built for it. The cooler, the tent, the sleeping bags, they were still exactly the way he had packed them away some three years ago. Just dustier.

Darlene wasn't camping. And if she'd gone off on a trip, on a purposeful trip, she would have called him to care for the animals. She would have made her bed and washed her dishes.

Something was wrong, and Phil didn't know what to do about it.

He sat in the recliner. Ashes jumped up into his lap and settled down with his fluffy white head on Phil's knee. Phil petted him and looked around at the familiar furniture. What used to be his furniture. He liked this bulky, easy-living rugged stuff far more than the dainty things Angela bought to furnish the new house.

He softly stroked the silky curls on top of Ashes' head and

pushed the chair back into its reclining position. He closed his eyes, thinking about Darlene, trying to think where she could be that she had to find someone named Patrick—some fairly rude guy named Patrick—to call him to ask him to care for her animals. Most odd. *Most* odd.

He opened his eyes and looked around. The cordless telephone was on the end table. If Darlene knew she was going away for a couple of days, she would have put the phone in the charging cradle.

If anybody knew anything about Darlene's activities, it might be their daughter, Lari. He picked up the phone and dialed her.

"Hi, Mom."

Phil heard her soft voice and he could see her in his mind's eye as clear as if she were standing in front of him, with her shiny brown hair and her sparkling brown eyes. She looked like his side of the family.

"Hi honey."

"Daddy! Hi. You're at Mom's. What's up?"

"Did your mom say anything about going away for a few days?"

"No. Why?"

"I got a funny phone call from a guy named Patrick who asked me to take care of Ashes and Tina for a few days because your mom had gone camping."

"Camping? I doubt it."

"Yeah. I know."

"Weird."

"Yeah. I'm at her house now, and nothing looks like she was prepared to leave for a while."

"Should we call the police?"

Police. The word pumped panic through Phil's blood. "I don't know. Do you know anybody named Patrick?"

"No."

"Was she seeing anybody?"

"You mean was she dating?"

"Well..."

"C'mon, Dad. She wasn't interested in dating."

"You sure?"

"Well, no, but I think she would have told me, don't you? I mean, did this Patrick guy sound like somebody Mom would be interested in?"

"No," Phil said. "He sounded too young."

"I think you should call the police."

"Maybe I will. But maybe I'll wait another day. I hate to overreact."

"Have you talked to Rocky?"

"No." Rocky. That word was as bad as the police word. "What about Carolyn? Could your mom have called your place and talked to Carolyn?"

"I'll ask her. Meantime, you call Rocky and then call me back. If she didn't talk to anybody, then you better call the police."

"Maybe. Okay. Bye."

"Don't worry, Dad."

"Okay. Bye."

Phil clicked off the telephone and sat back, stroking the sleeping dog. He didn't want to call Rocky. He didn't like Rocky. He didn't even know Rocky's phone number. He should have asked Lari to call Rocky.

And now he didn't want to get up. Ashes had fallen asleep in his lap and Tina was snoozing on the arm of the recliner. The house was silent, except for the rattle of the refrigerator motor and Phil felt peaceful among all the familiar, comfortable things.

And that made him mildly uncomfortable. He should be more comfortable among his own things in his own house.

He woke up the dog and took him out to the car. Then he got the cat carrier from the garage and put Tina in it, much to her dismay, and put her in the car. He got the dog's leash and the cat's litter box and their dishes and bags of food. Then he went through the house, making sure everything was secure. He put the phone into the recharger and left a note propped up against it. Darlene would see it and call him as soon as she got home. He turned on a living room lamp and locked the front door behind him.

Angela wouldn't like having Tina and Ashes as guests, but Phil would. He'd missed them. Maybe he'd get himself a dog. Oh yeah, he reminded himself. He couldn't have a dog. He had a baby instead. Maybe when Peaches was older. Yeah. He'd bring home a puppy.

Ashes jumped into his lap and looked out the window as he drove home. Tina yowled.

~ ~ ~

The phone was ringing when Phil brought Tina's carrying cage into the kitchen, Ashes dancing around his feet.

"Hello?"

"Phil? What's this about Mom?"

Rocky. Phil could see his set jaw, his disdaining look, his attitude as it came across the phone line. Rocky was too smart, too good looking, too well-equipped for life to want to sink down to his father's level in order to have a civil conversation. Phil tried to be the adult, to hold his temper in check and talk quietly and rationally to his son, something they could only pull off for short periods of time. Very short periods of time.

"Hi, Rocky," Phil said, inwardly sighing.

"Lari said you should call the police."

"Maybe I will."

"What's the deal? I mean, what *exactly* is the deal?"

That old feeling flared up inside of Phil. Maybe one of the reasons he never liked Rocky was because Rocky never respected him. Phil understood that Rocky could be mad at him, but Jesus Christ, Darlene got over it, couldn't Rocky? "The *deal* is this. Some guy called here this morning, said your mom had gone camping and wanted me to take care of Ashes and Tina."

"And so?"

"So I went over to the house and it didn't look to me like your mom had planned to go anywhere, especially camping, so I called Lari. Has she talked to Carolyn?"

"Yeah. Carolyn didn't know anything. She's going to go ask her crystal ball or magic cards or chicken entrails or something. Are you going to call the police?"

"I don't know."

"What do you mean you don't know?"

"I mean if she was in trouble, nobody would have called."

"Then nobody would have known. It might have been days... a week, maybe before we'd have thought something was wrong, and by that time, Ashes and Tina would have starved."

It was true.

"And Mom might be long gone. I think the phone call was her cry for help," Rocky said. "If you don't call the police, I will."

"Okay," Phil said. Maybe this was why Rocky didn't respect him. Rocky had more sense. "I'll call the police."

"You have the animals?"

Phil looked at Tina, who blinked back at him from behind the wire of her carrier. "Yeah, they're here with me."

"Keep me posted," Rocky said, and hung up.

"Jerk," Phil said.

"What the hell?" Angela glared at Ashes, then at Tina, then at Phil with her hands on her hips.

"Something's happened to Darlene," Phil said. "So I brought the animals here for a while."

"Something? What kind of something?"

Ashes backed away from her and stood on top of Phil's feet.

"Doggy!" Peaches squealed and ran for Ashes, who dodged her and escaped into the other room. Peaches followed. Angela sighed.

Phil opened Tina's cage and the cat skulked out of the kitchen and down the hall, running belly to the ground, looking for a place to hide.

Phil tried to ignore the tight-lipped look on Angela's face and started to tell her the story.

Then Angela sneezed. Again. And again. In the living room, Ashes yipped, then barked. Peaches began to scream.

"Shit," Phil said.

Darlene was on her fourth beer and feeling downright sociable by the time Patrick and Molly got back from the store. Molly carried in two grocery bags, Patrick carried two cases of beer.

"Hi," Patrick said. "How y'all doin'?"

Molly eyed Darlene and Leathers with suspicion, as if it had not been her intention, nor did she consider it a good omen, that Darlene and Leathers were drinking beer together in a most friendly fashion.

Leathers was sprawled on the couch, the only piece of furniture in this part of the house that could accommodate him. Darlene still sat in the captain's chair, her feet propped up on one of the rickety kitchen chairs. She blew on her freshly-applied coat of pink nail polish, then waved her fingers in the air.

"We need fresh beers," Leathers said in his whiskey voice.

Molly put the food away, then disappeared into the back room. Life didn't seem to be going her way.

Patrick unscrewed the caps off three beers and handed them around. Then he straddled a kitchen chair and smiled at Darlene. "So," he said. "What are you guys talking about?"

"Tattoos," Leathers said.

Patrick laughed.

"What else?" Darlene said, then drained her beer and picked up the fresh one. She put the top on the nail polish and dropped the bottle into her purse, then slung the purse over the chair back.

Leathers pulled the white gauze off his forearm where the freshly inked tattoo had stopped bleeding. He smeared the ointment around on it a little bit and inspected his work.

"Yeah," Patrick said. "He's quite a work of art, isn't he?"

"Amazing," Darlene said.

"Darlene here thinks she might like to have a little design," Leathers said.

"Yeah?"

"Well," Darlene said, suddenly shy about being in the spotlight, especially anything about her body being in the spotlight. "If I could think of something that suited me, you know it would have to be fairly perfect. I mean, it's for the rest... well, I guess I don't have to tell you how permanent it is."

Leathers laughed, a good sound in the cabin. When he laughed his belly shook, and his jowls and his tattoos danced. Darlene wanted to make him laugh some more.

"Do you have any tattoos, Patrick?" she asked.

"What's for dinner, Patrick?" Leathers asked before Patrick could answer.

"Leftover rabbit stew."

"Best get on with it, boy."

"Yes sir." Patrick got up and began to work in the kitchen.

Leathers hauled himself off of the couch. "C'mon in," he said. "I'll show you my studio."

Darlene extracted herself from between the arms of the chair and followed him on unsteady feet. She was a little drunk, and that felt kind of good.

Leathers wore a loose pair of blue terrycloth drawstring shorts, which showed the entirety of his hairy back, the backs of his arms, his neck, his waist, his calves. He was a walking photograph of the cabin.

Darlene had not seen the back of the cabin, but she knew that this was as actual a depiction of it as the front of him was the exact image of the front of the cabin. It had been tattooed onto him in the springtime, when the rhododendrons were in full bloom, and the iris and azaleas and jonquil and the dogwood as well, for all of that was in bright color on Leathers' arms, chest, neck, back and sides. Even the hulks of rusting cars were pictured there, and the torn screen door and the stacks of moldy beer bottle cases.

As she followed him, she saw three fifty-five gallon drums and another woodpile. She saw a bow saw stuck in the branch of a tree, the snake of a hose amongst the thistles, a rope wound around another tree, its purpose long forgotten. She saw moss growing thick on the cabin roof, the smoke curling up from the crumbly chimney. The smoke—wasn't it the exact same way on his chest?

He turned to face her, and it was. The smoke was exactly the same on his chest. She wanted to shave him so she could see the picture better.

Shave him! The thought made her blush, and she giggled, and that sounded really drunk, and she giggled again, then she lost her balance and he caught her arm in his meaty hand.

"You okay?"

She nodded, her eyes watering. She tried to get herself under control.

"Maybe we better go back and sit down. I'll have Patrick make a little coffee. You can see the studio later."

She nodded, unwilling to trust her voice, and he guided her with shuffling steps, back to the main room where he deposited her on the couch and then flopped down next to her.

Her skin tingled where he had touched her. He stirred those long-dormant juices within her, and Darlene felt just a little bit embarrassed that her body was reacting in this way. She tried to remember that she had been kidnapped at gunpoint, that she had been brought here against her will, that these people could be dangerous, that her life might be in jeopardy.

But all she could really think about was how she wanted to run her fingertips lightly over those brightly colored tattoos. She wanted to wrap her fingers around all that hair. She wanted to shave it off gently and sudsily, the two of them sharing some mammoth bathtub. She wanted those big fat hands to explore her, she could imagine what it would feel like to hold his head, her hands tightly gripping fistfuls of that thick white hair while his mouth suckled one of her breasts.

Oh god, she was really drunk.

He wheezed when he breathed. "Coffee, Patrick," he said.

Yes, sir," Patrick said and put down the knife he was using to slice bread and went directly to the coffee maker. "Sure is nice to be working in a clean kitchen."

Darlene decided she wasn't going to say another word until she felt a little more normal. But as much as she wanted to deny it, she had to go to the bathroom. She hated the thought of going to the bathroom in this filthy place. And she wasn't sure she'd be able to get herself up out of this ruined couch. She wasn't so much sitting on it as sitting *in* it, its springs all having given up long ago under Leathers' considerable use. There's nothing uglier than a fat woman trying to get up from a frumpy couch.

Oh well. "I have to use the bathroom," she said, and struggled to her feet. She made it, and quicker than she thought.

"Through the studio and to your right," Leathers said.

Darlene concentrated on her walking so she didn't stumble or bump into anything. She liked the drunk feeling a little better when she was sitting down. She found the bathroom and while she was searching the wall for the light switch, the string from the light bulb above hit her in the forehead. She clicked it on.

It was bad, but it wasn't as bad as the kitchen had been. The worst part was the way the toilet gave way a little bit below her when she sat down on it. The floor was rotting through.

She finished, noticing that her arousal was more than in her mind, struggled back into her stretch pants, flushed the stained toilet and washed her hands. The towels all looked dirty, so she wiped her hands on her shirt and went back out into Leathers' studio. Idly, she noticed the big padded table, the easy chair, the stainless steel five-wheeled chair, the threadbare braided rug. Leathers' studio was neat and tidy. Not like the living room. Not like the bathroom.

There were two other doors, both closed.

Something was cooking in the kitchen and it smelled good. Darlene's stomach rumbled.

Food. Ashes. Tina. "Patrick, did you call Phil?" she asked.

"Yes, ma'am," Patrick said. "He said he'd take care of the animals for you."

"Did he say anything else?"

"Well, I told him you were camping and he didn't seem to believe that, but he said he'd take care of the animals for you."

"Thank you."

"Yes, ma'am."

Leathers was watching Patrick as a king would watch an underling. He never made a sound, or spoke a criticism, but Darlene had the feeling that Leathers had run this household with pointed remarks and an iron fist from this couch for years. She sank back down next to him on the couch and took time to look at him objectively, although the beer made objectivity a little blurry.

He was past sixty. His thick, neatly cut and combed hair was almost entirely white with a little shading of black in the back. It was clean and looked soft, but she could still see the comb marks along the sides. He was a big man, fat, yes, but also big. He stood at least six foot four, and weighed she imagined close to four hundred pounds. His skin was a light brown, as if he had some nationality or two mixed in with a delicate hand. His jowls and neck were the only places he could be considered flabby; the rest of him wiggled and jiggled, but he was just big. Big and solid and very colorful.

She wondered if the tattoos went on below the belt.

Of course they did, she reasoned with herself, and giggled some more.

"Let me see your arm again," she said.

He peeled off the gauze and wiped away the Vaseline with it. "Just filling in some color work," he said.

It was a bird, a tiny yellow bird, perched on an axe handle. Its mouth was open in song.

"Who did this work?"

"I did, mostly."

"And your back?"

"When's that chow going to be ready, Patrick?" Leathers asked.

"Half hour."

Leathers looked at Darlene, and she saw that he had dark brown eyes that were as clear and as clean as the eyes of a twenty-year-old. The whites weren't yellow, or veined, the clear brown irises weren't watery or faded. His eyes were mysterious and deep. She could lose herself in those eyes.

"Patrick, bring me that design book, will you, boy?" Leathers said, then smiled at Darlene and she felt her face grow as warm as her nether regions.

Patrick wiped his hands on a dish towel and dodged into the back room. He came back with a thick scrapbook that had pieces of paper sticking out of it on three sides.

Leathers laid the book on Darlene's lap and with one arm around the back of the couch behind her, encouraged her to open it.

"Go ahead," he said. "Pick a nice design."

Darlene had no intention whatsoever of getting a tattoo, in fact, it was about time she headed for home, wasn't it? but she couldn't resist opening the cover. The first picture was a pen and ink drawing of an elephant dragging a man by his foot.

"Not that," Leathers seemed irritated. He reached over and flipped half the pages, wheezing in her ear.

Patrick set a steaming white mug of coffee on the stained couch arm. "Want anything in it?"

"No, thanks. Black." The coffee smelled good and her stomach rumbled with hunger. She wished Patrick would put out some chips or something to munch on.

"This here," Leathers said, "is part of a series."

Darlene looked at a circular explosion of roses. Colorful and as accurate as any botanical artist could make it. There were old fashioned single roses, there were new hybrid double and triple petaled roses. There were leaves of all the shades, from dark glossy green to light and gently spotted. Some petals were gently withered, some buds still green. It took her breath away.

"Series?"

"Yeah." He signaled her to turn the page.

The next page was the same, with daisies. All kinds of daisies, including Black-eyed Susans, the tiny purple ones with yellow middles, the distinctive lacy green foliage from thick and sturdy to fragile and fern-like.

She turned the page again.

Patrick brought a cup of coffee to Leathers, and stood in front of them, looking down at the book.

The third page was filled with iris. Little tiny woodland iris, tall, giant Dutch-grown bearded iris. Purple, yellow, brown, white, triple-headed, single throated, all manner of iris.

"See this here?" Leathers held his arm next to his body and pointed to the wildly pink rhododendron that covered his bicep and exactly matched its other half on his chest. "This is when I got started with the flowers."

Darlene wanted to touch the rhododendrons, but she didn't dare. "These..." she pointed to the iris. "These are tattoos?"

"Not yet," Leathers said, and Patrick went back to the kitchen.

The last in the floral series was a mix of lilies and dahlias. These

41

were and bolder than the others, both lilies and dahlias being hardier, sturdier. "This is so masculine," Darlene said.

Patrick laughed.

She turned back to the roses. She should have asked Patrick to remind Phil to water her roses.

Her first rosebush had been a wedding gift. She had always thought that rose gardens were a whole lot of spindly prickly things for too little loveliness, until she had a rosebush of her own. It was a Double Delight, and its fragrance would sweeten the whole house with only one red-edged white blossom. She still had that rosebush, twenty-four years later. It had moved with them five times, as had the others she had collected over the years. Darlene had finally joined the local rose society and became somewhat of an expert on their care. She fantasized about digging up the whole back yard and breeding her own roses. Having her own miniature test garden.

"Double delight," she said, pointing at a rose on the drawing.

Leathers grunted.

"Blue girl?" she pointed at another.

He nodded.

"Sterling Silver. Peace. Chicago Peace. I have all these roses."

"Hey Patrick," Leathers said. "She's lost in the roses."

"They're my favorite too," he said. "Let's eat."

Darlene and Leathers humphed themselves out of the couch. Darlene took a bowl from the top of the stack and helped herself to a ladle of stew from a big pot on the stove. Patrick had sliced some warm bread, and she cut a couple of hunks from the stick of butter to soften on the bread. Then she took her meal and sat back in the captain's chair at the kitchen table and waited for the others.

Leathers set the salt, pepper and Tabasco on the table, then his bowl of stew. Patrick brought a roll of paper towels.

"Go get Molly," Leathers said in a low voice.

"She's not hungry."

"Get her."

Patrick disappeared into the back room. A few moments later, a rumpled Molly emerged, and she flopped in a chair with a pout.

"Getcherself some stew," Leathers said.

"Not hungry," she said.

"Go comb your hair and get yourself some food," he said, a little more forcefully.

She rolled her eyes and got up, disappeared into the bathroom. When she returned, her hair was combed, the smudge of mascara under her right eye had been repaired, and she brought a bowl with a spoonful of stew to the table. She set it down, then she sat down, but she ignored it.

"Thanks, Lord," Leathers said, and then he began to eat.

Darlene poked around in her stew for a while. She'd never eaten rabbit before, and was reluctant to try it.

She picked out a carrot round and ate it. It tasted good and she remembered how hungry she was. Still suspicious, she ate a piece of celery, then a potato.

"Good," Leathers said, then grunted himself out of the chair and back to the stove for more.

Patrick was wiping his bowl out with his bread.

Leathers came back with a fresh steaming bowl and stood looking down at Molly. "Eat," he said.

"Not hungry."

Leathers sat down, pushed the bowl toward her.

She pushed it away.

"In my house, young woman, you will not come to the dinner table with that attitude," his voice began to rise, "and you will, by God, *eat!*" He slammed his fist on the table and everything jumped, including Darlene.

Molly picked up her fork and ate a carrot. Leathers scooped a big dollop from his bowl into hers. "All of it," he said.

She closed her eyes as if praying for strength to endure him, then she began to eat, slowly.

Darlene took a big spoonful which included some white shredded meat. Looked like chicken. It was delicious. "Delicious," she said.

"Patrick's a good cook," Leathers said, laughing a hoarse laugh. "Taught him everything he knows."

Patrick drained his glass of milk.

Darlene noticed that Molly was steadily eating her stew. She looked borderline anorexic. It was good that Leathers made her eat, if she didn't just throw it all up afterwards.

She watched Leathers shovel the food into his mouth, washed down by at least three glasses of milk and half a loaf of French bread slathered in butter. He punctuated his eating with a half dozen remarks to Patrick about matters that Darlene knew nothing about. This was his castle, his fiefdom. He and Patrick seemed to be partners in it, and Molly seemed to be some sort of a young stepsister of some sort, although she was clearly partnered with Patrick.

She's someone Patrick brought home one day as young boys sometimes do, Darlene thought, and she has just stayed.

Darlene watched Leathers push his empty bowl away after his fourth helping. She watched him burp politely into his paper towel, then discuss things of upkeep importance with Patrick. She saw how he handled Molly as a wayward child, she could see how he handled Patrick and Molly as a couple. He was forceful and dynamic, big and unashamed. He had decorated his less-than-perfect body in a manner perfectly in keeping with his personality and his artistic talents.

Darlene burped up some stew and some beer herself and realized that she was comparing Leathers to Phil. Phil, who never paid much attention to the children. Phil, who made a fine living and had all the right things, lacked substance of some sort. He certainly lacked a conscience. Phil, who was always just a little bit too good looking, too smooth, too cool. Phil, who had cheated on Darlene from day one—probably on their honeymoon. An odd couple, Darlene and Phil, although she loved him dearly for just exactly who he was.

But who he was, was no Leathers. Leathers was intriguing. Leathers, Darlene found to her astonishment, was incredibly attractive. She couldn't remember the last time she had been attracted to someone who was her age, or older. She looked at him, but had to look down when his eyes met hers. She felt herself blushing like a teenager. Must be the beer, she thought.

"That was a good dinner, Patrick," she said.

Taken as a signal, Molly dropped her fork. She'd eaten almost half of what Leathers had given her to eat.

"Thank you, ma'am," Patrick said.

"Yes it was," Leathers said. "Molly will now do the dishes." He looked over at her. "Without pouting."

Molly picked up all four bowls and took them to the sink.

"You know," Darlene said. "I really ought to be going."

Leathers looked at her with mild surprise on his face. "Going?"

"Home."

"Oh, no," he said. "You can't leave."

Darlene's chest tightened. "Can't leave?"

"No, no, no," he said. "We need your car."

Here we go again, she thought. She didn't know whether to get angry or to be afraid.

"Besides," Leathers went on. "Your animals are cared for, so you don't have to rush off."

"Yes, but—"

"*And,*" he halted her protest, "you haven't got your tattoo yet."

Phil was sitting in Darlene's comfortable recliner with his eyes closed when he heard Lari's little car idle to the curb out in front. He wondered if Carolyn would be with her. He hoped so. He loved Carolyn, and now that he thought about it, Carolyn was family, after all, so it would be entirely appropriate for her to be in on the family meetings. Carolyn said a lot of things that Phil didn't understand— she was into metaphysics, whatever that was. She had Tarot cards and worked up everybody's astrological charts. But while she said a lot of things that flew right over Phil's head, she also had a way of looking at things with a positive attitude that made the world seem to make sense.

Carolyn's world did make sense. She had explanations for everything, which set her soul at ease. She had faith and trust in some universal architect who took care of all the things for which there were no explanations. Phil admired that.

Their house was full of crystals and runes and things that Phil found odd, but it was their house and their lives. Lari and Carolyn had been married for four years. Their lives made a lot more sense to them than Phil's life did to him.

He heard one door slam. Lari was alone.

Phil hadn't invited Angela, because Angela didn't seem like part of his family. Angela wasn't crazy about Darlene, which was understandable, and she didn't like Lari and Carolyn being married lesbians, but most of all, Phil didn't like to have Angela see him with Rocky, because Rocky always made Phil feel inept. Guilty. Phil hadn't wanted this meeting, didn't ask for it, didn't need it. It was Rocky's idea, and that made it worse, because it was probably a good one.

He heard Rocky's throaty truck idle to the curb.

Phil's bowels clenched. He willed his muscles to relax.

46

Rocky's radio was on too loud, as usual. He killed the engine, jumped out of the truck, Phil could see him in his mind's eye, looking healthy and fit.

He heard them laughing together, this big sister and little brother, as they met in the street walked up to the front door together. Phil felt as though he hadn't laughed in ages. He was too old, too used up, too serious. These young people, these laughing people, they didn't understand life yet. Let them laugh, he thought bitterly. Let them make a few mistakes they'd have to live with. Let them learn. Soon they'll know. Life is no laughing matter.

A soft knock on the door, then the knob turned and the door pushed gently open. "Hello? Dad?"

"Hi," he said.

"Hi." Lari came over and gave him a hug. "What are you doing here sitting in the dark?" She turned on a lamp.

Phil hadn't even noticed that night had fallen. He'd been sitting in the recliner, reminiscing since afternoon daylight.

Lari had a new perm and her shiny brown chin-length hair was allover curls. It looked nice. She looked like she had come straight from work, where she was an administrative assistant in the county clerk's office. She wore a pair of white slacks and a soft green blouse. She was a knockout.

"Phil," Rocky said, and offered his hand. Phil shook it, and looked into Rocky's deep blue eyes. He was still wearing his blue electric company uniform. Rocky, at age twenty-one, had found security as a lineman. Phil had always found that odd. Rocky never seemed like the kind of guy who would seek out security.

Kids. Never a dull moment. Always a surprise.

"Any Diet Cokes?" Lari asked.

Phil shrugged.

"Put on a pot of coffee, Lar," Rocky said, then he sat on the couch and began picking at the afghan that stretched across the back of it. "Any news?"

"Don't you guys start without me," Lari called from the kitchen.

Phil shook his head.

Lari returned with a Diet Coke in her hand. The sound of a burbling coffee pot came from the kitchen. "So," she said. "What's the scoop? You have the animals, right?"

Phil nodded.

"Boy, I bet Angela loves that," Rocky said, snickering.

Phil ignored him.

Lari sat on the couch next to Rocky and the two of them looked at Phil.

"Well," he started weakly. He cleared his throat. "What do you think we should do?"

"I think we should call the police," Rocky said.

"Don't they need a 24-hour time limit or something before they'll consider it a missing persons case?" Lari asked.

Both kids looked at Phil. "I don't know," he said.

Rocky leaned forward, his forearms on his knees. "What *do* you know, Phil?"

"C'mon, Rock," Lari said. "Lighten up."

"Do you, for example, know the phone number this Patrick person called from? Did you look at your Caller ID?"

"It was just a number, just a phone number," Phil said. "I called it. No answer."

"We definitely ought to call the police," Rocky said.

"I just think we're jumping the gun a little here," Phil said, that feeling of panic beginning to grow again. "She was here this morning, and I'll bet she'll be back tomorrow."

"So you want to give it twenty-four hours," Rocky said.

"Well, yeah, it seems reasonable."

"They could kill her in twenty-four hours," Lari said.

"They could kill her in twenty-four minutes," Phil said. "But nobody says that she's in trouble."

"We're giving them a twenty-four hour head start."

"Who? Giving who?"

"Okay, okay," Rocky said. "I say we call the police right here, right now, have them come over here and we tell them what we know and see what they think."

"Good idea," Lari said. "Dad?"

Phil looked at them, so young and fresh. He felt so tired. He looked at their pink faces and just knew that his face was as yellow and as dried up as an old book. "Sure," he said. "Let's see what the professionals say." He handed the cordless phone to Rocky.

"Coffee, Lar," Rocky said.

~ ~ ~

Phil had never faced police before. Two of them, a man and a woman, acting proper and polite and official with all their guns and badges and radios and gear made him nervous. They both sat on the edge of the dining room chairs Rocky brought over for them to sit on, and took notes in official looking little books while their radios squawked softly and the squad car sat out in front of the house.

Phil looked out the window and saw the neighbor kids looking at it.

Rocky dealt with the police, giving them all the information, except about the telephone call. Phil filled that in, and the fact that he came here and got the animals. Yes, he told them, he had a key to the house, always has. Lari looked through Darlene's desk and found the license plate number to her Ford.

Both police officers seemed to think that Darlene would show up the next day, and on their way out, handed Phil a business card. He was to call them the following day, or if he got another telephone call, whichever came first. He stammered out an agreement.

And then they were gone.

Phil rubbed his eyes with relief. Their presence was so intimidating, so enormously space-consuming. Those two blue uniforms seemed to take up the entire house. He had found it hard to breathe while they were in the room.

The kids were laughing again. Phil sat down in the recliner and tried to get in on the joke, hoping it wasn't poked at him.

But Lari's face was red.

"God, Lar," Rocky said. "Get a grip."

"What?" Phil asked.

"Lari started drooling over that cop."

Phil remembered him as being bald and with a face that looked like it had been punched too many times. He couldn't quite imagine... then he remembered. Lari, being a lesbian, would have been attracted to the *female* cop. Would he *ever* get that right? And the female cop had been attractive, with her red hair and green eyes, except for all that blue and leather and officer attitude. Under different circumstances, Phil would have made the most of the situation.

"She was pretty cute," he smiled.

Rocky looked disdainfully at his father. "Yeah, I'm sure *you* noticed."

"Shut up, Rock." Lari elbowed him. "She *was* cute. Thanks, Dad."

Phil would never be able to adapt to the new world. He tried, he just wasn't able. He always thought he'd have a son he could admire women with. Instead, it was his daughter.

And Darlene was missing. The presence of the police made it more real. It was dark outside, and there was no word from her, and Phil was beginning to believe they were right to be worried.

The phone rang and all eyes locked on to it. Both kids looked at Phil as if he were in charge.

It rang again.

Phil nodded at it. It was standing on the coffee table.

Rocky picked it up and clicked it on. "Hello? Oh, hi, Angela, hold on just a minute."

Phil took the phone. "Hi, honey."

"That Patrick person called again."

Phil's dinner threatened to come up.

"Oh?" He looked over at the kids. They were talking quietly to each other.

"He said he just wanted to make sure that Darlene's animals were cared for. He said he didn't want anything to happen to those animals, Phil, and it sounded kind of menacing, kind of like a threat. Who is this person? Where is Darlene? What is going on?"

"I'll be home in a few minutes."

"I don't like strangers having this phone number, Phil. Did Darlene give it to them?"

"I think she did." He looked up and saw the kids looking at him.

"I think you should come home now."

"I will. I'll come now." Phil hung the phone up. "He called again," he said.

Lari's mouth fell open, and then tears filled her eyes. Rocky's face turned into a mask of tense determination. "And?" he said.

"Well, I'm not sure, except that Angela felt that he made some sort of a threat, or something. I don't know, she's pretty agitated. I think I better go home and see if I can find out exactly what he said to her."

"Is he wanting ransom money?" Lari asked, then hicced and a

tear fell down her cheek.

"I don't know, honey."

"Well, what exactly did she say?" Rocky asked.

"She said that the Patrick guy called again and wanted to make sure that the animals had been taken care of. Then she said that he sounded menacing, and it scared her." Phil stood up. "I'm going to go talk to her."

"I'm coming with you," Lari said. She picked up the phone and dialed. "Hi," she said softly, "did I wake you?" Phil always tried to picture that she said those soft words to her husband, but of course, she was saying them to Carolyn. "I'm going over to Dad's for a while. I'll be home later. Yeah. Yeah, me too." She smiled and clicked the phone off.

Phil wrote another note to Darlene and stuck it under a butterfly magnet on the refrigerator. He left a lamp in the living room on, and the three of them trooped out into the dusky evening and got into their respective vehicles.

Ten minutes later, when they all walked into his house, Phil found Angela with a wad of Kleenex and a faceful of tears sitting on the couch. Her blonde hair was in a ponytail and with no makeup on, she looked about twelve. Phil was self-conscious about having a wife as young as his kids.

Ashes was locked in the laundry room where he was barking and scratching at the door. Tina blinked languidly at him from atop the dining room table.

Lari let Ashes out and he pranced to the living room. Rocky picked up Tina and Lari picked up Ashes and the two sat on straight back chairs with the animals in their laps and faced Phil and Angela. Phil had a strange feeling of unreality, as if he could close his eyes, rub them, count to ten, open them, and the house would be empty and quiet, a sensibly-aged Darlene reading a romance novel and drinking a cup of Earl Grey next to him.

"Okay, honey, tell me what he said."

"No," Angela sniffed. "First you tell me what's going on."

"We don't know, Angela," Rocky said.

"We only know what I told you before. Except that now—"

"The police—" Lari began.

"Police!" Angela's hands grasped at the throat of her papaya-colored Gap sweatshirt. Then she sneezed twice and looked at Phil, pointing at Tina.

"We thought it would be best to call the police," Rocky said patiently, while Phil locked Tina in the bathroom. "We had to report her missing and find out what they thought."

Phil didn't like the tone of voice Rocky used when he spoke with Angela. He talked down to her as if she were an airhead. Rocky didn't like Angela; he acted like she was beneath him, like he had to treat her as a child. Phil couldn't blame him in a way. She had been The Other Woman. Rocky viewed her as The Homewrecker. But it hadn't been Angela's fault. That's what none of them understood. It had just been bad luck. Phil knew Angela hadn't gotten knocked up on purpose, but Rocky always thought she had.

"We need to know what this Patrick person said to you on the phone, Angela," Lari said. "We might want to call the police back if there's any new information here."

Angela nodded, then took a deep, ragged breath. "Okay," she said. "I'd just gotten Peaches to sleep. I was in the bedroom reading. The phone rang. I answered it, and a man said 'This is Patrick. I want to make sure that someone took care of Darlene's animals.' I said, 'Yes, they're here and they're fine. Where is Darlene?' He said, 'That's not your concern. She's fine, she's having a good time, but I wouldn't want anything to happen to her animals. She'd be really unhappy about that.' *Then* he said, 'We'd *all* be really unhappy about that.' I said 'Who are you, who are you people? Where is Darlene and why isn't *she* calling us?' and he hung up."

"That's it?" Lari said.

"It's the *way* he said it, Larissa," Angela said.

Phil saw Lari cringe. Angela flatly refused to call her Lari.

"It was menacing. It was threatening. This is no good," Angela said. "This is no good at all." She looked at Phil. "We need to be thinking about Peaches here."

Rocky sighed audibly in response. "As if Peaches was the one in trouble. Call the cops, Phil," Rocky said.

Angela visibly shrank from Rocky's verbal slap.

Tina yowled in the bathroom.

Phil checked the Caller ID on the phone. "Just a phone number. I think it's the same one as last time," he said. He pulled the policeman's business card from his shirt pocket and flicked at the edge of it with his forefinger.

"No, wait," Lari said. "Let's talk about this for a minute first." Ashes struggled from her lap, trotted over to Phil and lightly jumped up into his lap, turned around once and curled up, his delicate little nose resting on his back leg. Phil stroked his tiny little foot. "What was the purpose for this phone call?" Lari got up and began to walk around the living room. "Why did he call? What did he mean to accomplish?"

"Who cares?" Rocky said.

"Because if he just wanted to make sure that the animals were cared for, that's one thing," Lari said. "But if he wanted to scare us, that's different."

"If he has our phone number, does that mean he can get our address?" Angela asked, her eyes wide.

Rocky nodded slowly.

"Can't we find him first? Can't the police go to the phone he used to call us from?" Angela asked.

Rocky frowned. "Maybe. Call the police, Phil."

Phil looked at Lari, who shrugged. He went into the kitchen and dialed, leaving the three kids to themselves.

Patrick cut the lights and idled up the weedy drive. He turned off the Ford's engine, got out and shut the door softly behind him. The cabin was dark; he didn't want to wake anyone.

He opened the screen door and held it with his foot, he turned the loose knob on the door, holding it gently so it didn't rattle. He knew the kitchen so well he wouldn't bump into anything. He could walk around in the dark with no problem.

Leathers' voice startled him. "Where you been, Patrick?"

"God, Leathers, you scared me."

"What you doing sneaking around, boy?"

"I didn't want to wake anybody."

"Where you been to?"

"The store."

"Where's a store open this late?"

"Elkton."

"What'd you buy?"

"Ice cream. Want some?"

A match flared and Leathers put its head to a candle. "C'mere, Patrick," he said.

Patrick set the grocery sack on the counter and sat down at the kitchen table. The stainless steel tray was at Leathers' elbow. Patrick's guts tensed and he took a firm grip on himself.

"You're not thinking of anything stupid, are you boy?"

"No, sir," he said, the roaring sound beginning in his ears.

"We've come a long way together, haven't we, boy?"

"Yes, sir."

"Been a lot of places, done a lot of things."

"Yes, sir."

"Don't be stirring up trouble just because of that skinny little piece of ass in there," Leathers said, ticking his head toward the back where Molly slept. "She's not that great."

"No, sir."

"We understand each other then?"

"Yes."

"You haven't lost your concentration now, have you?"

"No, sir."

"Let's see about that. Turn on the light."

Patrick stood, his knees wobbly. He turned on the kitchen light, then sat back down.

Leathers slid the tray over. There were two fresh scalpels, hemostats, Neosporin, gauze and about a dozen small steel ball bearings.

"Take that shirt off."

Patrick swallowed, trying to get his concentration up, trying hard, trying desperately, because if he whimpered, it would only be worse. He unbuttoned his shirt.

Odd that Leathers thought it was Molly that was fucking with his mind. But it wasn't her, it was the woman, the fat one. She had given him the makings of a plan, and his excitement over the plan was going to destroy him.

"Left shoulder," Leathers said.

Patrick turned, but that shoulder hadn't healed yet from the last time and it was really sore.

"Count down, Patrick." Leathers' soft fingers removed the gauze pad that covered the incisions, and Patrick could feel the little ball bearings Leathers had inserted under his skin as his fingers ran lightly across them. Leather's touch over those knobs gave Patrick the stirrings of an erection.

"Beautiful work," Leathers said to himself. "Beautiful."

Patrick began his mental countdown, but his concentration just wasn't there.

Not until it began to hurt bad. Not until Leathers was well into his work, Patrick's brief erection gone, did the coldness slide down over Patrick's mind and his emotions and then he didn't feel the pain at all.

When Leathers was finished, he bandaged up the shoulder, then dished himself up a big bowl of Rocky Road and ate it noisily.

Patrick sat in the chair for a while longer, his mind empty.

"Feed that to the dog before you go to bed," Leathers said, then heaved himself up and went into the other room.

Patrick looked at the tray. All the ball bearings were gone. He picked up the handful of bloody strips of flesh and skin and went to the front door.

The dog was waiting.

TUESDAY

When Darlene awoke, her muscles were stiff from sleeping on Leathers' studio table all night. It was vinyl, so she stuck to it, and though it was padded, it wasn't soft, and it was high, so even in her sleep she knew that if she rolled over, she might fall to the floor. Her scalp itched, her teeth felt furry, and she had a sour taste in her mouth.

She slipped into her shoes and folded the faded gold blanket Patrick had given her, then made her way quietly to the bathroom.

She winched at the bright unfiltered light from the bare bulb, and she realized that she was a little headachy and hungover. She relieved herself on the rickety toilet, then hunted around until she found a clean towel. She washed her face and finger-brushed her teeth with toothpaste, swished it good and gargled a bit. When that was done, she felt a lot better, but she still needed a shower, and she needed a change of clothes.

It was time to go home.

In her mind's eye, she saw her cell phone on the charger, sitting on the nightstand by her bed. Stupid. Never again.

Her purse was still slung across one arm of the captain's chair in the kitchen where she'd left it, and she got a brush and ran it through her hair. She opened the refrigerator and looked for something to eat, but even though the refrigerator seemed clean and she couldn't smell anything bad or see anything moldy, it was against her better judgment to help herself to someone else's larder.

She checked her watch. Seven o'clock. This household probably didn't rise until noon. Or later.

Darlene looked around the kitchen for her keys. It would be too easy for them hang them on some kind of a peg. They were probably still in Patrick's pants pockets, in his bedroom.

She could sneak in there.

No. God no.

She remembered the magnetic Hide-A-Key box that Phil had given her. It was still on her kitchen counter. She'd meant to put her extra set of car keys in it, but just hadn't gotten around to it. Actually, she hadn't done it because the box was dirty, and under the car was dirty, and she didn't know where to attach it anyway.

Well, she'd have to walk. The main road couldn't be more than a couple of miles. She could walk that. She might be fat and out of shape, but it was mostly downhill. She'd take her time, and she would make it. She'd get to the main road and put out her thumb and get a ride to a telephone and be home talking with the police long before any of these people were even out of bed.

She looked around to see if there was anything she should take with her. Nothing but her purse. It was probably chilly outside, but the walk would warm her up. She wore black stretchy leggings and a green print polyester overblouse, so she'd be reasonably comfortable, but her shoes... she wore flimsy little black slippers with no arch and hardly any sole at all. They were good for around the house, and even a quick trip to the store or to the post office, but they were not walking shoes. She'd feel every pebble. Oh well. She would have to make do.

She picked up her purse and shouldered the strap. Then she carefully opened the door, pushed the screen door back, and stepped into a wet, fresh Oregon morning.

The air was warmer than she thought it would be, and the cloud cover hung low, so the air didn't have that cleansed smell; it still smelled like the rotting wood of the cabin. But the grass was wet and the shrubs were wet and drops still fell from the trees. The soft June morning sunlight brightened the colors of all the flowers.

The flowers! They were fabulous! She'd been too distracted the day before to actually look at the landscaping around the junk in the yard, but someone in this house had a green thumb and tended these plants with love. The rhododendrons she'd seen depicted in Leathers' tattoos were even more brilliant in real life, she noticed with a wry smile. And the azaleas that bordered them were at their peak. Now that she was seeing the beauty instead of all the rusted junk, she saw that the entire yard was ablaze with flowers. It looked like a greenhouse, with its canopy of trees. It could be a test garden, it could be a nursery.

Who had the green thumb?

Leathers, certainly, but she bet Patrick did whatever work there was to be done.

She looked again at the mess of junk. Someone had their priorities clearly defined, that was for sure. Tend the plants and let the junk rust.

Well, she reminded herself, it's time to be going. She adjusted a bra strap, pulled the legs of her pants down and took off toward the opening in the weeds she had driven through.

"Look at this one," Leathers' scratchy voice said from behind her.

She jumped, startled. Blood flushed to her face in embarrassment. She felt like she'd been caught doing something naughty.

"I've got a mutant branch here on my Mr. Lincoln rose."

He spoke as if they'd been looking at his roses together all morning. He spoke as casually as if it were the most natural thing, the two of them in his rose garden at seven in the morning.

She wanted to ignore him and keep on walking. She wanted to respond to him in some way, tell him she was going.

But then she also wanted to see the mutation.

The smelly old yellow dog came up and sniffed at her shoes. She resisted petting him.She turned and saw that indeed, there was a blood-red rose with a white edging to the petals.

"Some of the petals have these white streaks," he said, holding it out to her. "Come look."

She came closer. The rosebush was flowering vigorously, and the mutant cane didn't come from the rootstock as sometimes happens, but was a regular branch of the grafted rose. She came closer.

Leathers wore a faded orange pair of drawstring shorts, rubber sandals and a torn tee shirt that had a marijuana leaf on the back of it. He was freshly showered and shaved, he smelled of some musky cologne. His hair was neatly combed.

"It's a virus," Darlene said when she saw the white streaks.

"Virus?" Leathers straightened up and leaned against the house. He coughed into his hand and then wheezed. She saw perspiration stand out on his tanned forehead.

"I think so. I seem to remember something... You know those

roses that have all the streaks? I think Carnival is one. Anyway, there are red and yellow streaks, and sometimes there are white streaks."

"Yes."

"Well, they're purposely inoculated with a virus to produce those streaks."

"Is it contagious, the virus?"

"I don't know. I don't think so. But it isn't a mutation."

"Are you sure?"

Darlene looked at it again. She had always hoped for a mutation in one of her own roses; she'd heard the Chicago Peace rose began as a mutation from the celebrated Peace rose. "I'm not sure, Leathers, you could take a cutting and see what happens."

"Why would a virus only attack one cane?"

Darlene inspected the other blossoms. They were rich, dark red with that classic, heavy Mr. Lincoln fragrance. No sign of white.

"I don't know. Maybe it will spread to the others. I'm no expert."

"You sound like one."

"I'm not. I just like roses. I'm learning all the time how to care for them, but I don't know much yet."

"Look at this one," Leathers said, and he moved down the row.

Darlene saw that the entire side yard was filled with rose bushes, something she had completely failed to notice earlier. It was almost like the test garden she had dreamed of in her own back yard. She could get lost here.

"No, Leathers, I'm going to leave now."

"Leave?"

"Yeah, I'm going to go. It was fun being here with you three, but I've got to be getting home."

"Did Patrick give you the keys?"

"No, I'll walk to the main road and I'm sure I'll get a ride."

"I'm sorry." He said it softly, and Darlene wasn't sure she understood him.

"Pardon?"

He came to her with his arms out, like he wanted a hug.

What the hell, Darlene thought. He was letting her go. She could give him a hug.

But when his arms wrapped around her and she felt him drawing her closer and closer, her knees became rubbery and something emotional rose from her feet to the top of her head. She reached around him as far as her arms would go, and he buried his sweet-smelling, warm, damp face in her neck and rocked her back and forth, back and forth. He emanated an immense amount of heat.

Darlene felt as if she had just been saved. She felt as though she had been near death and had not noticed it until just this very minute, when the touch of another person snatched her from hell's evil clutches. She had been so lonely, so *lonely*, she longed for this touch, this hug, this contact with another human being.

Sobs shook her and she barely stood, Leathers holding her up as she cried and wet the shoulder of his tee shirt. "Oh God," she said, "I need this."

"Me, too," he whispered, and when it had passed, Darlene was embarrassed and shy. She disengaged herself from him, and backed off a few steps.

Leathers' eyes were moist as well, and that tugged on her heart.

"Roses always do that to me, too," Leathers said and the tension diffused into the steaming Oregon morning.

"Can I have my keys?"

He smiled sadly and shook his head.

"Why? Why do you do this? Why do you live out here like this?" Darlene felt the flood emotion he had loosened in her turn to anger, and she wanted to lash out at him.

"Come look at this rose," Leathers said, nodding his head at the bluest rose Darlene had ever seen.

She crossed her arms and looked at him. She was angry, and she was confused.

"Look," he said again.

She took two wary steps toward him.

"I bred this rose."

Fear and anger fell away and curiosity took its place. "Really?"

"I crossed a Blue Girl and Sterling Silver. And then I bred the result back again to the Blue Girl."

"What did you name it?"

"I haven't named it yet. I'm still testing it."

Darlene bent over and examined it. The foliage was dark green and glossy. The rose was delicately scented, its petals thin and translucent. "It's wonderful."

"I'm going to enter it in the trials some time."

"I would."

They stood for a silent moment in the quiet rose garden morning, smelling, feeling, absorbing.

"Why don't you come in and let me fix you breakfast before you go?"

At least he wasn't going to force her to stay. She was no hostage. She wasn't in any danger, either. Weird as it seemed, they really just wanted her car. Too strange, but then... she looked around the yard. Strange. She looked at Leathers. Very strange. She looked at her emotions. Strangely intriguing. She looked around the rose garden. "All hybrid teas?"

"Floribundas in the back, a few old English roses back there too, but I like the hybrid teas. Come on."

She followed him back into the house.

Leathers moved gracefully around the kitchen; he was obviously a man who liked to cook. He brewed a pot of coffee, strong, the way Darlene liked it, and she sat in her captain's chair and sipped the brew while she watched him slice potatoes, whisk eggs, chop onions, green peppers and tomatoes. He wheezed as he talked, emphysema, she assumed. The veins in the calves of his legs were like blue snakes under the skin. Tattoos covered one thin thigh, she caught glimpses of it as the leg of his shorts flapped when he moved. The other leg had yet to be illustrated. She wondered if he would be able to tattoo over those varicose veins. The thought made her shudder.

He talked about his garden, punctuating his monologue with appreciative remarks about how clean the kitchen was.

Darlene got up to refill her coffee cup and before she knew it, the cheese grater was in her hand and she was making little orange noodles onto a paper towel.

Leathers opened the oven and turned the potatoes, then he heated oil in the omelet pan.

She watched him cook an omelet and with a practiced flourish, slid it onto a plate. Then he added two spatulas-ful of butter-roasted potatoes and handed it to her with a direct look into her eyes and a warm smile.

She smiled back, blushing. Leathers liked her. He was flirting with her. It made her feel young and attractive for the first time in years. Hundreds of years, it seemed.

She waited while he made himself an omelet to match, then he brought his plate to the table, and freshened their coffee.

"Thanks, Lord," he said, then shook Tabasco sauce all over his food. Darlene watched, amused, and tried a little dab on the corner of her eggs.

A door slammed from back in the house. A moment later, Patrick and Molly stumbled into the room, obviously surprised to see Darlene and Leathers having breakfast.

Patrick looked guilty. Molly looked haughty. Patrick wore jeans and a sweatshirt that said "Harvard," on it, Molly wore a pair of short shorts and a Disney sweatshirt with a picture of Dumbo. They both carried duffel bags.

"Hi," Patrick said.

Leathers put down his fork and looked at him.

"It's a nice day, we're going for a drive."

"Where to?" Leathers asked.

"Reedsport," Molly said. "Or maybe up to the dunes."

"In *my* car?" Darlene couldn't help herself.

Leathers shot her a look that said *Let me handle this*, and she abruptly quieted, closing her mouth and obeying him without thought.

"When will you return?" he asked.

"Before dinner," Patrick said.

"And what is on the dinner menu?"

"Why don't you fix your own stupid dinner for once in your stupid life?" Molly said.

Darlene saw Patrick wither.

Leathers wiped his mouth on his napkin. He pushed away from the table and stood, like a mountain, in the room. "I'll see you outside for a moment, Patrick, if I may."

"Yes sir," Patrick mumbled, then he shot Molly a scathing look and followed Leathers outside.

Molly pulled out a chair and sat in it, nervously tapping her foot against the duffel bag. She stole a potato slice from Leathers' plate and took a bite, wrinkled her nose and put it back. "Ugh," she said. "Tabasco." She wiped her tongue on the sleeve of her sweatshirt.

She looked at Darlene. "What you lookin' at?"

Darlene looked down at her plate. She wanted to go home.

Molly stood up and began to pace the kitchen. "I wonder what they're talking about," she said. "Me, probably."

"Me, probably," Darlene said. "Or maybe neither of us. Maybe they're talking about roses. Or omelets. Or this place."

Molly looked at Darlene with suspicion. "What's the matter with you?"

Darlene snorted. "You steal me and my car and expect me to act as if everything is normal?"

Molly frowned at the toe of her shoe. "It's pretty normal for around here."

"Yeah, well, I don't doubt that." Darlene looked at her breakfast. What had been steaming hot and delicious a few minutes ago had turned cold and unappetizing. She pushed it away from her. "Listen," she said. "Why don't you guys give me a ride out to the main road when you leave? I'll hitch a ride back home."

Molly gave her the same snort in return. "Sure," she said. "You'd be on the phone to the cops in a half a second. Then what do you think Leathers would say?"

"Hey, the car's paid for. You need it, you take it. I'll call the insurance company, file a claim, get a new one. You guys steal some new plates for it and you're in business. I don't care, I just don't want to walk all the way out to the main road in these shoes."

"I don't think so," Molly said.

The door opened and Leathers came back in. He didn't even glance Molly's way. He came back to the table, looked at his plate of food, picked it up along with Darlene's, and put them both in the oven.

Patrick stuck his head inside the door. "C'mon," he said. Molly jumped up, grabbed both duffel bags and ran, clacking in her sandals and tiny shorts to the door.

A moment later, Darlene heard the car start.

Another moment and she was alone with Leathers.

"So now everything's different, isn't it?" Molly took a piece of gum from her purse and stuck it in her mouth. "Now you've changed your mind, haven't you?"

"Be quiet for a moment and let me think," Patrick said.

"What did he say to you, anyway? What's the deal with you guys, that's what I want to know. What's the deal? He has some kind of a hold on you, Patrick, he has you wrapped around his fat little finger."

"Shut up a minute, now," he said.

She flounced back into her seat, popping her gum. "I knew it. I knew it all along. I should never have gotten my hopes up. You'll never leave that guy. You have no idea what's good for you and what isn't. You're weird. You're both weird." She chewed. "You're all three weird. That lady, she might be the weirdest. God, is she fat! She's even fatter than he is."

"I'm asking you nicely now, Molly, to be quiet while I think."

"Gawd," she said, and began poking around in her hair. "You know, Patrick, we've lived together now for what, three months? I've never seen you without your clothes on. It's weird, Patrick, that you're so touchy about that."

Patrick pulled off into the parking lot of a general store.

"Get me a Diet Coke, babe," Molly said.

"Get it yourself," he said. "I've got to make a phone call." He counted the change in his pocket, then opened the door and got out.

She sat fuming for a moment, then opened the ash tray and then the glove compartment to see if maybe Darlene kept a little stash of cash in there. Nothing.

She picked up the car's registration and looked at it. Darlene Martin. Springfield address.

Molly looked at Patrick at the little half phone booth attached to the side of the building. She folded the registration and stuck it in her back pocket. She didn't know how important it was, but it gave her some feeling of control over Patrick, over the car, over Darlene, over something. She never had any control over anything, and this probably didn't give her any either, but at least she had it.

She slammed the glove compartment closed and got out. Without a look at Patrick, she marched into the little store. A moment later, she came out with a paper bag.

Patrick was smiling as he hung up. He put an arm around her waist and pulled her to him.

She whooped. "Hey cowboy."

He nuzzled her neck. "What you got there?" He tried to peek into the bag.

"Beer."

"Good call," he said, giving her a kiss on the forehead. Then he let her go. "Let's go to the coast."

"All right!"

The party mood had returned. Molly didn't dare ask why. Maybe they'd have sex on the beach. Maybe she'd give him a good blow job on the road. Maybe then he'd listen to her and they could get away from that awful man and that awful place. A young couple had a right to start out fresh. They had a right to go to Arizona and begin a proper family. She sneaked a glance over at Patrick. He was smart, he was cute, he had a wonderful smile. They'd make fine babies together, Patrick and Molly would.

Patrick was a good guy. He wasn't exactly what she'd been dreaming about all her life, but he was good. He'd do.

Phil disconnected the telephone, then bounced the receiver against his forehead. He was glad he hadn't gone to work on time. He was glad that Angela hadn't answered that phone call.

Damn. Damn.

He punched in Lari's phone number. Maybe he could catch her before she went to work, too. He didn't know what to do by himself. He didn't want to do anything by himself. He wanted all decisions on this to be done by the committee. He wasn't going to take the rap from Rocky for anything he might do on his own.

"Hello?"

"Lari?"

"Hi, Daddy. What's up? Have you heard anything? Have you heard from Mom?"

"Lari, can you come over?"

Pause. "I'll be right there." Pause. "She's all right, isn't she? Isn't she, Dad?"

"I don't know, honey. Just come over."

"Rocky?"

"I'm calling him next."

"Your place?"

"Your mom's."

Lari hung up and Phil put the phone back in its charger. He'd have to look Rocky's number up in Angela's directory. His guts were hot and tight and he felt as though he might cry. He'd never felt so weak, so powerless, such a know-nothing. He had no idea how to handle this, no idea at all.

And Angela was about as much help as Ashes and Tina put together.

Ashes didn't have a fenced yard to run in, so he was a lot of work, and Tina, the upset cat, had urinated in Angela's house slippers. And now this. And now this Patrick. Damn.

Life had turned to shit. But then, he sort of deserved it. In a way, he was glad that it had finally arrived. He'd been waiting. He'd been waiting for his punishment. And here it was. He just hoped to God that Darlene's death wasn't going to be a part of it.

Phil looked up Rocky's phone number and punched in the numbers.

Elizabeth Engstrom

Molly popped a beer for Patrick and then one for herself and turned up the radio. The Ford was a good car, it wasn't a Camaro or anything, but it was a good, inconspicuous car. Patrick stomped on the gas and Molly sat back, smiling, lip-syncing the music. "Can we stop and see the elk?" she asked.

"We can do anything we want."

Molly wanted to say, *Then turn this stupid red car around and head for Arizona*, but she didn't. She'd wait. Patience didn't come easy to her, but she knew she was on the right track here with Patrick. He'd do just fine by her, she knew that. He'd do just fine.

When they got to the Dean Creek protected elk preserve, Patrick pulled into the parking lot, but there weren't any elk to be seen.

"They never have any horns, you notice that?" Molly said.

"Antlers," Patrick said.

"How come they never have any antlers?"

"Don't know. Maybe they're female."

"Females don't get horns?" She began to giggle. "Females don't get horny?"

Patrick smiled at her, finished his beer, and grabbed her, shoving his hand between her legs. "This female gets horny, I know that for a fact."

Molly squirmed around, rising up off the seat. "Let's go find us a place, Patrick," she said, then she pulled his face down and kissed him hard.

"The beach," he said, and he adjusted himself and they drove back onto the highway.

The miles rolled beneath the tires. Molly's kept herself occupied designing her new little ranch style house in Arizona with cactus landscaping. She'd have big cartoon characters on the walls in the baby's room, just like she'd seen in some magazine. A little boy, a little Patrick Jr.

She sneaked a peek over at him. He seemed unusually preoccupied, which was fine. She didn't have to have all of his attention all of the time. She left him to his thoughts. Whatever he was thinking, it was good for her, she could tell.

They drove alongside of some big, slow-moving river. Molly wished she liked Oregon better. She'd like to like this place, it was real pretty and all, she just had desert in her blood.

As they came up over the top of the coast mountain range, big black clouds thundered at them.

Patrick scanned through the radio stations until he found one broadcasting the news. Sure enough. Thunderstorms moving onshore from the coast. So much for walking the beach.

"Bad news, babe," she said.

"Yeah, what should we do?"

Go to Arizona, she wanted to say, but didn't. "How far north, do you think? Think storms would be in... like in Florence, or Depoe Bay?"

"I don't know. Let's just get to Reedsport. Maybe they'll blow on by."

"Maybe lightning will strike Leathers and burn that ugly shack down."

"Don't talk like that," Patrick said.

Molly finished her beer. "More beer," she said.

When the rain hit, it hit hard. Patrick slowed to a crawl as the center line appeared and disappeared. The windshield wipers slapped back and forth double-time, but that didn't help, the air seemed to be a solid sheet of water.

Then lightning crashed around them and Molly shrieked in the blue light. The headlights of a gigantic log truck came around the turn, flashed through the wall of water on the windshield. It looked as though it was coming right at them. It looked as though it was just about to hit them.

Molly screamed again and grabbed the wheel.

"No!" Patrick yelled, and stepped on the accelerator to move away from the truck, but Molly wrenched the wheel from him and spun it to the right. Patrick slammed on the brakes, and the car hydroplaned sideways, missing the huge semi's wheels by a thin sheet of water.

The engine died. Patrick tried to calmly start it, although his hands were shaking and his heart was pounding so hard he thought it might just give up and stop. He wanted to hit her. He wanted to slam her fucking head against the window until one or the other shattered.

The car started, he straightened it out and got going again, leaning forward to see the center line on the road.

"Don't ever do that again," he said quietly, red chords of anger pulsing in his vision.

Molly bit her nails.

Patrick pulled off at the first turnoff, shut down the engine, the lights, moved the seat back and stretched his legs. The tension of driving in the rain had given him a headache and the back of his neck hurt. His shoulder was sore as hell.

"I want—"

"Please be quiet," he said. "I don't want to hear you talk for a few minutes."

The car was anything but silent with the relentless thrumming of the rain on the roof. It sheeted down the fogged windows.

"What're we—"

"Please." Patrick said. He rubbed the back of his neck and listened to the rain. He began his countdown. Within moments, the coldness came over him. His emotions flattened out, the pain disappeared, Molly ceased to exist. He dove into that place, that stress-free place that was neither pleasure nor pain, here nor there, high nor low, dark nor light. It was void, empty, cold, blue, and quiet, except that if he listened just right, he could hear the buzz of Leathers' tattoo needle.

"No stress," Leathers said as he picked up their dirty breakfast dishes and put them in the sink, "I decided to learn to live with no stress. I left civilization, bought this old shack and moved in. No stress."

Darlene didn't want to argue with him, but he didn't look all that healthy to her. He had stress, she was sure of it. He just disguised it. The symptoms were all there, with his excess weight and the state of the cabin and probably even the tattoos. "No stress? How can you live without stress? Stress is part of life."

"The only stress I have is that little minx, that skinny little twat that Patrick drug in. She's not good for the boy, but that's his problem. When she begins to be a real problem for me, if he hasn't seen her true colors by that time, then I'll simply have her leave."

"That easy?" Darlene said. "Things that cause you stress... you just show them the door?"

"That easy," Leathers said. "Beer?"

It was long past breakfast. Darlene had been listening to Leathers talk about his roses for hours. Although she had been doing a fair amount of talking herself. In fact, she had told him her whole life story, it seemed, and they were just getting around to talking about him. Her mouth was dry. A beer sounded good. "Sure."

He twisted the top off two and then sat down again. He didn't seem to have a problem with the kitchen chairs. They squeaked and groaned under his weight, but he used them anyway. Darlene felt safer in the sturdy chair with sturdy arms.

"Stress is an attitude, Darlene," Leathers said. "And our minds are constructed so that we can only concentrate on one thing at a time. Live in the moment. So if your powers of concentration are fit—exercised regularly and vigorously—then you have no stress."

"How do you do that?"

"Do you have stress in your life?"

"Sure. I thought everybody did. I thought a little stress was good for people. It motivated them."

"Stress is negative. It is a terrible emotion. I can help you live without stress. No stress, no guilt, no negative emotions. It's easy. Want me to show you how?"

"Maybe later." Darlene sipped her beer and watched him. He seemed convinced that what he spoke was the truth.

"I'd like that," he said, leaning toward her until she could smell the beer on his warm breath, mixed with that after shave. The intensity in his eyes was electrifying. "I'd like that very much."

She felt her face grow warm. She wanted to lean forward the remaining few inches and touch her cheek to his. She wanted to feel his soft lips. Instead, she sat back coolly and sipped. "So what do you do for money?" A personal question, but then they were beginning to get a little personal anyway. And money was Darlene's primary source of stress. She couldn't remember the last time she had enjoyed talking with another person this much. Leathers was clever, entertaining, and just a little bit flirtatious. He seemed to enjoy her company as much as she enjoyed his.

"Social security, a little disability from the Navy and a few investments. I paid cash for this land and now and then Patrick brings in a little money. So it's just groceries, utilities and taxes. Doesn't cost much to live if you know how to do it. Biggest expense is probably rabbit food."

"Rabbit food?"

"Raise chickens and rabbits in the back. Good meat, good eggs. We eat a lot of eggs, rabbit and chicken. And the manure is pure gold for the garden."

Darlene smiled. It was hard for her to believe she had been brought here as some kind of a hostage. Carjacked. Leathers seemed like an old friend. "And so now and then you steal things to keep going?"

"Steal?"

"My car."

"No, that was Molly's doing. She's got a noodle up her ass to go to Arizona. No, I wouldn't do anything like that, but as long as she'd done it, well... we could use a car for a few days."

"That's all you want it for? A few days?"

"C'mon," Leathers said and stood up. "I'll show you the livestock."

"No radio, no television, no clocks," Leathers said as they walked outside. "No stress. But Patrick, well, he's young, and he likes that music stuff, and he likes to have a car now and then. He's young. He gets into mischief."

"Is he your son?"

Leathers coughed. "Thinks he is."

Burbank, the old yellow dog, joined them on their walk. Darlene threw a stick for him, but he just slowly wagged his tail at her as if he appreciated the gesture, but wasn't interested.

Leathers petted him and talked to him like an old friend. Darlene wanted to, but she could smell him from ten paces.

"Here," Leathers said, and they came around the corner of the house to a rabbit condominium that any bunny would be proud to call home. A shingled roof and a framework of 2x4s held a long cage partitioned off into separate units.

"This is the buck. The daddy. His name is Ranger. Then the two does. This one is Heather, she'll be having a litter next week, and this here is Sweets. She's got nine babies in her nest box."

Darlene could see woodshavings and rabbit fur moving gently in a wooden box.

"These are fryers, but they're not quite old enough for the freezer yet," Leathers said. He was looking at a cage with about seven or eight bright-eyed bunnies looking up at him with curiosity.

"You butcher them?"

"Patrick does."

Next to the rabbit cage was a little slant-topped box inside a wire cage. "Hello, girls," Leathers said, and opened the top of the cage and then lifted the slant top of the box. Two red hens sat in straw boxes. They squawked and flapped and scattered when he tried to reach beneath them, but they moved away and he brought up two big brown eggs.

"This always seems like a miracle to me," Leathers said. "A daily miracle." He regarded the chickens, smiling. He laughed at them preening. One began flapping dust up under her wings and he laughed like a little boy. "I love chickens," he said. Then he closed their house up and gave them a scoop of feed from a plastic bucket. He fed the rabbits, too, and watered them while Darlene watched.

When he was finished, he was breathing hard and perspiration ran down the side of his face. "It's hot," he said.

She agreed.

"Over here is the rose nursery."

Darlene saw furrows of the darkest, loamiest, most delicious looking earth ever, and every few inches a piece of rose stem stuck out of the ground. Each piece of stem sported budding leaves.

"Nice soil," she said.

"Bunny poo," Leathers said, and they both laughed.

Then a big raindrop smacked Darlene right on top of the head. And another one.

They both looked up at the sky just as the black cloud obscured the sun and turned the yard to twilight. Lightning flashed in the distance and a moment later they heard the rumble.

Darlene felt a little panic. She should have left long before. She couldn't walk out in the rain, not in a thunderstorm, she couldn't do it. She didn't want to do it.

"We better get inside," Leathers said, and she reluctantly followed him in.

She didn't want to overstay her welcome. But that was a pretty silly feeling, wasn't it?

She ought to go home, but then, if she was stuck here, she was stuck. There were worse places to be stranded. She leaned a little closer to Leathers as they walked back to the cabin.

Phil and Rocky sat in Darlene's living room trying not to look at each other until Lari arrived. The tension vibrated like gelatin between them.

Phil opened the draperies and early morning sun made the room smile. It made Rocky scowl.

Phil sighed with relief when he heard Lari's car, and he jumped up to open the door for her. She was fresh-smelling and dressed for work. He hugged her, then she sat down next to Rocky, leaving Phil standing in the middle of the living room. He quickly sat back down in the recliner.

"He called again," Phil said.

He was met with stony stares.

"Did you call the police?" Rocky asked.

"No," Phil said. "I called you."

"Why?"

"Because we have to make a decision here."

"There's no decision to be made, Phil. Call the cops." Rocky sat back and crossed his arms over his chest.

"Wait a minute," Lari said. "Go on, Dad. What did he say?"

"He said he wanted ten thousand dollars tomorrow and he would tell us where to find her. He said she was all right, and she would be all right through tomorrow, but if we called the police, or if we didn't come through with the money, he would leave her where she was, and nobody would find her. He said she would starve to death."

"Fuck," Rocky said.

Lari stared at him, her mouth open, her eyes beginning to puddle.

"You know that's an old kidnapper's ploy," Rocky said. "I say we call the police."

"No," Lari said, wiping her eyes and getting a grip on herself. "We think this through first. We don't do anything too fast. Does anybody have ten thousand dollars? I don't."

Rocky shook his head.

"Angela," Phil said. "Angela's got her inheritance."

"Yeah," Rocky said. "Angela should put up the money. This whole fucking thing is her fault."

"Wait a minute, Rocky..."

"No, *you* wait a minute, Phil." Rocky stood up and paced the length of the living room. "I can't help but find you to blame for this whole mess. If you hadn't been such a jackass, Mom would be home now instead of out with a bunch of—"

"Wait Rocky," Lari said, reaching for him. "One thing has nothing to do with another."

"You don't think so?"

"No, I don't," Lari said. "I don't think Mom had anything to do with this." She finally grabbed hold of his uniform shirt and pulled him down to the couch next to her. She grabbed his hand and held it tightly. "She's the *victim*."

"You wrecked her," Rocky said to Phil. "You and Angela. It's only right that the two of you pay."

"I'm not to blame for this," Phil said, his face growing hot. He'd taken just about his limit from Rocky. It was time he stood up to his son. Rocky was out of line.

"Well then this may be the only fucking thing in the world that you're NOT to blame for. You and your little pony-tailed bit of skank."

"That's enough," Phil said. He tried to visibly relax as he watched Rocky tense. He didn't want to make a bad situation worse.

Then Rocky's muscles went slack and his face screwed up into the seven year old Rocky that Phil remembered back in the days when life had a little stability to it. Rocky's shoulders shook and tears fell down his face. "She's my *mother!*" he yelled.

"Nobody knows that better than me," Phil said.

"It's about fucking time you remembered." Rocky swept the moisture off his face with the palms of his hands and reassembled his attitude.

"And Angela is my wife," Phil said quietly.

"Lucky you," Rocky sniffed.

Phil let Rocky's outburst slide with no outward reaction. Lari looked at him with that expectant look. Phil was still the adult. "I'll talk to her," was all he said.

"You know," Rocky said after a minute. "Only ten thousand dollars. That's kind of insulting, isn't it? I mean don't people usually ransom other people for millions?"

"Famous people. People who have millions. Mom is just... just an average person."

"She's my *mother*," Rocky said. "But that's what I mean. Why her? What's behind this? What if she *is* just on a camping trip and will be home on, say, Friday, which is why he wants the money on Wednesday so he can be solid gone by the time she comes home?"

"What are you saying, Rock," Lari asked, "that we need to delay him?"

"Buy time."

"I don't know," Lari said. "What if they're not feeding her? What if they have her chained to a tree or something out in the woods?"

They all looked out the window at the rain that was coming down in a steady, classic Oregon downpour.

"Carolyn said she's not in any danger," Lari said.

Nobody dared respond to that.

"She said that this is a time for unusually rapid growth and fulfillment for our karmic unit."

"Lari..." Rocky said.

"I'm just telling you what Carolyn said."

"And you believe that shit?"

"It's not shit."

"It isn't putting my mind at ease."

"I know," Lari said in a small voice. Then she looked up at Phil. "I say we spend Angela's money."

"*You* say that," Phil said. "I don't know what Angela will say."

"We'll pay her back," Lari said.

"My ass," Rocky said.

"*I* will. Somehow. *Somehow*, Dad. We don't have a choice."

"Call the police," Rocky said. "That's an option. Don't forget that option."

"I haven't forgotten, Rocky," Phil said.

"Listen," Rocky said. "This guy is a young, opportunistic little fuck. You know he's an amateur, or he would have made his ransom demand the first call, or the second call, instead of doing the 'are you taking care of the animals' stuff. He had to think about it first. He was testing the waters. He had to get his courage up. He's not going to hurt her."

"If he's such an amateur, then he's likely to be irrational," Lari said. "He could make some stupid decisions that a pro wouldn't."

"This whole thing is stupid," Phil said. "Let's us not be so stupid."

"Okay," Rocky said. "How about this? You go to Angela and get the ten grand while I call the police. We'll play both ends against the middle."

Phil looked at his kids. They both looked at back him and seemed to be of like mind. "Okay," he said, and handed the phone and the policeman's business card to Rocky.

"And when this whole thing is over," Rocky said, "I'm going to find that Patrick guy and beat him to death." He looked at Phil. "To death," he said again, for emphasis. "Horribly, painfully."

"Okay, Rock," Phil said. "That's enough."

"And if she's been hurt..." the implied threat was directed squarely at Phil. Phil ignored him.

Lari looked at her hands, the corners of her mouth turned down.

Rocky picked up the telephone and roughly punched in the numbers. He looked at Lari, still downcast. He elbowed her. "Hey, maybe they'll send over that butch redhead."

She elbowed him back. "You love the thought of it, don't you?"

"Yuck," he said. "You're my sister."

Phil watched them banter back and forth without really hearing what they were saying. He was glad the tension was broken, and he was trying to figure how in the world he was going to seduce that money out of Angela's account. He had to make it good; he had to make it very good.

"Okay," he said. "Let's talk to the police, and then I'll go talk to Angela."

Rocky looked at him with that damned knowing look on his face. Rocky knew he didn't want to ask Angela for her money. Rocky knew that Angela thought Darlene and Rocky and Lari–especially

Lari–were not quite up to her snobbish standards. Rocky knew that for Phil to get Angela to open her bankbook was going to take some major groveling.

Phil felt himself slip even one notch lower on Rocky's scale of respect.

~ ~ ~

Two men came this time, big policemen who again filled up Darlene's living room with what seemed to Phil to be a threatening presence. He kept telling himself that intimidation was half a police officer's job, but it wasn't until the shorter, younger one laughed a couple of times with his kids that Phil began to settle down.

When did he become so high strung? When had he lost his sense of humor?

Maybe yesterday, he thought. Maybe when he found out that Darlene might be in some kind of trouble.

The taller cop was a little closer to Phil's age, and his hairline was receding at just about the same pace. He pulled up a dining room chair and focused on putting Phil at ease, which made Phil feel old and special, like one of the old folks people had to be extra gentle with.

Stop it! He told himself. *You're being way too sensitive.* Sensitive. Ha. Now there was a word Darlene would love to hear somebody say about him. She would never have thought he had a sensitive bone in him. But sensitive was exactly how he felt. He felt like a raw nerve, jangling and twitching in Darlene's recliner while the other four people in the room talked of trivial things, and when they talked about Darlene, the police seemed to talk about just another customer, just another customer, when in fact the woman in question was Lari and Rocky's *mother* for God's sake, and she had been Phil's *wife* for twenty years, so have a little *respect*, fellas, and FIND HER.

I'm losing it, Phil thought, when he realized he was on the verge of yelling at the policemen, excused himself and went to the bathroom.

He washed his face in stinging cold water and reminded himself that they were only police officers, and to them she *was* just another customer. He had to be as clear as could be about this thing, but perhaps he wouldn't be able to leave the whole thing up to them. Perhaps if he cared so much, he couldn't just relax and leave her fate to bureaucratic paperpushers who might lose her file or let it become pre-empted by something more serious, something more important.

Take charge, Phil said to himself, and a new energy surged through him. He went back into the living room with a renewed sense of self.

"Now," the older cop said, "how did this Patrick guy propose to make the exchange?"

"He didn't say," Phil said. "I assume he will call back tomorrow."

"Okay," the cop said. "You made the right decision by calling us. I want you let us handle this, do you understand?"

Phil was insulted, as if the cop thought he couldn't understand plain English.

The policeman turned to the kids. "Do you understand? I don't want any of you getting hurt over this. Let the professionals handle this. We can get your mom back and we can get this guy, but you have to leave it alone and let us do it, okay?"

Lari nodded, wide-eyed. Rocky pulled at a thread in his phone company uniform pants. "Yeah," he said.

The cops stood up. "Someone will be at your house early tomorrow morning," the older one said to Phil, "to make a hookup to your phone. He'll stay with you until the kidnapper calls. If you hear anything before that, call us immediately."

Phil nodded. He had absolutely no faith in these local yokels. Wasn't kidnapping a federal crime? Shouldn't they be calling in the FBI?

They shook hands all around and then the blue suits left.

Lari sat wringing a sopping Kleenex, moisture under her nose, her eyes red. Rocky had his arm around her shoulders, and periodically gave her a little macho pull toward him.

"I'm going to stay here tonight," she said.

Phil nodded. "I think that's a good idea," he said. "In case anybody calls."

Rocky nodded, chewing on the inside of his lip.

"I'm going to go talk to Angela," Phil said. "It wouldn't hurt to have that money standing by."

"You can bring Ashes and Tina home," Lari said, her voice breaking. "It would be nice if they were here."

Phil didn't trust himself to speak. He looked down at his hands, then cleared his throat. "You think you want to stay here until she comes home? Might be a couple of days."

"Tomorrow," Rocky said, his jaw set. "She'll be home tomorrow."

Phil nodded. "The animals would like to come home."

Lari reached for the phone. "I'll call Carolyn."

"Maybe she could come stay with you," Phil said.

Lari began talking softly into the phone.

Phil stood up. So did Rocky. They awkwardly faced each other. "I'm going to go talk to Angela," Phil said. Rocky nodded. "Then I'll bring back the animals." He knew he was babbling, repeating himself, but he didn't know what else to say. He was burning to be alone, to think things through.

Rocky held out his hand. Phil took it and shook it, and they looked into each other's eyes. "I'm going to work," Rocky said. Phil nodded.

Then Phil dropped his son's hand and went out the front door.

The rain came down in a steady drum. Phil hunched his shoulders up and high-stepped to his car. He started it, turned on the windshield wipers and the headlights, then drove two blocks away, pulled over and parked.

He had to think.

He wasn't willing to let the ineffectual, politically-driven useless Springfield police handle this. It was too damned important. But even the police said that there was nothing to be done until the call came in. Then they'd spring into action. Phil could see it—he had seen it a zillion times on television. They'd mock up a briefcase, stash it, stake it out and then nab the bad guy after the exchange.

Well, hell, Phil could do that. Only he'd forget about nabbing the bad guy. The bad guy could have the money. Phil just wanted Darlene back safe and sound in her little house with Ashes and Tina. Life was not right without her there. Life was unbalanced and scary without her there. Phil was a single parent without Darlene, and while the parenting chores were almost nil now that the kids were adults, there were still birthdays and holidays, and someday Rocky would get married, and there would be grandkids... Angela was not parent to Rocky and Lari, she was more like a sibling. Phil didn't know how to do it without Darlene.

God, he missed her.

Maybe this was exactly the challenge that Phil needed. If he brought Darlene back single-handedly, perhaps... Vague hero dreams flashed through his head. Respect from Rocky, respect from Lari. Angela would get hot and rake her nails up his back when he screwed her like she used to, when she used to think he would make a fine catch. Darlene would be firmly installed back in her recliner, knitting grandbaby things with Ashes on her lap and Tina snoozing on the arm of the chair. Order would be restored. Life would be better than ever.

He'd go talk to Angela about the ten thousand dollars, and he would not take no for an answer. He'd give the jerk the cash and he'd get his wife back.

Oops. His ex-wife.

Phil gritted his teeth and started the car. It was easy to be a hero parked alone in his car on a quiet street in the rain. Let's see how he did in front of Angela.

~ ~ ~

An hour later, he was back at Darlene's house. He knocked and when Lari opened the door, Ashes danced in.

"Ashes, honey!" The dog yipped at Lari and jumped up at her knees. She picked him up and let him lick her all over her face. Tina yowled in her carrying case, so Phil set it down along with the bags of food, and released her. She walked around calmly, smelling things. Then she jumped up on the recliner and stretched toward Lari. Lari petted her.

"How'd it go?"

"Fine," Phil said. "Angela said we could have the money."

"She did?"

Phil nodded. It had been astonishingly easy. In fact, this was a side of Angela he had never seen. When he told her about the ransom, Angela had said that she had ten thousand in the bank and she'd draw it out tomorrow if he wanted. It had been that easy. Phil had been stunned. His fallback position was to put a second mortgage on the house, but he didn't even need to mention that.

It was only on his way back to Darlene's house had he realized that Angela now had a leg up on Lari and Rocky and Phil. Now Angela could demand a little respect, and she'd get it, she'd earned it. She was no longer the odd one out. She had leverage and had used it judiciously. She would probably never even remind anyone of her generosity. She wouldn't have to.

Superiority was a cheap buy at ten grand.

"But we don't need it yet, do we?" Lari spoke slowly, as if she suspected something.

"The police don't seem to think so." Phil held out his hand and Ashes licked it. "He's happy to be home."

"Yeah," Lari said. "They both are."

"Is Carolyn coming over?"

"Later."

"Good. I'm glad you're not going to be alone. You okay?"

"Yeah," Lari said, and she looked better. "I'm just worried. Freaked out."

"Yeah," Phil agreed. "Well, I better go. Tomorrow might be a bitch."

"Yeah. I called in sick, so I'll be here."

"Okay." Phil turned to go.

"Daddy?"

He turned back. Her pretty green eyes were filling with tears again. "Let the police handle this, okay? They're professionals."

"They're professional idiots, honey."

"I know, but they know more about these things than you do." She set the dog on the floor and reached up for a hug. Phil hugged her close and felt dangerously close to tears.

"We'll get her back, and that's all that's important," he said. Her newly-curled hair smelled like beauty shop chemicals.

She sobbed and gripped him even tighter.

In a moment, she relaxed and he extracted himself. "You going to be all right?"

She wiped at her nose with that soggy tissue. She nodded.

"What time will Carolyn get here?"

"Soon. She's calling in sick too."

"Okay. I'll be home if you need me."

She nodded again. Then she smiled. "Rocky's thinking about getting married."

The news was so unexpected, so incongruous that Phil didn't understand right away.

"Sorry?"

"Rocky's got a girl. He's thinking about marrying her."

"Marrying?" Rocky was about as far away from marriage material as Phil could imagine. "Well. Well, maybe that would be just fine," he said. "You're sure?"

"He's thinking."

"I can't worry about Rocky now."

"Oh Daddy, it's nothing to worry about."

Yes it is, baby, he wanted to say. Just another thing a parent worries about. "Well, I'm going to go now. Bye, Ashes. Bye Tina."

The animals both looked up at him with home-contentment in their eyes.

"It's all going to turn out fine," Lari said. "Carolyn said."

"Carolyn's a smart cookie." He kissed her on the cheek and walked back down through the rain, wondering when they turned the corner, trying to pinpoint just when it was that the children began to console the parents.

Rain hammered the shack and Leathers emptied pans as quickly as they filled up with the rainwater that leaked through the roof. It wasn't long before they were both doing it, and laughing.

"This isn't stressful? What happens when it begins to leak over your bed?"

"I had Patrick put one a'them blue tarps over my bedroom roof," Leathers said in that soft backwoods accent that sounded to Darlene like something that would come out of West Virginia. "No, it ain't stressful."

"Your house is falling down around your ears and that isn't stressful?"

Leathers laughed, his dry, whiskey rasp that sounded good in this dismal place. "This place'll outlive me," he said, then he coughed, a loose, jelly cough, and Darlene believed him.

They drank beer after beer until Darlene found everything to be funny, and so did Leathers. Darlene emptied the pans when they began to overflow, and Leathers made a fire in the little woodstove, which took the damp chill from the room.

Leathers kept the table supplied with snacks, from crackers and cheese, to chips and salsa, to canned anchovies and cream cheese on sourdough bread. They drank beer and ate away the afternoon. Darlene talked and talked, freewheeling and young under Leathers' ministrations and attention.

Late in the afternoon, though, the beer began to take its toll. She got up from the table and walked to the front door. The rain came down in a steady drone. She was suddenly depressed that she couldn't get home to her animals, to her shower and a fresh set of clothes. She was stuck here at least until Patrick and Molly returned, and even then, maybe she would be stuck here another night.

"I feel like a nap," she said.

"Me, too," Leathers said. "Come with me."

Darlene followed him, wary, ready to refuse whatever idea he might have. They walked through his studio, still a place of curiosity and intrigue to Darlene. She wanted to examine every stainless steel tool and secret stashed in the little cabinet full of drawers. Leathers opened the door on the left. He flipped the light switch and two bedside lamps came on.

"Why don't you lie down in here? I'll take the couch."

A waterbed. It looked inviting; Darlene was tired beyond belief. "Good," she said, and Leathers closed the door behind her.

The bedroom was nothing like the rest of the house. It was neat and clean. The two dressers and one overstuffed chair were old and looked like vintage Goodwill, but the doorless closet was filled with neatly hanging clothes, and items on top of the dressers were carefully arranged. There was no dust, there were no clothes thrown in heaps, no trash in the corners.

And there was a small bathroom with a clean shower, toilet and mirror.

Darlene pulled off her clothes and got into the shower without a thought. She found soap and shampoo and lathered herself up and rinsed off. Fresh smelling multi-colored towels were neatly folded and stacked on a shelf, and she helped herself to a turquoise one. She watched herself in the full length mirror as she dried the rolls of flesh around her waist and just below it, as she rubbed the towel around her breasts, across her back. She saw the dimpled skin of her hips, her buttocks, her upper thighs. Not pretty. Unfair, that heavy men like Leathers can still be attractive, but even a few extra pounds on a woman turn her into an item of ridicule. Then she used his deodorant, ran his comb through her clean, wet hair and crawled into his bed.

What a relief. She barely had time to consider why Leathers' quarters looked so nice and the rest of the house looked and smelled so ratty, before she fell into a delicious sleep.

"Darlene?"

She dreamed it was Larissa, standing by her bed. "Mommy's sleeping," she mumbled, but when did Lari start calling her Darlene?

"Darlene?"

It was Phil, at the edge of the bed. He was worried about her. Had she been sick? "Leave me alone for a little while," she said to him. "Just let me be myself for once."

"Darlene, are you asleep?"

"Go away," she said, but the words came out with such clarity that it woke her up. She wasn't in her bed, her bed was never this warm or this soft.

It was too dark. Her bedroom was never this dark. There were nightlights, and streetlights, and city noises—

Her heart pumped so hard and so fast that she saw light globes float before her eyes.

"Darlene?"

Then she recognized the voice. Leathers. She remembered. Her heart began to slow, she took a deep breath, her muscles relaxed a bit.

"Yes?"

"Are you awake?"

"Yes. What time is it?"

"I don't know, but Patrick should have been home by now."

Darlene thought about this information. It didn't seem to be a disaster, although her mind was still a little bit sleepy and maybe she didn't know all that Leathers knew that would make him worry. "So?"

"So Patrick said he'd be home by dinnertime. It's long past dinnertime."

"What time is it?"

"I don't know."

"Oh yeah. You said that. Well..." He seemed like a little boy, worried over some imagined disaster. She blinked her eyes, rubbed her hands over her face. She tried to be alert, but sleep still crouched in the corners of her mind. "Does he usually come home when he says he will?"

"Always."

"What about Molly?"

"I think she's talked him into doing something bad."

"Maybe it's the storm. Maybe they got trapped in Reedsport and couldn't get home. You don't have a phone, do you?"

"No." His voice was low, depressed.

Darlene pulled the covers to her chin and sat up, suddenly

aware that she was naked and in Leathers' bed. He was sitting on the wooden waterbed frame, the room was dark, this situation was way too intimate for her liking. She ought to go home. "Is it still raining?"

"Yes."

"Why don't you let me get up and dressed?"

She felt his hand on her back, his soft hand, and goosebumps rippled across her skin and down her arms. She pulled away from his touch. "Please?"

He stood.

"Can I borrow some clean clothes?"

"Help yourself," he said, and closed the door behind him.

She rolled out of the waterbed then turned on the light switch. She rummaged in his drawers until she found a stretched-out pair of sweat pants that were too big in the waist and tight in the thighs. Then she found a huge sweatshirt that let her breasts hang free without being obscene. She rinsed her face again, combed her hair that had dried squished down on one side and used his toothbrush.

Reasonably presentable, she opened the door and went into the studio. Leathers was in his recliner, shaving the hair off his right forearm.

"Sit down here," he said, indicating a low stainless steel stool on wheels, the kind that doctors use.

"What are you doing?"

"I want to color in the green leaves on this azalea." He finished shaving, then wiped the soap off onto a towel. "See?"

Darlene could see the details of the azalea very lightly drawn. It was all outlined in fine black lines with no color added at all.

"You'll have to do it," he said.

"Me? I'm no artist."

"I'm right handed."

He squirted green ink from a squeeze bottle into a little paper cup, the kind that fast food restaurants put ketchup in. He mixed in a little yellow, a little black, stirring it with a toothpick. Then he assembled the electric needle.

"I can't do that, Leathers."

"Of course you can," he said, working with what seemed to Darlene to be some kind of an antidote for his worry over Patrick.

"Are you worried about Patrick?"

"Uh-huh," he affirmed, his fat, sausage fingers deftly handling the tools that had colored so much of his body. "Okay," he said. He dipped the end of the apparatus into the ink. "It's only two needles, so it will make a very delicate line. You dip it into the ink like this, load it up good, see?" He turned on the high intensity lamp, trained it on the armrest.

Darlene took the needle from him, pulling the cord out so she could handle it easily.

"Now you just start it and color inside the lines. You need to load up on ink often, or the coloring will be uneven. Just try, you'll get the hang of it."

Darlene touched the trigger and buzzing filled the room. The needle vibrated in her hand. "Leathers, I don't think..."

"Of course you can," he said, then he sat back and closed his eyes, the azalea on his wrist in the warm spotlight.

Darlene closed her eyes, opened them, took a firm grip on his hand, dipped the end of the needle, then scratched the buzzing little thing into an azalea leaf.

It bled.

"It's bleeding," she said.

Without opening his eyes, he handed her a soft paper cloth. "Keep going."

She adjusted herself for more comfort. The electric needle was heavier than she thought, but within a few minutes, she had the hang of it. She began to think about the way Leathers looked, as if he was deep in a trance. Maybe he was meditating to the pain. Maybe he was meditating to the sound of the needle. Maybe self-mutilation was his way of escaping stress.

She began to understand how it worked. Her third leaf was better than her second, which was better than the first. Soon she realized where the light was coming from on the scene, and left blank areas along the edges of the leaves, where she could lighten the ink and come back and give them a little more depth.

She got into it. The needle and the towel. Dip the needle, scratch the skin, blot the blood, view the work. Dip the needle, scratch the skin, blot the blood, view the work.

When she was finished, she could barely straighten up. She'd been hunched over the azalea for far too long.

"Leathers?"

"Huh?"

Had he been asleep? How could he sleep? "I'm finished."

He sat up and looked at the coloring. "Good," he said.

"See these edges? I'd like to lighten the ink and come back and do them."

"Do them now," he said, and relaxed again, closing his eyes.

Darlene looked at the row of squeeze bottles. She took a dab of white and mixed it in. Too much. Another dab of green, a little yellow, she fiddled with the inks until she had what she thought was right.

It didn't take her long to finish the edging on the leaves, and when she looked at it, it hardly showed. Maybe it wasn't worth the effort. Solid would have been good enough.

Leathers smiled when he saw the finished product. "You're an artist," he said. He wiped alcohol over the area, waved his wrist around in the air for the alcohol to dry, then he smeared Vaseline and wrapped gauze lightly around it. "It swells a little," he said, "then it scabs. And when the scab falls off... a beautiful tattoo. By Darlene."

Darlene wasn't sure how to take his praise. This was as bizarre a thing as she had ever done. And the work had made her hungry.

"Ready for dinner?" he asked.

She nodded. He seemed to be back to his old self again. Whatever it was that had bothered him about Patrick and Molly coming home late seemed to have resolved itself during the inking. Too weird, she thought. Too weird.

But then she was in the kitchen, clearing off the remnants of their afternoon snacks, and he was heating oil in the big black cast iron pan, she was chopping onions and he was tossing a salad, and pieces of chicken were breaded and browning.

Rain fell steadily.

They ate with their fingers, Darlene knowing that she shouldn't be eating this much grease, knowing, too, that Leathers was killing himself as well. But never had she felt so free of social constraints, never had she felt so stress-free. She felt like she was on vacation with her new best friend, and when he brought a bottle of vodka out of the freezer, she laughed and matched him shot for shot.

They played cards after dinner, and ate ice cream, and when the rain stopped, they went outside and looked at the stars. They walked around the yard, the rabbits glossy-eyed and alert, the old dog following them at a fair distance. The yard was alive with rose perfume. Every now and then they would stop and listen, and they could hear the scurrying sound of creatures in the woods.

Rats, probably, Darlene thought, living in all this trash.

Leathers took her hand in his big soft one and they walked back to the house, their shoes squishing with water from the damp grass and weeds.

When they got back inside the house, Leathers went in the back and came out with a fresh pair of socks. Darlene took off her slippers and put on his dry socks. Then he sat next to her on the couch, and she could feel his heat.

"Bed time," he said.

She didn't know what to say. She wanted to say something about Patrick, but she didn't want to depress him. She wanted to say something about the weather turning nice so that she could leave in the morning, but she didn't want to make him mad…. or however it was that Leathers got.

Then he put his arm around her and brought her face to his and kissed her so lightly, so gently on the lips that she lost all thought. He broke the kiss off, but didn't move away. Their lips were but millimeters away from each other, and they just breathed in each other's essence. Then he kissed her again, sucking gently on her upper lip, and then her lower lip, his tongue exploring the corners of her mouth.

She'd never been kissed like that before. She felt her body respond in a dramatic, almost embarrassing way. She was too old for this, this teenage hormone thing.

"Oh," Leathers said softly. "You make my heart beat."

That did it. Darlene was lost. It wasn't hormones, it wasn't teenage. It was loneliness, the deep, awful, echoing chamber of loneliness she'd lived in since Phil left, since years before Phil left, since their marriage had run its course long, long ago. And now, almost fifty, she had found herself to be attractive again, by someone who didn't care that she had love handles instead of a waist, she had hams instead of thighs. That her hair was squished down on one side. That her clothes were as shapeless as she was, that she wore no makeup.

Leathers' loneliness matched her own. And their needs met with thundering cymbals.

"Oh God," he said. "It's been so long." He heaved himself out of the cloying couch, then pulled her up. He took her by the hand to his dark bedroom, where he stroked her face with his hands, and then he kissed her again. He lifted the sweatshirt over her head, and she pulled his tee shirt off.

He radiated so much heat she couldn't believe it. His skin was smooth; somehow she thought she'd be able to feel his tattoos, but she couldn't. He was hot and smooth and hairy. And big.

She was glad there was absolute darkness in the room as she pulled off the sweatpants, pulled down the covers and got into bed. She felt like a virgin. She felt like a fool.

He sloshed the bed as he got in next to her, and his hands were soft and gentle.

She sucked her stomach in as his hand explored her, but of course that didn't help. And he didn't seem to mind that she had much more flesh than she needed.

His hands were as skilled as his mouth, and soon she forgot everything about what she looked like, where she was and who she was. Her hands found his tender places, and she sat up and kissed the sweet, heart-shaped end of his enormous erection. She had only had three lovers in her life, and not a one had a penis anything like this.

Leathers seemed to anticipate her moves, her body's desires. He whispered gently in her ear and she lay back, trying to relax, but her nerve ends were feverish. She wanted to move, she wanted to help, she wanted to *do*. "Shhh," he said to her again, his fingers sticky with her juices as he lay them across her lips, and she kissed them, and licked them.

He heaved himself on top of her, then rolled them both over on to their sides, and with gentle little rocking motions, entered her a tiny bit at a time.

Then he grasped her backside and pulled her to him, and lying totally still, with nothing moving except the throbbing of their hearts and their parts, Darlene felt the orgasm building up from deep inside of her.

"Oh," she breathed quietly as it shuddered through her from the bottom up. "Oh!" She forgot everything except the sensation of being young and in love. She forgot everything except Leathers' deep brown eyes and how they looked when he peered into her soul.

He waited until she had finished, and was urgent for more. Then he rocked her and swayed her, and spoke quiet little instructions and words of pleasure into her hair.

And when he came, it was with such force that it carried her along with it, another stunning, surprising orgasm that left her not only breathless and perspiring, but weak with wonder.

"This is confusing," Carolyn said as she frowned down at the dining room table.

Lari folded the newspaper, got up from the couch and went over to her, looked at the colorful spread of Tarot cards laid out in front of Carolyn.

Carolyn shook her head. "I just don't get it," she said, then rubbed her eyes.

"What's the problem?" Lari began to rub her wife's shoulders.

"Everything seems to conflict. There doesn't seem to be a single thread I can follow. First, I get that your mom is all right, then I get that she's in terrible danger, but then it's danger of her own making, then I see that she's in physical danger, then I see death, but then she's all right again. It doesn't make sense.

"Did you throw the cards for Patrick?"

"Yes, but I see nothing. I've never seen cards so blank before."

"Maybe that's not his real name."

"Wouldn't matter. It's the entity. The Patrick is a blank person. Emotionless, I guess. No personality. No identity. Dead. No, something less permanent. Temporary loss of identity? I don't get it. This is weird, like I've never seen before."

"Maybe there's somebody else involved," Lari said. "Can you throw the cards about someone you're not sure exists?"

"I can try." Carolyn gathered up the cards while Lari sat down in the chair next to her. She cut the deck several times, then lay the large cards out carefully, one at a time, squinting and shaking her head at each new card.

"A man," she said. She lay down more cards. "Well, he's pretty clear." She finished the sequence, then stood up to look at them more carefully.

"What?"

"This is not good," Carolyn said.

"What?" Lari scanned the cards, but their symbols and placements were meaningless.

"He's incomplete," Carolyn said. "That's about all I can say."

"Incomplete? What does that mean? Deformed? Retarded? Paraplegic? What?"

"Skewed," Carolyn said with a shrug. She looked down and studied the cards. "I have no idea." She gathered them together and left the bunch in a pile. "I don't like looking at them." She looked instead into Lari's deep brown eyes, saw the lines of worry. "I don't know what to tell you," she said.

"Should we worry?"

Carolyn smiled a sad smile and hugged Lari to her. They rocked back and forth in each other's arms for a moment. "Let's light some candles," she said, "and hold your mom gently in our thoughts."

WEDNESDAY

Darlene woke to the singing of birds. She opened her eyes slowly and saw sun slanting through the scarlet-flowered rhododendrons that obscured the windows. Cobwebs of soft dreams continued to surround her. She smelled the warm, earthy scent of their lovemaking, and remembered shyly that those soft dreams were mostly made of how and where to move and not move in this liquid bed so as not to have his juices leak out from her. In her dreams, his seed had mystic healing properties.

She stretched, feeling luxurious. The bed was warm and soft. She felt brand new.

The Leathers furnace snored softly beside her, the corner of a sheet wrapped around his groin, the rest of him exposed to her examination.

In daylight, without fear of being rude, Darlene took her time and looked at the tattoos closely. They were extraordinary works of art. Nothing like the heavily-outlined cartoons of naked women, clawed panthers and bloody skulls she'd always equated with tattoos, these were actually skin illustrations. They were executed with a light, sensitive touch. The colors and shadings blended with Leathers' naturally light brown skin, and each image led to the one next to it.

Along the back of the arm that she could see was the doghouse, stuck in the back of the lot, almost obscured by bushes. In real life, it was as raggedy as the rest of this place, with its mossy shingles and a dirt-encrusted opening where the muddy dog had gone in and out a zillion times over the years. On Leathers, the scene was depicted with exact accuracy, even to the brown around the door, but on living, breathing skin, the doghouse took on a new importance. It became art.

Darlene would never look at another doghouse the same way again.

The lower part of his right arm was not colored in. She wanted to pull off the gauze that covered her color work on the azaleas. It had come loose during the night.

She sat up, bringing the sheet with her, and gently pulled on the gauze. It came away.

Leathers was right, the work was swollen, and had begun to scab. But she could see the design, she could see the unevenness of her first attempts, and she could follow her progress as she got the hang of it.

She couldn't wait to see it when it was completely healed.

What was she thinking? That would take days. She wouldn't be here in days. She wouldn't even be here in a couple more hours.

It was time to go home.

Homesickness gripped her stomach and she pulled back from him. She missed Ashes and Tina. They wouldn't be happy without her at home. And she wanted to call Lari and catch up on her life. This had been a wild and weird adventure, but it was over now, and she wanted to go home.

"How does it look?" Leathers didn't clear his voice or let her know in any way that he was awake.

Startled, Darlene pulled away from him. "Like you said. Swollen. Scabbing."

"And how do you look?" he asked.

She didn't understand the question, and then he rolled over and opened his eyes.

He grabbed her arm and pulled her back down, and looked at her, their faces inches apart. "You look gorgeous in the morning," he said.

She struggled in the awkward position, thwarted by the unstable waterbed, wanting to get up, to get away from him. "I have to brush my teeth," she said.

"Brush them, and then come back to me."

She got up and made it to the bathroom in record time. She didn't want him to watch her flab moving as she crossed the room, and she could feel wetness running down her legs from their lovemaking the night before.

She peed, brushed her teeth, then rinsed off quickly in the

shower. She came back out, freshened and wrapped in the turquoise towel.

"That color," Leathers said, sitting up. "That exact color. That's the color we will put on you. It's perfect. You're lovely."

Darlene smiled indulgently. "I have to go now, Leathers."

His face grew serious. "Wait right here," he said, then he rolled out of the bed and walked boldly, nakedly, unselfconsciously into the bathroom where she heard the water running and the toilet flush. He had tiny little buns below his huge torso, and his legs, though not skinny and bird-like as she expected, were well-formed and looked like they belonged to someone who used to play tennis. His thighs were muscled and still tight, his calves thin and snaked with veins.

He was tattooed everywhere. Everywhere except below his knees. Not all of it was colored, and the drawings stopped higher on one thigh, but other than that, he was covered in ink. And uniformly brown. She thought he might have a tan, but there was some ancestry there that made his skin dark. Brown eyes, white hair. Latino, maybe. The designs on his lower back and buttocks reminded her of something Asian. She'd have to look closer at those.

Graying hair spread across the tops of his shoulders and down across his shoulder blades. It was coarse hair that had lost its curl through the years, giving his back a gauzy appearance.

When he opened the bathroom door, Darlene couldn't help but stare at her first full view of his front. He was quite extraordinary. The same coarse gray straight hair covered his chest from his neck down to his nipples, then it tapered to a V and below his ample belly, merged with a thick crop of graying pubic hair. His nipples were large and sensuous, his belly round and Buddha-like. His heavy, circumsized penis traveled confidently under its protective shelf of abdomen, and when he lifted a leg to slide back into bed, it was all she could do to keep her hand from snaking out and cupping those glorious testicles in their diaphanous pouch.

He was colored with ink from his neck to his knees. All except his genitals. They were pure and untouched by needle and ink. The effect, she discovered, was highly erotic.

He snuggled under the covers, then reached up, grabbed her and pulled her down, shrieking, back into the bed. Warm hands felt her ample hips and slowly wrapped around her and brought her close to him. Then they unwrapped the turquoise towel.

"You're wonderful," he said with that husky voice, and kissed her with a minty tongue.

This wasn't what she wanted to do, but it was nice. It felt so good to be touched, to be appreciated, and it was likely to be a long time before she had another lover, so she closed her eyes and listened to the zinging sensations her body was treating her with, let the tiny, airborne thought of pregnancy or disease float through and on out again, and settled back to enjoy his attentions.

But he was rougher this time, more exuberant. He pinched her nipples, and pulled her hair, pulling her head back, farther and farther until she could only see the headboard, and her throat was completely exposed to him. When she whimpered and complained, he gripped her arms with hands so strong she was afraid he'd leave bruises. Then he pounded her and pounded her, his weight threatening to rupture the waterbed and she wondered if he would leave her to drown if it did. She wanted him to stop, but he had such a tight hold on her that she couldn't move, and she dared not complain.

Then he began to make these sounds in her ear, sounds of passion, sounds of love, and he began to lose control. When he began to whimper, her passion flourished, and in spite of herself, in spite of her feelings, her body greedily devoured him. He came, and she gripped him tighter yet, riding him until she came. When her shuddering stopped and her muscles quit twitching, she disengaged herself quickly and pushed him away.

She turned away from him, perspiration drying coldly on her skin, her breath ragged, her feelings hurt, her mind awash with conflicting, confusing thoughts.

"I'm going to teach you how to concentrate, Darlene," Leathers said. "It will make all the difference." He got up. "Come on," he said. "It's a beautiful day to be in love."

It's a day to be at home, Darlene said to herself. This situation has run its course. It's not fun anymore. She wanted nothing more to do with Leathers. She was certain he meant her no harm, but he was pretty creepy. She needed to get home to tend to business. Phil might start to worry about her, and once that started, then Lari and Rocky would get involved. She didn't want to worry anybody.

She heard Leathers puttering around in the kitchen, so she

showered again, then dressed in her dirty clothes. She tidied the bedroom, hanging his clothes that she had worn the previous day on a hook behind the bathroom door. She made the bed, smoothing the worn, hand-made quilt into place and plumping the pillows.

"Whole grain beet pancakes," he said. "I overwintered the beets in the garden, and now they're just right."

The reddish mixture swirled around in the blender. Darlene had never heard of such a thing, and she really wanted to get out into the morning sunlight, but she didn't want to just walk out on Leathers and his pancakes. And she was really hungry. She cleaned the table and swept the disgusting floor while Leathers heated the cast iron griddle. Then he made syrup from brown sugar, water and maple extract, and the maple smell wafted through the house.

The pancakes weren't red, although they were a bit pink, and when he'd cooked up a huge plate of them, they sat down to eat.

The pancakes were delicious, and she ate two big ones. That was enough. She had a long walk ahead of her.

Being this fat was fairly new to Darlene. She'd never been skinny, but she'd never been fat either, not really, not before Phil lost interest in her. And then when they divorced, and he remarried, well, the thought of another man in her life was absurd, so she felt justified in sitting in her recliner with Ashes on her lap and eating all day long and into the night.

And now... And now she felt like there were possibilities in her life. There was hope for her love life, she could see.

"What's your real name?" she asked.

"Bob," he said. "Bob Leathers."

Bob. She should have known. She had a history with guys named Bob. It was her father's name, and the name of the boy who stole her virginity in high school. It was also the name of the guy she was involved with when good looking Phil Martin calmly discussed his proposal of marriage, and made her an offer she couldn't refuse.

Bob. Every time she met a Bob, she looked a little closer, a little deeper. Every time she met a Bob, she automatically blushed a little bit, as if they all shared some memory of her, since she had been intimate with three—now four—of their number. She looked for recognition in their faces, as if she assumed they shared some genetic memory because they shared the same name.

Bob. Bob Leathers. Another one. Three of four of her lovers had been named Bob. Uncanny. Darlene had never given a thought to numerology until this very moment, but now she was going to have to look into it. She'd ask Carolyn: What was this thing with guys named Bob?

She wondered if their mothers all had something in common. Something to make them name their sons Bob, something that made these sons all grow up to be similar in some respect that was terminally attractive to Darlene. What kind of woman named her son Bob, anyway? And did Darlene have anything in common with the women who went along with their husbands and named their first born sons Jr.? Rocky's birth name was Phil Junior. How about the mothers of daughters named Larissa? Would she have more to talk about with those women than she would with someone who named her daughter Sophie?

Guys named Bob were the shapers of her destiny, she had to face it. The thought made her smile, and she looked down at her pancakes so the current Bob couldn't see her grin and question her on it. Interesting, how they could share so much of themselves in bed, at night, and yet she couldn't tell him about something this funny, this casual, this thing about guys named Bob.

Intimacy is easy, she thought. It's the casual part that's tough.

"So it really is Leathers?" she asked when she had recovered.

"Yep." He stabbed another three pancakes, slapped them down in the pool of syrup on his plate and slathered them up with butter.

She watched him eat, repulsed by his gluttony. Butter and syrup dripped down both sides of his mouth and wet his chin. He had a tiny piece of pancake on the side of his nose, and his fingers were sticky with syrup.

She wanted to go home.

"Well," he said between bites. "Today we turn the compost."

"Isn't that something Patrick does?"

Darkness clouded over Leathers' face. He set his fork down. "Patrick is dead," he said.

"Dead?"

"Gone. He won't be back." He pushed his plate away and mopped his face with a paper towel.

"Of course he'll be back," she said. "They just got tied up because

104

of the storm. They'll be back today."

"They won't," Leathers said, "and I've dealt with it, so let's drop the subject."

"Well, I don't think you should be thinking of him as dead."

"He has become a stranger. Strangers are not welcome here."

"Oh, come on." Darlene couldn't believe she was hearing him say this about Patrick, the boy who might as well be his son. "Your feelings are hurt, that's all. He'll be back. You two care for each other."

"Darlene," Leathers said, and she felt like Molly must have felt when he gave her the dressing down over eating. "What is, is. What ain't, ain't. Patrick ain't here. You are. Let's get on with it."

Darlene set her fork down and let the cold, heavy silence flow over the floor. She wanted to pick up her feet so it wouldn't get on her shoes. After a moment, she said, "I've got to go home. I'll clean up the breakfast dishes, and then I'll walk on out to the main road."

He looked at her questioningly. He shook his head as if he didn't understand. "Go?" he said.

She nodded.

"No, you can't go. Not now."

She smiled, feeling that indulgent look on her face again, hating it. "I have to. I have a house, and animals."

"Your animals are cared for."

"My children will worry about me."

Leathers waved that aside with his big paw. "I love you," he said. "Darlene. I love you."

"Pardon?" This was like a scene from a bad movie.

"You can't leave. I can't let you. I won't let you. I need you."

Darlene coolly watched his emotions tornado through him, from desperation to resignation back to desperation again.

"I can't live here by myself..." Beads of perspiration erupted on his forehead and ran down the side of his face. His breath came in irregular wheezes. He got up unsteadily from the table, a dazed look in his eyes, and went into the studio.

A moment later, she heard the tattoo needle.

Darlene quietly cleaned up the breakfast dishes, not quite sure of her own emotional state.

When dawn finally grayed his bedroom window, Phil watched with less relief than he thought he would. His muscles were sore from lying tense all night, waiting for just such gray. Angela breathed softly next to him, the quiet sound of a woman with a clear conscience.

He looked over at the clock radio. The red digits read 5:03. The bank didn't open until ten.

He willed his muscles to loosen for the zillionth time. He relaxed, his body sinking gently into the firm mattress, and then he re-rehearsed the morning in his mind. Before he was finished, his fists were clenched, his arms stiff, his back ached, the toes of one foot were trying with frustration to pull off the toes of the other.

He turned over, punched his pillow, and tried to meditate himself to sleep. It didn't work.

He kept seeing Rocky's face. He'd been looking at Rocky's face in his mind's eye all night. He'd seen Rocky's hate, his disrespect, his disdain. Rocky had always been like that; he'd hated Phil since the day he was born, it seemed.

But now, Phil was thinking something else. He was thinking that maybe Rocky hated him because Phil had been such a jerk to Darlene.

He had been, too. He married her in college because he wanted some stability. He wanted a home, and Darlene was the homemaker type. Darlene provided a good home, and did it happily, and then she gave him two great kids, but he had been a jerk. He knew she had always suspected about his affairs, she just chose ignorance over confrontation.

That couldn't have been much of a life for her. What kind of a partner had he been?

Kids are perceptive, he knew. Peaches knew the minute anything was amiss in the household, and she acted accordingly.

No wonder Rocky hated him.

Phil began to actively detail the plan that had been swirling around his mind since it woke him in the dark of the night.

He owed it to Darlene to do his best for her. He owed it to Darlene and he owed it to Rocky. Lari, having chosen the unconventional lifestyle, was a little bit more forgiving, but maybe he needed to make a few fundamental changes in his life if he didn't want to see the same look in Peaches' eyes when she was twenty.

He churned in bed all night, his mind clenching around this one idea. He worked on it, honed it, perfected it, discarded it, picked it up and worked it some more. Until, by God, it could work.

He lay in bed and waited for the alarm to ring.

Then he would get up, get Peaches up, dressed and fed, so Angela could sleep in. That would help put her in a good mood. He would call his secretary, have her cancel his appointments again, he would call the police, he would go to the bank, and then he would sit and wait for the kidnapper to call.

When Morning Edition on NPR began its morning spiel, Phil got out of bed, showered, shaved and fetched the baby.

He changed her, dressed her and put her in the high chair to amuse herself while he fixed them a breakfast for which he had no appetite.

He called the office and talked to the secretary. His load was light this time of year. He was ahead of projected sales, so the boss wouldn't have a problem with him taking a few days off. He lay the police officer's business card on the countertop and fiddled with it.

He read the paper, then cleaned up Peaches and played with her for a while. At eight o'clock, he made sure Angela was still sleeping, then put the baby in front of the television, went into the den and dialed the police.

The officer whose card he had wasn't there, so Phil left a message for him.

Within moments, he called back.

Phil snatched the phone on the first ring. He didn't want Angela up.

"Hello?"

"Phil Martin?"

"Yes."

"Lieutenant Jenricks, Springfield police."

"Lieutenant," Phil said. The name was not familiar. "Do you know—"

"Yes, I have your file here."

"The kidnapper called this morning." Phil's heart began to thump and he found that his breathing was ragged. He kept his mouth far away from the receiver so the cop couldn't tell he was lying.

"I see."

Phil's heart pounded anew. Did the cop believe him?

"What did he say?"

"I'm supposed to take ten thousand dollars in a gym bag and put it in the newspaper recycling box at the Roseburg mall at precisely six o'clock tonight. Then I'm supposed to wait for his call at the pay phone at the Rice Hill burger stand."

"Did he say anything else?"

"No."

"Well, since the kidnapper might know you, you'll have to make the drop. Do you have a gym bag?"

"Yes."

"Okay, we'll pick you up about four o'clock, and we'll make the delivery. We'll get your wife back, Mr. Martin, and we'll get this guy, too."

Phil almost corrected him on the wife/ex-wife thing, but then he didn't bother. He had until four o'clock.

He hoped he could be finished with his own plan by then.

By the time he hung up, he could hear Angela talking with the baby. He stayed in the den for another half hour, staring at his hands, looking through the contents of his desk drawers, just wasting time, until he was certain she'd had some coffee. Then he went into the kitchen, made small talk, nuzzled her a little bit and tried to pretend like everything was normal.

He hovered by the telephone until ten o'clock, when he approached Angela, who was reading a magazine in the living room, Peaches quietly playing with a vast mess of colored toys.

"Hon?"

"Hmmm?"

"This would be a good time for you to go to the bank."

"Bank?"

"The ten thousand dollars."

"Oh. Now?"

"Please?"

"Oh yeah, sure. Okay. Hm. I forgot."

Phil closed his eyes and willed himself to say nothing. *How could she have forgotten?*

She put on a different pair of shoes, gathered up her purse, a lightweight jacket, her sunglasses and left, spouting instructions for Peaches.

Phil paced until Peaches became bored. Then she became so demanding that he didn't have much time to dwell on what he'd done.

What he'd done was entirely, horrifyingly illegal. But did the police ever need to know about that? Was there any way they could prove or disprove that the kidnapper called or didn't call this morning?

Of course there was. The kidnapper could tell them. They could look at the phone records. These days of computers, the police could find out anything. Privacy had become a joke.

Phil was certain he would fry for that phone call he had made. He was going to send police and tax dollars on a wild goose chase while he ransomed Darlene himself. The police would screw it up, he just knew it. They would get her killed. Phil wouldn't. He'd pay the scumbag his blood money and get the children's mother back.

And somehow, he would have to repay Angela.

Angela was gone for hours. He tried his best to entertain Peaches, but she was not to be entertained. She was grumpy and temperamental. She threw things, she screamed, she cried for a graham cracker, then in spite, she crumbled it into the carpet right in front of him.

Phil tried bathing her, tried television, tried reading to her, tried putting her down for a nap.

She was having none of it.

Where the hell was Angela? Phil was too old for this.

Just as he was ready to dress Peaches warmly and take her out into the cold spring day where she could run around the park, Angela's Kia pulled into the driveway.

She had groceries. And two fancy shopping bags. No wonder

she'd been gone so long. Phil said nothing, just carried the bags in and set them on the kitchen counter while she cooed and tickled the baby who was suddenly all smiles.

Angela opened her purse and handed him three small bundles of bills.

"That's it, huh?" he said.

"Ten thousand dollars," she said. "You owe me."

He kissed her on the cheek. There were six five-hundred dollar bills. He didn't think the kidnapper would want five-hundred dollar bills, but he didn't think to tell Angela to keep the bills to hundreds and smaller. Oh well. The rest was in hundreds. He put the money in the gym bag and set the bag on the floor by the door. As soon as the phone rang, he wanted to be ready to grab the bag and head out. He gratefully relenquished Peaches' care to Angela while he put the groceries away.

Peaches settled right down and played quietly.

At noon, the phone rang. Phil spit coffee at the sound of it. It was Lari. Phil told her there'd been no word.

At two, Rocky called. Phil told him there'd been no word.

If Patrick didn't call soon, he'd have to go to Roseburg with the police. Or else call it off.

At two-thirty, the phone rang again.

"I have a collect call from a Patrick." The operator said. "Will you pay?"

He was calling collect? Good thing Angela didn't answer. She would never have accepted the charges.

"Yes, operator. I'll accept."

"Sorry," Patrick said. "I'm calling from a pay phone and didn't have any change."

"That's all right." Phil was having a hard time believing this.

"Got the money?"

"Yes."

"Called the police?"

"No." Phil tried to say it realistically, without too long a pause, without saying it too fast.

"Good. Okay. Bring the money to Florence."

"Florence?"

"Yes, just north of the Driftwood Shores Hotel is a little beach park. There's a big trash can there. Put the money in a... in a little cooler, like one of those little Playmate coolers, and put the cooler in the trash can. Then go home, and I'll call you."

"What about Darlene?"

"What about her?"

"Can I talk to her?"

"Just bring the money to where I said, and when you get home again, I'll call you and tell you where to pick her up."

"She's all right?"

"Of course she's all right. What kind of a... I gotta go."

The line went dead.

"Patrick? Patrick, wait." But he was gone, and Phil knew it.

Phil sat down for a moment, then went back into the den, closed the door and dialed the police.

"Lieutenant Jenricks? He called again, and called it off."

"Called it off? What do you mean?"

"I mean he called and said that the exchange wouldn't work the way he had it planned, so to hang on to the money and wait, and he'd call us back."

"We're going to put a wire on your phone."

Phil felt a sense of privacy invasion, and said, "No, I don't think so. I mean, I have a choice in this, don't I?"

"Well..."

"Then I think I'll just let you know when something else develops."

"Mr. Martin?"

"Hm?"

"Don't play footsies with these guys. It's your wife's life."

"Yeah, right," Phil said, and hung up.

He smiled down at the phone. He'd never felt so in control before. Not that what he'd done was a monumental task, he reminded himself, it's just that he had refused to be intimidated by the blue-suited police force, and a lieutenant at that. Perhaps he could get on the other side of the psychological game with this twit, Patrick. Calling collect. What a jerk. Surely he could get Darlene away from this geek without much trouble.

He smiled at his Rambo attitude. Rocky would like it.

There are social agencies, Darlene thought to herself as she finished wiping down the kitchen surfaces. She'd get home, notify some authorities, and somebody would come help Leathers get along. He didn't need much; mostly he needed companionship and someone to do the heavy things he didn't have the health for.

He was in the other room hurting himself, and that made her feel bad. She knew it wasn't her fault, she knew that Leathers was not her responsibility, but he was childlike in a way, and he needed to be cared for. If Patrick wasn't going to do it, then somebody was going to have to.

Strange that Patrick would just take off like that. She thought they'd just gone to the coast for a couple of days. She felt certain that he would drive her red Ford through that hole in the weeds any moment.

Or, if not any moment, then some time soon. Even if they had taken off, it wouldn't take long for a smart kid like Patrick to understand the likes of that Molly girl. And yet... God seems to have made somebody for everybody. He had to make somebody for Molly. Maybe it was Patrick.

Who had God made for Darlene?

Nobody, that's who. Darlene was the exception.

Unless she wanted Leathers. He was a Bob, wasn't he?

She gave the table a final swipe and then rinsed out the sponge and put it by the sink. She dried her hands and then walked gently through Leathers' studio. He was hard at work on his thigh. Etching drawings into his skin upside down.

In his bathroom, she washed her face, then ran his brush through her hair and noticed that it fell softly and waved around her face. With a little of the right kind of trim, maybe she didn't need to go through all the folderol of curlers any more. Why was she stuck with a hairstyle from the nineties?

She looked closer. It wasn't her hair at all. And it wasn't the lack of makeup. It was her face. She looked softer. She looked more feminine, and it wasn't the lighting, either. It was the man. Not Leathers in particular, but a man in general. The way she felt just being around a man, a man who liked her, a man who wanted her. It made her feel good about herself. It made her feel like a woman, a desirable woman.

That was not a politically correct thought, and Lari would pitch a fit if she knew what Darlene was thinking.

She closed her eyes and leaned against the sink. How many years had it been?

Or had she ever felt that? With Phil, maybe, many years ago. Then again, maybe Phil never wanted her. He only wanted what she could do for him.

Leathers wasn't the man for her. He wanted too much; he was dependent and a little bit nutso, but that wasn't the point. The point was that he had reawakened something important in her. He had reminded her what it meant to be a woman. She had to have that touching, that loving back in her life. She *would* have it.

She grinned at herself in the mirror, then opened the bathroom door. She'd do what she could for Leathers. He had made a profound contribution to her life, just in the last twenty-four hours.

The needle had stopped buzzing. He was sitting in his chair, taping gauze to his thigh when she came back through. He smiled at her. But that piece of pancake was still on the side of his nose, and there was still stickiness on his chin. He wasn't at all attractive to her any more.

"I'm going to go now."

"Okay," he said.

She leaned up against the edge of his padded table. "I will come back to visit," she said, "and I'll bring you help, too."

His eyes narrowed. "Don't bring strangers here, Darlene."

Her face got red. "I didn't mean anything by that," she said, "I just thought—"

He smiled and held up his hand. "I know. I know. Come on. Let me show you my pride and joy before you go."

He hauled himself out of his chair, then took her by the hand. He gazed around the clean kitchen, gave her hand a squeeze in appreciation. She closed her eyes in indulgence. She could do this.

They went outside.

The day was clear and bright, sunlight glinting off raindrops that still covered all surfaces and dripped from the trees. The ground was swampy, and Darlene's slippers were soaked through with her first steps in the high grass. The weeds had blossomed with purple, white, yellow and blue flowers. Tall grasses were tasseled, and each tassel was crowned by a clear, sparkling drop of rain. Through the trees, she could glimpse patches of dark blue Oregon sky. A slight June breeze rippled the trees and the grasses and sent more raindrops down on their heads.

Darlene slid her hand out away from his.

They took their time walking through the rose garden, Leathers touching each plant. Burbank followed.

"Do you work?" Leathers asked.

"I get alimony from Phil," she said. It's not much, but I don't need much. Pays the taxes, insurance and buys food. If I want more, I have to work. I do some part time stuff at a temp agency, doing this and that."

"Patrick used to work sometimes," Leathers said. "When he did, payday was always a celebration. He'd stock up on beer. Ice cream, too. That kid was an ice cream nut." Leathers' voice sounded thin.

He was grieving, Darlene realized. She was glad to be here for him.

"How do you pay your bills?"

"Nothing's due."

"But when you pay them, how do you do it?"

"Patrick."

"What about now?"

"Nothing's due."

"I know, but when it is?"

"When it comes due, I'll know."

A whole new concept to Darlene.

He led her through the roses, past the doghouse, the rabbits and the chickens, along a path that wasn't really a path at all, but just a lower spot in the weeds. Darlene's pants were now wet to the knees.

She didn't like not being able to see where she stepped. There might be dog poop, or tree branches to trip over, or snakes or something.

But Darlene forgot all her hesitations when she saw Leathers' garden.

"Pretty busy at harvest time," he said.

The garden was at least a half acre, and perfectly tended. Not a weed, not a plant out of alignment. Rows were as straight as they could get, paths were perfectly kept with matted straw.

Behind them, one of the chickens loudly proclaimed an egg.

Darlene would die for a garden like this. She had always wanted one, but never had the time to garden when the kids were little, and now that they were grown, she had a little tiny city lot.

This was a dream garden. No wonder Leathers was so brown all over.

"You must be out here all day long," she said.

"Usually, yes." They walked along the rows of tomato cages. The plants were thriving, already in flower and topping out over the tops of the cages.

"Bunny poo?" she asked.

He smiled, nodded. "And chicken."

The field was kept at bay by black plastic, held down with a variety of odds and ends, a toilet tank cover, a few boards, some old bottles and jugs filled with water. On the side of the garden opposite from the tomatoes, rows and rows of corn were already a foot high.

"So early!" They were barely selling starts in the grocery stores. In the back, berries were in bloom, asparagus was sprouting, rhubarb had gigantic leaves and artichokes were ready to be picked.

"I have a root cellar over there," Leathers pointed at a big mound on the far side of the corn, twenty feet from the edge of the garden.

"Can I see?"

"Sure."

She walked along the well-laid path. Trellises were set up for beans, and the peas were already up and filled with white flowers. Little pods emerged along one whole side.

At she neared the mound, she saw it was covered with tar paper. The root cellar. There was even a door. It looked like the door had once belonged to the lower half of a horse stall.

When Darlene was a little girl, she read about springhouses, where jugs of milk and cream were kept cool by the water that ran through. Since then, she'd always wanted to have a springhouse where she could sit and read the hot summer days away. A root cellar, by definition dark and earthy, held much the same mystique. No complete garden should be without its root cellar to keep carrots and potatoes fresh. This garden needed a couple of chairs and a table to go along with its root cellar. This would be a fine place to sit on a summer day.

She stepped carefully through thigh-high weeds around to the door. She heard a rustling, and her skin crawled as she thought of mice and rats having burrowed in and gotten in to the overwintering vegetables. Was this where Leathers had kept the beets they had in their breakfast pancakes?

She stepped again, onto something soft and squishy, and in jumping back from the icky feeling, her feet slipped out from underneath her and she went down hard.

Teeth snatched her left hand in a wretched vise.

At first it barely hurt. She heard the bones crunching, and felt them crinkle and collapse, but she felt no pain.

Then pain thundered. It hurt like the demons of hell were chewing on her. She screamed. One scream was all she had, though, then she couldn't catch her breath. Her hand was on fire, and whatever had it wouldn't let go.

It sounded like chains.

She turned toward Leathers, and saw him huffing his way toward her, but her strength was evaporating. She was afraid to faint, afraid to lower her head into the tall thistly weeds. Why didn't it let her go? *Why didn't it let her go?*

Sound began to muffle, like cotton in her ears, and the pain receded, as did everything else. She saw Leathers, but he was further and further away. The ground came up to her in slow motion as she sank down, and her horrified eyes clamped on the thick metal teeth that had sunk right through the palm of her hand. She moved her arm, and the chain rattled.

She thought she would throw up, but before she could concentrate on that thought, her neck went limp and she lay with noodles for muscles, mute and deaf in the grass.

"Holy Jesus," Leathers said, "Holy Jesus." The words barely made it through the cotton in her ears as the big man in the orange shorts arrived, panting and sweating.

He pulled on her arm and it didn't even hurt. He squeezed both ends of the rusted metal trap and the jaws relaxed. Her hand fell out of it and flopped on the ground. She could see the blood running out, but she felt no pain, no pain at all. She felt nothing.

"Come on, Darlene," Leathers said, and pulled on her other arm, but she had no strength, and she couldn't hold on to him. "Darlene, come on, let's go back to the house."

"Just a minute," she said, and it sounded like mumbling to her. It sounded like she had both her ears plugged and could hear her voice only inside her head.

"Stay with me, Darlene, don't go. Don't go."

Go where? she wanted to say, but then she knew. She felt like going to sleep. But first, she wanted to throw up.

He took off his tee shirt and began to wrap her hand.

Then, with a scream she didn't know she had in her, the pain shot back, and she had all her faculties, she had all her sensations, her limbs again worked and her muscles contracted.

She wailed.

"Good," he said. "Stand, and let's get back to the house. Damn traps. I forgot about the traps, I swear, Darlene, I forgot all about the damned traps."

He hoisted her up and she leaned on him, holding her crudely wrapped hand. Blood had already soaked through the tee shirt. "I'd carry you if I could, but I can't. You'll have to walk. Walk now, honey, and lean on me."

One step at a time, each step an eternity, each step shooting pains up her hand, her arm, her shoulder to her brain, each moment filled with the threat of unconsciousness. Eventually she was on Leathers' bed, her arm propped up on a pillow. She felt so dizzy she was barely able to lie there.

"Rusty old varmint trap," Leathers wheezed as he went about collecting things to clean her up. "I leave that stuff to Patrick. I forgot about the traps. I had no idea there was one by the door there. I had no idea."

Darlene just wanted to watch the blood drip from her hand and go to sleep. She wanted Leathers to leave her alone so she could sleep.

Sleep was the best idea she'd ever had.

"Don't leave me now," he kept saying to her. "Darlene? Don't leave me, honey."

Leave? I'm not going anywhere, Darlene thought. Not now. Not when I can sleep. I'll probably never leave here again, she thought, smiled softly and closed her eyes.

"Darlene? Drink this, honey."

Leathers held a water glass filled with brown liquid. Whiskey. She pushed him away.

"Drink it," he said, wheezing with exasperation, the authority in his voice unmistakable.

She drank and it burned her. She wrinkled up her nose and looked at him.

"Finish it."

"I'll throw up," she said, and tears involuntarily leaked out of her eyes.

"No you won't. I need you to drink the whole thing," he said.

She held her breath and gulped. And gagged. But the alcohol stayed down and soon began to warm her.

She looked over at him, sitting on the stainless steel stool, and saw him cleaning a pair of pruning shears with alcohol. "I don't want to hurt you," he said.

She nodded, and with no choice but to trust him, watched him sharpen the shears with a file.

He smiled at her. "This is perfect," he said.

Phil went into the den, pulled an old spiral notebook from the desk drawer and began writing. He wrote down what he had done and what he was going to do, just in case something terrible happened and he didn't come back. He wrote it in as much detail as he could. He was an educated man, but he was no writer. He was unsure of spelling and punctuation, so he kept it simple. The last thing he wanted was for Rocky to ridicule his suicide note.

Suicide note? Is that what this was?

Sure seemed like it.

So he put in a few words of appreciation for Angela, Larissa and Rocky, and wrote how much he'd loved Darlene, and what a fine life they'd had and mentioned yet one more time how their breakup had been nobody's fault, particularly not the kids'. He told them all how proud he was of them, signed it, and put it in an envelope. He licked it closed, and after a long hesitation, wrote on the outside "To be opened in the event of my death."

That seemed overly dramatic, and he felt a little bit foolish when he did it, but that was the only appropriate thing he could think of to write on it.

Then he put it in the very front of the middle desk drawer.

"I'm going out for a while, honey," he said to Angela, who was on the floor picking up all of Peaches' toys.

"Okay," she said. "Let's order pizza for dinner tonight, okay?"

"Sure." He kissed her on the top of the head, took the gym bag with the money in it and left.

He drove by Darlene's house. Lari's car was in front. Good.

He stopped at the grocery store and bought a little Playmate cooler, a six pack of Diet Coke and a Snickers. Those were for Darlene.

Then he turned on talk radio and headed for Florence.

After a couple of miles, he slowed down, turned off the radio and slid down in the seat a little bit. He relaxed. This reminded him of when he and Darlene used to take long drives just for the hell of it. They'd go to the coast for the day or to Seattle for the weekend, for no particular reason, except they enjoyed the drive. He and Angela would have to do that sometime soon. Peaches was old enough to enjoy a car trip.

At Veneta, Phil pulled into a convenience store parking lot. He threw the gym bag in the trunk; he didn't want to think about it. Then he got himself a bag of pretzels. He and Darlene always shared pretzels on their road trips. He popped himself a Diet Coke and got back on the road, ready to cruise through the beautiful coast mountains.

He and Darlene had shared some pretty spectacular times, not the least of which was the adventure of raising the two kids.

Rocky, too smart for his own good—it's never good to have a kid who is more intelligent than both parents combined—and good looking to boot. It had taken Rocky a long time to find his place in life, and Phil wasn't sure that he had found it yet. He was too smart, too good looking, he didn't fit in anywhere. He was named Phil Jr. when he was born, but that didn't fit him, never fit him. He nicknamed himself Rocky when he was about two.

But now, at twenty-one, he wore his blonde hair longish, but neatly cut. His strong jaw and even white teeth and blue eyes gave him that California surfer look that girls liked, but Rocky was not one for casual relationships. He went about solo most of the time, and only dated one girl at a time. Rocky was a boy that Phil could be proud of, and he was. But Rocky also intimidated Phil, and it seemed to Phil that he did it on purpose. Rocky wasn't a perfect kid, he was just too smart for his own good. He needed years to mellow those smarts into something useful.

Phil was surprised that he would go with such a secure job as the electric utility. Rocky seemed too individualistic for that large-company union mentality.

Larissa, another odd one, (were they all?) had been clearly a little boy in dresses. When Darlene finally stopped making her wear lace and frills (about the time Rocky was born, and Darlene didn't have the time or the energy to fight with her about it), and Lari settled in to her own style of clothing and friends, the whole family breathed easier. It was really no surprise when Lari announced her homosexuality; everybody had suspected it for a long time. Phil was happy that Lari had found Carolyn, a little tiny pear-shaped blonde girl who was so smitten with Lari that she had stars in her eyes. Lari looked much like Darlene, with the soft brown hair and warm eyes.

Lari and Carolyn. Phil and Darlene had gone to their wedding ceremony, or their Holy Union, as they preferred to call it. Angela was offended at the thought of it, and Carolyn's parents weren't there, either, but it was a beautiful, simple, candlelit ceremony in Lari and Carolyn's living room. Carolyn wore a simple white dress, and Lari wore a pair of white slacks and a white silk blouse. They both looked ethereal, and Phil found himself with a lump in his throat as they exchanged vows and wedding bands.

He and Darlene held hands throughout the ceremony, though they'd been divorced for three years, and he'd been married to Angela for two. It was a family affair, and for some reason, Phil felt that Lari and Carolyn would weather the good times and the bad times well. And, so far, so good. They'd been married now for over a year, and still honeymooning.

Phil crunched a pretzel and washed it down. He passed through Walton and began the climb up into the coast mountains. Spring was a beautiful season in Oregon. All the deciduous trees had their fresh, light green foliage, and all the evergreen trees had those tender little ends of fresh growth that looked so sweet, Phil always wanted to bite them.

A little nagging guilt chewed at Phil's stomach.

He felt like he was in some way being unfaithful to Angela by spending so much time thinking about Darlene. It's just that he and Darlene had such a history together. And there were the kids, Darlene and Phil's kids. Angela tried to enjoy their company, but there was rivalry there. Phil thought about the step-family paradox, the new family blending with/competing with the old family. Phil dealt with it by ignoring it. Let everybody work it out themselves.

How did other people do it?

It didn't matter. Nothing mattered much in the long run, and for the moment, nothing mattered as much as getting Darlene back from that loony. She wasn't built to withstand high drama.

He smiled. She wasn't built for speed, she was built for comfort.

He frowned. Angela was built for speed, and boy oh boy, she wanted speed in the bedroom. When he was feeling romantic, she wanted to get it in, get it off and get it over with as quickly as possible. It hadn't been like that before they were married. When it was on the sly. When he was married and she was a secretary in the firm, and very attracted to him.

Now that she had him, he wasn't as attractive to her any more, he could tell. She was too young to be married to a fifty-year-old fart like him, and nailed down with a baby to boot.

Phil smiled wryly to himself. Laughing coworkers had told him the day before his wedding that he'd just had the last great sex in his life. And that had been horribly true.

To Phil, she was just another hot little number who needed an experienced man to show her what could be done with a nimble little body like that. Women went wild with a man who took care, paid attention, gave them skyrocketing orgasms. They were easy to come by, those women.

But this one had caught him. Caught him big time. Phil didn't see it coming, but when Angela set her sights on him, she did whatever she needed to do in order to get him.

No. That's not right. He believed her birth control failed. He had to believe that. He couldn't believe that she got pregnant on purpose. He refused to believe that.

So there they were. Phil, fifty-one, with a twenty-four year old wife and a two-year-old daughter.

Darlene, on the other hand, was soft and warm and giving, even though he knew they hadn't been sexually well matched. Their years together had been good ones, and Phil couldn't explain what had happened to dissolve the marriage, except that he just lost interest. Panicked, Darlene tried everything she knew to fix it, to rekindle it, to repair it, but that only made Phil feel less inclined to stay around and watch her decline and more inclined to look at the firm young legs walking around the office. It wasn't anybody's fault, except perhaps Father Time.

Life.

Sometimes it was good, sometimes it was shit, most of the time it was flat-out baffling.

"Patrick?"

"Hmmm?" Patrick was propped up in bed with three pillows. His eyes followed the nonsense on the fuzzy motel television screen, but his mind was on ten thousand dollars and everything he could do with it.

"Wanna get married?"

"Hmm?"

Molly crawled over the newspapers that were sprawled on the wrecked bed, crawled up Patrick, wrapped her arms around him and looked up into his face. "Wanna get married?" she asked again.

"Married? No." He shrugged her away from his sore shoulder.

"No? How could you say no? What do you mean, no?"

Patrick took her arms and gently rolled her off him. He plumped up the pillows and resumed listing the things ten thousand dollars would buy him. "I don't want to get married," he said. A little electric cart for Leathers would be the first thing. If Patrick wasn't going to be there to help, Leathers needed some way to get out and around if he wanted to. Yeah, one of those little golf carts would be perfect.

Patrick wondered if any of the tomato plants had set fruit yet. He wondered if he'd caught any nutria or possums or rats or anything in his traps.

He missed the place. He missed Leathers. He felt a little sick to his stomach and realized, with dismay, that he was homesick.

He shoved Leathers out of his mind. Leathers had that woman now. He'd be all right. He felt Molly's hand sliding across his belly and under the elastic of his pants. Now there was something to take his mind off the farm. He turned over and grabbed her by the hair.

"Married!" he said and she began to giggle. "Is that all you women think about?" He let her unbutton his jeans, and then, careful not to let them slide down revealing what Leathers had done to his buttocks, he forced her legs apart and entered her, listening to the crinkle of the newspapers beneath them.

The thought of all that money aroused him to an incredible peak, and with scarcely a thought about the woman beneath him, Patrick humped and pumped and then came, in a long, drawn-out whoosh. He lay there on top of her for a moment, until she began to move and he remembered where he was and who he was with. Then he swallowed and rolled off her. He got right up, pulled up his jeans, grabbed some fresh clothes and went to the bathroom, locking the door behind him.

In the shower, he soaped up and sluiced down, running his fingers gently over the intricate network of scars that covered his entire body. He gently probed the latest development, the bumpy pattern across his shoulders, soaped and rinsed the rawness that hadn't quite sealed yet, then dressed carefully, buttoning his plaid shirt to the wrist and to the neck, and walked back into the room, toweling his hair with another.

"You're gorgeous," Molly said.

"Yeah?"

"Yeah."

He walked back into the bathroom and combed his hair. This shirt was old and thin. After tonight, he'd throw away these clothes and buy all new ones.

She stood in the doorway, watching him. Her blonde hair was a frizzled tangle, her mascara was smeared. Her lips were still swollen from passion, and the flush he'd put on her face was the most attractive thing about her. "What're you doing?"

"Going out."

"Without me?"

He turned, gave her a kiss on the forehead. "I'll be back before..." he looked at the ceiling, calculated time and distance, added in a little measure for emergencies, disasters, tried to figure how long it would take before she realized he wasn't coming back, then added an hour. "Nine o'clock."

"Nine o'clock! Tonight? Where are you going, Patrick? What are you going to do?"

"I'm going to take us to Arizona, cupcake. You just wait here like a good girl. Be patient. Remember. Good things come to those who wait."

She pouted. She hooked a finger into one of his beltloops. "Take me with you, Patrick, I don't want to stay here by myself."

"I can't, honey. You watch television, now, and take a nap. Before you know it, I'll be back."

"Arizona, really?"

"Really."

"Married, maybe?"

He smoothed his hair in the mirror. He shrugged his shoulders. "I won't say no," he said. "Down the road."

"I know," she said. "That is kind of a futuristic thought, isn't it?"

He gave her firm little buns a stinging swat with the flat of his hand.

"Ow."

"Be good," he said, and walked out of the door.

The sky to the east was clear, but huge black thunderclouds were rolling in from offshore. Boy, he was glad he wasn't out there in some small sailboat or something. The wind had picked up and was blowing salt, sand and the scent of adventure toward him.

He jangled the keys in his hand, trotted down the motel steps and got into the red Ford. He fired it up, put on the radio, and peeled out of the parking lot. He was headed for Florence and Easy Street.

"There are three kinds of pain," Leathers said. "Pain of the heart, pain of the flesh, and pain of the soul."

Darlene felt the throbbing in her hand, tried not to think about what it had looked like when he unwrapped it, bits of grass and weeds, mud and rain, dirt and slugs and God knows what else imbedded in her flesh by the force of those wicked, rusted triangular teeth. She needed to get to a hospital before she died of blood poisoning. She needed a phone. But how would she get to one? No way she could walk out of here now. No way.

"I'm going to teach you about pain," Leathers said. "Pain can become your friend."

The kind of friend I need is one with a car, Darlene thought. Where the hell is Patrick? She prayed that Patrick would come to his senses now, now, NOW and turn her little red Ford around. She needed him. She needed him bad.

"When you know your pain, you know yourself. I've taught Patrick, taught him well. Patrick knows his pain. He knows himself. Pain is a great teacher."

She listened to Leathers talk about physical pain, but what she felt was a different pain, a pain that had taken seed and was beginning to grow. It wasn't pain of the heart, and it wasn't pain of the soul. It was terror, a cold, cold pain. Terror that she would never see the outside of this room again. Terror that she would never see Larissa, or Rocky again. Or Ashes or Tina. Or Phil.

"Knowledge of your pain can give you control over your life, control over your body, control over your emotions."

Tears leaked out of the corners of her eyes and ran into her ears. Her chest heaved with a sob, but that only jiggled her torn hand and made it hurt. She was going to die right here in this bed. She would die of blood poisoning or infection or some damned thing and Leathers wouldn't even be able to get her carcass out of the bed and into the compost pile.

She cried, and that hurt and that made her cry some more.

"No one can touch you if you know yourself. No one can hurt you once you've become a friend with your pain. When pain becomes a friend, a good friend, an old friend, then to hurt is to love." Leathers talked and she sank into a mire of misery.

"Pain will never leave you, pain will never lie to you, pain will never die. Pain is good."

He set up the spotlight next to the bed and turned it on. He began talking as he adjusted it. "There is acute pain, and there is dull pain. Know how the sharp edge of a coffee table can hurt when you walk into it? Well, put a piece of cloth over it. Would it help? Not much. How about two layers? How about a hundred? A hundred layers of cloth would help, wouldn't it?"

He brought in the stainless steel tray, with its loud instruments, gauze and mysterious jars and set it next to the light. He lit a small white candle and placed it on the tray.

"Well, if we take the low-level, throbbing pain, and divide it into layers, then we can wrap some of those layers around the acute, sharp pains and dilute them. If you can learn to deal with one, you can deal with all of it."

He wheeled over to her, pruning shears in hand, and as the panic rose from her bladder to her throat, she swallowed rapidly and tried desperately to listen to what he was saying instead of thinking about blood poisoning. Or what he was about to do.

"All right now, Darlene, I want you to feel the dull, throbbing ache in your hand. Dive into it. Concentrate on it. It's made up of chords of vibrations. See them. Visualize them."

Darlene saw them. Sometimes they were vibrating, vertical shafts of colored light, sometimes they were jagged concentric circles.

"Isolate one of those chords. Separate it from the others."

Darlene saw them, but she couldn't do anything with them. She couldn't manipulate them. Well, wait, she could fixate on one and make it stand out, and the others receded, but she was afraid that if she opened her mouth and spoke, she would lose the whole thing.

"Now see what happens to it when I do this," Leathers said, and he tapped her hand with the handle of the shears.

The chords screamed in intensity of color, their vibrations went wild. She lost sight of them, they turned dark and went right off the scale of her vision. After a moment, they settled down, and she could see them again.

"Those are the layers," Leathers said. "This is how we're going to save you, Darlene. You have to be able to deal with the pain, otherwise you'll die in this bed. You'll die of fear. Understand?"

She tipped her head in a slight nod; she didn't want to lose sight of the pain chords. It was amazing how little her hand hurt when she could see the pain as opposed to just feeling it.

As if he could read her mind, Leathers said, "Know how your problems and worries are always bigger at night? In the dark? How noises are amplified and how afraid you can become, just because it's dark?"

She didn't think she needed to answer. She was listening to him and seeing the chords as they moved back and forth, depending upon what part of her hand throbbed. He tapped it again, and this time—was she gaining control?—they didn't wave off the scale.

"That's because you can't see. When you can see things, it takes away much of their mystery. Pain is fear, Darlene, and when you can see it, it's not that much of a mystery. Are you with me?"

Darlene remembered the time she had been hypnotized at a party. Vaguely aware of everything, completely aware of the hypnotist's voice, knowing at all times that she could open her eyes and smile and show the crowd that it was all a farce, yet not wanting to, wanting, instead, to stay just exactly where she was, doing what she was told. It had been a wonderful experience. This was much the same. She nodded gently, not losing sight of the pain.

"Okay then. We're going to begin what I call the countdown. I have to cut away the bad flesh and the broken bones, and it isn't going to be nice. But I'll do it quickly and I'll sear it with this flame. You're going to be all right, but you've got to stay with me. Are you with me?"

Darlene nodded carefully. She could see those chords. They were beautiful. She didn't want to lose them.

"Okay, honey, concentrate now. I'm going to begin work on the count of five, so there won't be any surprises. If you lose control, you just speak up and I'll stop, but the quicker I can do it, the better it will be. I'm thinking three or four cuts with the shears, then the cauterizing. Ten seconds. So I'm going to count backwards from five, then I'm going to cut. Are you with me?"

Panic tasted sour in the back of her throat, and for a moment, that sensation superceded the visualization.

Leathers noticed. "You can only concentrate on one thing at a time. This is important. Ready? Five."

Darlene saw the chords, tried to pick one out.

"Four."

They kept moving around, like they were slippery.

"Three."

She grabbed one with her mind, but it changed colors. She held on to it.

"Two."

She separated it into its different parts, and it seemed as though she could pry apart the strings of it like rubber bars in a jail cell and step through.

"One."

She stepped through, and felt a pressure on her hand. She found herself in a small room that seemed to be made of blue ice. Light poured in from an indeterminate source, refracting off the glass-smooth surfaces of the walls, the ceiling, the floor. Featureless, mysterious, cold, *boring...*

"Finished," he said, and pain screamed back at her.

She wet herself.

She yelled. She kicked her feet. Somewhere in the periphery of her senses, she heard something. She focused in on it, her mind warping loosely out of shape.

"Concentrate," she heard, and for a moment, that word seemed familiar, as if she had heard it before.

"Concentrate, Darlene."

She had heard that word before. She zeroed in on it. Concentrate. Concentrate.

And without meaning to, she saw the chords of pain, and they were like a crazy quilt, kaleidoscoping everywhere.

She demanded order, and it came.

And the pain vanished.

After a while—she had no idea how long—the pain chords were diminished, and she opened her eyes. She turned her head and looked at what was left of her hand, which lay exposed in a sea of bloody shirt.

It was black and blue, swollen and torn, scratched and covered with lint embedded in black crusty blood. A row of surprisingly competent stitches led from her forefinger to her wrist. She had a thumb and a forefinger. Half her palm and the other three fingers were gone.

Her hand looked like a crab's pincer.

The room smelled like burnt flesh.

When Leathers shuffled, wheezing into the room, he carried a blue speckled enameled basin filled with something hot. Steam rose.

"We're going to soak it," he said, and Darlene felt a flood of relief. Maybe he did know how to take care of her.

"Infection is our worst enemy," Leathers said, "infection and pain. Pain is the worst enemy of mankind, because people fear it. That's why we deal with it here and now."

"What's in there?" Darlene indicated the pot.

"Epsom salts."

Darlene nodded, closed her eyes.

He set the bowl on the floor.

"I'm going to soak your hand, Darlene. The water is hot. It's not going to burn you, but it will feel as though it is. Don't give up on the pain. Embrace it. Love it. Welcome it. Use it. Concentrate. Concentrate. Concentrate."

She felt him lift her arm, and saw the colors change, saw the bands widen, narrow, saw the jagged edges sharpen, soften, change, undulate.

"Okay now, start your countdown."

She didn't want to go back into that blue room. She didn't like it in there, but she didn't know what else to do. She prepared for it, listening to him count from five, and she tried not to be afraid.

Then she felt the hot water on her wrist, and it was okay, it was okay, and slowly he lowered her hand.

It felt like all the blood rushed to her hand. It felt like it was going to explode from internal pressure more than it felt like burning.

"Concentrate, Darlene," Leathers' low, dry voice said.

"Concentrate."

She stepped into the blue room and waited.

When next Leathers touched her arm, it was as if Darlene was awakening. Had she slept? How could she sleep? The water was cold and he was taking her hand out.

"Good," he said. "I'm going to heat this up and we're going to soak it again. Then we'll do it again in the morning, okay?"

"I have to go to the bathroom," she said.

He helped her sit up and she wobbled to the bathroom. Every shift of her weight made the hand feel like it was going to explode. Twice she had to hold on to him while blackness swirled around her sight. He talked to her in low level sounds, soothing words, something real for the talons of her mind to catch on to, to hold her consciousness in the room and to keep her knees from buckling. She made it to the toilet and sat down. He left her there, leaving the door open a modest amount.

From her seated position, she took off her wet and smelly clothes and washed herself. Then, the last vestiges of her modesty wrapped in a towel, her hand again feeling like it was going to burst from throbbing internal pressure, she made her way slowly back to the bed.

Leathers had changed the sheets. The soaking solution had been reheated. Darlene felt as if there were hope.

She sat on the edge of the bed and slowly put her hand into the hot water.

"Concentrate," he said. "Don't do it without seeing the pain first."

The pain was remarkably easy to see, now that she knew what to look for.

"It works," she whispered.

He stroked her head, sat down next to her on the edge of the bed, kissed her shoulder. "Of course it works," he said. "Pain is beautiful. Just wait. I have so much more to show you." He pulled her head down to his shoulder and roughly stroked her head. "Thank God you're here. I have so much to share. So much pain. So much beauty."

When he arrived in Florence, Phil's agitation grew to enormous proportions. Which beach park? How far north of Driftwood Shores? What if he got the wrong park and some beach comber picked a nice cooler out of a trash can, found a ten thousand dollar bonus and that was the end of Darlene?

Relax, he told himself, but relaxation came hard for Phil, and it was all but impossible now. He hunched over the steering wheel as he drove north, then turned west at the Driftwood Shores sign. He turned north when he got to the sprawling, beachfront complex, and sure enough, there was a little tiny grassy area with two picnic tables, a water fountain, and a trash can.

Phil pulled into the parking lot. This must be where Patrick meant. Phil got out and walked around. Patrick couldn't have meant anywhere else.

He took the cans of soda out of the cooler, got the gym bag from the trunk and transferred the money. Then he held the cooler next to him and leaned against the car. Ten thousand dollars was a lot of money. He was afraid it would fall into the wrong hands. He was so afraid.

Was the kidnapper watching him? He slowly turned three hundred sixty degrees, but he could see no one. Unless somebody was in the hotel looking out the window. Or way down the beach with a pair of field glasses.

Phil did not want to just put the cooler in the trash can and then drive for an hour or more back home. He would much rather give the money to the man face-to-face.

The sky darkened as if a curtain had been pulled across the sun, and indeed, the western horizon was obscured with low black clouds. A chill wind blew salt spray across his face, and skittered fallen leaves across the tops of his shoes.

He looked down into the garbage can. It was just an open fifty-five gallon drum, with a plastic liner. Some fast-food wrappers and a newspaper were in the bottom.

He looked around again. If it was going to storm, it was unlikely that anybody would be coming to this park. Anybody but the kidnapper.

He held the cooler high over his head, like the Wimbledon trophy, and turned all the way around.

"If you're watching, you prick," Phil said, "I'm doing it."

Then he put the cooler in the bottom of the trash can and tented the newspaper over it. Nobody would see it unless they moved the newspaper. Nobody would see it unless they were looking for it.

Then, with his heart wrenching, he got back into the car and headed for home, driving faster than he should.

He felt as if he had betrayed Angela with his guilt-driven devotion to Darlene's well being.

He felt as if he had betrayed Darlene by not letting the police handle it.

He felt as if he had betrayed himself and his kids by wasting half a century being such a schmuck.

Patrick slowed to a crawl as the rain battered the Ford and the windshield wipers slapped at it double-time. He pulled in to the parking lot at the beach park, and let the headlights illuminate the sheeting rain.

He turned off the radio. He turned off the headlights, then the windshield wipers, then the engine. He had planned to just pull up, grab the cooler and get gone, but with all the rain, he couldn't hear. He couldn't hear if he was about to be nabbed by the cops, and he wanted to be prepared. No way did he want to get shot or beat up. If he heard someone say "Hands up," or "Freeze," or whatever it was that they said, he wanted to comply immediately without any misconception on their part.

The beach park was empty in the storm's premature twilight. Nobody was going to come along unseen. They had to already be there.

He opened the door and rain drenched him in an instant. He closed his eyes against the faceful of salty wind and fresh rainwater and ran the three steps to the trash can.

He shined his flashlight in the can, saw the cooler outline plastered by a sopping newspaper. He grabbed the cooler, pulled it out, wiped off the wet paper and threw it back into the can. Then he shined his flashlight around the area, but the sheeting rain absorbed the light and he couldn't see far.

He went back to the car, threw the cooler onto the passenger seat, wiped the rain from his face, started the car and slowly drove out. It took all his willpower to not drive away like a maniac. But he couldn't see very well in the dark, in the rain, and because he didn't want to attract attention to himself, he drove slowly and carefully.

He turned left, then right on Highway 101. He drove through

Florence, to the dunes, on down to a little campground off to the left. He pulled in there and parked.

No headlights followed him.

Could it be? Had he pulled it off?

He shivered in his wet clothes. He looked at the cooler.

He opened it.

Three packages of cash sat in the bottom.

He closed the cooler with trembling hands.

What now?

Leathers, that's what. He needed to give some of this money to Leathers.

A strange pang tightened his heart. He could put a new roof on that shack with this money. He could take Leathers in and get some medical attention for his respiratory problems. He could buy a car, a legal one. He could do all of those things with this money.

Well, he likely wouldn't do any of them, but he had to give some of it to Leathers. He owed him. Big time. Owed him big time. And he couldn't ever just take off without saying goodbye. He thought he could. He always thought that was the way he'd have to do it, he never thought he'd be able to leave Leathers the normal way normal people did it, with tearful hugs and goodbyes and visions of rosy futures all around.

But now that he'd done this, now that he had himself a little bit of a future here in this cooler next to him, well, then he could hold himself up tall and shake Leathers' hand and tell him goodbye and thanks. Thanks for everything. Thanks for being my savior, my brother, my father. Thanks for feeding me and teaching me the right things. Thanks for giving me a kick in the ass when I needed it, and thanks for... Patrick felt that pang tighten the breath out of him... thanks for loving me. Thanks for raising me as one of your own. Thanks for giving me all you did, and teaching me about life, and helping me to know myself and here's a kick in the face for your trouble.

The hard grip on his heart moved up to his throat and its only release was leaking out his eyes and down his face. Pain.

He wiped his face with the palms of his hands, started the car and slowly drove out of the park and onto the highway.

He had too many things to say to Leathers. He didn't know how he was going to be able to make it all up to him. But he had to do something. Maybe he would just give him all the money and then walk out of his life. Maybe he would give him five thousand dollars. Maybe Leathers wouldn't want any of it, but Patrick had to try. He had to make amends for thinking he could just walk out on the best man God had ever created. He had to make it up to him before it was too late.

Oh Jesus, what if it was already too late? What if that Darlene lady got home and called the police and they put Leathers in jail? The pain intensified. It hurt his chest, it hurt his stomach, it hurt his throat.

Patrick stood a little harder on the gas pedal. Oh God, let him be there when I get there, he prayed. How could I be such a fool, such an idiot, such an ungrateful creep?

He never even thought of Molly as he passed her motel. The storm hit full blast before he got to Reedsport, and it followed him inland.

Over the coast range, the wind and rain was even wilder, and branches and boughs and other forest debris flew in front of him. He thought about pulling over to ride out the storm, but he was too agitated. This storm could just rip the roof off the cabin, he thought, if it wasn't so heavy and soggy. That cabin really needed a new roof, a roof that didn't leak. Maybe before he left, he could buy some shingles and some sheathing and some felt and put a new roof on for Leathers. That would be nice. That would be good. A nice kind of going away present, a thank you present. Yeah, a good idea.

The pain in his soul threatened to become unbearable, and Patrick began his countdown.

A blast of wet leaves borne by black rain blew into the windshield, covered the headlights, covered the lines in the road, and Patrick, trying to visualize colored chords, intent on getting to his quiet, insulated, secure and painless place, completely missed the turn.

He reached for the windshield wipers and without touching the brakes, without even slowing down, the car sailed across the center line, off the shoulder of the road and flew in a graceful arc over the embankment.

"Leathers," Patrick whispered when he saw the swollen and muddy Umpqua river in his headlights.

Then the car hit the river going sixty miles per hour, and the windshield smashed, letting the river water in to swirl around Patrick, whose chest had merged with the steering wheel.

The car spun slowly on its nose, then the river gently pushed it over onto its top and carried it, like all the other storm detritus, toward the sea.

THURSDAY

Darlene dreamed about pain. She saw the shards of light, the shafts of colors pulsating in time with her heartbeat. The pain looked like fire in her veins. It ebbed and flowed and lit up her skeleton like the overlay in a textbook.

Now and then she opened her eyes, but the stripes and jagged ends of the pain superimposed themselves upon everything, and confusion made it hard to concentrate.

And there was another sound, as well.

One time her mind said to her "rain," and that was a familiar word, she knew that she had known that word, that concept, but she couldn't quite put her finger on what it meant. Another word was "fever," and that one sent a different wave length of color through her sight. Sound colors were horizontal, whereas pain colors were vertical—vertical and sometimes circular with jagged edges, like an evil saw blade.

If she concentrated hard enough, she found she could rest between heartbeats. The pain only hurt on the downbeat.

She could even sleep, if she tried, on the upbeat.

She divided the pain into even tinier chords, trying to see which ones faded out with the rush of infected, white-hot blood to and from her head.

She remembered her hand.

Did it hurt when the rush of blood went to the destroyed tissue, or did it hurt when the poisoned blood from the festering flesh rushed back to irritate and infect the healthy cells?

Was she dying?

No, she was waking up.

It was raining. She was in Leathers' bed. She could hear his tattoo needle above the drum of the rain on the roof and the ping of water dripping through the roof into pans.

"I'm cold," she said, but her mouth didn't work right, and a strange sound came out. It looked like one of the pain ribbons wafting out from between crusty lips. She knew he couldn't hear her over the sound of his needle.

"I'm cold," she said again, and this time it sounded more human, but the sound of the needle didn't stop.

She closed her eyes and waited for him to come cover her.

It was good to have a man again, she thought, and then the pain bore down on her with her next heartbeat, and she dove into it, headfirst.

~ ~ ~

"Darlene? Darlene?"

The sound came to her from a long echo chamber. "I'm here," she said. "Don't drop me. Don't lose me." But her mouth was somehow befuddled and her lips didn't work right.

Something cool on her forehead.

Darlene was afraid to open her eyes. She felt oddly suspicious and distrustful. If she didn't open her eyes, she could stay in hiding. Whatever was out there would eventually go away and she could go back to whatever it was she had been doing.

Which was—what?

Then her heart beat again and the pain thudded into her cranium and her eyes flew open.

Leathers. Leathers came into focus, and she reached up with a trembling, timid hand and grasped for him. She caught the edge of his tee shirt and clung there with weak desperation. Where had she been?

He sponged her face again with cool water and it felt good. She was thirsty. He gave her something to drink. It was delicious, thick like nectar. He spoke in low tones, and she couldn't understand any of it, but the sound of his voice smoothed out the jagged edges of the pain. She caught the word "roses," and she smiled, thinking of her rose garden at home, her beautiful rose garden. Some day she'd till up the rest of the back yard and experiment with breeding roses like Leathers did. Then from May through August, when they were in full bloom, the rose scent would permeate the air in and around her house. Lovely. Lovely.

"Roses." She smiled. "Yes."

Molly moved and newspaper crinkled beneath her. Her eyes shot open and she looked around the room.

The motel television was still on, one of those morning news programs smiling its way into her hangover. She sat up, rubbed her eyes, her cheeks, crawled over the bed and the newspaper to her watch on the nightstand.

7:30. She got off the bed and stumbled to the window. A gray morning. Oregon drizzle.

No Patrick.

She should have known.

She went to the bathroom, the slowly dawning realization that he had dumped her beginning to clot in her belly. She came back into the bedroom, turned off the TV, turned out the lights, closed the drapes, pulled the covers back on the bed and climbed in.

She hated motel beds. They all felt the same, cold, hard, impersonal. She scrunched around a little bit, but it didn't help, so she just curled on her side and lay there, listening to the sounds of traffic outside on the wet street. Now and then someone passed by the window as they checked in or out, and now and then she heard a car start in the parking lot.

Patrick had dumped her. Not only dumped her, but stranded her here in this stupid motel somewhere on the coast. She didn't even know where she was.

Patrick. Damn him.

The clot in her belly made its way up her throat and behind her eyes.

She had known that eventually Patrick would do this. He was just like all the others. Just like all the others.

A big sob sucked in some of the starchy pillowcase, and the tears cut loose.

She cried to the tune of "What's the matter with me?" and "Why doesn't he want me?" and "I'll do better next time, Patrick, just come back to me," until she was cried out. Then she slept.

When she woke again, it was noon. She got up and scrounged around looking for money. There were fourteen dollars in her purse, she found another five in a pair of Patrick's jeans. She shoved it all into her pocket along with the room key and trotted across the street to the Safeway.

She came back with a big grocery sack full of day-old pastries. She put the chain on the door and ignored the maid when she knocked. She turned the television up loud and sat cross-legged on the bed, eating one Danish after another, one doughnut after another, one bear's claw after another. Before she was halfway through with the cherry pie, it all came up, and she barely made it to the bathroom, where she retched and heaved until the whole episode was over.

Over. Over. It was over.

Over.

She washed out her mouth, ran a brush through the tangles on her head, swiped at her runny mascara with the moistened end of a towel, put on her baggy denim jacket, stuck the gun in her pocket, and went out the door.

"You're gonna take me to Arizona, huh?" she said to the drooping rain. "You asshole."

She stood by the ice machine at the corner Seven-Eleven until a young kid in a small car drove up. He popped inside the store and when he came out with a Pepsi, she opened the passenger door, pointed her gun at him and said, "Let's go."

The color drained from his face and he dropped his soda, which spilled all over his pants.

"Take it easy," she said as he fumbled with his keys. "I'm not going to hurt you. I just need a ride."

"God," he said. "Why don't you take a bus or something?"

He's right, she thought. This is a stupid way to get around. She waited until they were off highway 101, headed inland. Then she said, "Okay, pull over here."

The kid breathed a sigh of relief. "I'm glad you weren't going much farther," he said. "I've got to meet my mom, and then I have a dentist—"

"Get out," Molly said.

"Huh?"

"Get out. I'm taking the car."

"It's not my car."

"No," she said calmly, cocking the .38, "it's mine."

He scrambled out of the car, leaving the engine running.

Molly climbed into the driver's seat and tried to remember the things she learned in her one day of high school driver's ed. Adjust the seat and the mirrors, fasten the seat belt, put on the turn signal, foot on the brake, put it into gear.

She did all those things with the gun in her lap, while the kid stood outside and looked in the window. He made her nervous.

She waited until there was no traffic, then she gently pulled out onto the blacktop. Nice and easy. She looked back and saw the kid standing with his hands at his sides. Just standing. So long, kid.

Within a couple of miles, she had a handle on it. Driving was actually pretty easy. She still held the steering wheel in a death grip, and her muscles were stretched like wires, but her breathing was a little more relaxed and as long as nothing unexpected came along, she'd be just fine.

She knew where she was headed—it was a damned good thing she had lifted the registration from the red Ford—and she had a vague idea how to get there. The only question was whether she should stop at Leathers' place on her way to Springfield. Would Patrick be there? What would she say to him if he was? Maybe she should go directly to that Darlene-person's house and see if anybody there would be interested in trading knowledge of her whereabouts for a one-way bus ticket to Arizona.

Plane ticket, Molly, she told herself. First class.

She smiled, feeling personal power push against the inside of her chest. It felt great. She took a deep breath, relaxed her grip on the steering wheel a little bit, rolled down the window and turned on the radio. The sun shone down brightly, and cool, fresh Oregon wind whistled through the car and around her head. The storm had cleared the atmosphere just like her binge this morning had cleared her senses. She felt free, totally uninhibited and unencumbered. She pressed a little harder on the accelerator.

This was a day just like the day she had first met Patrick. She'd been in Portland, getting high and wasting time with Bruno. They lived in a ratty condemned building that didn't even keep the rain off them in the winter, and Molly had developed a cough that was beginning to worry her. Still yet, when she took the right kind of deep breath, something squeaked deep inside.

Then on that one day—it had been a Sunday, she'd been reading the funnies—Bruno brought home some scrawny little dark-skinned woman. She had her hands all over him, and they were grinning like Cheshire cats. They were so coked up they could barely see straight, and he hadn't even brought a taste of it home for Molly.

That was the end of the road for Bruno. Molly threw her things into her duffel bag and slammed out. As she stomped down the hall, she heard them laughing in the room behind her, and the tears flowed unchecked out of her eyes and down her face. Fuck men. Fuck men. Fuck men. They're all hounds. Hounds.

And there she'd been, outside, again, with no money, and no friends, and nowhere to go. Again.

Oh well, she thought. Something will turn up. It always does.

And so it had.

She followed the signs to the freeway and stuck her thumb out just before the on-ramp.

A car slowed, then stopped, and when she ran for it, a guy beat her to the door, opened it and held it for her. Then they both got into the back seat.

"Where to?" the man who was driving asked.

"Curtin would be fine," the guy said.

"I'm going to Arizona," Molly had said, and elbowed the guy who'd horned in on her ride.

"'Fraid I can't take you that far," the man said, "but I can take you to Curtin, no problem."

"Thank you sir," the guy said, and Molly gave him another scowl. Just like a guy to let the girl attract the ride and then leave her out of it.

They had ridden in silence for two and a half hours, Molly sleeping on and off. The driver took the Curtin off ramp and stopped the car. The guy next to her got out, grabbed his backpack and her duffel bag.

144

"Hey," she said.

"C'mon." He coaxed her out.

With another look at the driver, she shrugged her shoulders. He probably wasn't going much farther anyway. She followed the duffel bag, and the car sped away into the day.

She squinted up at the guy who had kidnapped her. He held out his hand. "Hi," he said. "I'm Patrick."

"Molly," she said, and shook his hand.

"Need a place to stay?"

She nodded. "I'm going to Arizona," she said.

"Really? I've always loved Arizona."

He was tall, and slim, and kind of cute, she thought as she followed him past the truck stops, the little grocery store and out onto the lonely country road. He looked tidy.

Fortune had smiled on her that fine Oregon day, she thought, as they had walked down the country road together, thumbs out, waiting for a ride. The sun was shining, the breeze was blowing, the weeds were blooming and the clouds were magnificent.

Molly had felt clean to be rid of Bruno and his bad habits, and she had a real nice feeling about this Patrick guy. A real nice feeling.

They talked about Arizona, the place of her dreams, having come from frozen Minnesota and the weirdest family imaginable, and then he had flagged them down another ride, this one with country and western music, that took them directly to Leathers' driveway.

Leathers.

Molly had been scared to death of him, but Patrick put his arm around her and it wasn't long before she realized he was just a sick old man. A sick old man in a run-down shack.

Patrick, she discovered, could turn into quite a find, if she could get him away from that weirdo. He was calm, and nice, and he worked hard. He had some funny ideas about things—mostly about pain and about that old man. The pain thing scared her at first, when he began to talk about it, but he never tried to hurt her, so she finally just ignored him when he began to talk about it and eventually, he stopped. Molly never did figure out how Patrick and Leathers got together or what it was that Patrick thought he owed him, but Patrick reminded Molly of her uncle, her sweet young uncle who always treated her kindly and with respect.

He was easy to sleep with, too, not kinky at all, not too demanding, just straight and easy to please. Except for that weird modesty thing. He never took his clothes off in front of her. Never. But she could live with that. It was no big thing. Patrick was a rare find.

Best of all, he'd been to Arizona.

They would lay awake at night, feeding each other little spoonfuls of ice cream, and he would talk about the desert. He talked about the stars and the coyotes and the moonlight that reflected off the desert landscape until it was nigh to daylight. He talked about the mountains, the Superstition mountains that were still full of the lost Dutchman's gold. He talked about cactus, the cholla cactus, the kind that jumped out and grabbed you with its barbs. Apaches used to roll a victim in cholla cactus until the man was wound up in a ball, all stuck to himself, and then he would just slowly die, baking and hurting in the desert sun.

Molly wanted to see the cactus, the gold, the Superstitions, the desert moon. Her heart pounded with yearning as he talked. She could see it all in its majesty. She was born to live in Arizona. She was meant to be in Arizona. Patrick found the threads of her dreams, picked them up and continued knitting right where she had left off so many years ago. In him, she had found life, love, a future. Even in spite of the hold Leathers had on him, Patrick had real possibilities. He had great potential. And he might even have married her some day. Oh, they'd have made nice babies together.

And then he walked out, the shit.

No, she decided, keeping the little car carefully controlled and on the road. If she ran into Patrick at Leathers' place or anywhere else, she wouldn't say anything to him. Nothing at all. She'd just put a bullet in his fucking brain.

Phil had never been at home when the cleaning lady came. Angela got up, fed, bathed and dressed Peaches, then handed her to Phil while Angela showered and dressed. Then the two of them left. Phil couldn't leave; he was waiting for the phone to ring. Waiting for Patrick to call. Waiting. Waiting all evening, all night, all morning. Still waiting.

In the meantime, the cleaning lady, a nice woman with a serious overbite and a bit of a pot belly, dusted, vacuumed, washed windows, cleaned the kitchen, mopped the floors, wiped off every surface in sight, including the telephone, and tried to stay out of Phil's way.

He tried to stay out of her way, too, but every time he walked into a different room, she was in there, trying to get out of his way. It was unnerving.

Angela should be here. Phil wasn't used to being alone. And yet, Angela was becoming a little bit unnerving, too. Not once had she mentioned the money, but her attitude had changed. Phil felt it in the way she just handed him Peaches to entertain that morning. The balance of power had shifted.

But Phil had no energy to puzzle over Angela. Patrick should have called by now. He got the money, right? He should be calling.

Unless he didn't get the money. Maybe Phil left the money in the wrong trash can. Maybe Patrick never got to it. Maybe somebody else got it first. Maybe Patrick wasn't going to call at all. Maybe Patrick never had Darlene, and Phil was merely a first-class chump.

Every now and then he picked up the telephone receiver to see if it was working, then he put it down quickly, just in case Patrick tried to call.

He wanted to go to Darlene's house and wait with Lari, but he couldn't leave the phone.

When Lari called, Phil's heart almost stopped.

"Daddy?"

"Yes, baby?"

"I'm going nuts."

"Me too, honey. I gotta go."

"You'll call me first thing, right? I mean first thing?"

"Of course. Gotta hang up."

"Okay. Daddy?"

"Yes?"

"I love you."

"I love you too, baby."

"Don't worry, Daddy."

"Gotta go."

"Okay. Bye."

He hung up, a warm feeling for Lari, nestled up against the cold stone that was Rocky. Those two kids might as well have been members of totally different species.

The cleaning lady left at two o'clock, Angela with a sleeping Peaches came back at three. Angela rustled around in the bedroom with the packages she had brought home, then she emerged, wearing jeans and a blouse, and began to move around in the freshly cleaned kitchen.

Phil sat at the breakfast bar and watched her. She was as attractive as ever. Her fine bone structure was always a wonder to him, her hands were like tiny fragile butterflies, her feet the same, her ribs, when he hugged her, like the ribs of a child. Her blonde hair, shiny and bouncy, framed her healthy, pink-cheeked face.

"No word yet, obviously," she said.

He hung his head. She opened a beer and set it in front of him. He gulped it gratefully.

Time dragged.

They ate dinner, or pretended to. Phil pushed the pork chop around on his plate, Angela ate a tiny salad, as usual, Peaches was cranky.

After dinner, they went into the living room, and while Peaches cried herself to sleep in her bedroom, Angela worked on a silent needlework project, Phil clicked the remote control incessantly. Finally, Angela took it away from him and set it on the coffee table.

Just as Phil stood up, ran his hands through his hair and was ready to say something, something loud, the phone rang.

He looked at her. She raised an eyebrow.

He walked calmly to the den when he felt like running. He breathed deeply, then picked up the phone.

"Hello?"

"Mr. Martin?"

"Yes."

"Lieutenant Jenricks, Mr. Martin. We've found your wife's car."

Phil wasn't sure what that meant. His anxiety level didn't lessen, and it didn't jump, but it did take a lateral lurch.

"We should get together to talk about this, Mr. Martin. Would now be a good time?"

Phil looked through the doorway at Angela. "Why don't you meet us over at Darlene's house?" He gave the policeman the address, then hung up.

Angela raised that eyebrow again.

"They found Darlene's car," he said.

From the look on Angela's face, he knew that this was not good news. Angela was uncannily intuitive.

"I'll stay here," she said, and he was grateful that he would only have to confess his foolish behavior in front of the police and his kids, and he could talk to her about it later, in the privacy of their dark bedroom.

He called Lari, asked her to call Rocky, then grabbed his jacket.

He kissed her cheek on the way out.

~ ~ ~

The lieutenant arrived before Rocky did. He was a big man in a cheap suit, with thick gunmetal-gray hair and bushy eyebrows. He looked like a cop. He sat on the couch, Phil sat in the recliner with Ashes in his lap and Tina lounging in her personal spot, the depression that she'd made on the top of the recliner. Lari and Carolyn sat cross-legged on the floor, Lari's hands white, her face pale. Again, the official presence, even though he wore a brown suit instead of a uniform, again the seriousness of the family plight. Now and then Carolyn touched Lari, and Phil could see the communication between the two, and it warmed his heart.

"He probably died last night during the storm," the lieutenant was saying. "We don't have an official statement on that from the coroner yet. But it was Darlene Martin's car, and there was a cooler on the front seat with ten thousand dollars in it." The lieutenant looked to Phil for an explanation.

Phil's face grew red and hot, and he looked at his hands.

With his usual bad timing, Rocky showed up. No smiles greeted him. He closed the door quietly, touched the top of Lari's head as he stepped carefully behind her, then sat next to the policeman on the sofa.

Phil indicated Rocky. "My son. Lieutenant Jenricks."

The two shook hands, and then eyes were again on Phil.

"I gave him the money," Phil said. "I put it in the cooler and took it to Florence and put it where he told me to. Then I went home and waited for his phone call, like he told me to. But... nothing." He looked at his hands again, and a hot lump behind his breastbone told him he was on thin emotional ice here. He was about to cry.

"Daddy..." Lari said. Her voice made his emotional state even graver.

"You did this all on your own initiative?" the lieutenant asked.

Phil nodded.

"Excuse me," Rocky said, with his irritating way. "Against everybody's advice, wishes, and better judgment, you took it upon yourself to endanger our mother's life by acting on your own?"

"Rocky, they found the money, and they found Patrick," Lari said. "He was dead. He was driving Mom's car and he had an accident."

"Drove over a cliff into the river," Carolyn said.

"Which wouldn't have happened if the police had grabbed him when he picked up the money," Rocky said, his face red all the way to the roots of his blonde hair.

The hot feeling behind Phil's breastbone turned from sadness to anger in one beat of his heart.

"*Listen to me*," he said, his voice low and sounding more in control than he felt. "You can accuse me of many things, Rocky, some of them true, some of them skewed by your own perception. I am many things. I may not have been a great father. But I acted in what I thought was the best, most expeditious way to get your mother back. I complied completely and totally with the kidnapper's wishes. I know you didn't want me to do that and I know the police did not want me to do that, but I didn't want to gamble on her safety. You can think what you want about who I am and what I may have done in the past, but this time I acted with only one thought in mind, and that was to get your mother home safely. I figured the police could deal with the kidnapper after that."

Phil took a deep breath, then addressed Rocky one more time. "You can accuse me of many things, Rocky, but don't you dare accuse me of trying to harm your mother. In any way. Ever."

Rocky crossed his arms over his chest slowly, then sat back on the sofa. The redness left his face.

Phil realized he had spoken directly to Rocky, looking him in the eye for the first time in a long time. He had reason to defend his actions, these actions at least, and he had done so with grace. Maybe he had even moved up a notch or two in Rocky's estimation. Hard to tell with that kid.

"Be that as it may," the lieutenant diffused the tension after a respectful pause. "You've interfered with an ongoing investigation, Mr. Martin. I don't know if charges will be brought against you, but you might want to engage an attorney just in case."

Phil nodded. He expected that.

"Charges!?" Lari was indignant. "You're kidding, right?"

"I'm afraid not, ma'am."

"Charge him for—"

Phil held up his hand. "It's okay," he said, and she quieted down. She clearly had more to say on the subject. Carolyn tapped a little code on Lari's knee. Lari looked at her, but didn't smile. Then she looked at the floor.

"Anyway," the lieutenant went on. "We're back to square one." The lieutenant shuffled his feet a little bit on the floor, cleared his throat, then spoke again. "We're going to want you to account for your whereabouts since the last time Mrs. Martin was seen."

Lari looked up at the lieutenant with her mouth open.

Phil held up his hand and silenced her before she began.

"No problem," he said. "I'll write it out."

"Good. Drop it by the office."

Phil agreed.

"Find her purse or anything in the car?" Rocky asked.

"Nothing." The lieutenant seemed relieved that was out in the open and over with. "The lab is still going over it, but there was nothing in the car, nothing in the trunk."

"What about the guy? Any identification? Any address? Anything in his wallet?"

"He had a Portland address on his driver's license. We're checking on that." The lieutenant paused, and it was obvious he had something else to say. Everyone waited. The lieutenant took his time.

"Was there something else?" Rocky asked. Rocky, always pushing.

"As a matter of fact, yes. I'm not sure what it means, and I don't want to worry you, but perhaps it's a clue..."

"We're already worried," Lari said. "Let's have it."

"This Patrick had a curious pattern of scars."

"Scars?" Rocky leaned forward. "What kind of scars?"

The lieutenant ran his hands over his face, and rearranged himself on the couch. "Artwork," he said. "He had pictures drawn all over him, only they were made of scar tissue."

"Burns?" Carolyn asked.

The lieutenant shook his head. "This is difficult for me to talk about. I've never seen such a thing in my life. They were flowers. Dozens of flowers, all different types, shapes and sizes. It was like thin strips of flesh had been surgically removed from the boy, and when it healed, it healed with raised pink scar tissue. His whole body was covered with them."

"His whole body?" Rocky asked.

Lari started chewing on a fingernail.

"And in places, things were inserted under the skin to... to, I don't know, add texture, I guess."

"Things?" Rocky was on the edge of the couch, and his face was too close to the lieutenant's. Phil was afraid Rocky was going to grab him and shake him.

"Ball bearings, pieces of wire, glass beads."

"What does this mean?" Lari asked. She had Carolyn's hands in a white—knuckled grip.

"I don't know that it means anything," the officer said. "I only bring it up because some of the wounds were fresh."

"Fresh?" Rocky was losing control of himself.

"Within twenty-four hours."

Rocky looked at Phil, his mouth set in a grim line. "So Mom might be with someone who's carving her up?"

"We don't know that," the policeman said.

"And the only one who knows where she is drowned in the fucking river." Rocky looked at Phil. "You should die for this."

"This is a tense time for everyone," the policeman said. "You folks hang together and be a family now. You need each other for support."

Rocky snorted.

"In the meantime," he stood, and everybody else scrambled to their feet. Ashes hit the floor and ran to Rocky. "We're looking for her, and we'll be in touch if we learn anything new." He walked toward the door, shook hands with Phil. "Play by the rules from now on, okay?"

Phil nodded, closed the door behind him.

The tension in the room was thick. Phil picked up the phone and called Angela. He told her he'd be home within a half hour, and tried not to eavesdrop on what the kids were talking about while he was on the phone. It was difficult. He also wanted to keep Angela talking. He didn't want to face the kids, face his failure.

But Angela was not a phone talker, and the click on her end meant he had to be a father again. What a system. Why did they make ordinary guys into father-gods to these kids? What did they want from him? He shut off the phone and set it on the end table.

All three of them looked up at him.

"I did what I thought was best," he said, and was pleased with the way that statement sounded in the room. He hadn't had to clear his throat, his voice was calm, well-modulated, forceful. He stated a plain fact, and there it sat. The ball was now in their court.

When had it become him against them? Or had it always been so?

They said nothing. After a moment, Rocky stood up, walked to the door. "Keep in touch," he said as he left.

That was probably the only thing he could have done to rip Phil's heart out.

"Want some coffee, Daddy?" Lari asked, but Phil could see that she didn't really mean it. She wanted him to leave. He wanted to leave. He wanted to move to Mexico.

"No thanks, baby, I'm going to go." He stood up, a weary man, gave Lari a hug, gave Carolyn a kiss, and then he left Darlene's comfortable house and drove toward his own sterile one.

Rocky had never gotten over the divorce; Phil knew that. Rocky had romantic ideas that daddies and mommies ought to live together in peace and harmony forever. But some day he'd know. Some day he'd find out that real life didn't always work that way.

Phil wasn't exactly sure what had happened between him and Darlene. Their relationship had just run its course.

Angela, one of the secretaries at the firm, had caught Phil's eye, and she was all too willing to work late and have some hot sex on his desk. Or in the conference room. Or in a motel, in the car, down by the river, in the woods.

But that was nothing new. Phil had a way of attracting women, and if he had a fatal weakness, it was that he couldn't find anything wrong with screwing these young dollies. As long as he brought home the paycheck, as long as he was a husband and a father, what was the harm? It wasn't as if he was in love with them or anything.

Darlene, increasingly frustrated by Phil's lack of attention to her and the things in her narrow life, began to gain weight, which made Phil all the more susceptible to young supple girls with Crest smiles, flat tummies and perky breasts.

Then it happened. That thing Phil had thought would never happen to him.

First, Angela avoided him. For a couple of weeks. Almost a month. Long enough for a research assistant on the fifth floor to catch his eye.

Then one day Angela came to work with a puffy face and she hauled him unceremoniously into the conference room and locked the door.

He took her in his arms and she hugged him back for a minute, then pulled away, walked across the room and said, "I'm pregnant."

Phil felt as if someone had hit him in the stomach with a baseball bat. He just continued to look at her and the honesty with which those tears poured forth tore at something inside him and he knew for certain at that moment that she had not done it on purpose.

Within seconds, he computed a fresh life with a fresh wife and a new baby versus his stale existence with Darlene and made a decision.

He crossed the room, took a weak and clinging Angela into his arms again and said, "We'll get married." She cried harder. "Want to?" he asked, and she nodded against his chest. After a few moments, when her crying had subsided, and she had a whole pile of soaked tissues in front of her, he settled her into a conference room chair, sat next to her and holding her hand, dialed the company attorney and arranged a speedy divorce.

Then he took Angela home to her apartment, made love to her and told her to plan a wedding. Small. Tasteful. Inexpensive.

Then he went home to face Darlene.

He marveled at her innocence, sitting on the couch, the dog on her lap, as she watched television. He coaxed her into going out to dinner at her favorite restaurant, and while she was flattered and played coy with him, he had terrible news to deliver. He found it horribly difficult to make conversation, so he let her carry it.

Over coffee, he took her hand and kissed it. She smiled at him. "Darlene," he said, "there's been an accident at work." What a stupid thing to say.

She frowned.

Flustered, he just blurted it out. "I've met someone," he said, "and now she's pregnant." He couldn't believe how bad he felt. He felt sick, he felt faint, he couldn't believe how awful he felt. When he finally looked up, little tears were making tracks in Darlene's carefully powdered face. She bravely met his gaze. "I need to marry her."

Then she nodded, and pulled a tissue from her purse. "Okay," she said, and the simplicity of it cut him even deeper.

"Do you want me to move out tonight?"

She shook her head. "There's no need for that," she said. "Whenever. I'll call the realtor in the morning, and we'll put the house on the market."

They held each other that night, and he woke up more than once to hear her weeping. That, too, made his stomach feel weak, but the die was cast.

Phil and a suitcase moved into Angela's tiny apartment where they played house for a month. Angela was happy, but she wasn't the giddy, bubbling little girl she had beeen. Before the month was up, they were quietly married in a judge's chambers with Lari, Carolyn,

Angela's widowed father and one of her girlfriends from work in attendance. Phil and Darlene's house sold quickly. Darlene found her little house, and Phil sank his proceeds into a nice house east of Springfield where they awaited Peaches.

Angela's father died about a month before Peaches was born. Seeing Angela through her grief was perhaps the one and only thing Phil had done in his life that made a difference to anybody. He and Angela grew close over their tears and discussions of birth and death and the meaning of life.

An only child, Angela received the sum total of her father's estate, which didn't amount to riches, but was a nice, tidy sum, and Phil had been on unsure footing ever since.

Angela was good for him. She was highly independent. Maybe too independent. Darlene had been way too dependent, and Phil found Angela, young Angela, to be a breath of fresh air. Phil had nothing to complain about, marriage-wise. Nothing.

He pulled into the driveway, his heart heavier than ever over Darlene's plight and the role he chose to play in it. The automatic garage door opened and the car slid into a perfectly kept garage, the kind of garage he'd always wanted; the kind of garage he never had when there were kids in the house.

The tapestry of pain focused into colored chords, then coalesced into stripes, like pillow ticking. Darlene watched the pain as it changed shape, changed dimension, became flatter, harder, more singled and defined.

Light. Bright, intense light. She could see it through her eyelids, but she hesitated to open them, afraid it would hurt her eyes, and her body couldn't take another ounce, another inch, another high C of pain. Bright light might tip the scales and upend her all over again.

She moved her right arm, shifted her weight. Water moved beneath her. Waterbed. She moved the muscles of her back. They were tired, they wanted her to turn over onto her side, onto her stomach.

She shaded her eyes with her hand and opened them. The intense light came from the end of the bed. Leather's work lamp. The windows were dark. With her eyes open, her hand didn't hurt as much. "Pain is fear," she remembered hearing him say. She wasn't afraid now.

She looked over at her hand. It was wrapped in towels. She gently sat up in the wiggly bed and unwrapped it.

It was horrible. Mangled. Swollen. Bruised, black and blue and yellow and green. It was swollen all the way past her wrist. Pink and red tissue puffed out painlessly around amateurish yet solidly practical black sutures. The cut itself was black with dried blood.

Leathers had amputated three fingers and half her palm, leaving the forefinger and the thumb. Horrible, but it wasn't as infected as she imagined. She vaguely remembered Leathers plunging her hand into steaming hot water to soak. That had hurt like holy hell, but he helped her concentrate, and the soaking helped avoid infection, she was certain.

She still needed a doctor to look at it, to look at the way Leathers cut it, the way he stitched it. She would probably need surgery if she was ever going to use the remains of her hand again.

She needed to get to a hospital.

Sweat started to run down the side of her face again, and she felt way too warm. She could smell herself, the sour smell of a fever. She needed a hospital, she needed it now, and she didn't know how she was ever going to get to one.

She covered her hand with the towel and lay back, sweat making dark spots in the gray tee shirt she wore. She reached behind her head and tried to plump the pillow, but between the waterbed and the pain, moving was difficult.

And there was something else. Something that tugged on her foot.

Both feet.

She tried to sit up, but her damaged hand felt like a bowling ball and the bed shifted beneath her. She kicked, then kicked again.

Her ankles were tied.

Sweat poured off her face as she thought about this situation, her heart pounding, panic rising.

She sensed Leathers' presence before he spoke. She stopped fidgeting and looked toward the door. He stood there, freshly groomed, with a tray. On the tray was a jelly glass filled with roses. "You're awake," he said in his dry, rasping voice.

"Untie me," she said.

"I'm not finished."

Again, she tried to get up, but she felt weak, and her hand hurt and the action of the waterbed and the size of her belly with its slack muscles kept her from sitting up. She floundered helplessly. She lay back, took a deep breath, wiped the perspiration from her forehead and said, "Un*tie* me, goddammit."

Leathers set the tray on the bedside table and picked up a banana. He peeled it, broke off a piece and offered it to her. She glared back at him. He popped the piece into his mouth and chewed, looking down at her. Then he reached down with his big, banana-smelling paw and touched her forehead.

She winced and pulled away from his touch.

"Your fever is gone."

"Untie me."

"Anger is soul poison, Darlene," he said.

She closed her eyes and took a deep breath. He was right. If she got mad and lost control, nothing would be accomplished. She just wanted to get out of this damned bed and get home.

"Did you see it?"

She nodded. "It's horrible."

A puzzled look crossed his face. "Horrible?"

She nodded. "What did you expect? It's mutilated."

"*Horrible?*"

Darlene began to wonder what was the matter with him. Then a smile crossed his face and he relaxed. "Oh," he said. "Your hand." He nodded at the swathing of towels. "I saved your life."

"You don't get it," Darlene said. "None of this would have happened if you hadn't kept me here *against my will.*"

"I never kept you here," Leathers said.

"Then UNTIE ME!"

He turned off the high intensity lamp and the room softened.

"I gave you my best," he said, bent over and untied the rags that held her ankles.

She pulled her feet up and away from him. "Best?"

Leathers sat down on the stool. "The rose," he said.

"Rose?" Fragments of memory began assembling themselves in her mind. Why was the working lamp in the bedroom? And the five-wheeled stainless steel stool? Pain-shattered memories of buzzing, of being told to hold still, hold still, HOLD STILL, of the pressure of soft fingers on her leg, vibrations that perturbed the shards of pain she saw...

"Ah," he said, nodding, smiling. "So you haven't seen it." He took another chunk off the banana, offered it to her, then at her refusal, ate it.

Darlene began to feel sick to her stomach. He reached over, whipped the sheet off her leg, and there was a tattoo of his singularly bred blue rose, a brambled stem twining about her ankle, the beautiful blossom large and delicately drawn on her calf.

Darlene's breath caught in her throat. Tears pushed against her eyes. She was speechless. She was furious, she felt betrayed, he had no right. This was true mutilation. Invasion. Assault!

She closed her eyes tightly, then opened them again, and it was still there, covered with a shiny coating of Vaseline.

"Do you like it?"

"No," she said, her voice tiny, "I hate it." She looked up at him and realized that she was afraid of him. She felt weak, even weaker than before, weaker than she thought possible, powerless, defenseless, and she wanted to sink into the bed and wake up at home with Tina curled up next to her and Ashes snoring softly on the foot of the bed. Lord please, she prayed, let this nightmare be over.

"Why did you do that?" A sob choked out with the words. She hated that demonstration of weakness, and she stuffed the tears. Stuffed them hard.

"You told me to."

"I did?"

He nodded, a stricken look on his face.

"I must have been out of my mind."

Leathers put his half-banana back on the tray, stood up and shuffled out of the room.

"I *was* out of my mind," she called after him. "And YOU KNEW THAT." He disappeared into the studio. "You had no right," she called after him. "No RIGHT!"

A moment later, she heard his tattoo needle buzz.

"No right," she whispered. She didn't know what to do. She didn't know how to feel.

She could see him in there, scraping ink into his own skin, dealing with her rejection of his artwork. She felt guilty for hurting him. He was right, he had saved her life. And he hadn't kept her here. He had given her his best. She owed him. What did it matter that she had a tattoo on her leg? She was not going out to high teas with society ladies in their fine dresses. She was not on the prowl, looking for a man to marry, a man who might take offense at the illustration, she was not a young woman any more. Her time for impressing people was over. It didn't matter what happened to her body now, wasn't that obvious? She sat in that damned recliner day after day after day eating whatever she felt like, until she had ballooned into a grotesquery. She was just waiting for something to happen, kidney failure or a cancerous lump that she could neglect to treat.

Marking time, that's what Darlene's life had come down to, she realized with a gasp of reality. What matters a tattoo?

Leathers' feelings mattered much more than that.

She pulled up the covers, pulled up her leg and looked at it again. The rose was beautiful. Masterful. It was drawn with such a delicate hand she felt sure she could smell it.

And she had loved the rose illustration in his scrapbook. It was a finely detailed illustration of a trellis, with an overabundance of roses, lovely roses, beautiful roses, all her favorite roses.

And she owed him.

Owed him? her mind screamed. You were kidnapped, abandoned, injured and now defaced. How could you owe him?

"Because I think he loves me," she whispered, as she touched the edge of the greasy Vaseline protectant. She could do anything, she thought, anything at all, as long as she was loved.

FRIDAY

The sound of a car's engine revving startled Molly from a twitchy dream that starred her father. Her father. What a jerk. She awoke with a bad taste in her mouth, grumpy and disheveled. She'd gotten used to sleeping with Patrick in a nice bed, with sheets and all. It didn't take long to get used to something like that, and now going back to sleeping in back seats was harder than ever.

She never dreamed about her father when she slept in a nice bed, either. Only when she slept in corners, in boxcars, in the back seats of cars, on floors, in bus stations.

She peeled her skin from the vinyl seat and sat up. She was parked across the street and down the block from Darlene's house.

Molly had pulled in and parked there the night before. She wanted to go up to the house and talk to the people she could see through the lighted windows sitting around in the living room, but she didn't know what to do or what to say. She got out of the car and looked through the windows. A man, Darlene's husband, probably, two girls and a guy, probably her three kids. They were having some kind of a family conference. The blonde guy left, then the man left. The blonde guy was pretty cute, too. Molly had wanted to follow him, to see where he went. Maybe she could talk to him privately.

But what would she say? What did she want? Why did she come all the way here, anyway?

Maybe she hoped Darlene would be home by now, and would give her a helping hand to Arizona. Maybe those people didn't know where Darlene was, and would give her a few bucks for the information.

Molly, get real, she told herself. These people would slap you in jail for what you did. You stole that woman along with her car. And then you stole this car. The police might come along any minute

163

now, check the plates and toss your sweet little ass in jail.

Not Patrick. They wouldn't throw Patrick in jail. Patrick was getting away with everything. Men get all the breaks. Fucking men.

She felt for the gun that she'd stashed underneath the seat in front of her. It was still there. She rubbed her eyes and face. She needed a shower.

She slumped back down in the seat and picked at her cuticles. She was hungry, too, and the car was about out of gas. She was almost out of everything.

How could everything be so hard? Getting to Arizona hadn't seemed like such a difficult task. All she wanted to do was soak up the sun and the dry heat. Arizona wasn't all that far away. It would have been so simple for her and Patrick to jump in that red car and go, but no, it couldn't be that easy for *her*. Nothing was easy for her. Everything seemed to be easy for everybody else, but for her, everything was hard, hard, hard. Like chewing nails. Like pulling teeth.

And it was all because of the guys. Guys had it easy, maybe because they made all the rules. Guys had a network of some kind, they had some kind of a secret handshake, where they knew each other's hearts, somehow. If they had hearts. Guys helped guys, and the girls had to just play along or something.

She looked around. The stupid little car. Her duffel bag was in the front seat, she was in the back seat with Patrick's jacket and a faded pink towel she had found on the floor, that she'd covered her legs with during the night. She had maybe five bucks, she was hungry, out of gas, dirty and needed to pee.

Pretty dismal.

She climbed into the driver's seat and pulled the mirror toward her. God. Black mascara rimmed her eyes until she looked like some sort of a demon. She wet her finger and wiped at it, but that just smudged it and brought great black marks off to the sides of her eyes. She licked the corner of the towel and tried to work at it with that, but she was afraid of damaging the tender skin under her eyes. She didn't want big bags under there when she got older.

She fingered through her ratty hair, opened the door, grabbed her duffel. Now or never, she thought, and she walked up to Darlene's house and rang the bell.

In a moment, a pretty little dark-haired girl answered the door. Molly looked at her, intimidated.

"Yes?" Lari prompted.

"Hi. I'm, uh, I'm a friend of Patrick's." Molly saw the look of recognition cross the girl's face. Damned guys. They were the ticket to everywhere. "Can, uh, can I use your bathroom?"

When Molly was finished using the toilet, she looked around the bathroom, at the plastic flowers and the crocheted dolls. This didn't look like that girl at all. She poked her head out of the bathroom door. The girl was in the living room, talking on the telephone. Calling the police, probably.

"Hey," Molly said.

The girl looked up at her. "Mind if I take a shower?"

"Fresh towels in the bottom drawer," the girl said, and Molly thought she might like this girl.

She took a long, hot, luxurious shower, helping herself to a fancy little soap in a seashell and lathering up her hair twice with shampoo, then using the expensive-smelling conditioner on it and letting the conditioner soak in to her split ends while she steamed her skin. Patrick's leaving had made her feel dirty.

She toweled dry, then searched through her bag for clean clothes. She settled for a pair of cutoffs and a wrinkled tank top. She found some clean socks, and then used the wide-toothed comb in the bathroom drawer to comb her hair. She didn't bother with makeup.

She looked at herself in the full length mirror on the back of the bathroom door. She looked the same, but she felt brand new. She felt like she could do whatever she needed to do now, take the next step, whatever that might be. She turned and looked at her butt. She could lose a little weight.

What was the next step? Kill Patrick, probably. Patrick. Asshole. She scowled at herself in the mirror, then opened the door.

The girl still sat in the same chair, phone in her lap.

"Thanks," Molly said. "That was great."

"Yeah."

"I'm Molly," Molly said and sat on the couch.

"I'm Lari."

"Lari?" Molly smiled. "Great name."

"Short for Larissa. That one never fit."

Molly nodded. She didn't know what she was doing here.

"I called my brother," Lari said. "He's coming over."

"The cute one?" Molly should have bitten her tongue.

"You know my brother?" Lari's eyes slitted in suspicion. "What is the deal with you? You know my mother, you know this Patrick guy, you know my brother? Who the fuck are you, anyway?"

"I don't know him," Molly said. "I saw him last night. He was here, right?"

"I think I better call the police."

"No. Don't."

"Well you just sit tight until Rocky gets here."

"Rocky. That's a good name, too. Rocky and Lari."

Lari smiled. "He's Phil Junior, but he never liked that. So one day when he was just little, he was watching cartoons and announced to the family that his new name was Rocket J. Squirrel."

Molly smiled. Maybe she ought to dip back into the bathroom and put on some makeup. She fluffed at her stringy, wet hair. She was a mess. "I dreamed about my father last night," she said, and then winced. "I guess that was a pretty stupid thing to say."

Lari was silent, leaving Molly's words hanging in the air.

"Is Darlene your mom?"

Lari nodded. "You know my mom?"

"Yeah."

Lari bit into the side of her thumb, then pulled at the loosened skin. They were quiet again. Waiting for Rocky, Molly thought. Waiting for the guy to come and get everything going. Waiting for the man to come ask the questions, get the answers, get the ball rolling. Molly would be a lot happier when he got here. She could negotiate with a guy. This girl just made her nervous.

"Want something to eat?" Lari asked, finally.

"Like what?"

Lari shrugged. "Fruit. Yogurt. Bagel."

Molly shook her head.

"Coffee?"

"Have a Diet Coke?"

Lari smiled, got up and went to the kitchen. She returned with two Cokes.

"Is that your sister?" Molly pointed to a framed photo on the end table.

"My wife," Lari said.

Molly frowned. "You're a lesbian?"

"Bingo."

"What's that like? I mean... I.. well, I don't want to be nosey, but I guess I've never understood."

"Were you in love with Patrick?"

Molly thought about that for a while. She wasn't sure she'd ever been in love with anybody before. "I don't know. Maybe."

"Well, it's like that. I'm in love with Carolyn."

"So, when you sleep together—" Molly couldn't help herself. She couldn't imagine it.

"So when we make love you mean?"

Molly nodded.

"So when we make love, we do what pleases the other person. That's what making love is all about."

Molly frowned again. She'd never thought of that before. She liked sex all right, but it was messy and a hassle. Usually the guys were too rough and inconsiderate and it was over before it had really ever begun. No boy she'd ever been with had tried to please her, and she could please them just opening her legs. She looked down at her hands and tried to think what it might be like to be in love. "I guess Patrick and I weren't in love."

"I'm sorry about Patrick," Lari said.

"Yeah," Molly said.

Wait a minute. Sorry? How did this Lari person know that she'd been dumped? Did Patrick go back to Leathers' and announce to everyone that he had left her? Did that mean Darlene was here? "How do you know about that?"

"The police told us."

Molly's face flushed with fire. She put a foot out to steady herself, even though she was sitting down. "Wait a minute," she said. "The police? The police told you what?"

Rocky knocked, then opened the door. "Hi," he said.

167

The pain in Darlene's hand lessened until she saw it as a red, glowing basketball that surrounded her wrist. She kept it propped up on a stack of pillows as Leathers worked on her leg. At first, the sound of the tattoo needle was distracting. She couldn't concentrate on the pain in her hand, the pain of the tattoo needle and its irritating buzz all at the same time, but he spoke soothing words to her, talked to her about the pain, talked to her about seeing the colors, the shards of light. All pain is the same, he said, pain of the heart, pain of the soul, pain of the flesh. It all has one distinct voice.

Soon she could hear the pain as well as see it. It sounded like a high pitched whine that harmonized with the needle's buzz. All pain was the same, it just floated above her body on a thin layer of relief: the hand, the leg, the past, it all hurt the same, nothing stood out any more, she could see it, and hear it, and perhaps she could discard it as well. It seemed as though she should just be able to make it disappear, but learning to do that might take a while. Getting acquainted with it was taking its own time. Pain had its pace, she discovered, and she had to honor that.

He'd worked through most of the night, stopping occasionally to stretch out beside her and snore softly for a while. Then she would awaken to the sound of the needle and the gentle pressure of his fingertips as he stretched her skin, moved her leg, softly asked her to turn over. She found that when he was concentrating completely on his work, a sense of peace settled throughout the room, and she could sleep, dreaming of people acting on a stage of colored pain.

He helped her to the bathroom, he brought her fruit and soup, and never suggested that they might end up running out of food. There seemed to be an inexhaustible supply, and the only worry that Darlene had was that Lari would be missing her by now, and Phil's new wife would probably be getting her fill of Ashes and Tina.

But what did that matter? What did any of it matter?

Darlene remembered her step-father as he lay in his recliner, dying. Lung cancer took him when he was in his mid-seventies, took him slowly, and he wasted to a smelly death for almost two years, right in that damned recliner.

Darlene had that chair taken out back to the field and burned when he had finally breathed his last.

And then she took a look at her mother. A woman busy with her children, busier taking care of a retired husband, busier still, when he became ill and cranky. And suddenly, he was dead and she was alone at age seventy.

Darlene had always looked at her mother, as she did now through burning hazes of pain, and wondered at her vitality. Surely, she could see that she had maybe ten years to live at the very most; she was elderly and not all that well herself. When did one finally sit down and say "what's the use?" and give up? Her step-father had done it the last time he sat in that recliner. He wasn't going to fight his cancer, he wasn't going to fight for life any longer. He was finished with all of that.

But Darlene's mother was going to use her life, right up until the final moment, and the last time Darlene talked with her, she was still playing bridge, still dancing, still vivacious, feminine, involved, interested.

Darlene took after her step-dad. Or maybe her real dad, the one named Bob, the one who walked out on her when she was little. Odd, that when faced with the two differing role models, that she would opt for the one who gave up. Darlene's mother would never give up, she would want them to shove tubes into her until there was nothing left but hardened skin stretched over useless tendons and brittle bones. She would want to suck the last ounce of life out of herself and everybody else.

Not Darlene. She bought a recliner when Phil left, and sat in it, watching television and eating, with Ashes on her lap and Tina on the chair's arm, uninterested in life, until this odd thing that brought her to Leathers' shack.

Darlene, in her late forties, had been ready to give up. What's the use? What's the purpose? She inspected herself daily, hoping for some lump in her breast, some purple lesion on her skin, blood in the toilet, some sign of a fatal illness that she could bravely refuse to treat, something that would remove her from this plane, this planet, this life that had cheated her of so much.

What kind of life was left for a fat woman pushing fifty? She'd given her all to Phil and the kids, and when it was over, all she had was a garden full of roses and two animals who were aging much faster than she was.

Darlene's life had stretched before her as a desert expanse, populated only by roses, soap operas, double chocolate fudge ice cream and a dozen little deaths.

The purpose for life is to perpetuate the species, she had decided, and that done—with Rocky more successfully than with Larissa, as Rocky would breed and Larissa would not—she had been used and was ready to go.

And then: Leathers. He took each day as it came, the gifts, the trials. He expected nothing and gave everything. Was that her problem? High expectations? Standards too lofty? She would rather be dead than average?

When she had awakened and first discovered that he had tattooed her while she had been delirious with fever, she had been horrified, and rightly so. But when he returned to the bedroom, a new bandage on his thigh, he gently, wordlessly, tied her ankles again to the bed and began working on her illustration that now stretched all the way to her thigh. It was the trellis, tangled with a profusion of roses.

Darlene didn't resist. Resistance would be useless anyway. She was in no position to fight him, she was too weak to leave, she was giving up, only not to bone cancer or brain tumor or any of those noble things she had prayed for. She was giving up to Leathers, the way Leathers gave up to life, and she would trust that it would all turn out in the long run.

He was odd, but he wasn't going to hurt her. In fact, he loved her, and she could put up with a lot as long as she had someone who loved her.

Leathers finished working, turned off the needle and the pain ballooned in her hand again. It throbbed with a heat that looked to her mind's eye like a candle flame, yellow on the periphery, an inner layer of red, then blue, and white-hot at the core.

He gently rubbed Vaseline on the newest flower, untied her feet, wiped his hands on a cloth, then lay down beside her.

"How are you feeling?"

How long had it been since anybody cared enough to ask her that? "Okay. My hand hurts. It doesn't hurt so much when you're working."

"I know. I'll rest and then do some more."

"Roses," she said.

"Roses," he said, putting his hand on her cheek, and turning her face toward him.

He looked different when he lay next to her. He looked soft, vulnerable, sweet, tender. Darlene felt a bit of a sob well up inside her, and she had to squeeze her eyes shut to force it down.

"I have a rose jones," he said.

"Rose jones?"

"Yeah, don't you know what a jones is?"

She shook her head, noticing again what a deep brown his eyes were, how clear and shiny. His skin wrinkled up in a smile.

"A habit. An addiction. Can't live without it. You know. A jones."

She laughed. "Rose Jones. Sounds like somebody I ought to know."

"Sounds like you. Rose Jones. What's your last name? Martin? Darlene Martin? You're more of a Rose Jones."

"Rose Jones," she laughed, her hand forgotten until she wanted to wipe away the tear that had leaked out of the corner of her eye. "Ow."

"Rose Jones. That's you. Especially when you wear those short skirts and show off the trellis on your leg."

"Short skirts. I'm too old for short skirts."

"Too old? Never. You'd look mighty sexy in a little black skirt that came down to about..." He zeroed in on her thigh with a pudgy finger, "here."

She ignored him, lost in the new concept. "Rose Jones," she said. "Maybe that's who I really am. Maybe all my problems all this time have been because my mother named me Darlene and I was really a Rose."

"I'm sure of it. All your problems are solved. All your troubles are over. You are now Rose Jones, and you have a whole new life, and a whole new outlook."

She smirked. If only it were that easy.

"And a new lover."

No, he was no longer her lover. She would let him tattoo her, but she wasn't going to have sex with him anymore. That part was over. She was marking time. Marking time. Soon she'd heal enough to get home and leave this whole adventure behind her.

Within moments, he was sleeping, his bulk sinking deeper into the bed as his spirit went soaring.

"Rose Jones," she whispered into the room. It fit. She looked down at Leathers, his eyes closed, his white hair spiking out over the pillow.

Who'd have thought?

Now, here she was, with a badly damaged hand, her perfect excuse to give up and die. It could fester with gangrene or blood poisoning, she might go insane with the infection and then die from some brain fever. This was it. This was her opportunity. Darlene hadn't been afraid of Molly's gun, because what could that young thing do to her that she hadn't already done to herself?

But now, as Rose Jones, she was afraid to look at her hand. She was afraid she'd see gangrene or the red line of blood poisoning or feel phantom fingers because of the way Leathers had cauterized the heel of her palm after he'd cut away the stumps. She needed a hospital. She didn't want to die. She wanted to take another look at herself, she wanted to take another peek at life.

It was time to go. She thought she could walk out now, walk out to the main road and flag down a good Samaritan. She wanted a doctor to see to her hand.

When the sun was high in the sky, and Leathers snored softly beside her, Darlene ventured gingerly out of bed. She rolled her feet to the floor, then stood, holding on to the headboard while the rush of pain from her hand clouded her vision.

When it passed, she went to the bathroom and cleaned herself up.

She examined the tattoo which now circled the lower part of her leg from her ankle midway to her knee and extended almost to her hip, an incredible profusion of roses, delicately drawn and tinted. But it was strange, the added weight of color to the lower part of that leg. At first glance, it looked like some mottled skin disease had affected her. It seemed unfinished, but then what would finished mean? The entire leg illustrated? Both legs? Her whole body?

It didn't matter, she was ready to leave, and the tattoo would remain as it was.

"Rose?" Leathers called softly from the bed.

She opened the bathroom door and peered out. She felt silly answering to that name. Silly, but it made her smile. "Yes?"

"Come back to bed."

"In a minute." She closed the bathroom door and finished dressing, in her damp and smelly leggings and green polyester blouse. The pants hurt the fresh tattoos, and she thought this might be a good way to get her leg infected. Then she'd really be a mess.

She came out of the bathroom and stood next to Leathers' side of the bed.

"You're dressed," he said.

She just looked at him.

"You should have gauze on the tattoos. The dye in your pants is not good."

"It'll be all right."

"Are you leaving me?"

"I'll be back."

"You won't," he said, and his eyes squinted shut.

"I will, Leathers, I promise. I need to see my kids so they won't worry, and I need to see a doctor."

"You'll forget."

"I don't think so," she said. "You've marked me."

He opened his eyes and they were soft and brown and trusting, like a child's. She loved the brown of his eyes and the white of his hair against his dark skin. He was beautiful. She sat on the waterbed frame next to him.

"The tattoo isn't finished," he said.

She just looked at him.

"Please let me finish it. I was just about to add some texture to it. It will be the work of my lifetime. Please let me finish it. Please."

She looked down at him and he appeared as a troubled little boy. A strange little boy, the odd one in the crowd that always stood apart, the one that made you want to reach out to him.

She reached out and touched his soft hair.

"Rose," he said.

"Rose Jones."

"Perfect."

"I like being Rose Jones."

"You belong here."

She thought about Ashes and Tina and Lari and Rocky. And Phil. She wasn't even sure what day it was, but she knew they'd be worried.

"Do you have children?"

"No. My only regret."

"Regret? I wouldn't spend too much time regretting it. It's overrated."

"No, I don't think so. I can't imagine anything better."

"There are many things better."

"Nothing more important."

Rose thought about that for a minute. She could feel his hand on her back. It felt warm and nice to be touched. "Maybe not. Maybe it is really important. I'm not sure I did a very good job of it."

"There's a difference between people who have had children and people who haven't," he said. "A difference of perspective."

She waited for him to go on, but he didn't. His hand was up under her blouse now, and it felt really good the way it relaxed her. He massaged her gently. "You feel cheated out of a greater understanding or something?"

"Yeah."

"You had Patrick."

"Not for long, and he was grown, anyway. I just put a few finishing touches on him, and look what he did... Never even said goodbye." His hand massaged the back of her neck and played with her hair.

"See what I mean?" Rose said. "You put your heart and soul into kids and they just take it for granted."

"That's the perspective I'm talking about. I think if I'd had that done to me all along, been the selfless person that a parent needs to be, then I would understand how he could do something like that." He pulled her around, and she let herself be upended until she was on the bed and in his arms. She could feel his swelling penis against her leg. "It's godlike," he whispered into her hair.

"What is?" She felt her passion rising up through her. She ought to be going, but when was the next time she was likely to have someone make love to her? Never, probably. And it felt so good.

"The perspective. God is the ultimate parent," he began to unbutton her blouse, "and he's used to dealing with us ungrateful idiots. You could have the right perspective on our relationship to God, whereas I never could."

His hand was pulling down her pants and her breath caught in her throat. She worked at his clothes, and taking his beautiful strong penis in her one good hand, she stroked it, kissed it, and even though she knew she shouldn't, she knew there was something wrong with this, something wrong with him, it felt so good, it felt so goddamned *good*.

This time, as the first time, he was gentle and attentive, and tears leaked out of her eyes as they made love.

Later, he got up, got her a warm, wet towel, and then he carefully cleaned the lint from her leg, reapplied Vaseline and wrapped it lightly with gauze. "There, my rosebud," he said, giving her ankle a gentle squeeze.

Darlene watched him with those hot tears still pushing at her eyes.

"I'll be back," she said.

"I can't count on that," he said. "I have to believe you will never come back, or I'll go insane waiting. I'll be so disappointed when you don't return. This way, if you do come back, it will be icing on the cake of my life."

"How would you live? How did you live before Patrick?"

Leathers looked down, shrugged. "I've always been looked after, I guess. It just works out."

Darlene found her pants tangled amidst the sheets. She extracted them, sat on the edge of the bed and pulled them on, gently, one-handedly, over the gauze bandage. "I like being Rose Jones," she said.

"Then stay," he said, as he stood there, mountainous in his own bedroom, wheezing with emotion. "Stay and be Rose Jones here with me."

Darlene smiled sadly at him and shook her head. She'd thought about it, but couldn't imagine living here, but then it was going to be hard giving him up, too. In a few short days he had wormed his way into her. For the first time since college she felt like a woman, a desirable woman, and she had so much to give... She could cook, shop, drive, fetch medications. She could give this place a real going over, both inside and out, she could turn this place from a rundown shack into a home.

But she couldn't live without her kids. Or without a phone. And that isn't how Leathers wanted to live.

Leathers couldn't compromise, not to that degree. She looked up at him when she stood to pull up her pants. He was watching her with a quiet desperation, then he hitched his shorts up and went into the next room.

She heard the tattoo needle begin to whine as she brushed her hair and made herself ready to leave.

He didn't look up as she passed him. She touched the top of his head as he awkwardly added details to the rabbit hutch on his side. "I'll be back," she whispered, her heart twisting with the lie. She felt like she was treating him the same way Patrick had. She felt as if she was kicking sand in his face after he'd loved her and cherished her.

He needed her. He needed her, and she was walking out on him. She found her purse and walked out the door.

At noon, Phil announced to Angela, "I'm going to the office."

"Good," she said. "You're about to drive me nuts, with all your pacing and snorting. Peaches is picking up on the energy and it isn't good for her. The people at the office need to be annoyed for a while. Better yet, go to the range and hit a bucket of balls."

That sounded like a good idea. He'd do that first. Expend a little of this nervous energy. He was about to drive himself nuts. Then he'd go irritate everybody at the office. He was so worried about Darlene he was afraid he was going to lose his mind.

"You'll be here, right?" he asked.

"I'll be here," she said, turning the pages of her magazine, "waiting for my ten thousand dollars. I'll call you if anything happens."

He backed out of the garage, but instead of turning left, he turned right and headed toward Darlene's house. He didn't know what he expected to see there. Her car, perhaps, still dripping with river water, hairs from that boy's head caught in the spiderweb crack in the windshield? Darlene, her cellulite gloriously caught up in those ludicrous stretch pants, bending over to pull a few weeds from between the roses? Lari, sipping a cup of coffee on her mother's front porch, with a ready smile and an inviting wave?

Yes. Lari. He could just sit in her cool, calm company and hate himself and it would be just fine.

He turned the corner and saw three police cars. Blue uniforms were examining a little white Honda parked down the street from Darlene's house. Rocky's truck was in Darlene's driveway, along with Lari's car.

Phil slowed way down and crept along. This police business didn't seem to have anything to do with Darlene, unless she was in the house. But the kids would have called him, wouldn't they? They would have.

No, there couldn't be any good news, not yet, and Phil wasn't up to spending any time at all with Rocky. Not now. Let Lari handle Rocky. Phil needed to go to the range and slam some golf balls right out of the park first.

Or else shoot himself.

I'll just be sitting here waiting for my ten thousand dollars. Bitch.

He drove out of town and was well on his way toward the driving range when that suicide thought hit again.

He slammed on the brakes and pulled off into the first big parking lot he saw. He pulled down the visor and looked into the mirror.

His father's face looked back at him.

His father. Harold Martin. Marty, his barfly friends called him. Too smart for his own good, never made anything of himself. Always in the basement, tinkering with motors and screws and pieces of metal. Always doodling little mechanical drawings on pieces of paper. Always drinking. Always drunk.

Phil was an only child, and his mother exhausted herself working two jobs to pay the bills. Phil felt guilty that she worked so hard. His father felt no guilt, so Phil felt it for him. Marty could never understand why Phil preferred homework to the fantasyland of gadgetry in the basement.

"C'mon, boy, let me show you something," Marty would say, a thin hand on Phil's shoulder.

Phil would shrug it off. "Ball game," he'd say. Marty would show severe disappointment, sometimes he would look hurt, but Phil couldn't help that. Phil wanted to get out of the house. Phil thought that if there were two of them tinkering in the basement, his mom would leave. Leave or give up. Or die. As long as there was just the two of them, their tension kept a balance. But if Phil hung out too long with his mom, it seemed his dad went overboard drinking and gambling. He was afraid if he went into that basement and was tempted by all that creative inventive stuff, his mom would go off the deep end. He didn't want that, so he kept out of the house.

Social skills were Phil's strong suit.

Girls.

Phil wanted to have a wife and kids, and he wanted to support them in a solid way. He wanted his children to respect him the way he could never respect Marty.

Phil's mother did leave, give up and die, all in the same day when he was seventeen. Phil finished high school and got a job selling magazine subscriptions door to door. It was a piece of cake, especially to the housewives. He had charm and he knew how to use it.

Marty electrocuted himself one night while drunk in his shop.

Phil sold their tiny home and went to college, majoring in marketing. The college social scene began to drag on him, so he found and married Darlene and they raised two fine children. He supported them well, acted the part of husband and father, and he did it better than his dad. He did everything right.

So how come when he looked in the mirror, he couldn't see a difference between himself and Marty?

Marty drank, Phil did not. Phil made a living, Marty did not. Did either of them have respect from their kids? No. Did either of them have a satisfying marriage relationship? No.

Phil used to. Darlene had been a good wife for many years, and still might, except for a little accident at work.

God, he missed Darlene.

Fine time to realize that Phil, you jerk.

So here he was, on the side of the road, thinking about suicide, running so far away from his father that he had become him. They looked the same, they had the same failures, the same problems.

Phil had found his niche, selling office equipment. He liked dealing with the executives, he liked flirting with their secretaries. He'd made a fine living, but so what? What did he have to show for it except equity in a house? Where was the meaning in that?

Phil looked up and realized he was in a tavern's parking lot. Sam's. The door to Sam's opened as two men in jeans and tee shirts came out. Phil saw the cool, darkened interior, with neon beer lights over the bar.

A cold beer sounded better than a bucket of balls.

He parked and locked the car. He'd drink a toast to the old man, and maybe somewhere inside there, he'd find a little forgetfulness, a little blessed peace.

Peace. Maybe that was what had eluded the Martin men for so many years.

"Listen," Molly said, after she'd caught her breath. She blew her nose again with trembling fingers. Patrick was dead. How could that be? He was dead and he had ten thousand dollars with him. How could that be? "Can I talk to you alone?" she asked Rocky.

Rocky looked at Lari. Lari shrugged.

Good, Molly thought. She could get him away from that little dyke. Lari made Molly nervous. She had everything, and none of it was pegged to any man. Maybe that's why she had everything.

Molly had some thinking to do about that whole scenario. But for now, she had a mission. If she could get the guy by himself, maybe she could work him a little bit. Get enough money to get out of town and away from the police. She was in deep shit and she just wanted to get out.

Molly stood up, and as she did so, she looked out through the living room windows and saw police cars. Policemen were swarming over the little car she'd stolen from that kid. Boy, that didn't take long. How did they do that?

Rocky stood up and followed her into the kitchen. He sat on a barstool and picked up a pencil that had been on the counter. He played with it nervously.

Molly moved close to him, stood just a little too close for casual conversation. She felt as though the three of them had been skirting the issue of Darlene, not a one of them willing to divulge what information they had. Molly didn't know if Darlene had come home or not, didn't know if these people knew about Leathers or not, didn't know exactly how much they knew about Patrick.

Patrick.

The thought of him closed her throat. She cleared it and put Rocky foremost in mind. Rocky. He was some kind of great looking guy. And he didn't flinch when she moved close, even though her nose and eyes were red. A good sign.

"So?" he said.

"So," she said, and put her hand on his shoulder. His muscle was firm, his skin warm through his shirt. He didn't move or shrink from her touch. His self-assurance was a little bit disconcerting, and she removed her hand, then moved to stand in front of him. "So, I need some help, and I thought you might be the one to give it to me." She smiled, hoping that the sexual connotation was not lost on him.

It wasn't, but neither did he rise to the bait. "Ready to get out of town?"

She nodded demurely, or what she hoped passed for demurely, then reached out one finger and traced it down his bicep. "Bus fare," she said. "That's all I need."

"To?"

Molly shrugged. "Out of town, like you said."

Rocky nodded. "How much?"

Molly shrugged again, moved closer, began to rub Rocky's shoulder. He didn't close his eyes in ecstasy, didn't even show that he knew she was touching him. "Couple hundred."

"Why should I?"

She kept rubbing.

"Do you know where Darlene is?" he asked.

Bingo. She had him. He *didn't* know. Maybe her information was far more valuable than a bus ticket. Far more valuable.

"Yep," she said, moving back to face Rocky. She leaned against the counter, this time with her arms folded across her chest. She was pretty proud of herself, ferreting that information out so cleanly. She could write her own ticket here.

Rocky leaned toward her, a menacing look in his eye. "Is she all right?"

Molly nodded. "She's fine."

Then he stood up and walked back into the living room.

He wasn't supposed to do that. Shit. She wanted to deal with him, and with him alone. On her terms. She held all the cards here, they would deal on her terms.

"Hey," she said. "Where are you going?"

"To discuss this with my sister."

"I don't want to discuss this with her. This discussion is between us."

"This is a family matter," Rocky said. "Or, if you prefer, it can be a police matter."

Bust. She lost the hand. How did that happen so fast? She followed him into the living room, holding her head up, trying not to look as cowed as she felt.

"She knows where Mom is," Rocky said to Lari. "She wants two hundred dollars to tell us."

"What?! You're kidding."

"Bus fare," Rocky said. They looked at each other and began to laugh.

Molly felt her face grow hot. They could laugh all they wanted, but she still had the information they needed. "I don't understand what's so fucking funny," she said, feeling the pout grow on her lips. Here she was again, the outsider. Outside all the inside jokes, the inside information.

"You're a cheap date," Rocky said, and they started to laugh all over again.

Molly scowled.

"No, really," Lari said, trying to straighten up. "Two hundred is very reasonable..." she couldn't stop the giggles "...we'll be happy to pay it." She looked at Rocky and gasped out the words "fire sale." They both laughed again, tears pouring down their cheeks, tears of comic relief, tears and laughter of life-threatening tension giving way. Lari felt on the verge of hysterics, and knew that Rocky felt the same way.

"I hate this," Molly said.

Rocky wiped his face, gave a last laugh or two, then began to calm down. "Two hundred really is far more reasonable than ten thousand."

"Ten thousand?" Molly wasn't making the connection.

"Ransom," Lari said. Molly's face was blank. "Patrick wanted ten thousand dollars to tell us where Darlene was."

Molly sank down to the rug. *Patrick had held Darlene for ransom? What were they talking about?* "What are you talking about?"

They both stared at her, all humor gone from their faces.

There was a long, silent moment.

"You mean you weren't in on Patrick's scheme?" Rocky asked. "All those phone calls? The ransom demand?"

Molly shook her head no. She couldn't believe that snake had schemed to get ten thousand dollars and leave her broke in a stupid motel room. This was far more sobering than his death. It was good that he died. It was good. Snake. Fucking snake. And he had the balls to say Arizona and marriage both in the same sentence. Fucking snake. Molly's face was hot with humiliation.

Then Rocky said, "Okay, enough bullshitting. Let's get down to it. Nobody's going to call the cops, okay?" He looked at Molly. She nodded. He looked at Lari. Lari nodded. "All right. Now just exactly what the fuck is going on here?"

"Will you help me?" Her voice sounded young and hurt.

"You mean buy you a bus ticket out of town?"

Molly nodded.

"If it means getting our mother back in one piece, then yes, we'll help you, for Christ's sake. Just talk."

Molly did. She told him all about her young uncle, her father's little brother, the one who lived with them.

Only this time when she told it, she told it in more intimate detail than she'd ever told anybody before, maybe even more detail than she'd ever admitted to herself. Maybe it was the shock value she wanted to impart to these two middle-class people, maybe it was the lesbian sitting on the couch that she wanted to impress, but she told them of Stewie, her uncle, ten years older than she, who would steal into her bedroom at night, lie next to her on her bed and talk about the desert, while touching her in ways that made her feel wonderful.

It had started one night when Molly was in seventh grade. She knew about sex, some of her girlfriends had been having sex with their boyfriends for a year already, some of them even before they started their periods. They felt that was safe, no periods, no pregnancy.

Stewie was twenty-three, and he had been in the Navy. He came back looking so handsome, Molly just about swooned every time she saw him. He worked in their yard all day long, and he was tanned and his hair was sunbronzed and his teeth were white and his eyes were sparkling blue. He was gorgeous and all her girlfriends used to walk by the house just to talk to him. He'd lean on his shovel, or his rake, or kill the lawnmower engine and talk with them, smiling.

Molly would watch the girls smile and blush and giggle, elbowing each other as he teased them, and she smiled inside, knowing that he was hers. They could look all they wanted to, but he belonged to her.

She flirted with him more outrageously than they did, and she became more insistent about it. One night, when her parents were out for the night, and Stew was watching television and drinking beer, Molly came down from her room dressed only in bra and panties, took the beer from his hand and sat in his lap. She kissed him, full on the lips, and the beery breath sent shivers up her spine. He smelled so masculine.

She knew he had misgivings at first, but she wanted him to be hers, so she teased him until his jeans had a huge lump in them, and in mystery, she touched it.

"That's it," he said, and he got up, then pulled her along with him to her bedroom, where he closed the door and unbuckled his belt.

Suddenly, she was afraid, but he settled her with gentle, calming touches. Then he began to kiss her and she was lost.

He always promised her he'd take her to Arizona with him, and then one day he went without her.

She stopped eating.

She knew that the extra flab on her thighs was what kept Stewie from taking her with him, after he professed such love for her. There had to be a reason he would only touch her in the dark. There had to be a reason he just left—*he just left*—without even saying goodbye.

He hadn't wanted to hurt her feelings. She was fat and he found her repulsive, and she vowed that she would be thin the next time he saw her. Thin and beautiful and ready for desert adventures. He'd be proud to take her with him on the back of his motorcycle. She'd look good. She'd look real good.

Since he was family, she knew he'd be back.

Only he hadn't come back. So she decided to go to Arizona to look for him.

Her father never noticed that she stopped eating. He never noticed how good she looked. She just wanted him to notice her for once. She even pranced around in her underwear some, but her mother shooed her upstairs, and still her father never noticed.

But her mother noticed. Her mother ranted and raved and

screamed and cried, as Molly's face grew more slender, as her thighs approached normalcy. Her facial features took on an elegant look, and Molly took to prancing around her bedroom in just her underwear, mugging for the mirror and liking the hipbones that protruded just like the runway models. If she'd been taller, she could have been a model.

But no word from Stewie.

Molly stopped going to school. She'd leave the house in the morning, as usual, then come back home, sneak inside and go up to her room. As long as she was quiet, her mother never knew she was there. She'd read, she'd fantasize about Stewie, she'd touch herself the way he had touched her, she'd look at pictures of desert creatures in the National Geographics she'd found in the basement. She'd memorize maps of Arizona. She'd trace the routes she'd take as she explored the desert, with its Indian reservations and silver and turquoise jewelry, its reptiles and relentless sun, its cloudless, pale skies and red rock formations.

Arizona was a lifetime away from Minnesota, and that is where she intended to be.

Then one night, they had the showdown. Molly would have eaten dinner if her dad had asked her to. She would have eaten if her father had just once mentioned what a beautiful young woman she had become, how proud he was of her accomplishments, her dreams, her ambitions.

But at dinner one night, with just the three of them in their shabby, pitiful dining room, when Molly had messed with her food and actually gotten through the whole meal without putting a single bite in her mouth, her mother began to cry.

"Okay, that's it," her father said. "Molly, I want you to eat that food that your mother prepared."

"I did."

"She didn't," her traitorous mother said. "Not one bite."

"I did so," Molly said, put a touch of mashed potatoes on the end of her fork and put it in her mouth, just to prove it. It tasted awful.

"You're flunking school and you're beginning to look like a goddamned skeleton," her father said. "I want you to clean that plate and I'm going to school with you tomorrow to see if we can't salvage something of your education. No daughter of mine is going to embarrass me in this community. Your mother and I have worked too hard."

Molly locked her calm eyes onto his raving eyes, picked up the plate of beans, potatoes, gravy, meat that she had shredded, and green jello with fruit cocktail inside it, held it aloft like a serving tray, then threw it against the dining room wall.

The plate broke and the mess slid down the flowered wallpaper.

She looked at her parents' shocked faces with triumphant satisfaction and walked out the front door.

She was free. She didn't need money for food, she could just hitch a ride, and soon she'd be in lovely Arizona, where all she'd need was a sturdy pair of shorts and a tank top. All year round.

It took three months of miserable rides, scummy guys and back alley sleeping to get to Portland, Oregon, and that's where she met Bruno, cokemeister and all around badass. Without Bruno, she would have died of the clap. Without Bruno's bouts of common sense, she would have died of starvation, coked out and wasting away. But Bruno made her eat. Bruno would get clean now and then and work on his ravaged body, and he would drag her back to health along with him.

For five years she lived with Bruno. She'd almost forgotten about Arizona, that dream along with the others lost in the drugged-up gray rainclouds of the Pacific Northwest.

And then he brought home that little bitch, and Molly found Patrick with his thumb out on the freeway.

By this time, she had remembered Arizona, and she had remembered Stewie. She needed to get clean, she needed to get herself together, she needed to get to Arizona and find out just exactly what there was about that place that drew her so.

And then a few months with Patrick and her plans were about to be derailed again.

Patrick. Dead. He had betrayed her, held Darlene's family up for ransom, and then died. Good. He'd been a lousy lay anyway. Never even took off his clothes.

Tears were falling freely down Molly's face by this time, while Rocky and Lari sat watching her with stone faces. Lari got up once and brought her a roll of toilet paper so she could blow her runny nose.

"Patrick wasn't too keen on going to Arizona," she said. "I mean he didn't have a car or anything, and there was something funny going on between him and Leathers." She looked up at Lari. "I mean they weren't queer or anything, you know, I don't think they were at least..." She blew her nose again while she considered that possibility. "No, no, I'm sure they weren't. Maybe they were related somehow. I don't know. Anyway, Patrick worked his ass off for Leathers, all the time, I mean all the time. He worked in the garden and he butchered the rabbits and he cleaned Leathers' bedroom and bathroom, and he did all the cooking. Jeez, he did everything around there, like a slave. Sometimes he went out and got a job too and brought home beer and stuff. And *still* he had this kind of weird devotion to the fat man. And they had this weird thing about pain."

"Pain?" Lari asked, with a worried glance at Rocky.

Rocky ignored her, he was zeroed in on Molly.

Molly shrugged. "They used to talk about it a lot. I thought it was weird, but I just ignored them."

"Did they ever hurt you?"

"No *way*. I wouldn't put up with that, not for a second." She sniffed, fluffed her hair, stretched and felt a little better after pouring her heart out, even if it was to these two unfeeling yuppie kids. "But I think Leathers used to hurt Patrick. He had some funny lumps and things. I could feel them through his clothes."

"Scars? Were they scars? Did you ask him about them?"

"Eeew, yuck, no, you don't ask people about their *scars*, Jeez. That's kind of personal, don't you think? So *anyway*, back to the subject, that's why I stole her car. I thought if we had a car, Patrick and I could go."

"*You* stole her car?" Rocky sat up as if awakened. "Mom's car?"

Molly nodded. "And she came with the car."

Lari smiled. "What do you mean, you mean she wouldn't give up the car? She wouldn't let you have it?"

"I didn't drive," Molly said. "I needed her to drive."

"You hijacked her."

Molly shrugged.

"Did you have a weapon?"

Molly nodded. "A pistol."

"Loaded?"

"Of course. What do you think I am? A jerk?"

"So where is she now?"

"Your mom?"

"*Yes*," Rocky ran his hands through his hair in frustration. "That's who we're talking about, right?"

Molly nodded. "Can I have something to drink?"

Rocky sprang out of the chair, stomped to the kitchen, came back with a Diet Coke.

"Thanks." She opened it and took a long drink. "That fucking Patrick." She shook her head. "Fuck him."

"*Where is she?*"

Molly looked at them. "Tell me about Patrick," she said. "Tell me what he did."

Lari looked at Rocky. "Do you think Dad ought to be here?"

Rocky snorted. "While some lunatic might be carving up our mother?" He took a deep breath and sat back. Slowly, the purple faded from his face, and he looked calmly back at Lari. "Why would we want Phil here?"

"Well, because he's our father, for one thing, and because he's been so upset by this, and he went so far as to do that money thing."

"Does 'tits on a boar' mean anything to you?"

Lari frowned her disapproval at Rocky's crudeness.

"Useless," Rocky said. "He's a useless man."

"He's your father, Rocky."

"Yeah, well, I would have been better off with an anonymous sperm donor. Mom should have had more sense than to marry a cheating asshole like him."

Lari sighed. "We've beat this dead horse before. You expect too much from him. You've always expected too much."

"And you don't."

"He's just a guy, Rocky, just a guy. Don't you get that? He's no more or less qualified to be a father than the next boy or man on the street. He's just a guy. You've got him set up to be some sort of a... a... paragon of goodness or something. He can't compete with your idealistic picture. He's *just a guy*."

"I hate that he hurt Mom the way he did."

"Yeah, I know," Lari said, putting a hand on his knee. "But

that's between them, and there's nothing we can do. Have your own relationship with him. Try looking past his failings and seeing his strengths."

"There aren't any."

"There are," Lari sighed. "He's no superhero, but he's an okay guy, and you're missing having a relationship with him because of your attitude."

"I'm not missing anything worthwhile."

"Hey, no shit," Molly said. "Fathers are—well, I have a couple of friends who got good ones."

"I don't," Rocky said. "Fathers are a fucking disappointment."

"But *you'll* be different," Lari said, mocking him.

"I'm getting a vasectomy," Rocky said.

Lari stared at him with her mouth open.

"Can we get back to talking about me, please?" Molly said.

Three men sat at Sam's bar drinking beer and watching a football game on the big screen television.

The bartender nodded at Phil as he walked through the door, then cleared away dishes and wiped down the bar.

"Light draft," Phil said.

The bartender poured a cold one and set it on a napkin in front of him, took Phil's money, then turned around and leaned against the bar to watch the game with the three other guys.

The quarterback threw the bomb, the tight end caught it in the end zone.

The bartender threw up his arms and cheered, two of the other guys did as well, while one hung his head and moaned.

The bartender set five shot glasses on the counter and filled each with vodka. "Round on the house," he said.

Phil looked at the shot of vodka and didn't think he ought to drink it. If he did, and the bartender's team won by a wide spread, he could get into a lot of trouble.

He sipped his beer, letting the shot sit there, and gradually got involved in the game with the guys. The Eagles were playing the Packers. Phil remembered when he was a kid, he used to watch a lot of football at a friend's house. That kid's dad, an ex-marine, was a football fanatic, and the Green Bay Packers was his team. He learned to love the Packers and the memory of those days tugged Phil's heart as he watched.

Philadelphia had just scored.

The bartender looked at him. "It's football season in here three hundred sixty-five days a year," he said. "What's your team?"

"Seahawks," Phil said. He got blank stares. "But I like Green Bay, too," and the man two stools down reached over and shook his hand.

"This isn't football season," Phil said.

"An old game," the bartender said. "I tape them, then show them all over again. I just don't happen to mention which year it is, and well... you can get into it if you try."

Phil smiled, finished his beer.

The Packers had the ball and were marching it right down the field, one first down after another.

He ordered another beer, and he poured the shot of vodka into it. Maybe this is exactly what I've been needing, he thought. Some football watching time. Some time with the guys. Some time away from Angela. Some time to myself. He reached down and turned off his phone. The simple act gave him a sense of recklessness. He liked it. He wanted more.

Maybe I ought to go fishing one of these days.

Wonder if Rocky would want to go.

Another cheer went up. Phil looked up in time to see the replay. Philadelphia had recovered a Green Bay fumble and had run ninety-eight yards to score again.

Out came five shot glasses.

Phil downed his along with the rest of them, then set to his boilermaker. This is good, he thought. I need this. And I'm not going to think of Darlene or Patrick or Rocky or Angela for the next—he looked at his watch—hour. Then he'd turn his phone back on and return to responsibility.

"Okay," he said, feeling the warmth from the booze and the camaraderie. "What's the score? And what quarter is it?"

~ ~ ~

Philadelphia won, and with one quick trip to the back room by Sam, the Giants began to play the Chargers. Phil became buddies with the three guys at the bar, and as the second game progressed, the bar began to fill up with laughter and raucous cheers.

Now and then the door opened, letting in vivid shafts of bright light, and a new presence would lend its atmosphere to what was beginning to feel like a real good time.

Then a woman took the stool next to Phil. He knew it the moment she slid onto the barstool.

He turned and looked at her. A blonde, maybe forty. She was

dressed in a business suit and ordered a club sandwich and a beer.

"Football fan?" Phil asked.

She nodded. Smiled. She liked his looks. Not an uncommon reaction. Phil smiled back and turned a little bit toward her, and began beaming his charm. Within five minutes, he'd know if he could pick her up. He always knew, and the answer was usually yes. He had good luck. Or a good line, or something.

This woman could be his, he realized, and he proceeded accordingly.

She ate her sandwich and drank her beer, joining in with the spirit of the crowd, warming to him, touching his arm now and then. Phil smiled and laughed with them all, enjoying the freedom and relaxation, and hardly knew that he was getting drunk until he looked at his watch and realized that he ought to be getting somewhere.

He looked back at the blonde. He had time. There was no place he had to go that was so desperately important that he couldn't spend a little more time in the company of a mature woman. She'd be a breath of fresh air after living with that young, immature—

Angela.

Phil's stomach turned over in disgust. His body reacted before his logy mind caught up with it.

This was what had turned him to shit in Rocky's eyes. This, exactly this. This is what had turned Darlene into a fat caricature of what a wife ought to be.

If he picked up this woman, and went back to her place, or to a motel, or God knows what, he'd be traveling down the same old road. Soon Angela would hate him. She wasn't as magnanimous as Darlene had been. And Peaches would grow up hating him just like Rocky.

Where would it end?

Phil's past opened up in as clear a revelation as if he were watching a film. He always thought he was blessed with good looks and an easy charm, and now he could see that it was his curse. Taking the blonde on the barstool next to him to bed was the easy way for him, contrary to what all his buddies had told him from high school on. Finding willing women had been difficult for them, but what was difficult for Phil was resisting the easy breach of ethics.

The boilermakers, the camaraderie, the cloying closeness of the bodies in the bar began to work on him. He felt dizzy, he felt sick.

He threw some bills on the bar and asked Sam to call him a cab. No way could he drive.

No way could he drive. No way would he drive. He was too drunk to drive, but not too drunk to know it.

He was surprised to see that night had fallen, and the air was cold. Phil got into the cab, shivering, and then forgot his home address. Then he remembered Darlene and his fear for her safety and his mood plunged from the melancholy drunk to the dangerously morose.

"Just take me to Autzen Stadium," Phil told the cab driver.

Football seemed to be in Phil's blood at the moment.

The cab driver stopped at the chained gate. The stadium loomed deserted and spooky across the barren parking lot. Phil fumbled some bills at the driver and got out. He walked across the wide expanse of blacktop, back toward the University of Oregon, back toward the footbridge that spanned the Willamette River. The footbridge that spanned the rapids of the Willamette River. The cold, deep, swirling, dark, black, dangerous, lethal Willamette River.

He knew he shouldn't be going there in this condition, but he newly realized he had options in life.

Life had dealt him certain hands, and some of those he could play and some of those he certainly had the power to fold.

He played Darlene and Lari and Angela. He had folded over Rocky.

And now he was just marking time.

Marking time.

Maybe the time had come to quit the game altogether. He didn't know. He'd have to take a look at the river and see.

Darlene felt as though one end of a long rubber band was tied around her waist, the other end attached to the slumping shack in the woods. No, it wasn't attached to the shack, it was attached to Leathers.

She walked through the calf-high grass, her shoes squeaking with water before she reached the parting of blackberries where the cars drove through into the yard. Leathers' area of influence extended far beyond that.

She knew she had been in bed with infection, with a fever for a couple of days, she knew she was heavy and out of shape, she knew that she dreaded doing whatever it was she was going to have to do to get a ride home, or to a phone, but she didn't know it was going to be so damned hard to walk down that road.

Her hand throbbed so hotly that zingers of pain shot up her arm. Her head pounded, making her dizzy and queasy and lightheaded. Her newly illustrated leg felt swollen and uncomfortable, and the weeds hid myriad threats, from snakes to holes to traps that had her nervous at every step.

And what would happen when she reached the road? She would stick out her good thumb and catch a ride? With a rapist? With a murderer? She had no protection. Could she just refuse a ride? How long would it be before someone stopped for her?

Darlene stopped and listened for a moment. She could see the grasses moving in the breeze, but could no longer hear them. She felt that empty feeling in her stomach, that cotton in her ears and knew she was about to, about to—

She sat down, her knees weak, sweat running into her eyes. She put her head down and took deep breaths.

Slowly, her hearing came back, and the cotton stuffing that

194

seemed to surround her brain dissolved.

She couldn't walk all the way to the road; that was a ridiculous idea. She wasn't well. She'd have to get herself better first. Then she could go.

Unless she was just getting sicker and sicker. Unless her damaged hand would be the death of her.

Well, if it was, it was already too late. She wasn't going to make it.

She looked down the lane that wasn't a lane, the driveway with barely any broken weeds to mark it. She couldn't see the road, she couldn't hear the road, she couldn't see the buried white car that marked the turnoff. It could be a mile farther. Two miles. There was no way she would make it.

She looked behind her. She had hardly come far at all. The hedge of blackberries was perhaps fifty yards behind her, and beyond that, a cool canopy of trees, mossy and damp. A shack that had somehow become very familiar, almost home, and Leathers.

Leathers.

A man so desperate with longing that only Darlene knew its depth. Only the longing she had felt during those long evenings when Phil was out with his girlfriends, and after the divorce, when she watched the late shows on television, could match Leathers' loneliness.

She remembered how her future stretched out in front of her, empty, like an abandoned warehouse, with dim light filtered through dusty, cobwebby windows. Desolate. Hopeless. Lifeless. Loveless.

She thought about her recliner, her television, her double chocolate fudge ice cream. Desolate. Hopeless. Loveless. Lifeless.

She thought about Leathers and what he must be going through right now. Losing Patrick. Losing her. Gouging himself in his loneliness. Desolate. Hopeless. Loveless. Lifeless.

Maybe he was right. Maybe she belonged here. Maybe together, they could become whole.

The compromises she would have to make—she touched her pants where they covered her new tattoo—would be different than the compromises she had made for Phil. Did that mean they were worse?

Leathers could compromise too. They could learn much from

each other.

   She stood up carefully and walked slowly back to the shack. This return trip seemed much easier; the rubber band helped.

SATURDAY

The cold woke Phil. To his sick astonishment, he was still down by the Willamette River, huddled shivering next to a log. The heels of his shoes were dug into soft earth, and his hands were inside his shirt, next to his skin. His clothes were soggy and kind of slimy. His head pounded, his stomach felt like it was filled with rocket fuel, his eyes were dry and there was something gritty on his tongue. Like he'd been eating river moss or something.

He was hung over, freezing, and about as miserable as a man could get.

Dawn lighted the overcast sky, and just as soon as he was wide awake and properly ashamed of himself, it began to rain.

He scrambled stiffly up the weedy bank to the bike path, where trees gave him some shelter. He brushed himself off as well as he could, tucked his shirt back in, straightened his clothes, and then tried to wade through his foggy mind and figure out the best way to get home.

He walked through chilly morning drizzle toward the university, head bowed, scraggy looking, feeling like a bum, and tried to remember the last time he had slept off a drunk outside. College.

He was relieved to find some cash in his wallet, and called a taxi from the Seven Eleven store.

But when he climbed into the cab, he visualized pulling up in front of his house, walking into its pristine interior, meeting up with Angela, who, no doubt, would have a few things to say.

He gave the driver Darlene's address.

Both Lari's and Carolyn's cars were in the drive. Phil used his key and entered as quietly as Ashes would let him. He knelt on the floor and petted the dog and then the cat, who came yowling for attention.

Someone was asleep on the sofa. He hoped it wasn't either Lari or Carolyn. He didn't want there to be any trouble in their relationship.

He took a long hot shower, shaved with Darlene's razor and a fresh blade, brushed his teeth with her toothbrush, then threw his clothes into the washer.

He made a pot of coffee, and was finally feeling just about normal, when Carolyn, tousled and adorable, came padding out of the bedroom in her blue terry robe and slippers.

"Phil," she said. "Hi."

"Hi, Carolyn."

"When'd you get here?"

"About an hour ago," Phil said.

"Early riser?"

"You might say."

"Angela was looking for you."

"I bet." Phil remembered turning off his phone in the bar. It wasn't on the counter in front of him with his wallet and his keys. A vague recollection of throwing it into the river made his face flush.

Carolyn poured herself a cup of coffee and sat next to him at the breakfast bar. Phil wore only a towel around his waist.

"My clothes are in the washer," he said.

"I wasn't going to ask," she said, smiling.

Phil felt a surge of affection for Carolyn. She was a good friend and a wonderful daughter.

"Who's on the couch?"

"Molly."

"Oh."

"I guess Lari ought to explain Molly to you."

"Oh?" Phil sipped his coffee and wondered if there was a love triangle crisis among Lari, Carolyn and Molly. He also wondered how long he should wait before he could ask Carolyn to take him to his car. He should have had the cab driver take him to his car.

"Molly is a friend of Patrick's."

Phil almost choked.

Carolyn patted him on the back as she walked behind him. "Want a bagel?"

A thousand questions clotted in Phil's foggy brain. He sat, open-mouthed, while he tried to think of words to put to the first one.

"Bagel?" Carolyn smiled.

"Please."

Carolyn held up her hand. "Before you even begin, Phil. I don't know anything. Ask Lari."

"What *do* you know?"

"I know that when I got here last night, Lari and Rocky were fighting—"

"Rocky was here?" Phil loosely remembered driving by and seeing Rocky's truck.

Carolyn nodded. "And Molly was trying to get some money out of someone to tell them where Darlene was."

"Is Darlene all right?"

"All Molly said was that the last time she saw Darlene, Darlene was eating omelets with Tabasco and laughing a lot." Carolyn picked the bagel halves out of the toaster. "I don't think she's in a lot of danger."

Phil's psyche relaxed one notch.

"Lari got mad, threw Rocky out, threw Molly a pillow and blanket and went to bed. I turned out the lights."

Phil spread Darlene's homemade strawberry jam on his bagel.

"And then Angela called about two o'clock in the morning and woke us all up."

"Sorry about that."

"She might have called the cops. You been home yet?" Carolyn took her bagel out of the toaster and began to nibble at it, standing at the counter.

"No. I'll call her." They ate in silence, Phil feeling like he owed her an explanation. "I got drunk."

Carolyn nodded. She sighed. "I can understand it. This whole family needs to blow off a little steam."

"I woke up down by the river."

Carolyn grinned at him. "Really? Shit, that's great. I haven't done that since..."

"College."

"Yeah, college. Good for you, Phil. Feel better?"

"Feel like hell."

Carolyn laughed, gave him a pat on the bare shoulder and went in to check on his clothes.

Phil poured another cup of coffee for each of them. When he was dressed, he'd wake Lari. Or maybe he'd just wake Molly. He tried not to think that Lari and Rocky had Molly here before he turned off his phone and they hadn't called him. Maybe they were cooking up their own Operation Rescue. Lord knows he'd tried his. They were certainly entitled to their attempt.

"Clothes're in the dryer. Your shirt will be ready in just a few minutes."

"Thanks. You know, I don't remember Darlene liking Tabasco sauce."

Carolyn sobered. "Do you think the girl lied?"

Phil shrugged. "At this point, I have no idea what to think."

"I know you don't believe in fate," Carolyn said after a pause.

"I don't disbelieve it. I just don't give it much thought."

"Well, in light of what's been going on around here, perhaps it wouldn't be a bad idea."

"Meaning?"

"Everybody seems to be taking this thing very personally. Feeling responsible. Blaming others. When in reality, perhaps it's nobody's fault and nobody's responsibility. Perhaps it's just one of those things."

"We just want to do what we can."

"Of course," Carolyn said, and polished off her bagel. "But Lari and Rocky shouldn't be fighting over it, and you and Rocky shouldn't be at each other's throats over it."

"Rocky and I... This is just another of a long list of irritants for him. He's been mad at me since the day he was born."

"I know. I guess what I'm trying to say is that we all want to feel as though we have a lot of personal power, when in reality, we don't have any. The universe operates on its own timetable, within its own cycles, and we're such a tiny piece of it that we can't understand the whole perspective because we can't get a wide enough view."

Phil sipped his coffee and looked out the window. Carolyn was the metaphysician in the family, and while he had little use for her crystals and Tarot cards, what she was saying made a strange sort of sense.

"It's no accident that girl is asleep in the living room," Carolyn said. She interlaced her fingers. "Events all come together at the right time despite our efforts to help, hinder or thwart them."

"So you're saying there was a reason for me to go get drunk last night."

"Exactly. If you hadn't been so occupied, you might have been over here, and Lari and Rocky wouldn't have gotten said the things they needed to say. Maybe Molly would have responded differently, maybe we all would have jumped into the car and gone to get Darlene, instead of Darlene doing whatever it was that she did last night. Whatever it was, she needed to do it. Am I making sense? Everything is interconnected, everything has its own time table, and by taking personal responsibility for things, we become arrogant about our personal power, which is illusionary."

Phil finished his coffee and set down his cup. "So you think we ought to do nothing?"

"Oh, no, not at all. No, I think you should do exactly what you've been doing. Everything that you can do to find her and bring her home safely. *But don't take it so personally.* She'll be found in, as they say, 'the fullness of time.' And this whole episode shouldn't be viewed as a nuisance, but as a learning experience, a growth experience for everybody. I think you'll agree that we've all learned things about ourselves and each other during this."

Phil nodded. He remembered the blonde in the bar. That shame still burned inside of him. Rocky kept torching it.

"So then, even if the worst happened to Darlene, the entire experience hasn't been for naught."

Phil nodded. He liked her attitude, but there had to be a line drawn between taking responsibility for one's actions and leaving it all up to the gods. With each year that he grew older, that line came closer and closer to him. Carolyn wouldn't understand that, she was too young yet. Give her time.

The dryer buzzed and he went to get his clothes.

"I'll get Lari up," Carolyn said.

Phil finished the coffee and made a new pot. Soon he heard the shower going, and then Lari, all sleep-puffed, came in for her first cup.

"There's the phone," she said. "Call Angela."

"I will."

"Do it now," Lari said. "It's cruel to make her worry."

Phil picked up the telephone and dialed.

Angela answered on the first ring.

"Hi," he said.

"Hi," she said. "Where are you?"

"Darlene's."

"Is everything all right?"

"Yeah. I'm sorry about last night."

"Well," she said. "We'll talk about it when you get home."

"You didn't call the police or anything?"

Angela let a long silence go by. "I think there's enough of police calling going on around here," she said. "I figure if you'd gotten yourself killed, the police would have called me."

Phil smiled. "I got drunk," he said.

"Did you get laid?"

The question took him by surprise, and his face flushed red. "No, no of course not. I woke up down by the river."

"Hmmm. Did anybody see you?"

"I don't think so. I was pretty far down." Phil looked up to see Lari taking all of this in, watching him over the rim of her coffee cup.

"Is Darlene home yet?"

"Not yet, but I guess there have been some developments. I'll be home soon." He hung up.

Lari stared at him.

"I left my car at the bar," Phil said. "Can you give me a ride?"

"Yeah."

"And maybe you could let me know what's been going on here."

"You should meet Molly," Lari said. "She knows where mom is, but she wants two hundred dollars to tell us."

"Two hundred dollars? That's a far cry from ten thousand."

"Bus fare to Arizona or something."

Phil shrugged. "No problem. Let's give it to her."

"Be my guest."

"Do you have another suggestion?"

"Call the police."

"What did Rocky have to say about all of this?" Phil asked.

"Fuck Rocky."

"Hey, don't talk like that."

"Rocky's a jerk."

Phil couldn't argue with that.

"Anyway, Molly said that Mom was doing all right. I don't know where she is, and I don't know why she hasn't called or come home, but I'm sure Molly knows. And she doesn't seem to be too worried. So I'm not so worried anymore."

"Omelets with Tabasco sauce."

Lari smiled. "Yeah."

"Darlene doesn't like Tabasco sauce."

Lari's smile faded. "What are you saying?"

"I don't know," Phil said. "I'd like to talk to this girl."

"Wait until Carolyn's out of the shower. Then we'll get Molly's butt up and talking." Lari pulled a bagel out of its plastic bag, sliced it, put it into the toaster and slammed down the slider. "Want a bagel?" she asked.

Darlene lay on the padded vinyl table feeling fairly comfortable, despite the fact that she was three feet off the floor, despite the fact that she was almost flat on her back, despite the fact that her ankles and wrists were securely fastened to the table by inch-wide cotton web straps. There was enough give to the straps so that she could shift her position a little bit, but she was indeed firmly tethered.

Her pants were off; Leathers had been working on his masterpiece, as he referred to it, since she had returned to the cabin. He had greeted her with some weird fire in his eyes, desperation, now that she thought of it, and he had held her and cried, grateful that she had returned.

She clung to him, dizzy and unstable, and speaking soft words of love and comfort, he led her to the work table in his studio. Then he bound her good wrist and one ankle before she realized what he was up to, and since she had no fight in her anyway, all she could do was to surrender, heart pounding, sweat pouring into her eyes, panic bringing bile up the back of her throat.

Then he put a pillow under her head and covered her with a blanket and brought her soup and fruit and said that the restraints were only because he wanted to finish the work. He had to finish his work. Patrick hadn't let him finish, but Rose would, lovely, lovely Rose would let him finish his work before she left.

How long would it take?

It depended.

She found the concept of being tied down hard to contemplate. He put roses in a vase on the instrument table, so she could see them and smell them. He spoke words of love to her. He changed the dressing on her hand, her claw, and she saw that it was healing well.

"What did you do with my fingers?" she asked.

"Gave them to the dog," he said, and they both laughed, and she felt a surge of affection for him, forgetting for a moment, that she was tied to the table, kept a prisoner of Leathers' quest for mastery in his art, completion in his life.

She knew he wasn't going to hurt her. He was like a child, and as soon as he trusted her to not leave him, he would release her. She relaxed, ate some fruit with his help, and slipped into a light, restless sleep.

When she awoke, he was uncovering her leg. She felt the chill of the air, then the heat of his spotlight. He unwound the gauze and surveyed his work like a master craftsman, running his fingers over and over the delicate designs.

Then he began to work.

Darlene lay quietly, automatically sliding into the pain, recognizing that indeed, all pain was one, the pain of humiliation, the pain of loneliness, the pain of mistrust, the pain of the needle. It was all the same.

Leathers wheeled around her on his stainless steel stool, wheezing and commenting in short puffs to himself, the design growing ever higher on her thigh.

When she begged him to stop so she could go to the bathroom, he relaxed her bonds, gave her a bedpan and left the room.

A fat woman using a bedpan while tied to a table is not a pretty sight, but Darlene had no choice. Though Leathers gave her privacy while she maneuvered, her humiliation grew and with it, her own brand of desperation.

He came back, emptied the pan into the bathroom, tightened the straps, and began work again, this time higher and to the front of Darlene's thigh.

She lay quietly, the needle digging into her soft flesh. He wiped more frequently; she knew that blood was flowing freely. It hurt like holy hell. It felt like he was carving her up with an electric knife. Her jaws ached from being clenched and tears leaked out of the corners of her eyes and ran into her hair.

He worked until dawn. Finally, he put his instruments away, salved the artwork she had no stomach to view, covered it with gauze, then covered her with a blanket. He clicked off the light, kissed her cheek and without a word, went into the bedroom where she could hear the bed slosh as his bulk eased into it. She lay awake, listening to the birds greeting the new day, listening to Leathers' snoring, listening to the cabin creak as the insects that infested its rafters reduced it by another day's work, listening, finally, to the rain on the roof. While waiting to hear water drip from the ceiling onto the tile floor in the kitchen, she fell asleep.

A beeping noise roused Darlene from the grip of a dark dream, and Leathers stomped into the studio from the kitchen, flipped a switch on the autoclave.

"Omelets," he said, brandishing his spatula, and returned to the kitchen.

Darlene had to pee again, but did not want to face that bedpan ordeal. She pulled gently on each strap; they were secure. She wanted to cry, but the sadness wasn't there. She wanted to get mad, but all she felt for Leathers was a sort of pity. She wanted to be afraid, but if she didn't fear death, she couldn't fear Leathers. He wasn't going to harm her, not really. She just had to wait it out. Maybe she should begin to talk to him about trust. Maybe he would listen and trust her enough to let her go. At least to the bathroom.

But would she get back onto the table once he released her? Not on your life.

So she lay there, feeling fairly comfortable, despite the fact that she was three feet off the floor, despite the fact that she was on her back, despite the fact that her ankles and wrists were securely fastened to the table by inch-wide cotton web straps.

A few minutes later, Leathers appeared with a basin and soapy water. He loosened her straps enough so that she could brush her teeth and wash her face, then he left her alone again to wrestle with the bedpan.

When she had finished, exhausted and sweating from the exertion, she winced as he tidied her up, then he brought in a breakfast tray, complete with a vase of roses.

She watched in amazement as he talked and laughed and spoke words of love and affection, smoothed her hair, wiped her mouth, helped her to eat, seemed hardly to notice that she was in a position anything out of the ordinary.

After breakfast, she heard him put the dirty dishes into the sink and wash his hands. Then he came back to her, opened the autoclave with a pop and backed up as steam roiled out. With oven mitts he pulled a stainless steel tray out and set it on the counter.

"Leathers, please," she said.

"Not now, Rose."

"Leathers..."

He tightened the ankle straps with a jerk, uncovered her leg, turned on the high intensity lamp and trained it on Darlene's calf. Then she watched as he picked some things out of the autoclave tray and set them on his working tray. Different lengths of different gauge wire. A Pyrex dish of oval glass pebbles, like that of smashed safety glass. Darlene thought of the smashed windshield in the back yard. Another Pyrex dish of what looked like ball bearings in different sizes.

"This is going to be magnificent," he said, fitting a fresh blade into the scalpel.

Darlene tasted panic.

He kissed her big toe. "Start your countdown, darling," he said as he held her leg firmly and began the first incision.

Just as Molly got her tiny hands wrapped around a steaming cup of coffee, her hair freshly washed and hanging down in brown-rooted blonde strings, her face clean of makeup and looking like a skinny twelve-year-old, Lari, Carolyn and Phil surrounded her.

Phil. Phil was the money man, or so it appeared. He would give her money, she would give him information, and they could all be on their way.

She was so tired of all this.

She sat on the floor in the living room, sipped her generously milk-and-sugared coffee, tore a chunk from her bagel and popped it, dry, into her mouth.

"So," Phil said.

She looked up at him. The other two girls looked at him too.

"You're a friend of Patrick's," he said.

Molly nodded. The bagel tasted good. She was suddenly starved. She ate another chunk.

"And you carjacked Darlene."

Molly nodded again.

"Will you tell us where she is?"

Molly nodded, held up a finger while she finished chewing her bread. She swallowed, then drank a sip of coffee to wash it down. "I keep telling you people. God, I tell you people over and over and over. How many times do I have to tell you people this same stuff? I need to get to Arizona. I think it costs about a hundred or a hundred fifty bucks on the bus. If you'll help me out with about two hundred dollars so I can get out of here, I'll tell you exactly where to go to find her. She's fine, she's having a good time, she's in a nice place, there's nothing wrong. She just doesn't have a phone and has no way of getting out of there."

"Is she locked up?"

"No, she's not locked up, Jesus Christ. She's in a remote place. Remote. Distant. Too far to walk, has no car. Patrick took her car, remember?" Jesus, what dolts.

"Two hundred dollars, that's extortion. That's kidnapping," Phil said.

Molly shrugged. "That's bus fare," she said. "Call it a loan from one friend to another."

"Okay," Phil said. "I'll get it."

Molly nodded her approval. "Good," she said, and ate another bite.

Phil stood up. "It's Saturday, right?"

Lari nodded.

"I'll have to go to a teller machine. I'll be right back." He jangled the keys in his pocket. "Oh. My car. It's at the—I left it at the bar."

Lari smiled. "I'll drive you. We'll go to the bank and then I'll take you to your car."

"Good."

A knock sounded on the front door, then the door opened. "Hi," Rocky said as he came in.

Everyone kind of froze in position, Molly noticed. She smiled to herself and kept picking hunks off the bagel and chewing them slowly. This was going to be good.

"C'mon in," Lari said coldly.

"You guys leaving?" he asked.

"We'll be right back."

"Where are you going?" He turned to Carolyn as if they had already left. "Where are they going?"

Carolyn motioned him back to Phil and Lari with a nod of her head.

"We're going to the bank to get Molly her money," Phil said.

"Do you need to go?" Rocky asked Lari. "Can't he go by himself?"

Phil winced. The only question he did not want to have to answer to Rocky. The one and only goddamned thing he didn't care for Rocky to know.

"I'm going with him," Lari said, and then Phil remembered that she was mad at Rocky and would offer no information.

"Stay here," Rocky said. "Let him go by himself."

"No," Lari said. "C'mon, Dad." She opened the front door.

"Lari," Rocky said. "We need to talk."

"Later. C'mon, Dad, let's get this thing over with."

Phil took a step away from the door. "What's going on here? Why are you two acting like this?"

"I don't want to talk about it," Rocky said.

Lari slammed the front door, stood looking at him with one hand on one well-grounded hip. "Oh you don't? Okay, Dad, let's wait a little while. Rocky wants to talk to me about something. Okay, Rock. Here I am. Talk."

He shot daggers at her.

Phil looked at Carolyn. She was picking at a thread on the arm of the couch. Molly was grinning, watching the sibling action. Molly probably knew what the fight was about, too. She looked up at Phil with too much delight. This fight was about him. His gut clenched and he wished he had his own car.

"Give me the keys," he said.

"Yeah," Rocky said. "Give him the keys." He turned to Phil. "Where is your car, anyway?"

"In the shop," Lari said.

Rocky ignored her, kept his eyes on Phil. "Is that where you spent the night? In the shop? Or with your latest piece of ass?"

Phil's face burned. Angela had called Rocky too, it appeared, and he just couldn't wait to throw it back into Phil's face.

"I went out and got drunk last night," Phil said, deciding to meet the issue head on. "It's not a crime, because I left my car and took a cab. I just didn't take a cab home."

"Uh-huh," Rocky said with such disdain that Phil wanted to take a chunk right out of his finely-formed jaw.

"Sit down, Dad," Lari said. "Sit down, Rock." She sat on the floor. Phil and Rocky looked at each other. Neither sat. "Okay, Rocky, what did you want to talk about?"

"Nothing. Jesus Christ, let's just get this girl her money and get her the hell out of our lives. Let's get Mom back here so everything will go back to normal."

"Rocky's thinking about getting married," Lari said.

"That's what I understand," Phil said, sitting on the couch next to Carolyn. That left Rocky standing alone.

Instead of sitting with the others, he brought a dining room chair out and straddled it.

"Are we going to meet this girl?" Phil asked.

"Maybe. Maybe it's not a girl."

Carolyn's head snapped up and she looked at Rocky, then looked at Lari. Lari got up slowly, she calmly walked over to him and slapped him. He backed up so fast to get out of her way that he tipped the chair over and almost fell on his butt. "Hey, what the fuck—"

"Don't you dare, don't you dare to *ever* insult me like that again. *Don't you dare.*" Lari spoke through clenched teeth.

"Hey," Phil said, taking parental control. He wanted them to have out whatever they needed to have out, but he didn't go for any kind of violence. Jesus, Darlene might even have a gun in this house. If she did, Rocky would know how to use it.

Rocky put a booted foot up on the chair seat. "It's so easy for you to sit in judgment of me, isn't it, big sister? You have your choices, but I'm not allowed mine."

"One has nothing to do with another. One is a choice, one is not."

"Camouflage," Rocky said. "You're masking the issue. You're trying to shirk responsibility for your choices by saying they're not choices."

"I choose Carolyn," Lari said. "I don't choose surgery."

"Surgery?" Phil said. "Who's having surgery?"

Lari glared at Rocky.

"Rocky?"

Rocky glared back at Lari.

"Rocky's going to get a vasectomy," Molly said.

Everybody glared at Molly. Molly just popped the last of the bagel in her mouth and chewed happily while looking around the room.

"A vasectomy?" Phil wasn't sure he heard right. "What— why on earth— I don't understand. Why would you do that? You're what, twenty-one?"

"I don't want kids," Rocky said flatly.

"Rocky, you're not prepared to make a decision like that," Phil said. "A lot can happen during your life."

"I don't want kids," he said again.

212

"What about your girlfriend?" Carolyn asked. "Have you talked this over with her?"

Rocky picked at the knee of his jeans.

Lari slammed her hand on the coffee table and everybody jumped. "That's just sweet," she said. "You're going to get a vasectomy and then marry some starry-eyed little girl who doesn't know that you will never be the father of the children she wants so desperately to have."

"*You're* not getting pregnant any time soon," he said.

"Watch yourself," Lari warned.

"You made a choice not to have kids when you married Carolyn," Rocky said. "Nobody is bitching about that choice. Yet when I make a similar choice, everybody acts as if it's a crime."

"I just don't understand," Phil said.

"Leave it, Dad," Lari said.

Rocky looked at him, a long stare. "Maybe you really don't. Maybe it's time you did."

Carolyn jumped up. "C'mon, Phil. I'll drive you to the bank. Let's let these two battle it out."

"No," Phil said, feeling braver than he had in years. "I think Rocky's got something to tell me."

"Damned right," Rocky said. "You're a miserable excuse for a father. You're a failure and a disappointment all the way down the line. I am embarrassed for you and ashamed of you. You wrecked my mother. You and your girlfriends and your fucking around. *You ruined her!*" His face glowed red and Phil thought for a moment that Rocky was going to forget himself and start to cry. That might be just exactly what the doctor ordered, he thought. Rocky needed a good cry. Phil thought Carolyn at least, would agree.

But instead of tears, Phil watched the anger and rage slide right off Rocky's face. Those were the same things he'd wanted to say to his own father, and never could.

Listening to Rocky throw those things at him with such vehemence was not comfortable, nor was it particularly uncomfortable. Phil had known how Rocky felt about him for years and years. The only thing new here was that Rocky was verbalizing it. Getting it out. Getting it out in the open air, getting it said to the person to whom it mattered the most, according to Rocky.

When Rocky was finished, the rain was the only thing they could hear.

Phil wanted to tell him about the woman in the bar the night before. He wanted to tell Rocky that he knew he had been a failure as a father, and he'd been given a second chance at fatherhood, and that this time he was going to do it right. He'd made a decision not to be like he had been. He wasn't going to ruin Angela the way he'd ruined Darlene. Peaches wasn't going to hate him the way Rocky did.

He wasn't going to turn into his father.

He hoped Rocky wasn't going to turn into him.

But he said none of those things. Rocky wouldn't want to hear them. This wasn't about Phil, Phil's life, Phil's choices. This was about Rocky. He waited until he felt an appropriate length of time had passed, to give Rocky's statement the weight it deserved. Then he said, "So?"

Lari laughed. "Exactly! So what, Rocky? So you're going to let your anger and hate and pain over your dad rule the rest of your life? You're sitting here saying what a miserable father he is, and now because of him, you're going to begin your marriage with a lie? You're going to give him that much power over your life?" She started to laugh.

Rocky's face began to turn red again. It made his hair look even blonder.

"You're a jerk," she said. "C'mon, Dad, let's go."

Phil leaned forward, toward Rocky. "Listen," he said. "I'm sorry that you feel that way. Not sorry for me, sorry for you. Sorry that you are so angry about everything. But I want you to know this one thing."

Rocky looked up at him, and Phil's heart bled with the hopeful look of the young son he saw there.

"Every day of your existence, I've tried to do the best by you that I could. I did the best I knew to do at the time. It wasn't always right, and given it to do over again, knowing what I know now, I would do a lot of things differently. But on a day by day basis, I did what I thought was best."

Rocky snorted. The hopeful child had hardened again into the angry young man.

"Now what does that knowledge—that knowing that I did the

best I could do *at the time*—what does that get me?" Phil went on. Rocky was looking at the floor. "It gives me peace. Great peace. Your anger is your problem, Rock. I'm sorry about it, boy, and I wish it weren't so, but your anger is your problem and it's affecting *your* life, not mine." Phil stood up.

Carolyn reached over to the end table and lit a candle. "Candles neutralize excess energies," she said.

Phil and Lari walked out the front door and ran through the light rain to her car.

Rocky tapped his boot on the floor and chewed on his lip.

Carolyn closed her eyes and tried to visualize rainbows around the house, guardian angels sweeping up the fragments of shattered dreams, the dust of spent anger.

Molly finished her cold coffee and went into the kitchen to search for another bagel.

As she passed Rocky, she touched his shoulder, and he felt warm and somehow childlike.

"C'mon," she said. "I'll toast you a bagel."

He followed her into the kitchen, but just sat with his head in his hands.

She split a bagel and toasted it, but he wasn't interested. She put it on a paper towel, pulled up a barstool next to him, then lined her thigh up with his and pressed next to him. The warmth of him through his jeans felt comforting to her, and she hoped it was comforting to him as well. She could almost feel his heartache, right through their clothes.

They sat together in quiet companionship until Carolyn came in for another cup of coffee.

"Forgive him, Rocky," she said quietly.

Rocky nodded. "I feel like a little kid," he said.

Carolyn walked behind him, placed both her hands on his back. "That's a good start."

Rocky looked over at Molly, pulled his leg away from hers. "I want my Mom back," he said.

Molly nodded. "As soon as I get my money," she said.

"He's gone to get it."

Molly shook her head. "In my hand."

"You don't think you can trust him?" Rocky gestured toward the door.

"You don't."

"I *trust* him," Rocky said. "I just don't *like* him."

"He's a guy," Molly said. "I don't trust guys." She ate some more of the bagel while Carolyn rubbed Rocky's shoulders. She remembered trying to rub Patrick's shoulders, and he would never let her. "Patrick wouldn't let me do that to him," she said to Carolyn.

"Why not?"

"He had ridges. Ridges and bumps, and I think they hurt him. Did I tell you that I never saw him naked?"

Carolyn looked down at her, slowly rubbing Rocky's neck.

"Don't you think that's weird?"

Carolyn nodded.

"You think Leathers gave Patrick those scars?"

Rocky slammed his hands on the countertop, then whipped around and grabbed Molly by the neck.

She gasped and squeaked, and then his big hands began to squeeze. "Tell me where she is, you bitch, or I swear, I'll pop your head off like a cork."

"I better stop by the house," Phil said. "I've got to see Angela."

"Really?" Lari said. "Why don't we just get this thing over with? That girl is pretty flaky."

"She'll be all right with Carolyn and Rocky for a while. Just swing by the house and let me—I don't know—just let me see Angela for a minute. I need to— I want to kiss Peaches." Phil didn't look over to see the small smile he was sure tickled at the corners of Lari's mouth. He didn't feel like smiling at all.

"Okay." Lari turned left and drove up the hill where the houses instantly gained a hundred thousand dollars in value. She pulled into her dad's driveway and turned off the engine.

"C'mon in."

"Nah. I'll wait here."

Phil looked at her, his insides jangling. Things never went the way he would have them go. Never. Angela didn't like Lari—or rather she couldn't get far enough past Lari's sexual orientation to find Lari and learn to like her. He kissed her cheek. "Okay, sweetie. I'll just be a minute."

"Hurry," she said, her voice barely above a growl.

Phil slammed the car door and trotted up the front steps. He fumbled with his keys, but before he could get it unlocked, Angela opened it from the inside. Peaches was riding one hip, hair brushed, red and white rompers on, fingers in her mouth. Her big baby blues stared at Phil with exact same dispassionate gaze her mother's had.

"Hi," he said.

"Hi." Angela looked at the car, waved weakly at Lari, then stood aside for Phil to come in.

He stood in the foyer, a stranger in his own home.

Angela waited for him to speak. He wanted to take her in his arms and hold her, whisper into her hair what he had been doing and what he was about to do, but she was an ice block, so that was out of the question. Instead, he brushed his thumb across Peaches' forehead. She pulled away from him and hid her face in her mother's shoulder.

"Where's your car?"

"I left it at the bar last night. Listen, Patrick's girlfriend is over at Darlene's house. Carolyn and Rocky are with her. She says Darlene is fine, but wants bus fare to Arizona before she'll let us know where Darlene is. So I'm going to go to the teller machine and get a couple hundred bucks. Lari's going to take me to my car, but if this girl tells us where Darlene is, we might go on down and pick her up."

"Where?"

Phil shrugged. "Elkton, maybe. The coast? I don't know."

"So you'll be back?"

"Yes, of course. Yes, of course I'll be back. I'm not exactly sure when."

"Will you call me?"

"I will."

"Don't *ever* do that to me again."

"I won't."

"I mean it, Phil."

"I promise."

"I'm not stupid, you know."

Phil wasn't sure what she was talking about. He touched Peaches' cheek again, this time getting a little smile. Angela took a step back, forcing Phil's eyes to meet hers.

"You're a snake. You cheated on Darlene, and I know that it's just a matter of time before you cheat on me. When you do, I'll rip this little girl out of your life so fast it will make your balls twitch."

Phil was stunned. He'd never heard this kind of talk from Angela before.

"You're not a great catch," she went on. He'd given her all night to work on this speech. He owed it to her to get it off her chest. "But we can have a good marriage and raise a fine daughter, if you play by the rules. Understand?"

"Yes," he said, his eyes meeting hers squarely.

"Play by the rules, Phil. You know what they are."

"I do. I will."

"Okay," she said, and took a step closer to him. "Kiss Daddy," she said, and Peaches reached over with both hands.

Phil took her and hugged her and kissed her angel-soft hair. Then he put his other arm around Angela and kissed her hair, too. He wasn't going to let them down. Not the way he let Darlene and Rocky and Lari down. He wouldn't do it. No way.

"I lost my phone," he said, "but I'll call you," Phil said, kissed Angela's cheek, then kissed Peaches' cheek and handed her back to her mother. He turned back to the door, opened it and stepped out. The nice thing about Angela was that she got mad and then she got over it.

He trotted down the driveway and jumped back into Lari's old car. "Whew," he said.

"Rough, eh?"

Phil snorted his assent. Then he said, "Nah, not really. She's okay. She's good. She's mad, but she'll get over it. I shouldn't have made her worry. She wants this whole thing finished, too."

"Yeah, that makes it unanimous." Lari backed out the drive and drove down the hill.

Phil took two hundred dollars from the teller machine and then had Lari drive him back to the bar, where his car was lined up in the parking lot along with all the Saturday morning drinkers.

"Meet you back at the house," he said, then gave her a kiss on the cheek and got out of the car.

He checked his car quickly for dents and scratches put there by perception-impaired drunks. It looked good. He got in, started the engine and drove slowly back toward Darlene's house, thinking about Rocky and how hard life seemed to be at times. Then he thought about Lari and Carolyn and how sweet life seemed to be at times. Then he thought about Darlene and Angela and how confusing life seemed to be at times.

All at the same time.

There was always something, wasn't there? If it wasn't something with his family, it was something with his job. If it wasn't something with his job or his family, then it was his health. Something. There was always something.

And now, there was something else. A police car in front of

Darlene's house.

Rocky. Damned Rocky called the police on the girl.

Phil parked and ran up the walk and into the house.

Lari sat on the sofa, holding Carolyn's hand. Rocky stood, both hands caught up in his hair. Lieutenant Jenricks sat on a dining room chair, looking serious.

Ashes barked and yapped as if it had been years since he'd seen Phil. Phil picked him up to quiet him down and walked into the somber room.

"Good timing, Mr. Martin," the lieutenant said.

"What's happening?"

"She's gone," Rocky said.

"What?"

"We found a stolen car parked out front yesterday morning," Lieutenant Jenricks said. "We impounded it and they're checking it out right now, down at the station, but when I heard about it, I just couldn't get the address out of my mind. It seemed like such a coincidence."

"Molly," Rocky said. "Molly came here in a stolen car."

"And?"

"And when the lieutenant rang the doorbell, she panicked, I guess, and took off out the back." He looked back at the policeman. "She was telling me about those scars on Patrick. I want you to tell me more about those scars."

"We didn't know she was gone," Lari said, "until—well, we don't know how long she'd been gone. Ten minutes, maybe."

Phil sat down in the recliner. He set Ashes on the floor, but he immediately jumped right back up into Phil's lap, turned around a couple of times and lay down, his tiny black nose glistening and twitching at the policeman.

"How could—" Phil looked at Rocky.

Rocky held up his hands. "Hey. Not my fault. You had to go get your car. You had to stop by Angela's. If you had just gone to the corner for the cash—"

"Cash?" the lieutenant's eyebrows shot up into brown chevrons. He sighed. "Okay. We all here now? Let's hear it. From the beginning."

"Is that Patrick guy, his body I mean, is it at the morgue?" Rocky cracked his knuckles. "Can we go see him? Can we go see his scars?"

"Rocky." Carolyn turned up her nose. "Ick."

"What good would that do?" Lari asked.

"I don't know," Rocky said, beginning to pace. "But it's Saturday, and Mom has been with the guy who did that to Patrick since last Monday."

"We'll get her back," Lieutenant Jenricks said. "Please sit down."

Rocky jangled.

"Sit *down*," the cop said, and Rocky perched at the edge of a chair, his knees bouncing up and down.

"Okay," Jenricks said, looking at Phil. "You go first."

Molly crouched behind the wire compost pile, her heart thumping in her chest like a wild rabbit's. Okay, she told herself. Okay. That is absolutely the last, the final illegal thing I ever do. I will never steal another car, I will never hijack another person, I will never steal food, I will never steal clothes. I am finished with that. Finished.

The back door opened and she hunkered down, her heart stuttering again. She opened her mouth wide, a trick she learned when she and her friends played hide and seek. She could breathe in tons of air without making a noise. Still, she felt out of breath.

Somebody was talking. Rocky and somebody. Maybe Rocky and a policeman. Maybe just Rocky talking to himself. Looking for her. "Shit," he said, scuffed his boots on the porch, then went back inside.

Molly grabbed on to the compost wire. She felt dizzy from the fear. She looked around for a place to sit, but it had been raining, and the ground was wet and muddy and smelled rotten. Well, of course, stupid, she told herself. Compost. Probably dog shit, too.

She settled back on her haunches and tried to think of what to do next. She had about five dollars and the gun. Her duffel bag was in the house, so that was lost. She had only what she wore, so she best not get it muddy.

Clouds darkened the sky, and then darkened it further. It was about to rain again.

She looked up at the sky and wondered what was so special about her that God had to be picking on her all the time. All the time. *All* the fucking time.

Then she realized that running away was just one more illegal thing. She should go right on in there and give herself up.

Jail.

Oh, God. Oh, no.

She heard a few drops of rain on the tin roof of Darlene's little tool shed. Then a few more. Then a steady drone. Molly stood up and walked back to Darlene's porch. She had no place to go, she had no resources, no money, no clothes, no friends. She didn't want to go to jail, but she didn't want to live such a hard life any more, either.

Life is a bitch, she thought. No matter what you choose, you're screwed. She picked up a little brown throw rug that was full of dirt and dog hair, shook it out, then sat on it, chin in hands, elbows on knees. She watched the rain beat the rose petals until they fell on the ground, and she waited for whatever was going to happen to her.

"I think you better come with me," Lieutenant Jenricks said.

"Pardon?" Phil was taken completely by surprise.

"We might have a better talk at the station."

"You're arresting me?"

"Taking you in for questioning."

"For what?" Lari said.

"Suspicion of murder."

"What?" Shock numbed all faces in the room. All except the lieutenant's.

"Listen, Mr. Martin," he said. "We have one dead guy and one girl allegedly missing and perhaps one dead woman. We know you've had dealings with the Patrick guy, and he was found dead in your wife's car with your money. Now unless I have some absolute proof that what you're saying here is true, that there was a kidnapping and a girl and a conspiracy, it all looks like an elaborate murder cover up. You hired Patrick to kill your wife, you paid him, and then killed him to cover it all up and get your money back."

Phil looked at the girls. They both had their mouths hanging open in disbelief.

"Kind of looks that way, doesn't it?" he said.

"Daddy!"

"You gotta see it from his perspective, baby."

"You have no proof," Lari said to the policeman. "You have no motive."

"Yeah," Rocky said.

"Yeah," Carolyn said.

"Yeah," Phil said.

"Well, we won't know about proof for a while yet. The lab is still going over the car. As to motive...well, that's one of the things we'll talk about at the station. I do know that you've been fairly uncooperative when it comes to letting the police do the investigative work on this. And, in fact, you have lied to us at least once." He crossed his arms over his chest. "Being stupid isn't against the law, Mr. Martin, but murder is."

"What about that stolen car?" Lari asked. "The one out in front? Molly stole it. She's Patrick's girlfriend. She's the one who was here, the one who knows where Mom is."

"Well," Lieutenant Jenricks smiled slowly, "all I know is that it was stolen by a young blonde." He looked at Carolyn. "Could have been you."

Carolyn gasped and shrank back from him.

"Unless you can produce this girl, and/or Mrs. Martin, I'm afraid I've got my number one suspect right here."

"There's no motive," Lari said.

"Did she have life insurance?" the lieutenant asked Phil.

Phil hung his head. He nodded.

"Let me guess," the lieutenant said in a snotty way. "You're the beneficiary, right?"

Phil tightened his face as if expecting a blow. He nodded again. "Only until the kids turn thirty-five," he said. "She didn't want them inheriting anything until they were thirty-five. She knew I'd respect her wishes, and invest the money wisely for the kids. *She didn't have anybody else!*"

Rocky leaned against the bookcase and crossed his arms. "You know," he said. "If I hadn't met that Molly girl, you'd be my number one suspect too."

He ducked just in time. Lari threw a marble coaster at him that put a dent in the wallboard just behind his head. "You sonofabitch," she said.

"And come to think of it," Rocky said, "I don't know why I would believe her, either."

"Shut up, Rocky," Lari said. "Just shut up. You sound like a jerk."

"C'mon, Mr. Martin," the lieutenant said. "Let's go have a chat."

Phil kissed Carolyn's cheek, gave Lari a hug. She clung to him and began to cry. He detached himself from her, nodded at Rocky and preceded the policeman out the front door.

The door closed and Lari sobbed. Carolyn put her arm around

Lari and glared at Rocky.

Rocky walked over to them, but Lari pulled away from him. "Don't touch me," she said. "Go call Angela. She better know about this."

Rocky snorted. "I'm not calling her. You call her."

"You are nonstop chickenshit," Lari said, wiping her nose and cheeks on the sleeve of her sweatshirt.

"Please, Rocky?" Carolyn said. "Angela doesn't like us very much."

Rocky looked at Carolyn's cool blue eyes and he felt a little ashamed of himself. He picked up the phone and looked at Lari. "I don't even know the number," he said. Lari rolled her eyes and told him. He dialed.

"Hello?"

"Hi, Angela, it's Rocky."

"Hi, Rocky."

"I'm at Mom's house with Lari and Carolyn," he said. He didn't know how to tell her.

"Yes? And your father? And the girl?"

"Well, that's just it. The girl took off when the police came back and so they arrested Dad."

"Phil's been arrested?"

"Well, he's being held for questioning. I guess he hasn't been charged yet."

"For what?"

"Murder."

Angela was silent.

"I guess they suspect him of hiring the Patrick guy to kill Mom and then killing him as a cover up."

"Oh God. You didn't find out where Darlene is?"

"That's just it," Rocky said. "The girl who knows took off."

"But she *was* there."

"Yeah, but she wasn't talking. She wanted money. She wanted two hundred dollars for the information. She ran away before we could give her the money and find out where Mom is."

"You mean she was there all that time and you didn't find out? You didn't learn a single thing about where she is?"

Rocky shuffled his feet. He gave Angela the lieutenant's name and phone number from the card still sitting on the coffee table and then mumbled a goodbye.

"Whew," he said to the girls. "She's... I don't know. I'm glad I'm not married to Angela."

"What was she saying?" Lari asked, still furious.

"She said that in all the time Molly spent here, she must have said something that would have been a clue as to where Mom is."

"She didn't," Lari said. "Don't you think I'm smart enough to key in on that stuff?"

"Remote," Rocky said. "She's in a remote place, but she's fine. That's all I got."

"Yeah, well, she also said that Mom was eating an omelet with Tabasco sauce," Lari said.

"Mom doesn't like Tabasco."

"Exactly."

"Fuck."

"Leathers," Carolyn said.

"Yeah, that's right," Lari said, reaching for the phone. "She's supposedly with someone named Leathers."

Ashes yipped and scratched at the back door. "I'm going to try to find somebody named Leathers," she said, dialing directory assistance. "Go feed the animals, Rocky."

Rocky, glad to be out of Lari's field of irritation, went into the kitchen, where Ashes pranced at the door and Tina sat on the counter, blinking her huge green eyes. "Hungry, guys?" He opened the back door and the dog shot out, ran past Molly, leaped down the stairs and lifted his leg on a rosebush.

Rocky stood in silent amazement and looked at the girl. Tina brushed up against her and she ran her hand over the cat's fur. She didn't look up at Rocky.

"They arrested my dad," he said.

Molly nodded. "Figures."

When Darlene awoke, the slant of the sun through the trees told her that it was late afternoon. She listened to the sounds of the woods, the creak of the trees, the rabbits restless in their cages, the hound scratching himself on the front porch. She heard water dripping somewhere, she heard the branches of something brush against the side of the cabin. She heard her stomach rumble.

Her leg lay hot, swollen and raw under its layers of Vaseline, gauze and blanket.

There had been times when she thought she would scream, when she would rip her hair out if he didn't stop whatever he was doing, it hurt so bad, it hurt *so bad*, but then he would speak harshly to her, and one time he pinched her—not hard, just enough to get her attention, and when he did, she fell through the chords of pain into the ice-blue room. It was quiet there, and pain-free. She couldn't hear Leathers as he wheezed and snorted and grunted while inserting lengths of wire under her skin millimeter by millimeter, manipulating it with needle nose pliers to follow the inked lines. She couldn't feel the scalpel slice horizontally through the layers of skin, making little pockets big enough to slip in ball bearings and pieces of God knows what. Leathers was creating a three-dimensional tattoo on her leg, and in the ice-blue room, she was far from reality. She relaxed in there. She could meditate, pray, pace. Eventually, she slept.

When she awoke, she listened to the cabin, listened to her body, listened to the despair that howled in her mind like coyotes. Leathers was outside, she could hear him walking and puffing. What if he died out there with her tied to this table?

A different desperation seized her. Desperation may be my tool for escape, she thought, then dared to bring up the next thought, the bigger question: what does a finished project mean? Her leg or her entire body?

Could she lie on this table while he inserted things under the skin of her breasts? Her nipples? The thought made blood pound in her ears.

Her nose itched and without thinking, she raised her damaged hand to scratch it.

Just tightening the muscles and tendons hurt like hell, and when the strap pulled on the wrist, the sharp pain made her gasp.

Then she looked at it. Blinked. Looked at it again.

She scratched her nose on the pillow and looked at her hand closely, carefully.

Leathers had cut away most of the palm along with the three damaged fingers.

Her hand was not wider than her wrist.

She could slip it out of that strap.

She looked at the other wrist. If she slipped off the one wrist strap, could she maneuver her swollen forefinger and thumb so she could undo the buckle on the other wrist strap?

Perhaps. She tried moving them. They were stiff and painful and not very serviceable. But perhaps she could see the pain, slide into the pain and make them work for her. *Make* them work for her.

The front screen door slammed and Darlene felt her face flush as if she had been caught doing something naughty. She heard Leathers rustle around in the kitchen, and when he emerged into the studio, he had two frosty beers in his hands.

"Thirsty?"

She nodded. She'd rather have a shot of vodka, but she wasn't going to say that. If she was going to engineer an escape, she needed her wits.

He held her head and put the bottle to her lips. She took a few long swallows. The cold beer tasted wonderful. Then he swigged on his and set both bottles on the instrument tray.

Then he opened the door to Patrick's room and went inside.

Darlene had never seen the inside of Patrick's room, but she could look squarely through the door.

Patrick and Molly's room matched the crusty bathroom and the wreck of a kitchen she had first walked into. Their room was as far removed and as different from Leathers' bedroom and bathroom as bleach from soot.

A stained, blue-tick mattress lay on the floor in the corner, with two dirty, uncovered pillows. Some dingy white sheets were pulled in from the edges and balled up in the center. Clothes lay half in and half out of boxes everywhere; shoes, socks, underwear were thrown everywhere. Darlene couldn't see the floor for clothes.

A half dozen dead plants were lined up on the windowsill. In front of the plants were lotions, oils, shampoos and hair preparations.

On one wall was a series of half-completed drawings—sketches, really, thumbtacked haphazardly.

But one drawing was larger, and it was in color, and it was right near the door where Darlene could see it in detail. It was surely Patrick's artwork.

A face in rapture, arms open, heavily feathered angel wings behind him. Blue sky, stars, clouds—it looked like a child's image of heaven, all enclosed in the small window-reflection of a single drop of dark red blood.

Eerie.

Poor Patrick. Maybe he had escaped. Just as she was planning to do.

She tore her eyes away from the artwork and followed Leathers as he kicked around in the clothes, looking for something. This was not the room of two people who had moved out. Patrick was probably coming back.

Unless he really had escaped.

Once Darlene escaped, would she return?

She amazed herself by not knowing the answer to that question.

Leathers came out carrying a staple gun. "Mind if I leave this door open?" he asked.

Darlene shook her head.

"Lets in more light."

"Patrick is coming back," Darlene said.

"Patrick is dead. I'll clean out his room one of these days." He set the staple gun on the instrument table. She closed her eyes, not daring to even think about what he wanted to do to her with a staple gun. He picked up his beer and finished it. Then he helped her drink more of hers. Then he wheeled the stool around and sat down, stroking her hair, her cheek. He kissed her neck. "How are you doing?"

"I'm sore, I'm hurt, I'm angry, I'm uncomfortable. I want you to untie me."

"It's not for much longer. Please, Rose, please, just hold out for a little while longer. I need to finish this."

Knowing she could escape—would escape—emboldened her. "Are you just going to do my leg?"

He hesitated just long enough for her to suspect a lie. "Yes," he said, pulling up the blanket and looking at it. "Just this one leg."

"Is that the truth, Leathers?"

He dropped the blanket and looked at her, his clear brown eyes soft and loving. "It is the truth," he said, then kissed her cheek. "One more day. By this time tomorrow, it will be finished."

Darlene felt the hot ball of emotion rise up through her throat, rasping it nearly raw. Tears squeezed out of her eyes. Leathers kissed them away, and she didn't pull away from him. It felt nice to have someone touch her face, her hair, treat her with some semblance of compassion and love, even if this same man also treated her as an object, a canvas, a subject.

"Shhh," he said, smoothing her hair, but she had started to sob and hiccup and she couldn't stop.

He wiped her runny nose with a tissue and stroked her.

"I miss my kids," she said.

"I know," he said. "I know. Shhh." And he lay his head next to hers, loving her and touching her and ministering to her until she was left emotionally exhausted and dried up.

"I'm going to finish now," he said. He wiped the tears from her lashes with the soggy tissue, and then wiped it across his own and blew his nose.

He had cried with her and she hadn't even noticed, she was so wrapped up in her own homesickness. The fact that he left his own tears in her hair touched her.

She drank the last of her beer, then lay quietly while he worked, thinking about Leathers and his big heart while planning her escape.

Rocky shook food into Tina's bowl and scooped some from a bag into Ashes'. He filled their water bowl from the kitchen sink, and set it on the little plastic placemat that had black and yellow daisies on it.

"C'mon," he said to Molly. "We've all had enough of this bullshit. It's time to finish this."

She put her head in her hands.

Rocky grabbed her arm. "C'mon."

"Let me go," she said.

"I'm through fucking with you."

She whipped around and Rocky found a gun pointed directly at his face. For a second he thought it was a toy. She was joking. Surely she was joking. No way was she going to shoot him in the face.

Then he looked at her expression. She'd had enough, too. Then he looked at the gun. It was real. It was definitely real. It was a revolver, and he could see the ends of the bullets in the cylinder. A loaded revolver.

He looked at her face again, saw its hard glaze begin to crackle. She'd had enough of this tough guy act, too.

He reached out and took the gun from her. She gave it up without a whimper. He put his arm around her and shuffled her into the house.

Lari stopped speaking into the phone mid-sentence when she saw Molly. She just clicked the phone off, changed her expression to that of a thin-lipped, reprimanding school principal and set the phone on the arm of the couch. Carolyn smiled.

"She was sitting on the back porch," Rocky said.

"It's raining," Molly said.

Rocky set the gun on the coffee table. "She's going to take us to

Mom now." He looked at her. "Right?"

She wouldn't look at him. He turned her toward him and tilted her chin up. She brought her thick brown eyes up to look at him, briefly, then pulled away. She nodded.

"Want to call the police?" Lari asked.

Molly stiffened.

"No. Let's just go get Mom."

"Tell Angela?"

"*No*, Lari, let's just fucking *go*. Come *on*, what's the matter with you?"

"Okay, okay," Lari said. She went into the bedroom and brought back a pair of tennis shoes. She sat on the couch and put them on. "Where is she?"

"West of Curtin," Molly said. "In a shack."

"Shack?" Rocky asked. He began to bounce on his heels, looking at Lari as if she were purposely tying her shoes slowly.

"Well, cabin, then. House. Leathers' house. It's just kind of run down."

"Who is this Leathers?" Rocky asked.

"A guy. A friend of Patrick's."

"Who else is there with them?"

"Nobody. Just them."

"If she's been hurt," Rocky said carefully, seriously, dangerously, "I'll kill you."

"Rocky, please," Carolyn said. "There's been enough of that kind of thing, don't you think?"

Rocky picked up the gun and stuck it into the waistband of his jeans. "I'll drive," he said. "Come on Lari, are you ready yet?"

Lari nodded. "Carolyn, would you stay here and mind the store?"

Carolyn nodded. "Call me as soon as you get her?"

Lari walked over and hugged Carolyn. They held each other for a long time, then whispered to each other. Rocky looked away. He looked at Molly, who stared. "C'mon," he said to Molly.

"What's going to happen to me afterwards?"

"I don't give a shit," Rocky said.

"That's not nice," Carolyn said.

Rocky looked at her with exasperation. "Okay," he said. "I care what happens to her. Where's that two hundred dollars?"

"Dad's still got it."

"We'll get you to Arizona, Molly," Carolyn said. "That's a promise from Lari and me."

Molly smiled. "Really?"

Lari nodded. "We're good for it. You come on back with Mom and Rocky, and we'll get Dad out of jail and give you your two hundred bucks."

"No cops?"

"No cops."

"Okay," she said, sounding close to tears.

"Let's *go*," Rocky said.

Lari gave Carolyn a parting kiss.

"Be careful," Carolyn whispered. "Try to get that gun away from Rocky. He's a little too emotional."

Lari nodded, and followed Rocky and Molly out of the house and into Rocky's truck.

"I-5 south," Molly said from the middle, where she sat between them on a little pillow between the bucket seats. She leaned not so much away from Lari as leaned into Rocky. She put her arm around the back of his seat to brace herself, as Rocky pulled out of the driveway and into traffic. She pressed her thigh to his.

When they were on the freeway, Lari said, "So, Rocky, when are we going to meet this fiancée of yours?"

Rocky straightened up, pulling his leg away from Molly's. Molly flounced back, the aural bond she was building with Rocky shattered by his sister.

"She's not my fiancée yet. I'm just doing a little thinking, is all."

"So when will we meet her? I'd like to."

"Don't start, Lari."

"Start what? I'm trying to be pleasant here, I'm trying to be nice, trying to be a sister, that's all. I'm interested in your welfare."

"You're interested in telling her... you know."

"I wasn't even thinking about that, you jerk. You're in love, I'd like to meet your girlfriend, that's all."

"I'm not in love."

"Men don't fall in love," Molly said. She turned and looked at Lari, and saw Lari looking back as if she were giving that statement deep consideration. "It's true," Molly said. "They like convenience, but they don't fall in love."

"They'll commit to convenience," Lari said, and the two girls laughed.

"You're not in love with this girl?" Lari asked again.

"What is it with you women and love?" Rocky said. "You think that's all there is in the world."

Lari touched Molly's arm. "One reason I am glad to be a lesbian," she said, and Molly laughed.

"Have you ever been in love?" Molly asked.

Rocky shrugged. "Can we talk about something else?"

"Sure," Molly said. "I'm just trying to figure something out."

"What?"

"This thing with your dad."

"What thing?"

Lari snorted. "Come *on*, Rock. Do either of us look like idiots to you?"

"What's there to figure out?"

"Your problem with him. You two seem to be a lot alike."

"Cut from the same cloth," Lari said.

"That's bullshit. We're nothing alike. He's stupid, for one thing. He has no morals. No character. He's a tomcat and a jerk."

"No," Molly said. "I mean deeper. Neither one of you seems to have much—I don't know—emotion or something."

"That's probably his fault, too," Rocky said. "He's a cold sonofabitch. And I probably got the gene."

"He's not cold," Lari said. "That's just the way you perceive him. If you were to look at him with a little more empathy—if you tried to like him a little bit more, I think you might be surprised at what you found inside him. He's a really nice guy, Rocky, you just expect too much."

"He hurt our mother, Lari, hurt her so bad she could have died. And now, with his juvenile heroics, he could have got Mom killed."

"He made a mistake. It's exactly the kind of thing you would have done, you know."

"No way."

"You think he *intentionally* tried to harm her?"

"He intentionally screwed around on her."

"Yeah, well he's not very original with that concept either. Don't judge him until you've been married twenty years. Now stop being a jerk. One of these days Dad'll be dead and then you'll have blown your chances for a relationship with him."

"Stewie," Molly said.

"Stewie?"

"Yeah, I gotta get to Arizona." She put her hand on Rocky's knee. "Hey, I have an idea. Why don't *you* take me? We could have a nice drive down there, it'd take, what, two, three days? Wouldn't it be fun?"

"Where in Arizona?"

"I don't know. Anywhere. The desert. Someplace hot. I need to find my uncle Stewie."

"That'd be nice," Lari said. "The two of you."

"Shut up, Lari," Rocky said. "Where's your uncle?"

"I don't know. How big could Arizona be? Oh. Turn here," Molly said, pointing at the Curtin exit. "God, I hope I can find the place."

Rocky and Lari both looked at her.

Once Rose began to think about the family, she couldn't stop. A squeeze began in her chest, and the pain moved from wherever it was Leathers was currently working on, up her spine and into her throat.

The homesickness felt bottomless, felt hopeless, she felt as if she would never see her little house again. The pain grew so intense it completely eclipsed Leathers.

There was only one avenue of relief, and Darlene opened her arms and fell back, fell through the chords of the pain and landed softly on layers of love in the blue room.

The contrasting freedom overwhelmed her for a moment. It was quiet here, and pain free. Darlene luxuriated in the absence of all sensory input, but soon she began to think again of the family.

She found that she wanted to talk to Leathers about Carolyn, about Lari, about Rocky, about Phil and Angela, but why?

Practice, perhaps. Practice for when she had the opportunity to have a relationship with another man. Another lover.

She could have a relationship with Leathers, if she wanted.

But he would never meet those members of her family, and there were only so many words. How could she recreate Lari for him? How could she accurately represent her daughter, their relationship, her passionate maternal devotion? And what about Lari's choice of Carolyn, and their mutual devotion—and how Lari broke the news of her homosexuality, and how the family dealt with that, then her eventually pairing up with Carolyn and the wedding and resultant partnership, strengthened by defense against local bigotry? How could she tell him about all of that?

And what about Rocky? She could never describe what a gorgeous child he had been, how he had grown up with a superior attitude that had got him into trouble more than once and would, doubtlessly, continue to for the rest of his life. Rocky had always been her son, never Phil's son. Rocky had been overly devoted to Darlene from the very beginning. He'd been attentive and affectionate and devoted, without being a "mama's boy." Darlene was never sure if it had to do with how much he loved her or how much he hated Phil. Rocky and Phil had butted heads the first time they met in the hospital on the day of Rocky's birth, and had every day since then. The source of that irritation in Rocky was a mystery to Phil but not to Darlene. She had carried him in her womb during those long nights alone when Phil was "on the road." She had held him and rocked him as tears flowed off her cheek and onto the breast that he suckled. Tears of pain, of loneliness, tears of anger over Phil's infidelities. Surely those tears, those feelings had tainted her soul, her body, her milk. Rocky had no choice but to grow up hating his father. How could Leathers ever understand the depth of affection between her and Rocky, the depth of that agony and guilt she carried over him hating his father so much?

How could she explain all of that to Leathers? He had never had children.

How could she explain all of that to anyone?

And Phil. She could never relate their young romance, the years they spent broke, then his ego blossoming as he discovered sales. He discovered that he could sell office equipment to women as easily as he could walk into their offices, and with that gift came an attraction that he was helpless to defend himself against. He bedded hundreds, she assumed, as the children grew along the same pace as their net worth, and out of self defense, she retreated, taking care of things on her own, not depending on him for anything—emotional or physical. Lack of challenges in their marriage meant lack of devotion to duty and to each other. How could she explain to Leathers how their relationship just kind of dissolved in her fingers like lace made of sugar?

She thought about marrying again, thought about having a long term relationship with a man—any man, and realized that Rocky and Lari and Carolyn and Phil, not to mention Ashes and Tina, were so much a part of her, that without knowing them, he could not know her.

She could try to reinvent Darlene Martin as Rose Jones, but

who would it be really? A shade? A shadow? A shell? A hollow misinterpretation?

What if she just forgot about all of them? People did. All the time. They just walked away and began new lives, and they invented history to satisfy any holes that might arise in their conversations. She could do that, but wouldn't that make her a traitor? She would be spitting in the face of all that was wonderful, all that was happiness, all that was sacred to her. Her children, their choices. They are what made her Darlene Martin. All those experiences with those people.

Darlene saw her family in a new way. Not that she would be nothing without them, but that she was so much more because of them. And to just leave them—to forsake them....

Maybe Leathers was right about raising kids. Maybe she had underestimated the importance of it.

She felt strangely drawn to the huge tattooed man who had such a bizarre lifestyle and had yet acquired wisdom. Wisdom wasn't just a product of years, she had come to realize. Some mature people still hadn't any sense.

Leathers pulled on her like a child would, he appealed to her maternal instincts. She wanted to mother him, help keep him safe from outside evil, outside forces that could hurt him. He needed someone to care for him, and it had been so long since she had been needed in that way.

He was also a caring, attentive lover.

His cabin was as far away, literally and metaphorically, from her living room recliner as it could possibly get. And that too, was attractive.

But what about the tattoo? What about the tying down, the against-your-will *surgery* he was doing?

Was it really against her will? He was working on her leg right now, right this very minute, when she knew how to escape. Didn't that make her a willing partner?

No, she said to herself. It's time to go.

She broke out of the blue room. The noise of the cabin, the sounds of Leathers as he worked, the clinking of metal on metal as he moved instruments around on his tray, the pain of her leg, the pain of her homesickness still lodged in her throat, came back with such force that she felt dizzy with the assault.

She blinked her eyes.

"Stop," she said.

"Hmm?" Leathers came over to her, smoothing her hair, his eyes clouded with worry. "Do you need something?"

"No," she said, and with more ease than she wanted to acknowledge, slipped her hand out of the strap. She turned, and with extreme difficulty, began to work at the other strap.

Leathers took a step backwards and watched.

"It's time for me to go." Until she said this, until she took action, she hadn't realized that he might just let her go, or that he could kill her trying to restrain her. She just hadn't thought of her options, she had just lay there like a trussed up turkey letting him do what he wanted instead of asserting herself.

And if she came back to him, and laid down the ground rules, she had a feeling that he would respect them.

He looked at her and his eyes filled with tears. "Right now?"

She smiled at him, painful tears filling up her own lids. She nodded. "I miss my kids," she choked out. The buckle gave way and with difficulty, she sat up. She steadied herself while the dizziness receded. Then, avoiding looking at her leg, she bent over and with her good hand, she worked at the buckles on the ankle straps.

Leathers nodded, his soft brown eyes seeing off into some distance Darlene couldn't see. "Kids," he said.

Tears overflowed her eyes and ran down her face and the squeeze in her throat eased up with each sob. Why couldn't she find someone to love who could share her family with her?

Maybe she could.

Straps unbuckled, she slid off the table and stood up, her legs unsteady. She stood for a minute, testing her strength, seeing her pants neatly folded across the back of his big chair. She took steps toward them, but he intercepted her, his big arms enfolding her.

"It isn't finished," he said.

"For me it is," she said and tried to disentangle herself from him.

"I'm so close," he said, holding her more firmly until she began to be afraid that he wasn't going to let her go after all.

"I'm sorry," she said, relaxing for a moment. Maybe she could lull him into a place of complacency and then she could make a break for it. She could never win in a struggle.

"What's the harm in just one more night? Just one more night," he said, and he sounded like a little boy. He held her to him, his heat enveloping her as cloyingly as his big arms. He held her head to his chest and she felt the vibrations as he talked. "One more session tonight, one more in the morning. Then we'll make love, Rose, my rosebud, my darling, and then if you must go, you must go."

She held her tongue.

"Please. I have to finish. Please, oh my God, please say yes."

"Let me look at it," she said, and he abruptly let her go.

She staggered back with the surprise of it, and he grabbed her arm to steady her. She looked up and smiled at him, and saw love and concern in his face and an intensity with which she was completely unfamiliar. Intensity. Passion. There was no passion in her world. Not any more.

She backed her way around the table and sat on his little stainless steel stool. Then, for the first time, she looked at her leg.

Mangled.

At least that was her first impression.

It was swollen and bruised and spotted with points of heat. It had scabs and blood smears and thin lines black with crusted blood and lumps and she felt lightheaded just looking at it. It was monstrous. It was an abomination.

It was permanent.

Leathers heavily sank to his knees next to her as if in prayer. "See the beauty," he said with reverence, his fingers gliding softly across the incisions. "Look beyond the reality and see the future. Please, Rose, see it complete. See it finished." He looked up at her again.

She looked at those beseeching brown eyes, and while all the flashing warning lights went off in her head, she wanted to believe him, she wanted to trust him, she wanted to love him so badly, that when he encouraged her again with a nod of her head, she looked back down at her leg.

And she saw a work of art so magnificent it took her breath away.

Was this a trick?

She closed her eyes, inhaled deeply through her nose, exhaled through her mouth and opened her eyes again.

It was a painting. An artwork with color shading and subtlety so rich she could see the morning sunlight on the roses. The texture of the petals as they unfolded to the clear morning air, the curling petals, the opening sepals, the little twist ties that held the thorny canes to the trellis. She could smell the rich dewy fragrance. She reached down with a tentative fingertip and traced the outline of one brilliant red rose, its first bud opening to the sky. It felt as velvety as it looked, rich with promise. She didn't dare touch the others. She was afraid of falling in love with them. She was afraid of falling in love with the artist.

The trite word "tattoo" didn't even begin to apply to this creation.

"Please let me finish," he whispered, and then the tears came again, loosening the knot in her chest, and they flowed down the bridge of her nose and dripped onto her knee.

Leathers rested his big head on her lap, and in a gesture as natural to a mother as wiping a baby's nose, she touched his head, stroked his hair.

After a time, she moved and he lifted his head. She stood up, heat flaring in her leg as she did so. Gingerly, she pulled on her black stretch pants, feeling every lump, bump, insertion and incision as she did so. She wished she had worn the bagged out sweat pants that she lived in at home.

Leathers sat in his chair and fiddled with the tattoo needle.

She sat back down and put on her slippers, then ready to go, needing to go before she lost her resolve or something, she went into the kitchen, grabbed her purse from the back of the captain's chair. She heard the needle begin to buzz.

It tugged on her. Her heart bounced.

She put her purse over her shoulder and fortified herself for the final goodbye.

Leathers was gouging deep scratches inside his thigh. There was no ink on the needle, but a trail of blood followed it as if it were a razor.

Darlene bent over and pulled the plug.

Leathers slumped as if she had pulled the plug on him.

"Please don't do that," she said, opened a gauze pad and tried to cover the bleeding gouges.

He grabbed her wrist with bone-crushing intensity.

Panic flared up in her and she pulled away, but he held her tightly.

242

"Please don't go," he whispered.

"Let me go."

"No, I can't. Stay with me, Rose, I love you. I need you. I want to finish the work."

"Let me go," she said, tears of rage and frustration pushing on her. Her breath caught in her chest, she realized that by resisting him she was only going to hurt herself.

She stopped. Relaxed. Stopped fighting him.

His grip was harder than ever. He was going to crush her good wrist. Tears of pain squirted out of her eyes. "Five," she said, starting her countdown.

"Am I hurting you?"

"Four." She nodded.

He relaxed his grip. She jerked her hand away, twirled and ran for the door. She was fat and out of shape, but she could outpace him any day. She pulled the swollen door open, burst through the broken screen door and ran out into the golden evening.

Tears came down her face, snot ran out of her nose, her breath hurt in her lungs and her chest was full of the pain of some kind of weird love and its loss.

She stopped in the middle of the yard and looked back at the tumbledown shack.

Heard the buzz.

She walked through that opening in the blackberries and toward her life. Her good life. Her comfortable life. Her stable, predictable, boring life.

She stumbled a bit. Her hand throbbed. Her pants rubbed her leg raw. Her head pounded. Her eyes stung.

She kept going forward, through the weeds, down the pathway, toward the road. Toward civilization, humanity, sanity.

"I can't believe you left him sitting there, bleeding," Rose said to her. "I can't believe you're throwing away our only chance at another love."

"Who says it's our only chance?" Darlene answered. "There could be lots of chances. With a normal man. With a man who can be a part of my whole life. There will never be another Leathers, that's true, but surely there's another Bob out there, somewhere."

"Maybe we should stay away from guys named Bob."

"Maybe we should."

She muttered and talked to herself all the way to the main road, wondering if she had gone over the edge, knowing that of course there would be no normal man willing to take her with all her blubber, half a hand, and a tattooed leg to boot. She sidestepped the larger rocks, feeling the smaller ones bruising her feet, trying to ignore the pain, conscious only of putting one foot in front of the other before she turned around and dove back into the safe, anonymous life of Rose Jones and Leathers.

In shorter time than she would have imagined, she reached the main paved road.

The sun had gone behind the wooded hills, leaving the valley in a nether dusk. Insects began to boil in their weird little gnat clouds, and Darlene slapped at a couple of mosquitoes. She turned east and walked along the shoulder, and when she heard a car come up behind her, she stuck out her bandaged hand.

A blue pickup. It braked and stopped. She walked as quickly as she could up to it.

A toothless man wearing stained overalls, a green John Deere ball cap and three days of whiskers smiled at her from the driver's seat. "Whereya goin?"

"Springfield," she said.

"Hop in."

Against her better judgment, but eager to escape Leathers' area of influence, and even more eager to get home, Darlene opened the door and got in. The cab smelled of old, unwashed man. She left the window down and let the wind blow her hair as they drove.

Rocky turned on the headlights as he passed through Curtin. He felt his muscles whine from the prolonged tension. He stretched his neck, flexed his arms. "How much farther?"

"Not too far," Molly said. "A few miles."

Rocky tried to relax, but his nerves were singing like high wires. He didn't know what to expect in this rural place. He remembered watching a video called "Deliverance," and didn't know if it was that kind of back country okie that had his mother, or what. He only knew he had the girl's gun inside his belt, and it was loaded, and he aimed to get his mom back from the criminals.

"Okay now," Molly said. "I got to tell you a little bit about Leathers."

"Who the fuck *is* this Leathers?" His voice came out high and hysterical sounding.

"Rocky," Lari said. "Settle down a little bit, okay? Jesus, you're gonna have a stroke."

Molly patted his thigh, an intimate gesture Rocky didn't quite know how to handle. "He's the guy with the cabin."

"Mom is with this guy Leathers?"

Molly nodded.

"Is he the guy who's into pain?"

Molly nodded again.

"Okay, so what about him?"

"Well, Patrick always said he was harmless, but he always scared me."

Rocky took a death grip on the steering wheel.

"Why?" Lari asked.

"Well, he was so big, and strange. He was always, I don't know, like a father to Patrick, I guess. He used to boss me around, too, but

245

he never hurt me. He scared me the most I think because he's one of the biggest guys I've ever seen. He's huge. And, he had all those weird tattoos."

"Tattoos?"

Molly laughed. "Wait 'til you see him."

"Did he hurt Patrick?"

"I'm not sure." Molly had wondered that many times herself.

Rocky spoke through gritted teeth. "If he has hurt my mother, I swear to god, I'll kill you with my bare hands."

Molly shrank down, putting her hands in her lap. "I don't think he would."

"You stranded her in this place with this weird guy for a *week* for Christ's sake. That's plenty of time."

"For what?"

"For something to happen. For anything." Rocky tried not to think about all the things that could have happened to his mother, but he couldn't stop the visions, couldn't stop running the sick scenarios. He kept envisioning some fat greasy tattooed man tying up his mother, raping her repeatedly, burning her with cigarettes, starving her, torturing her for his own pleasures, *injecting* things, for God's sake, under her skin.

When Molly said, "Slow down now," Rocky slammed on the brakes and almost threw them all through the windshield.

"Jesus," Molly said. "I said slow down, not come to a fucking halt."

Rocky kept driving slowly.

"Here," she said. "Turn in here."

Rocky stepped on the gas and shot through the weeds, bouncing Molly until her head hit the ceiling of the truck. "Slow down, Rock," Lari said, but Rocky was intent. He was close to the source of his fear and anxiety, and he aimed to rid himself of all of it, once and for all. The truck rocketed through the weeds and into the woods, headlights bouncing crazily along.

Finally, they broke through the blackberry hedge and straight ahead was the mound of beer bottles. Rocky stopped the truck. "This is it?" he asked. He didn't like the looks of this. Not at all.

"This is it," Molly said. "Park over there."

Rocky parked where she told him, turned off the engine and the headlights, took a deep breath and opened the door.

The cabin was dark. There was no sound.

"Wait," Molly said. "Let me go in first. Leathers knows me, and he doesn't like strangers coming out here."

"You wait here with Lari," Rocky told her.

"No way," Lari said. "I'm coming with you."

"I'm telling you, Leathers doesn't like strangers."

"Yeah? Well, I don't think I much like Leathers," Rocky said. He pulled the gun out, his heart beating so hard he could barely breathe, and led the way through the dark, wet weeds to the cabin's front door. He followed a path worn in the knee-high weeds, but even so, by the time he stepped onto the sagging porch, his shoes squished with water.

He pulled open the torn, cockeyed screen door and looked at Molly in the waning daylight. "What? Knock?"

Molly shrugged at him. "Your show," she said.

"Is he going to be standing on the other side of this door with a shotgun?"

Molly shrugged.

Rocky turned the knob on the filthy door and pushed. It stuck. He put his shoulder to it and the door shuddered open.

The cabin was dark except for a glimpse of light from the next room. A buzzing sound came from that room.

"What the hell is that noise?" Rocky whispered, out of breath from his heart hammering double time.

Molly smiled at him. "That's Leathers," she said.

Rocky's bowels felt watery.

Molly hit the wall switch and the kitchen lights came on. "Wow," she said. "Your mom really cleaned this place up."

Lari and Rocky both frowned at her.

"Leathers?" she called. "It's me. Molly."

The buzzing continued.

"Why don't you two stay here for just a minute," she said, holding them at bay with a raised hand. "I'll be right back."

She walked through the kitchen and disappeared through the doorway.

Rocky looked at Lari, who looked back at him, her eyes wide with wonder. The place was a dump, and he couldn't imagine his mother staying here five minutes, much less a whole week. And it wasn't that remote. She could easily have walked out, couldn't she? Unless she was being restrained.

Rocky's blood began to heat. She was in this house and he meant to find her. Now.

He walked through the kitchen, shaking off Lari's hand of better judgment. "Molly?" he called. "Molly, I want my mom and I want her now." He tried to walk loudly, so she knew he was coming, but when he rounded the corner into the other room, he was taken totally by surprise.

Darlene thought she saw Rocky's truck drive right past them just before they made the turn north onto I-5, but it was getting dark and she couldn't be certain.

She looked over at the craggy face of the driver who had picked her up. He looked a little bit scary; she was glad they were headed in the right direction. Wouldn't it be ironic, she thought, if Rocky showed up at Leathers' house just after she had left? Ah, life.

She kept her eyes on the farmer and kept her concentration on Ashes and Tina and Lari and Rocky and her roses and her little house, and how badly she wanted to get home. She probably had aphids all over her rosebuds, and surely the lawn needed to be mowed. Maybe there was some good mail. Darlene felt as if she had been away on a long, strange, not very restful vacation.

And her hand throbbed. She needed to take it to the doctor first thing in the morning. Perhaps there was even some kind of reconstruction something they could do so she wouldn't be totally without those fingers.

Good Lord, she thought. In the real world, with cars whizzing by on the freeway, the things she had done at Leathers' place seemed so strange. The tattoo on her leg, for example. She flushed with shame at the thought of it. *I can't believe I let him do that to me.* And the hand. *He gave my fingers to the dog. And we laughed about it!*

Dizziness struck her and she grabbed the door handle with one hand and put the bandaged one on the dashboard.

"You okay?" the driver said, but Darlene wasn't, and she couldn't tell him what the problem was.

"You want to go home? You want to go to the hospital?"

His voice came from further and further away. She reached out to touch him, but her ears were filled with cotton and her bandaged hand couldn't reach him. Little darts of darkness spotted her vision and they spread out, swirled, and she remembered thinking, *I don't want to hit my head*, so she lay it back against the seat.

~ ~ ~

Awareness came back slowly. First, the cold. She rubbed her bare arms. Her skin was cold and dry. She opened her eyes. The truck was silent. She was shivering. They were parked. She looked out the window. They were parked in the driveway of some big house. Darlene listened and heard no sound, and was afraid it was the cotton in her ears effect she'd experienced just before she fainted. She moved around. Her hand throbbed. She reached for the door handle and touched it. Her faculties were intact. She tried to remember. They were turning onto the freeway when she remembered her tattoo. Did she really have a tattoo of a rose trellis all up her leg? She remembered her hand. Had she really lost three fingers to a varmint trap? She remembered Leathers. Had she really slept with him in that nasty cabin, made love to his grotesque body? She remembered the ride with this grisly old farmer, or mechanic or whatever the hell he was. She remembered fainting just as dusk descended.

And now it was dark. Faints didn't last long, did they? Could she have been out more than a few minutes?

She heard voices.

Her instinct was to open the truck door and run for her life, but knew her legs weren't up to it. She felt weak and nauseated. Instead, she waited.

She looked at the big house again. The driver was talking to someone in the doorway. He pointed at her, then he went inside and they closed the door. *Oh Darlene*, she thought. What now?

She tried to open the truck door, but her muscles were still weak. She couldn't make a fist solid enough to pull the door handle. She intended to get out and go into the house, but then the door opened again and the two men came out. One was the driver, the other a young balding man in sweatpants and tee shirt. They came around to her side, and one of them opened the door wide. It was the driver. "Howya feelin'?" he asked.

She nodded. "Better."

"Here," said the other one. "Let's have a look." He moved into the dim interior truck light, and she saw that he was a decent looking man, clean shaven, with graying hair cut short and good teeth.

"No, thanks, I'm fine."

"This here's a doctor friend of mine," the driver said.

Darlene looked back at the man. "A doctor?" she said.

"Yep," the driver said, proud to have done the right thing. "Been treating my kin for twenty-odd years."

"You gave Teddy here quite a scare, passing out the way you did," the doctor said.

Darlene looked at the driver. "Teddy?"

"Timber Ted," he grinned his toothless mouth at her.

"What's your name?" the doctor asked.

Darlene's female intuition was waving red flags, flashing red lights. Something wasn't right. This guy didn't look, or act, or seem like a doctor any more than she looked like Rose Jones.

"Rose Jones," she said.

"Well, Rose," he said, "why do you think you passed out? Have you taken any medication? Why don't you let me have a look at that hand?"

"I'm all right now," she said. She looked at Ted. "Can we go now? I need to get home."

"Is there someone there who can take care of you?" the doctor asked.

"Well..." Darlene said. She thought she smelled beer on his breath.

"Why don't you come into the house and call?" He smiled. "Come on, my wife will make you a nice cup of tea, I can take a look at that hand, and you can call your family so they won't worry."

Wife. Phone. Tea. Doctor. Darlene ignored the red flags and flashing lights. She was just used to seeing doctors in clinics, that's all. They all had private lives, lived in houses with wives. Surely they had an occasional beer in the evening.

Phone. She wanted to call. She wanted a doctor to look at her hand. She wanted a cup of tea. She wanted to see another woman. She nodded. "Okay," she said. "Where are we?"

"Curtin," the doctor said, and helped her out of the truck. "Come on in."

Darlene got out, steadied herself with his arm around her, then walked the steps up to the front door.

She felt tired and sick. She wanted to lie down and sleep. She wanted someone to take care of her. She wanted a shower, and most of all, some clean clothes. She wanted to go home and have Tina sleep on her chest. She felt like crying.

The doctor opened the door and Darlene looked into a lovely living room. She stepped two steps down, with his hand on her arm, and settled into a plush sofa.

"Oh," she said. "I should call."

"Sit tight," he said, and a moment later, he brought her a cordless phone.

She dialed and listened to it ring. Carolyn, jangling with impatience, had run to the corner store for ice cream, the only thing that calmed her nerves. Ashes picked up his head and looked at the purring phone. Tina blinked her big green eyes at it, but nobody answered it.

Darlene clicked the phone off, and saw Ted looking at her. She didn't think she should be here with these two guys. Where was the doctor's wife? "Nobody home?" Ted asked.

She shook her head. She closed her eyes and rested her head on the back of the couch. In another minute, she heard the microwave beep and the doctor brought her a cup of steaming, aromatic herbal tea in a green mug on a tray. He set the tray down. It also had alcohol, scissors and a bowl of warm water on it.

He snapped on some rubber gloves. "Let's take a look at that hand," he said.

She held it protectively to her chest. "Why?"

"Because it's not the right shape," he said. "I'd say you've lost some fingers. Your bandage is not fresh, so your wound is a few days old. It's clearly a home bandaging job, *and* you fainted, remember?"

She nodded, held her hand out. He began to unwrap the gauze.

"Where's your wife?" Darlene asked.

"She's gone to bed," he said. "She had a headache. If you need her, I'll waken her, but as long as we're all right... ah..." he was getting to the gauze that had stuck to the ooze of her stitches.

Darlene looked away. She didn't want to see it.

"How did this happen?"

"Varmint trap," she said.

"Good God. When?"

When? Darlene couldn't remember. "Wednesday?" she said.

He took a pair of hemostats from his shirt pocket and gently picked the gauze wrapping from her hand.

"I'm not even sure what day today is."

"Saturday," the doctor said. "It's Saturday night." He finished unwrapping and piled the bloody bandages on the tray. "Well. This isn't as bad as I thought it might be. I'm even going to leave those stitches, even though they look amateurish and pretty silly. They don't seem to be infected, and they're doing the job. Who did this?"

Darlene looked at the crab-claw that had once been her hand. Only the thumb and index finger remained, looking stupid with the pink polish on the nails. Her hand hurt more when she looked at its purple, bruised, swollen ugliness with that long Frankenstein line of black and red stitches. It made her queasy.

Darlene looked into the doctor's face and suddenly began to trust him. He seemed to have her welfare at heart. "Leathers," she said.

"Leathers."

She nodded. "A friend."

"Well, he did all right by you." he worked with her hand, putting ointments on it. "I'd like to give you a couple of shots. One for tetanus and one for infection, just to make sure."

Darlene nodded. She knew she needed them, and it was probably not a moment too soon.

"Why don't you tell me how you happened to be hitchhiking?"

"Leathers doesn't have a car," she said.

"Do you?"

Darlene shook her head. "I meant to go home on Tuesday, but it rained. Then I did this..."

The doctor nodded. "Drink your tea," he said.

Darlene sipped. The tea tasted good, so good, it warmed her through.

The doctor put ointment on her hand and rewrapped it. "I put a shot of brandy in the tea," he said, "I thought you might need it."

She nodded, feeling the brandy warm her stomach, feeling lucky to have stumbled upon this guy.

The doctor finished wrapping her hand. It looked professional, competent. She felt much better. Then he took the tray into the

253

kitchen, and when he returned, he had two syringes. "One in each arm," he said, and she pulled up a sleeve. She winced, but the shot was swift.

"Other arm," the doctor said.

She rolled down the one sleeve, and pushed up the other one. She barely felt the pinprick.

"There you go," he said, and he smiled at her.

She smiled back, and then she suddenly felt ill. She felt like her throat was growing smaller, even as her tongue became larger.

"Wha's your name?" she asked, knowing that something was dreadfully wrong with her, and it probably had to do with him.

"They call me Doctor Bob," he said.

Darlene felt like panicking. Something was wrong with her. Something dreadfully wrong. What had he given her?

Antibiotic. Penicillin.

Oh, God. Darlene had been violently allergic to penicillin since childhood. She even had one of those stupid Medic-Alert necklaces, but she never wore it.

She grabbed for the doctor, who moved out of her way. "Penicillin?" she gasped.

Comprehension flowed over his face.

He stood up, grabbed Ted by the front of the shirt with a strong hand. "Call 911," he said. "Tell them there's a woman going into anaphylactic shock."

"*What* shock?"

"Anaphylactic. Hurry."

"What's the address here?" Ted asked, and Darlene could see the gravity of the situation in their faces.

"They can't come here," Doctor Bob said. "I'd lose my license for treating a human being. And I had a couple of beers tonight. Tell them she's in front of the mini mart. We'll take her there."

"What do you mean?" Ted asked. "Lose your license? You're a doctor."

"I'm a veterinarian, you idiot. Call *now*. Wait. Don't use the house phone, get the one in my desk drawer. Use that."

Darlene shook her head as her eyesight failed her. They were going to dump her. She slipped sideways on the couch and couldn't make her muscles work to right herself. She lay there blaming herself, luck and men in general. She said a prayer, wished for Leathers, and struggling for breath, her chest heaving, her eyes popping with the effort for air as her throat closed, Darlene slipped into semi-consciousness.

She felt the men grunt with her weight as she was hauled off the couch, carried out of the house and heaved into the pickup. She heard a loud, rasping noise but couldn't imagine it was the sound of her own breathing.

"Twenty years you treated my kin," Ted said.

"Competently," the doctor replied, his voice tight and righteous. "And charged you almost nothing."

"Ain't right," Ted said. "This ain't at all right."

Darlene's muscles had totally failed her. She bounced limply between the men, then they stopped under a solitary streetlight.

They hauled her out of the pickup and unceremoniously propped her up against a glass front door. Darlene listed to starboard and struggled for breath. She must look like a wino, she thought, but her awareness was so fuzzy, she felt hazy and barely real.

She felt like she was drowning, and she waited for that moment when the fear ceased and she could embrace the lungs full of water.

After settling her, Darlene heard the door slam as the doctor got back into the truck.

"I'm sorry," Ted said, and touched her shoulder. "This ain't at all right."

"Come on!" Doctor Bob called, and Ted left her, too. The truck started and spit gravel as they took off. Then Darlene heard the ambulance siren.

When the paramedics tried to talk to her, she hadn't enough breath to concentrate. They gave her oxygen, which helped her relax, and she thought she could go to sleep.

As she was being carried through the air once more, she wondered once again about her weird destiny with men, most apparently, named Bob.

Phil sat in a blue plastic chair in the police station and watched people pass by him for hours, his frustration level growing by the moment. Every time he asked someone what was going on, he was told it was a busy night and he needed to be patient.

"I can go home and come back in the morning," he said.

"No," was always the response. "It won't be much longer."

So he sat and helplessly watched bums, derelicts, police officers, drugged hippies and women who looked at him with suspicion, and tried to figure out what he had in common with these people. Hell of a way to run a city.

He saw where the carpet was seamed, he counted the panels in the wall. He counted the acoustic tiles in the ceiling and the number of little holes in each tile. He was thinking about counting the hairs on the back of one hand, or the number of lice in the head of the dreadlocked Rastafarian who sat in front of him. He completely forgot about Darlene's plight, and centered on his own. He was a little dehydrated, his alcohol binge from the night before still taking its toll. His mouth felt dry, his brain began to hurt all over inside his skull. And time slowed down so that he was looking at his watch every half hour and seeing that barely two minutes had passed.

He began to feel sick to his stomach, and he lounged there, in the blue plastic chair, in abject misery and self-pity.

He didn't even have the energy to fight with anyone about it.

He waited for someone to call his name and take him to the interrogation room. At least that would be different. He waited for Angela and an imaginary bevy of attorneys to rescue him. He waited for Molly and Darlene and Rocky and Lari and Carolyn to stride triumphantly through the door. He waited to be handcuffed and thrown into a dark, fetid prison cell with a monstrous, tattooed, toothless, brainless psychotic killer for a cellmate. He waited for his head to explode.

He waited. Miserably.

A bleeding man in a Hawaiian shirt. That's what Rocky thought when he first laid eyes on Leathers.

Leathers was ripping his skin with what appeared to be an electric knife in long, parallel streaks diagonally across the top of his left thigh, leaving oozing trails that looked like claw marks. Blood barber-poled down his calf. Molly stood next to him, watching.

"Hey," Rocky said, and Molly looked up, but the man did not.

"Hey!" Rocky said louder.

Molly jerked the plug out of the wall and the buzzing stopped. Rocky felt he could hear the cabin, alive with insects and bacteria, rotting all around him as he stood in the doorway. The place was being reduced to compost, even as they stood confronting a self-destructive crazy.

It was then that he noticed the tattoo needle. It wasn't a knife, and holy shit, that was no shirt.

"This is Leathers," Molly said softly.

Rocky took two steps and grabbed her arm so hard it hurt his fingers. He knew it was hurting her, he could feel the tiny bone in her thin arm. "You left my mother here with this—" at a loss for words, he gestured at Leathers.

Lari took a step toward Rocky, to keep him from breaking Molly's arm, but even she was stopped dead by the sound that came from the mountain of sadness in the big leather chair.

"Rose," Leathers said, his breath wheezy, his voice coarse.

"You're bleeding, buddy," Rocky said, and picked a towel up from a chair and threw it over the bleeding thigh.

"Rose," Leathers said.

"Leathers," Molly said. "Patrick is dead."

"Patrick is dead," Leathers said, nodding. "Patrick is gone."

"How did you know that?" Molly asked.

"Where's my mother?" Rocky asked, then saw two closed doors leading off the studio. Without waiting for a reply, he released Molly with a shove, strode over, opened one and flipped on the light switch. Patrick and Molly's disaster area. No Darlene. He closed that door and opened the one to Leathers' room. He looked in the closet, in the bathroom. No Darlene.

"This room is clean," he said to nobody. "Mom's been here."

He came back into the studio. Molly was kneeling next to Leathers. Lari stood, uncomfortable, by the door.

"Better sit down, Rock," Molly said.

"What's up?"

"She's dead," Leathers said. "She's gone." And a tear dampened the brown creases in his face.

Lari stumbled for a chair and sat down heavily.

Rocky felt a weakness shudder through him. He wanted to say "No!" He wanted to say "I knew it!" He wanted to shake the bleeding idiot-giant and get the truth, the whole truth and nothing but the goddamned truth.

He sank onto a five-wheeled stainless steel stool, his mind flapping with things to say, things to do, things to feel. He looked at his hands and listened to the old man cry.

"Where—" his voice came out dry. He cleared his throat and willed his voice to be strong. "Where is she?"

"Leathers?" Molly said. She smoothed his hair. "Leathers, where is Darlene?"

"Gone," he said.

"Gone, or dead?" Rocky asked.

"Dead!" Leathers shouted. He stood, his massive artwork shaking in passion. "She's dead. She's gone. She's dead. She's gone." In panic, he looked around, found his tattoo needle and tried to get it to work. He plugged it in and the buzzing began.

"No," Molly said. She unplugged it again.

"What do you want from me?" Leathers whined, imploring.

Lari, forgotten in the exchange, slipped off the chair and slumped to the floor, her eyes dazed and her face ashen.

"Where is she?" Rocky asked, his hands beginning to tremble. His mother was dead, his father was in jail. This was a nightmare that happened only to other people.

"I loved her," Leathers said.

"I don't think you're going to get any information out of him tonight," Molly said.

"Well then, by God, I'll get someone here who *will* get the information from him." Rocky stood up, stomping his boots. "Is there a phone?"

Molly smirked. "Of course not. Are you kidding? There's not even cell service."

"Where's the nearest service?"

"In Elkton. West."

"Stay here with Lari."

Molly nodded.

Rocky pointed at Leathers. "Make sure he stays put. I'll be back with the cops."

"Good," Molly said. "Somebody needs to take care of Leathers."

"Fuck Leathers," Rocky said as he walked out the door. "You take care of Lari."

Molly watched Rocky's back as he left. She heard the truck start and he gunned it, spinning the wheels in the wet weeds.

Soon all was quiet again, quiet except for the sounds the cabin made. Molly helped Lari to the couch, where she lay with her head on a pillow, silent tears running out the sides of her eyes and down her cheeks into her ears. Molly covered her with a knitted shawl and went back into the studio.

"Leathers?" Molly asked. "Have you fed the animals?"

Leathers looked up at her like he'd never seen her before. "Animals?"

"The dog. The rabbits."

Leathers looked at his leg.

Molly stood up and went outside. The big yellow dog slowly wagged his tail at her. He had something in his mouth.

"Hi, Burbank," she said. She scratched him between the ears, and wondered if his horrible smell kept the fleas away. Maybe that's why Leathers never washed him.

He seemed to grin at her.

"Whatcha got there, boy?" she asked, and he bobbed his head at her feet.

Then he dropped three rotting fingers on the toe of her shoe, pranced proudly and waited for her approval.

Molly stared at them for a long moment, noticing the nicely kept nails, the pinkish polish. She remembered admiring Darlene's nails that day in the car, that day she had kidnapped Darlene and brought her here to this house, to Leathers, to her death.

Molly knew if she didn't scream, she would faint. So she screamed. And then she threw up.

The police wanted Rocky to meet him at the Elkton store. He waited there for almost an hour, fidgeting, pacing, biting his fingernails. He finally called them back and told them to meet him at Leathers' place, and gave them the best directions he could. Impatience crawled up the backs of his thighs, clenched his buttocks and brought goosebumps and twitches to his back muscles as he verbally wrestled with the woman on the other line of the phone.

When he hung up, he wasn't convinced that she understood, but he didn't care. He couldn't stand there at that park, the first place he got cell service, and try to explain to her for another minute. The heebie-jeebies were upon him, and he had to get into action.

He jumped into his truck and sped back the way he had come, back to Leathers' place.

He missed the turn in his haste and went miles too far before realizing it. He could feel his face heating up, it felt like his skin was stretched tight. His hands hurt as they gripped the steering wheel, and when he made the u-turn in the middle of the highway going way too fast, the empty back of the truck fishtailed, and for a heart-stopping moment, he thought he was going to lose control and follow Patrick into the river.

The tires found their grip, though, and he slowed down.

Rocky felt as though his chest were being squeezed by a giant hand. He felt like a tube of toothpaste, and with another jolt, with the slightest bit more pressure, he was going to squirt. He'd squirt all the black nastiness that he felt sure was his true personality, the one he'd kept hidden all his life. The only person in the world he felt he could expose his soul to was his mother, and he had never done it, knowing, of course that she would always be there for him. He knew that someday he would have to open his heart to someone and let the sunshine and fresh air in to his rotten soul, and she was the only one who would understand him, she was the only person who loved him totally, completely, without reservation, and would accept him, black, bile-filled guts and all.

And now she was dead.

It wasn't possible. It was inconceivable. It couldn't be true.

He wouldn't allow it to be true. He had to have her. He had to have her back. He had to appreciate her, he had to let her know how much she meant to him, how much he loved her, how she was the only yardstick in his whole stupid life. Without her, he had no gauges at all.

His chest sucked in a massive sob just as the little white rear end of the abandoned car came into view.

This time he made the turn and humped over the ruts, still going faster than he should. The headlights bounced crazily and he bounced so hard in the seat that his head hit the headliner of the truck. He burst through the opening in the blackberry brambles, made a hard left turn and spun to a stop in front of the cabin.

The cabin was dark. It looked deserted.

If they've split, Rocky thought, *I'll be more than pissed.* He got out of the truck and slammed the door, leaving the headlights on. *In fact*, he said to himself, *I'll track them down like vermin and kill them where I find them.*

The smelly old yellow dog came wagging up to him on the porch.

He had something in his mouth.

At eleven-thirty, Carolyn went to bed with a bowl of popcorn. She didn't understand why nobody had called her. She didn't understand why Lari hadn't called. She didn't understand why Angela hadn't called. She didn't know who to call, she just knew that the waiting was gnawing a hole in her gut and the only way to fix that was to eat.

She ate.

At one forty-five, the phone rang. Carolyn had been listening to talk radio to try to keep her mind from wandering in places she didn't want it to go. She preferred to see angels and rainbows, she preferred prayers to far-right talk radio paranoia, but for some reason, her anxiety was chasing all that away. Talk radio helped.

She grabbed the phone, hoping for relief.

"Hello?"

"Is this Darlene Martin's home?"

"Yes."

"This is Wanda Fitzpatrick, a nurse at Sacred Heart Hospital. Mrs. Martin has been admitted as a patient."

"Is she all right?"

"She's stabilized. She wanted me to call."

"I'll be right there," Carolyn said.

She threw on a pair of jeans and a tee shirt, then called Angela. No answer. She left a message on Phil and Angela's voicemail and ran out the door. Halfway to the hospital, she wondered if she should leave a message on Darlene's refrigerator in case Rocky or Lari came back.

But then they were probably with her. How else would she have gotten to the hospital?

SUNDAY

I should have known, Molly said to herself. *Sleep with dogs, you're gonna get fleas.*

The warmth that had initially spread across her back with the impact of the bullet was evaporating, and in its place, a bone chilling cold began to seep through her, like ice crystals multiplying in her blood.

She was drooling on the floor, and willed her sleepy hand to wipe her mouth. Her fingers came away bloody.

Molly smiled. Was she in the movies?

She closed her eyes. The movie of the past three or so minutes rewound and began to play.

She had turned out the lights to help Leathers calm down. He was in his big chair, the one in his studio, and she sat on the stool next to him. The house was silent, the only sound she could hear was Lari weeping softly in the kitchen and the rabbits jumping around in their cages behind the house.

She had her hand on Leather's hot shoulder, talking to him slowly and gently. She'd seen Darlene's fingers, oh God, she'd seen those fingers, and she knew that Darlene was dead. She tried not to think about the fact that she was in that house alone with a murderer, with a maniac. But Leathers was no threat to anybody but himself at the moment. As she sat there, Molly saw that he was a clear danger to himself, and she had to make sure he didn't do anything permanent to himself until Rocky came back with the police and they could torture the true story out of the fat freak.

So she sat with him, talking to him, keeping the place dark so he couldn't cut himself. Or worse.

"How did you kill her?" she finally asked.

"I didn't kill her."

"How did she die?"

"She left."

A flicker of understanding began to illuminate Molly's mind. "Did you know that Patrick was dead? That he was killed in a car accident?"

She felt him tense under her hand. He hadn't known. She felt him begin to shake and knew that he was crying.

"Is Darlene dead, Leathers, or is she just gone?"

"Dead, gone, it's all the same," he said, his voice thick and syrupy.

"Big difference, Leathers."

"She's gone."

"What about the fingers?"

"Fingers?"

"Burbank is carrying around three of her fingers."

"Varmint trap."

Molly shivered. She used to watch Patrick set those traps. She saw how those metal teeth cut rats right in half. One of those would take off three fingers easily. She moved her hand to feel the pulse in Leathers' thick neck. With a blast of understanding, she saw him not as a murderous, creepy fat man, but as a pathetic, needy human being. She suddenly understood what Patrick had seen in him—a father figure, a comrade in need, an eccentric who needed friends, who couldn't live on his own, who used his weaknesses as a way to seduce those who had a need to help. He and Patrick had needed each other.

As if her past were being rewritten on a giant chalkboard in the sky, Molly viewed her time at the cabin in this new light, and she saw that Leathers and Patrick weren't perverted, or as sick as she had always chosen to think. They were friends, one older, one younger and healthier, who helped each other out. So what if they had a weird relationship? So what if they were into pain? They didn't hurt anybody else. Leathers was the sick one and Patrick was his enabler. Their system seemed to work for them. Who was she to judge? She, with her suspicious nature, was the pervert in the house. Leathers always made her eat, and take care of herself. He made Patrick work for his self-esteem, and Patrick knew it and respected him for it, while Molly only resented it.

Issued a total loser for a father, Molly was somehow granted a second chance, a second dad, and she had just about blown it.

She heard Rocky's truck. The headlights shone in through the threadbare curtains. She heard the truck door slam.

"Jones," Leathers said softly. "I'm going to name my new rose Jones."

Molly heard Rocky on the porch, and then she heard him scream. Funny, she always thought guys would just yell, but this one screamed. She should have taken those fingers away from Burbank when she had the chance.

Too late. Rocky shouldered his way through the door.

Molly stood up, her heart hammering in her skinny chest. "Sit still," she said to Leathers, but then there was Rocky, silhouetted by the truck's headlights. He had a gun.

"You fucker," he said, as he turned and pointed the gun at Leathers. "You killed my mother."

"No!" Molly screamed, and like a jerk, threw herself in front of Leathers just as fire spit from Rocky's hand.

She thought someone had taken a baseball bat to her back. Twice.

Then, unable to move her legs, she slipped from Leathers and landed heavily on the floor.

She tried to call his name, "Leathers?" but she coughed instead, and felt a little lightheaded.

She heard sirens in the distance, and Rocky's boots pacing back and forth. She didn't hear any sounds coming from Leathers at all.

She heard Rocky drop the gun on the floor. She saw the kitchen light go on. There was a big puddle of blood in front of her face. She brought her other hand up and rested her cheek on it. She didn't want to lie in a puddle of blood.

She turned her head and saw blood dripping from Leathers' shoulder, but if it was her blood or his blood, she didn't know. She listened again and heard his wheezy breathing.

"Daddy?" she said.

"It's okay," she heard, but she didn't know if it came from Leathers, or from a voice echoing back in her memory.

I should have known, she thought. *Sleep with dogs and you're gonna get fleas. Or fingers.*

She barked a laugh that hurt and multiplied the ice crystals.

They were working their way up the back of her neck. She heard voices in the kitchen. She heard electronic voices over a radio. She heard singing.

She wanted to get up, she wanted to know what was going on. She wanted to tell Patrick to put another log on the fire, Jesus Christ, Patrick, it's cold in here.

But the singing got louder, and she suddenly realized how beautiful it was.

She looked around and didn't quite know where she was, but the singing was so nice. She wanted to close her eyes and sink into the music.

"Daddy?"

"Here, baby." And there he was, the light of love shining in his eyes, and she jumped into his arms, leaving behind only dust.

They finally moved Phil to a little quiet room by himself instead of being a spectacle in the police station hall. This place looked exactly like the interrogation rooms in the TV police dramas, except maybe it was a little newer. He'd been sitting there for what seemed like days, when finally a door opened and a little squatty woman came in and told him he could leave.

"Leave? Why?"

"Your wife has been found."

"Found?" Nothing was registering.

She took a good look at him for the first time and Phil saw that tiny, flirtatious smile cross her face. She was attracted to him. It irritated him. "She's at the hospital, they said."

Relief flooded through Phil and swept away all resentments, thoughts of revenge and anger at the inconvenience. Darlene was safe. Thank God. "What hospital?"

The woman shrugged. "They just told me to tell you that you can go."

He stood up, stretched, and followed the woman out the door.

"Is there anything for me to do? Any papers to sign? Anything?"

"Nothing," she said. "Can I call you a cab?"

Phil nodded. He felt some kind of a strange letdown, and walked toward the door just as a police car pulled up in front.

Rocky. In handcuffs. A belligerent Rocky, mad, defiant, all those potentials suddenly cut loose. Not a pretty sight. He was being handled roughly by two uniformed cops, and that stoked his ire.

Lari, not handcuffed, emerged from the police car as well.

"Daddy!" she shouted, and ran to put her arms around his waist.

"Cocksucker," Rocky spit into Phil's face. "This is all your fault, you sonofabitch."

270

Then the policeman pulled Rocky through the glass doors, and the last Phil saw of him was his long blonde hair, tangled around crazed eyes.

Phil didn't know that man, but his throat burned with the aftertaste of Rocky's hate.

Lari leaned against him as if she were going to fall. He tightened his grip on his daughter and steadied her, then together they walked down the steps and he helped her into the cab.

"They found your mom," he said.

Lari started to cry. "Leathers said she was dead."

Phil wanted to cry, too, but instead, he said, "Well, she's not."

"Rocky shot that girl. I think she was dead when the ambulance got there. Leathers was still breathing, but he was shot, too." They rode the rest of the way in silence.

Phil wondered what was real any more. Didn't he know his son? He did, and he knew that Rocky had always had that potential. Violence. Severe violence. Unchecked hatred, bordering on madness. Another door opened up in Phil's future, one of attorneys and courtrooms and DAs and trials and evidence, and the extent of his involvement was completely up to him. How far would he go? How deep would he dive to try to salvage his son's affections?

Not far, he thought, and Peaches' sweet face floated up to smile in his memory.

The taxi stopped in front of Darlene's darkened house.

Ashes, of course, danced all over the living room to see Phil. Phil picked him up and he stood in the living room with Lari while they looked at each other in confusion.

"Hospital?" Lari said.

Phil winced. He had been thinking it, but didn't want to say the word. "Where's Carolyn?"

Lari shrugged. She checked the refrigerator. No message. "How about a pot of coffee?" she said. "Let's relax here. Someone will call."

Phil wanted to go home. His headache was coming back. It was the middle of the night, and he hadn't slept, except down by the river. He was exhausted and his eyesight began to have that twinkly aspect that spoke of lack of sleep. He didn't want to call and wake Angela, though. It would be better to just slip into the shower and then slip into bed.

Clean sheets. Clean body. Stretched out straight, head on soft pillow, blessed, blessed sleep. He still felt hangover-greasy. He wanted to shower. He wanted to sleep. He wanted to kiss his baby.

"I think I'll go home," he said, but as he opened the door, Carolyn drove into the driveway.

Ashes squirmed out of Phil's arms and began dancing again.

Carolyn gave Phil a deep hug. Then Lari joined in and they held on to each longer than was comfortable for Phil. "Your mom's at the hospital," she said.

Phil sat on the arm of the recliner. Lari and Carolyn stood with their arms around each other.

"Is she all right?" Lari asked.

"She's had some trauma," Carolyn said. "She's been through some pretty weird stuff, but she'll be okay. She's the same. You know, she's your mom."

"What kind of weird stuff?" Phil asked.

"Well, she's lost some fingers on one of her hands."

Phil's blood flushed through him with a burning heat. Some torturous bastard cut her fingers off?

"And apparently she found a doctor who bandaged it for her, but gave her a penicillin shot—"

"Penicillin! That'd kill her!"

"That's why she's in the hospital. She's okay now, she's still all swollen up, but for a while I guess it was touch and go. Her throat closed up and she went into shock."

"Can we see her?" Lari asked.

Carolyn looked as beat as Phil felt. "She's resting. I don't know about you guys, but I need to go to bed. Phil, you look like hell. Go home."

Phil needed no more encouragement than that. He stood up, opened the front door. Carolyn scooped Tina up and the big gray cat began to purr.

"Rocky shot the girl. Killed her," Lari told Carolyn.

Carolyn gasped, hugged Tina so tight the cat yelped.

"He shot the Leathers guy too, but I don't know the whole story there."

"We'll find out tomorrow," Phil said.

"Let's not tell Mom, okay?" Lari said. "Let's wait until she gets home. She needs to rest, and if she knows all that, well..."

"You're right," Carolyn said. "Let's let peace of mind flow through her right now."

Phil nodded. There was a time and a place to spread bad news. The hospital was not an ideal place.

He closed the door on them comforting each other and went home alone.

He showered, then slipped into Peaches' room. A sliver of light from the nightlight in the hallway haloed her fine, blonde hair. One thumb was in her mouth and her breath rasped in and out of a stuffy nose. He kissed his fingertip and touched it to her tiny ear. Then he went out, closed her door behind him and slipped into clean, cool sheets next to his warm, sleeping wife. He dared not touch her. Instead, he luxuriated in the feeling of bed. He willed his taut muscles to relax, and just before he drifted off, he saw the angry, crazed eyes of his son once again, and wondered what kind of a system God had made that had children perpetually, dangerously mad at their parents.

He thought of Peaches' soft ear and wondered if he had ever looked in on Rocky when Rocky was that age.

He couldn't remember.

Darlene awoke in her hospital bed to find Lari sitting in the chair at her bedside, her head dropped down and a thin strand of saliva connecting her lower lip to a dark spot of moisture on the collar of her shirt.

Darlene smiled.

The sun was not yet up; Lari must have been sitting there for a while.

Darlene took a quick inventory of herself. She felt pretty good, in spite of it all. Her hand was freshly bandaged, and an IV dripped steadily into her arm. She felt a little gritty, her eyes felt gummy and swollen as if she had spent the night crying, and she could use a shower.

"Hey," she said softly.

Lari started, then slowly raised her head. She wiped her mouth, rubbed her eyes, then rubbed the kink in her neck. "Hi," she said. "How are you?"

"I think I feel better than you look. How long have you been here?"

"I don't know. I got here about three, I think. I couldn't sleep. Are you all right?"

"Yeah. A little worse for the wear, but that's to be expected, I guess."

"We don't need to talk about it now," Lari said, "but I'd like to hear the whole story."

Darlene nodded, and tears bunched up inside like a sinus headache.

"Maybe we'll save it until we're all together and you can tell it all at one time."

Darlene nodded again, feeling her lips contract as she tried to hold in the tears.

"Don't cry, Mom," Lari said, and Darlene saw her daughter's eyes begin to puddle too.

Darlene nodded again. She swallowed, took a deep breath and regained control. "How is everybody? I saw Carolyn last night, although I don't think I looked so great."

Lari wiped her hands over her face. She looked down into her lap. "Everybody's okay," she said.

She's lying, Darlene thought. *I can always tell when Lari lies.*

"Dad's okay, he had kind of a rough time of it. He should be here fairly soon."

"Rocky?"

Lari fiddled with her hands in her lap. "He's okay, too." She bit her lip, then forced a smile. "He's thinking of getting married." The smile turned uncertain, then sad.

Married.

"Do you know about Molly? And Patrick?" Darlene asked, then held her breath. "And Leathers?"

"Everybody's fine, Mom."

Darlene knew the worst had happened, whatever the hell that might be. Lari was as transparent a liar as was ever born.

"Why don't you go home, sweetie, and get some sleep. I'll be okay, in fact, they'll probably discharge me today."

"Carolyn and I have been staying at your place with Ashes and Tina."

"Good. Go on now, get some rest. Everything's okay now."

"We were so worried," Lari said, and this time the tears spilled over her long dark lashes and landed on her cheeks.

Darlene stuffed her tears behind her anger. She knew that Lari probably had a good reason to lie to her, but she resented it just the same. Like the family telling a dying patient that she would be up and around in no time. She felt patronized, compromised and depersonalized. She felt old and of no use. A burden. The subject of family conferences. "Go home," she said.

Lari nodded, and stood. She wiped her cheeks again, then leaned over and kissed Darlene on the cheek.

"I'll call you when they tell me what time I can leave," Darlene said. "Maybe you can give me a ride."

Lari nodded, kissed her cheek, and walked out, her back hunched as if the load that had come off everyone's shoulders had resettled as one heavy lie on Lari. Darlene knew it wasn't Lari's fault.

Darlene also knew with concrete certainty that her kids didn't need her and she didn't need them, and she wanted to get out of this hospital and back to a life of her own as soon as possible. She was stupid to think that the kids needed her. They didn't need her—not for *her*. Perhaps they needed her for their own comfort level, but what about Darlene's comfort level? Children's comfort level for their parents was to relegate them to old age, convenient old age. Well, Darlene would have no part of it, not any more. She'd bought into that for too long. Leathers had awakened her, and she would not fall back to sleep again. She would not. She needed love and caring and passion, all those things that the kids thought they had exclusive rights to. Well, they did not.

Darlene dialed the IV drip closed, then gently pulled the needle from her arm, and got out of bed. Her red, swollen, bruised and textured tattooed leg glared obscenely in the white hospital room, next to the white hospital gown. She went into the bathroom, finger-brushed her teeth, then dressed in the same damned black pants and polyester shirt. Her face was still swollen from the allergic reaction to the penicillin, but it wasn't too bad. She ran her hands through her hair, and looked around for her possessions—of which there were none. Then she walked out of the hospital and into the early morning light of Springfield.

It was going to be a hot day. And she needed some answers. But where to begin?

Springfield on an early Sunday morning was as silent as the town gets. Even the air smelled fresh. The hospital grounds were expansive and beautiful with wide sidewalks. Darlene's freshly-bandaged hand throbbed as she walked toward home, trying to enjoy a little quiet time for a change, but those tight pants rubbed and rasped at the ball bearings and things under the skin of her leg. She tried to ignore it. She had plans to make. Property to dispose of. Relationships to reshape.

Could she make a life with Leathers? In that cabin?

Terrifying thoughts of him restraining her mixed with pleasurable memories of their lovemaking. She remembered his laser-like dedication to his artwork, to the exclusion of her feelings, her comfort, her fear and pain; she remembered his soft brown eyes and tender fingers smoothing her hair, touching her face, soaking her stitches. She remembered him talking her through the pain, introducing her to herself, to her limits, showing her the blue room, the way to deal with life's little tragedies as a whole, complete person.

There was so much wisdom in his one-day-at-a-time lifestyle. She could learn much.

She could teach him much. She could temper his strangeness. She could bring balance to his life.

Balance.

He could bring balance to her life.

Wait a minute, she said to herself. She stopped cold in the middle of the block in front of the closed bank. *He tied you down and mutilated you.*

Yes, that's how she ought to think of it, but somehow those words didn't fit together with the feelings.

He was an artist. He was creating. He had a right to be single-minded.

When was the last time she created something of beauty, of perfection?

When she created Rocky.

What if someone had wanted to interrupt *that* project halfway through? Would she have inconvenienced someone, would she have *tied someone down* in order to see her creation through?

Absolutely.

How dare she not afford him the same courtesy. He missed out on the children experience. Her body as canvas was his only opportunity at creating perfection.

And if she didn't resist, he wouldn't have to tie her down. They just needed to agree on a few boundaries.

Partner-hunger gripped her so tightly she could barely think of anything else. She had to get back to him before he gave up on her. He'd hurt himself, or declare her dead, or worse, he might replace her with the meter reader or someone. Good God, how could she have left him alone? He was like a child. He needed someone to care for him. He needed her. He needed her there now.

And she had something important to tell him. That sport on his

Mister Lincoln rose was probably a true mutant. The viruses, those were in tulips. She'd remembered that in the hospital.

Darlene's priorities clicked into place with a focus that she hadn't known since the children were small.

She ignored the throbbing in her hand which had spread to her head. She ignored the pain in her feet. It felt good to walk. She wanted to shower, change clothes, and then get back down there to reassure herself and reassure Leathers. He needed her and she'd been gone too long as it was.

When she turned the corner onto her street, her house looked familiar and yet like it already belonged to somebody else. Carolyn's car and Lari's car were in the driveway. Darlene remembered with a little smile how happy she had been to buy that house, how thrilled she had been to live in it, her own house, her own mortgage, her own independence, for the first time in her life. And now she was so detached she could move out tomorrow.

Which she probably would do. And put it up for sale. Take the money and run. She and Leathers could probably live for the rest of their lives off the equity in this little house.

She went in the back gate, around to the back steps. Tina was resting on a rag draped over the railing, paws tucked under herself as she sat in the early morning sunbeam. She stood and stretched when Darlene came through the door, meowed softly and held her head up for a scratch.

"You'll come with me, won't you, sweetie?" Darlene scratched the cat in all her pleasure spots and spoke quietly. Then she opened the back door and went inside the house. Tina jumped down and followed her.

Ashes danced so hard he growled when he saw her. She picked him up and he enthusiastically squirmed and wiggled and licked her all over her face. "Shhh," she said to him, not wanting to waken Lari and Carolyn. They were surely still asleep. The house was early-morning cool and silent.

Darlene could smell herself. She smelled like hospital and moldy clothes. She smelled like pain and sweat and the cabin. She took Ashes into the bathroom, closed the door and then petted him, played with him and talked to him in whispers about Burbank, his new brother, and how he was going to call her Rose from now on, and they were going to live in a very challenging place. And Burbank would have to have a bath, too.

Ashes watched her as if he understood every word. Then she took off her clothes, and at the risk of waking up the girls, she took a long, hot, luxurious shower, with plenty of scented soap and shampoo. She shaved under her arms and her legs, carefully circumventing the tattoo. She ran her soapy fingers wondrously over the magnificent artwork on her leg and thigh. It was healing but still swollen, and if she closed her eyes, she could read the outline as if it were Braille.

She remembered the pressure of his gentle fingers as he pulled at her skin. She remembered the buzz of the needle, the stinging chords of pain, the meditations. She remembered the delirium of the fever, the throbbing of her hand, she remembered his skin, so smooth and soft, his penis, so beautiful, so gentle. She paid special attention to soaping her crotch, hoping he would give her a nice welcoming home. Then she stood in the hot, steamy downpour, letting the water wash over her, cleaning away the hospital, cleaning away the angers, resentments, insecurities. She felt solid, centered and with purpose for the first time in many, many years.

She felt invincible.

The bandage on her hand was soaking wet when she left the shower, but she didn't care. Ashes was curled up on the tiny blue bathroom rug, and he lifted his little head and twitched his shiny black nose at her.

She dried herself slowly and carefully with a fresh towel, watching in the mirror as she did so. Her large dimpled thighs and buttocks weren't shameful any more. They were just exactly what they were. Fat. But they didn't have to be hated, or feared, and you know what? They didn't have to be fat any more, either. She lifted each pendulous breast and looked at it, felt it. She gripped two handsful of tummy skin. Yep, it could all go. It would all go. She didn't need insulation from life any more, she wanted to bring life as close to her soul as possible.

She rubbed antiseptic ointment into the artwork on her leg. In the bathroom lighting, with the mirror slightly fogged around the edges, her leg looked ethereal and spectral. It was a wonder. Phoenix plumage. The colors were brilliant; the hours he spent bent over it were awesome now that she thought about it. This was not a piece of art created in one day. This was a month or more of work compacted into a couple of days.

She ran a comb through her hair, plugged in the curlers. Then she unplugged the curlers and looked at them for a long time. She wrapped the cord around the unit and put it quietly into the trash can and got scissors from the drawer. Fifteen minutes later, she looked younger, fresher and ready for adventure. She fluffed out her short hair and let it dry.

Carolyn and Lari were still sleeping in the spare room, Lari snuggled up to Carolyn's back. Rose tiptoed into their room, got the suitcase from the closet. Back in her room, she dressed in a fresh pair of gray sweatpants and a t-shirt, threw all her underwear and casual clothes into the case, took the envelope of emergency cash from under the bed frame, snapped the suitcase closed and hauled it to the living room.

The living room. The television, the recliner.

The sight of it all made her queasy. It had been a nightmare, those years of sitting in that chair, watching that television.

She drank juice directly from the carton in the fridge. She saw a note there from the kids to call them if she came home. She took the note down and penned a reply on the reverse side. "Lari. Borrowed your car. Be back tonight or tomorrow. Mom." She petted the animals one last time, assured them that she'd be back for them, then lifted Lari's keys from the dining room table.

Phil stopped at the hospital gift shop and picked up some silk flowers and a tiny teddy bear for Darlene. As an afterthought, he also bought a pleasant, generic, say-nothing get well card for the guy who Rocky shot. He paid the woman and walked to the elevator, feeling old, gray-faced and leaden with fatigue and remorse.

He got off on the surgical floor and asked the nurse about the gunshot victim that had been brought in.

She gave him a raised-eyebrow look.

"My son shot him," Phil said, and couldn't believe those words came out of his mouth. He held up the get well card.

"Five twenty-seven," she said.

"How's he doing?"

"He'll probably go home tomorrow," she said.

"Good," Phil said.

The nurse pointed to her right and then went back to her paperwork.

Phil followed her direction turned down the hall.

Hospitals.

Phil had brief encounters with a variety of hospitals during his life. The birth of his kids, of course, a couple of childhood emergencies, one for Larissa, two for Rocky. One of his own when he burned himself lighting the barbecue.

Rocky, then about ten, had looked him square in the eye when he came home with no eyebrows and a heavily bandaged hand, and said, "You could have burned like a torch." Phil heard the words and agreed with him, laughing it off, but Phil also knew that Rocky would have enjoyed watching him aflame, running screaming around the yard. Rock would go stand over him after he'd fallen into a smoldering heap by the birdbath, the scent of juicy roasting flesh whetting the boy's appetite for dinner.

Hospitals.

He walked along the hall, trying not to look into the rooms, trying not to be nosy, wondering what had gone wrong with all these people that they had been turned to mysterious lumps and humps shrouded by white and diaphanous curtains, hooked to tubes and drips and beeps.

527. He knocked softly, then pushed the door open.

The bed by the door was vacant, sterile. The bed by the window held a mountain of a mound. His hair was as white as the pillow, his dark face a startling contrast. The head of the bed was elevated, and the television was on. One arm was casted and held straight out from the body with two steel rods, the other wildly colorful arm protruded from the threadbare polka-dotted hospital gown. At first, Phil thought he was wearing some colorful pajamas underneath.

He wasn't.

Deep brown eyes turned from the television to Phil, who stood staring in amazement.

"Hi. I'm Phil." He didn't know what else to say.

A smile began to line the huge man's face and Phil saw even, white teeth that matched the hair, that matched the hospital antiseptic white.

"She told me about you," Leathers said, his voice a hoarse gravel pit.

Phil didn't like the image that evoked. What was the relationship between this guy and Darlene? What had she told him? Did she confide the secrets of their bedroom? Did she tell him about Angela? Phil cringed inside.

"How are you feeling?"

"I'll heal." Leathers' eyes drifted back toward the television.

"Well, here," Phil said, uncomfortably, and he pulled the card from the little pink striped sack and realized that he hadn't signed it or anything. He started to put it inside the envelope, and then felt Leathers' deep eyes on him again and he wondered where the hell his glib tongue was. The easy banter that made him such a success in sales had left him uncomfortable and way out of his element.

He gave up and just put the card on the man's stomach, then moved it to the side of the bed, where it leaned up against him.

"I guess I didn't sign it," he said.

Leathers just looked at him.

"Well, listen, I just wanted to look in on you. The nurse says you're doing fine and should be going home maybe tomorrow. That's good news, huh?"

No answer. Just those eyes. If Phil had been a different kind of man, he could fall in love with those eyes. But now they made him nervous.

"My son's in jail," he said, his voice unexpectedly catching.

Leathers looked at the television.

Phil fidgeted for a moment longer. "Well, I'll be going. Take care, now." He turned and walked away, pushed open the silent door and went into the hallway. He was sweating, still that greasy, hangover, lack-of-sleep sweat. He felt like shit.

On the sixth floor, he asked at the nurse's station about Darlene's room.

The nurse gave him that same raised eyebrow. Did they teach that in nursing school? "Mrs. Darlene Martin?" she asked.

Phil nodded.

"Are you family?"

"I'm her husband. Well, her ex-husband."

The nurse looked down and smiled. She touched her hair. Phil had seen that preening gesture a thousand-thousand times. Usually it made him take a second look at whoever it was that found him attractive. This time it irritated him.

"Mrs. Martin is no longer here."

Phil wasn't sure what that meant. "Excuse me? She's been discharged?"

"No, she just left. Took her clothes and left. Early this morning."

"Was she all right? Was she—" Phil groped for words, but they failed him. He wanted to know if she was right in her mind.

"She hadn't been discharged." The nurse clearly got his message of disinterest. "I'm not a doctor." She went back to her paperwork, discharging Phil. Gone. Home, of course.

Phil felt his pocket, but of course his phone was still in the river.

"Can I use your phone?"

"Pay phone by the restrooms," she said without even looking up. "Just beyond the elevators."

Phil left the flowers and the teddy bear on the counter and walked quickly to the phone, fishing a quarter out of his pocket as he went. He dropped it in, dialed Darlene's number.

"Mom?" Lari answered the phone. Phil's heart sank.

"It's me, sweetheart."

"Daddy, she was here while I was asleep and she took my car."

"Did you see her at all?"

"I went to the hospital this morning; she was there then. She looked okay. Tired, still kind of puffy, but good. I came home and went back to bed. When I got up, there was a wet towel in the bathroom and a note on the fridge. She took my car."

"What did the note say?"

"That she'd be home tonight or tomorrow."

"Shit," Phil said.

"Daddy, is she okay?"

"I'm sure she is, honey. Sounds like she has something she needs to settle is all." Phil's guts churned, although he knew Darlene, and he really felt as if she would be all right. He just wished she would ask for help now and then instead of going off and doing everything her owndamnself.

"I should have stayed with her in the hospital, Daddy."

"It's okay, baby. Don't worry. She'll be back. You know your mom. She's all right."

"What about Rocky?" Her voice still held a tinge of that hysterical quality that wore him out.

"I don't know. I'll find out about arraignment and so forth. You just relax. You and Carolyn just try to enjoy your Sunday, and we'll all keep in touch about everything, okay?

"Okay."

"I'm going home to get some sleep now."

"Okay, Daddy. I love you."

"I love you too, sweetie." Phil hung up the phone and with heavy feet, walked to the elevator and pushed the button. Sometimes life was a goddamned nightmare.

When the elevator opened, two uniformed policemen, accompanied by Lieutenant Jenricks, stepped out.

Phil's body responded with a tense stiffening, as if he were guilty of something. Those damned authority figures. They were here to see

Darlene, he knew it.

Lieutenant Jenricks gave him a look, but Phil didn't bother to return it. He felt no obligation to tell them that Darlene wasn't there, he felt no obligation at all.

He nodded to them as they stepped out, and he stepped in. The doors smoothly closed.

The police were going to be disappointed. But not as disappointed as Phil. He'd like to sit down for an hour with Darlene himself. Barring that, he'd like to slide into bed for an uninterrupted ten. But that wasn't going to happen. He had to see to Rocky first, then go by and see the girls.

What on earth made him think that once the kids were out of the house that they would be out of his life? And what made him think that a divorce decree was going to cut the cord that bound him to Darlene?

Taken a step further, what made him think that a marriage license was going to give Phil-and-Angela what Phil-and-Darlene had?

It wouldn't have been a bad thing, he thought, *if Rocky had shot me in his moment of passion. That wouldn't have been a bad thing at all.*

He snickered to himself as he walked out of the air conditioned hospital into the heat of the day. What made him think that death would end all this?

Some big trucks had left deep ruts in the mushy ground. Someone had taken a chainsaw, or something, to the blackberry hedge that shrouded Leathers' house in privacy. As if to let trucks in.

Trucks?

Rose's heart pounded and her mouth turned dry and sticky. Pieces of yellow police tape flapped disconsolately on the ground. Don't know why they'd need to tape off the area, Rose thought. There weren't any neighbors to be nosing around.

The screen door hung on its solitary hinge, the front door was closed. She pulled Lari's car into the place where she had once, a million years ago, parked her little red Ford. She pulled in next to Rocky's truck. Rocky wasn't here, so why was his truck here?

She remembered riding in that other truck with that unwashed logger and seeing Rocky's truck pass by. It *had* been his truck. If she had taken Leather's easy going approach to life, if she had tried to understand him instead of fighting him, instead of pushing everything and trying to control it and make it go her way, Rocky would have come, picked her up and none of this weirdness would have happened.

No ambulances or trucks or whatever would have been coming through here. There wouldn't have been any yellow tape flapping in the breeze.

She got out and closed the car door. The place was silent. No, not silent. Birds talked, trees rustled and groaned, water dripped, moss grew, the earth drank. The cabin settled.

No smelly yellow dog came to meet her.

"Burbank?" she called, her voice an intrusion.

The sounds of nature paused.

Rose walked across the front, her tennis shoes squeaking with dew from the long grass before she reached the rose garden. It looked abandoned. She had been here only the day before, and yet some transformation had happened.

Leathers was gone. Leathers had left and with him went all the magic.

Weeds grew in the roses. The rabbit hutch doors hung open and the cages that yesterday were full of curious bunnies with their tall ears were now vacant and mournful. The wire door to the chicken run was open. There were no chickens scratching and clucking, laying and gossiping.

Someone had taken Leathers away, and because they thought there was nobody to care for the animals, they had taken the animals as well.

Rose felt like crying.

She walked back toward the front door, touching and smelling the dewy roses as she went. They were marvelous, even so.

If someone could take Leathers' animals away to care for them, perhaps she could dig up his roses and take them home. She could begin her rose garden with his genetic experiments. Perhaps she could even perfect that one he was working on. What did he call it?

Didn't matter. She might call it Leathers. Or Darlene. Or Darlene Leathers.

Jones.

She walked around to the front again, hating the sight of the yellow tape as it flapped everywhere in the trees and the bushes. She ripped it down with tears of anger in her eyes, and bunched it up next to her chest, holding it there by the clubby, bandaged damaged hand. Yellow streamers followed her as she went around the yard collecting the official trash. She wondered what had happened here. Something awful, she knew that. She looked again at Rocky's truck. Something so awful Lari had lied to her about it.

Carrying her tangled yellow bundle of police tape, she finally faced the front door. She held the screen open with her foot and turned the knob then shouldered the swollen door open.

It smelled different. It smelled like men's cologne, like chemicals. The delicate balance of the cabin had been disturbed, and it took Rose's breath away to feel it.

She dumped the police tape in the garbage sack by the refrigerator and looked around the room. She expected to see doughnut boxes and empty styrofoam coffee cups, but there was nothing to see.

Yes there was. Muddy wheel tracks from the front door.

She followed them into Leathers' studio.

And her heart died.

A hole in Leathers' big padded chair. Two holes, two small entrance holes that had blown stuffing out the back. Blood was smeared all around the holes and down the back of the chair, across the seat.

There was a big pool of blood on the floor, a big, black sticky stain, and in it were the discarded sterile wrappings of a variety of medical things.

Rose felt her knees weaken, and she sat down on the five-wheeled stool.

Someone shot Leathers as he sat in his chair.

Rocky.

Someone else called the police, but by the time the police got here, and an ambulance after that, Leathers would have had no chance of survival. None. Not if Rocky shot him at this close range.

Rose felt as if someone had punched her in the stomach. She felt a wailing grief rising up and out of her, and a noise escaped her mouth that sounded eerily like a wolf howling. Keening.

Then the tears came and she sobbed and wailed, mourning the good man Leathers had been, mourning her last chance at love. Rocky had stolen it from her. What business was it of his? It was unfair, unfair, *unfair*.

Eventually, the tears wore themselves out, and Rose went to the kitchen, filled a big pan with hot, sudsy water, and went to work on the blood. The chair came clean easily enough, except for the pieces of flesh imbedded in the hole which she had to pull out with her fingers. The rug was a total loss. With energy she didn't know she had, she moved furniture and rolled up the rug, dragged it through the kitchen and out the door, across the yard and then heaved it to rot amongst the blackberries. Then she went back in and mopped up the hardwood.

When it was as clean as she could get it, she washed out the pan, swept sweaty hair away from her face and tried to think what to do next. It hurt her head to try to think about it, and tears pressed close again.

She walked into Leathers' bedroom, which seemed exactly as she had left it. Maybe the police never even came in here. She kicked off her shoes, took off her clothes and slipped naked into the warm waterbed, smelling Leathers on the pillows, smelling their lovemaking on the sheets.

Rocky had stolen her life and Lari had lied to her about it. Who had asked them to interfere, anyway? They came here uninvited, shredded her life and left, going back to their own lives. Phil had gone to Angela, Lari to Carolyn, Rocky to his fiancée and there was nobody left for Rose. *There was nobody left for Rose.* A wail rose up and out of her. With pain as deep as the love she had once held for her babies, Rose cradled her soft belly with both arms and cried herself to sleep.

By five o'clock, Rocky had been bailed out and was sitting silently sullen next to his father as they drove to Darlene's house. Lieutenant Jenricks had released Angela's ten thousand dollars, and Phil had used it, along with a personal guarantee on his house as bond.

Rocky wished Phil had left him in jail. Now he felt indebted to both Phil and Angela. And where the fuck was Mom, anyway? She was what this whole damned thing was about. She was the reason he'd been in jail, she was the reason he was charged with murder, although he was pretty sure he'd get off on the temporary insanity plea, given the circumstances. Shooting his mother's kidnapper, the guy who cut off her hand? No problem. They'd let him off. He wasn't worried. But what the fuck had happened to her?

Rocky couldn't figure families. At least he couldn't figure his family. He wanted to move to northern Canada or someplace, so he wouldn't have to deal with any of them again. Except by long distance, and then only when he felt like it. They were a damned bunch of loonies—nobody talked to each other, nobody ever asked his opinion, nobody understood anybody else's opinion. Nobody even tried.

Mom had been okay, she'd been maintaining until Phil dumped her and married the pregnant little chippy. That's when Darlene's downhill slide escalated. That's when she became vulnerable and was just ripe for something like this to happen. And what did Phil care? He had his young skirt. And a baby, too, whether he wanted that or not. What business was it of his that his wife of twenty years was dying in a recliner?

What a horse's ass Phil was.

Rocky looked over at his father's profile. His hair, thin on top, graying at the temple, looked brittle. There were deep lines around his eyes and some slack puffiness at his jaw line. That face was as familiar to Rocky as his own, and yet he hated it with an intensity that frightened him. He wanted to put his boot right through that cheek. He wanted to feel fragile facial bones crunch. He wanted to see those glasses go flying, to shatter on the pavement. He wanted to crack open the top of that skull and see red and gray spill out. He wanted to watch nerves twitch and lips pull back in agony. He wanted to stomp on those delicate fingers that held the steering wheel and feel them crunch. He wanted to make his father wet himself. He wanted to make his father cry. He wanted to make his father humiliate himself, lose his self-respect in exactly the same way Rocky had lost respect for him.

Rocky's fists were clenched so tight his forearms hurt. His jaw hurt, his teeth hurt, his thigh muscles hurt. He felt like he was going to explode.

"Where are we going?" he finally asked, just to expel some energy.

"Your mom's."

"Why?"

"Because that's where Lari and Carolyn are."

"I'd like to get my truck."

"Where is it?"

"I don't know. Still at that place, I guess. At that guy's place. Unless the cops impounded it."

"Do you have the keys?"

"Yeah."

"Well, let's stop by your mom's and see what the girls are up to."

Just talking helped the tension, helped sate that hungry anger that wanted to snap indiscriminately at anything that moved, like a foam-jawed, rabid wolf.

He needed to do some pushups.

~ ~ ~

Lari hugged Rocky and held on to him. He felt strangely moved by her show of affection. Carolyn sat on the couch, her legs tucked up underneath her. She looked wounded, as if someone had stolen her dog.

When Lari let go of him and sat next to Carolyn, Rocky found himself shaky and close to tears. He sat on the floor and gathered up Ashes' fragile little frame and let him lick his face.

"Rocky wants to go pick up his truck," Phil said.

Rocky jerked as if his number had just been called. He felt it was inappropriate for Phil to say that right off. Shouldn't they talk about what happened down there or something? He made it sound as if Rocky couldn't wait to get back there to visit the scene of his crime.

Scene of his crime.

Obscene of his crime.

Obscene.

Obscene, that's what Phil was, with his flat statement to Lari, who was still red-eyed and weepy, and to Carolyn, who believed that the worst thing in the universe was personal violence.

So with no introduction, with no "this is what really happened there, girls," Phil announces that Rocky wants to go back down there, to the place where he shot that Molly girl dead, wounded the man—ugly, fat... talk about obscene!—and where his mother had been kept hostage for a week. That freak had held her hostage for a week and cut off her hand! Shouldn't we talk about this? What the fuck could Phil be thinking?

Rocky took a deep breath and let it out slowly. He looked down at the dog's wet nose twitching in his lap and he tried not to cry. He tried not to jump up and grab the bastard by the throat. He tried to calm himself, reassure himself that Phil had no idea, no idea whatsofuckingever. He had no idea what it was like to see half his mother's hand in a dog's mouth. He had no idea what it was like to see nothing but blinding rage, and feel the comfortable, powerful heft of that gun in his hand. He had no idea what it was like to be locked up in jail. He had no idea what it was like to have been bailed out by Phil and Angela, the only two people in the world for which he had not a glimmer of respect, and who now held the keys to his prison. Literally.

He had no idea.

Rocky breathed deeply.

Soon he felt hands, gentle hands, small, female hands on the back of his neck.

Carolyn.

"Just relax, Rock," she said soothingly. He tried. He felt her deft fingers poke into those painful hollows at the base of his neck, along his shoulders. They rubbed up into his hair along the spine, and down along the back of his shoulders, and down to the middle of his back.

The tears began to fall out of his eyes and land on Ashes.

"Just keep breathing," she said softly, but he began to sob and couldn't seem to stop.

She stopped rubbing him. Very gently she picked the dog up and put him on the floor, slid onto Rocky's lap and held him, rocked him, and he cried into her breast like a little boy with a broken heart.

Phil and Lari moved into the kitchen, where Lari started another pot of coffee. "Looks like it might be a long night," she said.

"You don't think she went back there, do you?" Phil asked.

"You mean to that place?"

Phil nodded.

"Why? Why would she go there?"

"Where else would she go?"

Lari wiped down the counter and thought about it. "I guess it's possible. But if she had to go back there, Dad, it was to settle something personal. We can't go get her. That would be intruding."

"What if we just went to get Rocky's truck? What if we didn't know she was there?"

Lari shook her head. "I don't think so."

"In the morning," Phil said. "I'll take Rocky there for his truck in the morning. And if she's there, well... She knows what happened there, doesn't she? I mean she knows about Rocky and Molly and that guy, right?"

Lari laced her fingers in front of her and wouldn't meet his gaze. "You didn't tell her?"

"She asked, and I told her that everybody was all right."

Phil shook his head. "That's why she went down there," he said. "She went to see him. But he's not there, so she should be back. She'll be back. She'll be back tonight."

"Revenge, you think?"

Phil shrugged, then shook her head. "She's not that type."

"I think something's happened to her, Daddy," Lari said.

"Like what?"

"I don't know. She's not the same. Her eyes look different."

"You saw her in the hospital, sweetheart. She had been traumatized. Hurt. That'd change anybody. But you'll see. She'll get home, settle in with Ashes and Tina and the rose garden and she'll be back to normal in no time. Back to her TV and her recliner and her soap operas. She'll settle right back. You watch." He held out his arms and she came close for a long hug.

The coffee pot dripped and groaned and they listened to it rather than listening to Rocky's heart breaking in the other room.

Rocky's voicemail was full of messages from Theresa, and she called again while he was listening to them.

"Rocky! You're home?"

"Yeah."

"You okay?"

"Yeah."

"You were on the news."

"Really?" This neither pleased nor displeased him. He felt empty.

"Yeah, listen, you don't sound so good. I'm going to come over, okay?"

"Nah, that's okay, I'm really tired. I think I'll just go to bed."

"I'll give you a massage. Don't say no now, because I'm coming." Silence. "Okay?"

"Yeah, okay, come if you want."

"Be right there."

Rocky put the phone down and wished she wasn't coming over. He wanted to be alone. He wanted to think. On the other hand, if Theresa was here, she could distract him and he wouldn't have to think.

He didn't know what to think. He didn't know what to think *about*, and if he *did* know what to think about—*Mom*, for example— he didn't know *how* to think about it.

He pulled a Pepsi from the fridge, popped it open, shucked his clothes on the way to the bathroom and stood under a hot, steamy shower spray, Pepsi in hand. When the can was empty, he threw it into the sink, then soaped up and washed his hair. Then he examined the ankle bracelet the cops had put on him. It would be a simple thing to cut that fucker off.

When he walked out of the bathroom, towel around his waist,

Theresa was pouring wine into two glasses in the kitchen.

"Hi, hon," she said, came over and kissed him.

"Hi." He was surprised at how pleased he was to see her. Life somehow felt normal with Theresa in his kitchen. He bypassed the wine and went for another Pepsi.

"Think you need more caffeine?"

He ignored her, snapped it open and drank it down, belched with obnoxious satisfaction, crushed the can and threw it in the garbage, hooked her finger with his and led her to the bedroom.

"Massage, you said."

She scooped up her glass of wine and let him lead her.

But the Pepsi kicked in about the same time Rocky got to thinking about his mom being back down at that dump with all that blood and all that stuff. All that nightmare stuff. All that pain, all that blinding red rage. Her hand... shit, maybe the stupid dog was still carrying her fingers around. The Pepsi kicked in about the same time he realized that Theresa's fingernails were too long and she was pressing too hard. Then he noticed that her skirt was off and she was pressing something else against his thigh; she had straddled his leg and was moving up and down, up and down, her breathing getting that rhythm that he knew too well.

"Stop it," he said.

"*Stop* it?"

"Yeah, I'm not into it tonight."

"I'm sorry, sweetie, of course you're not."

She said the words, but he knew she was disappointed. She flopped down on the bed next to him and trailed her nails lightly across his back, something he usually loved, but which irritated him tonight. He turned his face away from her, resisted the temptation to jump out of bed and... and tell her to leave.

She sensed his distance, sensed his agitation.

"Have a glass of wine, Rock. You need to relax. C'mere, let me give Smoky Joe a little kiss."

Maybe she was right. He rolled over and took her glass of wine. He sat up and drank it in one gulp, then held the glass up for more. She grabbed it and scooted into the kitchen, her tight little buns moving just right under those white cotton panties.

When she came back, she gave him his glass, knelt on the bed, sipped her wine, never taking her eyes off his, then slowly, gently, pulled his towel away.

Smoky Joe got longer and fatter and began to move as he inflated.

"That's what I like to see, sweetie," she said. "Now you just drink your wine and put your mind into the zone and let mama take care of her little baby boy here."

Mama. Baby boy.

Smoky Joe lost his appetite. All Theresa's coaxing and cajoling just irritated him further.

Rocky grabbed her face with his hands and pulled her up to him.

"Sorry," she said.

"It's not you. I've got things on my mind."

"Oh, of course you have, sweetie, being on the news and all. I'm sorry," Theresa said, and she started to coil the hairs on his chest.

He grabbed her hand.

"What?"

"I don't know, I just... maybe it would be better if you went home."

"I'll cook you some dinner."

"I'm not hungry."

"Well what then?"

"I need to think."

"About what?"

Rocky exhaled loudly. "Go home, Theresa. My mom was kidnapped, I've killed a girl, wounded a man, and I need some time to... you know..."

"Process."

"Whatever."

"I can help you. Here—"

"No, Theresa, go home."

"Rocky, if we're going to spend the rest of our lives together, we've got to go through the good *and* the bad together."

"Yeah, well, *if* is the key word in that sentence."

"Pardon me?" She moved away from him and sat up straight.

Fuck. "Listen, I just need some space right now, okay?"

"Sure," she said with exaggerated coolness. "Take all the space you need." She rolled off the bed, shimmied into her skirt, zipped it, fluffed her hair, slipped on her shoes, grabbed her purse, opened the apartment door, and without a backward glance, walked out without closing it behind her.

Fuck, Rocky thought. Women. He got up, wrapped the towel around himself again and closed the door. Then he grabbed the bottle of wine and swigged while he paced back and forth in his little apartment.

He paced and thought. Thought and paced. He thought about Phil, he thought about Theresa. He thought about his mother and that Leathers guy and that Molly girl and Lari and Carolyn and his fucked up life.

He thought about that monster and what he might have done to his mother, after what his father had done to her.

He drank and paced and thought and when the wine was gone, he got a half bottle of vodka from the cabinet.

He drank and paced and thought about Lari and Carolyn and what kind of a life they had. He drank and paced and thought about Theresa and what kind of a life they might have. He thought about kids and he thought about motherhood and fatherhood and he thought about a vasectomy. He thought about tattoos and he thought about scars. He drank and paced and thought until he couldn't do it anymore and then he picked up the telephone.

MONDAY

Rose's subconscious heard the front door open and her hammering heart jerked her up through the deep levels of sleep, to lie there, on the quivering bed, trembling, immobilized with fear. The house was dark and quiet, the pre-dawn light silhouetting the trees outside.

She was trespassing. She was alone, vulnerable, isolated. No one could hear her if she screamed.

Her heart pounded so loudly that she heard it echoing in the room. She could barely breathe, and what breath she had whistled in and out through her nose. She hoped whoever it was would get what they wanted and leave.

There was nothing to want. Burglars would find nothing, and they wouldn't stop until they went through the whole house. Vandals would trash the place and probably do damage to both her and the vehicles.

The car. She could make a run for Lari's car.

But where were the keys?

On the kitchen table, of course. What a dummy.

Maybe they'd just take the keys and the car and leave.

Heavy footsteps wandered around the kitchen. Only one set.

Maybe it was some friend of Leathers'.

That thought brought pounding new fears to her. Some other big, pain-oriented tattooed guy? And what would someone like that do with a naked woman in Leathers' bed?

Maybe it was someone coming to do harm to Leathers, someone who wouldn't even look before firing a few bullets into the lump in the bed.

Somebody like Molly's father.

She willed her frozen neck muscles to move and she looked

for something she could use as a defensive weapon. Wasn't there something heavy in here? Something. Anything.

Too late. Footsteps in the studio. Someone touching Leathers' tattooing tools. She heard them clink together on the tray. She wanted to scream. "Leave them alone! Don't touch them! They're HIS, not yours."

The cold, immobilizing terror began to warm up, began to heat into fear, and she knew that just beyond the fear was anger, pointed and deadly.

She heard him sit in the recliner, heard the crackling of the worn and cracked vinyl as it gave under his weight.

Then she heard him sigh.

A wheeze and a groan of discomfort.

Leathers?

"Leathers?" she whispered. *Oh God, dare she hope?* Then louder, "Leathers?"

"Rose?" The chair chirped as he got up.

Tears sprang to her eyes and she crawled out of the sloshing bed, and without bothering to cover herself, ran to the doorway.

He stood there, large as life, his left arm casted and held out in front of him.

In the dim light of the darkened cabin, she could see the glistening in his eyes, the way his beautiful hair was matted down on one side, the lines in his face, the sag to his jowls.

"Hi," he said.

She wanted to dance and laugh and cry and kiss him, but her body lurched to a halt. She stopped short of touching him. It felt as if her body recognized the person who had given it pain, hours and hours of pain, and it mistrusted him and held her back, even if her stupid emotions wanted to dive off the waterfall of love.

"Hi," she said.

His cast wrapped all the way around his chest, from his neck to the bottom of his rib cage. There must be fifty pounds of it.

"I'm tired," he said.

"Of course you are," she said, and felt suddenly shy about being naked in front of him. She stepped aside, grabbed one of his big shirts and slipped it on while he walked to the side of the bed. She had to undo his pants, then helped him down onto the bed, where he sloshed so heavily she was afraid the water mattress would burst under the burden. But it didn't. His casted arm stuck straight up. "Oh my," she said, "that can't be comfortable."

"It isn't," he wheezed as he turned and tried to find a position that didn't chafe. "I need more pillows."

She went into Patrick's room and returned with four limp, stained, coverless pillows. She got freshly laundered and neatly folded cases from Leathers' closet and dressed the pillows, then tucked them gingerly around his cast, supporting him in all the right areas. While she worked, she began to chatter in some nervous way that was completely foreign to her nature. "How did you get here? Did they let you out of the hospital so soon? Did you have surgery? How in the world did you get home? It's what, six o'clock in the morning?"

"I need sleep," he said. "Can't sleep in a hospital."

"I know," she said, slowing down, feeling maternal, smoothing the hair from his forehead, and she watched his eyes flutter closed and he immediately dropped into a deep sleep.

Rose smoothed the covers. "I'm glad you're alive," she whispered to him, then donned a pair of his drawstring terrycloth shorts and closed the bedroom door softly behind her.

She put the kettle on and made a cup of tea. Then she sat at the table with her gratitude and her confusion and tried to figure out the rest of her life.

The telephone rang, jarring the silence of Phil and Angela's bedroom. Phil had been dreaming. Dreaming about sleep. Precious, restful sleep.

"Phil?" Angela nudged him. She wanted the noise to stop.

He sat up and fumbled with the telephone. He looked at the digital readout. It was five forty-five. His alarm was due to go off in another fifteen minutes. "Hm? What? Hello?"

"Phil. Get up. Let's go."

Rocky. Phil cleared his throat, tried to unfuzz his tongue, although his mind was immediately clear and his heart hammered inside his chest. "Where are you?"

"Home. Come on. Let's finish this."

"Lari?"

"Pick her up, too. Come on."

"Yeah, okay, your mom didn't come home last night?" Phil wanted to delegate this entire project.

"No, she didn't. So let's go get her."

Phil sat up, rubbed his head.

"Forget breakfast," Rocky said.

Sometimes Rocky just went too far. Anger began to whoosh inside Phil. That same old anger.

"We'll grab something on the way."

The anger whooshed right on out again. Maybe the boy was making some progress after all.

"Okay," Phil said. He hung up the phone and looked over to see Angela looking at him. Her hair was fanned out across the pillow, her skin was rosy and flawless, her eyes a little sweet-puffy from sleep. He reached over and laid a hand on her warm, yielding breast. Urges stirred in him. He wanted to sleep in. He wanted to make love to his gorgeous young wife, then go back to sleep for a few hours. He wanted to make a little brother for Peaches and then cuddle Angela until next week.

But he couldn't. Rocky was waiting for him. And Darlene was... somewhere.

Phil felt so tired.

He felt young and horny and energetic when he thought of Angela and Peaches, and he felt old and used up when he thought of Darlene and Rocky.

Yes, Rock. Let's finish this.

Phil snuggled back down inside the covers for one last deep inhalation of Angela's sweet, early-morning scent. He pulled her to him and felt her nipple harden against his thumb. He felt his own reaction press up against her butt and he wanted nothing more than to slide right in there, taking advantage of her warm, sleepy willingness. Instead, he brushed her hair up off the back of her neck and kissed it. "I have to go," he whispered.

"What's happening now?" Angela asked.

He told her.

"Why would she go back there?"

"Women," he said. "Who can figure 'em?" Phil sat up, rubbed his face. He knew he looked like shit in the morning, with graying whiskers and puffy bags under his eyes. He grinned at her, but she just lay softly back into her pillow and pulled the covers up to her chin. "I'll get to the office by noon," he said, then got out of bed and into the shower, the memory of his office feeling like it belonged to the Phil of a different lifetime.

~ ~ ~

Rocky was pacing in front of his building when Phil pulled up. His eyes were still wild and his hands were shaking. Phil didn't like the looks of this at all.

Lari and Carolyn were drinking coffee on the front porch of Darlene's house when Phil pulled into the driveway. Lari got into the front seat and Rocky climbed into the back. Phil pulled away as everybody waved to Carolyn, still on the porch with Tina in her lap. They headed for the I-5 freeway going south. At Rocky's direction, he pulled off at a little cafe and they went in for more coffee and home-baked muffins. Phil felt hungry, but the muffin turned dry in his mouth and he had a hard time swallowing. There wasn't much talk. Nobody wanted to address the issue at hand; nobody wanted to say, "What do you think has happened to Mom?" or "Do you think Mom has gone crazy?" or "What are we going to do when we get there?" But that's what they were all thinking. Phil was thinking it and he knew by the look on their faces, they were thinking it too.

Finally, Rocky stopped tapping his spoon against his saucer and he spoke. "There's a syndrome," he said, "about people who fall in love with their kidnappers."

Lari made a face at him. "Mom's not falling in love with any kidnapper."

"You don't know that."

Phil had never seen Rocky jangling so hard.

"Of course I do. I talked to her. She's got her head on straight."

"Then why did she go back down there?"

"You don't know that that's where she went. And if she did, it was to get revenge, I bet."

The dry muffin turned to dust. Phil put it back on his plate, and noticed that the others weren't eating, either. "Let's go," he said.

They stood up as one. Rocky threw a bill on the table and they got back on the road.

Revenge. Nobody wanted to hear that word. This family was having enough trouble with the law.

Phil drove ten miles per hour over the speed limit, and still it took forever to get to the Curtin exit.

He sped through the little town, visions of rescuing Darlene at the crucial moment—before she'd done harm to herself or that guy—running through his head. But that guy was still in the hospital, and would be for a while. So what was she doing? Laying in wait?

Nobody spoke. He just drove, his sense of urgency filling the car with a zingy tension. Rocky leaned up against the back of the front seat, staring holes through the windshield. Nobody spoke, and he had a feeling that he wouldn't be able to hear anybody if they did have something to say.

"Here," Rocky said, putting a firm hand on Phil's shoulder. "Turn left here."

Phil slowed down, turned onto the rutted weedy path. They jostled across the field, and he saw the jagged hole hacked through the blackberries, and bits of yellow police barrier still stuck to the brambles.

He slowed even further and rolled quietly through the hedge.

Lari's car sat parked quietly next to Rocky's truck.

She was here.

Phil parked his car next to Lari's car, and turned off the engine. "Now what?" he asked.

The three sat in the silence of the ticking car and didn't move. Nobody wanted to know what was happening inside Darlene's head inside that cabin.

"You guys stay here," Lari said. "I'll go see if she's all right."

That was fine with Phil, but Rocky said, "No way." Then Phil too, had to open his door and walk with them to the front door of the ramshackle place. He couldn't imagine Darlene living here for ten minutes, much less a week. And come back to it? She had something in mind, that's for sure.

Rocky stepped up onto the sagging porch. "Be careful here," he said, and bounced up and down. The porch dipped alarmingly, and Phil knew it wouldn't hold all three of them at once. He held the screen door open while Rocky shouldered open the sticky door, and then they filed into the cabin, Phil bringing up the rear.

"I hate this place," Lari whispered.

"It's evil," Rocky said.

Phil just wanted to do a quick search and get the hell out. He stood in the middle of the kitchen, looking at the open doorway and felt like a trespasser. He couldn't bring himself to walk through that door, and it didn't look as though the kids were too excited about going any farther, either.

"There's nobody here," Rocky said.

And then, without warning, a voice spoke, an authoritative voice, a deep voice. It said, loudly, "Darlene?" As both kids turned to look at him, Phil found it had been his own voice.

Then Lari did it. "Mom?"

And Rocky. "Mom? Are you here?"

That was good. They could yell and holler and never have to go into the next room. They would not have to explore this wretched place, they could stay a certain length of time—maybe ten more seconds—and then they could each get into their respective vehicles and go on home.

That would leave Darlene—where?

With no car, no truck, no wheels.

Phil sagged.

Then they heard a sound. Footsteps. Bare feet on wooden floor.

Lari moved closer to Phil.

A door opened. Closed.

All three looked at the doorway, and in a moment, Darlene appeared there, wearing an oversized red and white checked shirt and a pair of orange faded terrycloth shorts that came down to her knees. Her hair had been hacked off short and it was roostertailed from sleep.

"Mom!" Lari said, but made no move toward her.

And then Phil saw a softness about her that he had never noticed before. An attractive, unattainable, ethereal softness. In the midst of this very strange scene, the woman he had been married to for over twenty years had suddenly become a complete stranger. A stranger to him, a stranger to his children. To their children.

"Mom, you okay?" Rocky said. He made no move toward her, either. He recognized the strangeness, the distance, too.

She nodded.

"Darlene, come on home," Phil said, his voice tight.

She shook her head, then ran her fingers through her hair. "What are you guys doing here anyway?" she asked, and Phil knew at that moment that they had lost her. Sadness opened in his gut and he fell right through.

"You took my car," Lari said, her voice catching.

Rose looked at her feet, nodded. "Oh yeah," she said. "I forgot. Sorry. You can take it." She pointed at the keys on the kitchen table.

Boundaries. She had never established boundaries with her kids, and this was her reward.

"You're not coming?"

"No."

"Yes you are," Rocky said. "Something's happened here, and you need to talk to somebody about it. You need to get out of here and get some distance. Come on home with us, see Ashes and Tina and get a little perspective."

"Some counseling, Mom," Lari added.

"Then if you want," Rocky continued, "you can come back... after a month, say."

Darlene laughed. Phil fell another two stories. She laughed so easily, as if what Rocky said was truly funny. Actually, Rocky sounded just like Phil.

"No, you guys go on. I'll come by one of these days."

"How? You've got no car," Lari was close to tears. She moved toward her mother. Darlene opened her arms for a hug, and moved in toward Lari.

That's when Phil saw her leg. His hand shot out and gripped Rocky's arm. Rocky pulled back violently like he was going to hit Phil, but stopped when he saw the intensity of Phil's stare. He followed Phil's eyes, looked at Darlene's leg and began to tremble.

Darlene's eyes locked onto Phil's while Rocky's gaze roamed her tattoo. "You guys go on home now," she said evenly and clearly, and then kissed Lari's forehead and pushed her back toward the two men.

"C'mon, Lari," Phil said.

"What the—" Rocky said. Phil knew with a bolt of empathy exactly how Rocky felt. Darlene was gone. She'd made some choice, and that choice was away from them. "No," Rocky said. "I'm not leaving here without you," he said, his fists trembling with growing rage. Dangerous rage.

He took a step toward Darlene. She took a step back.

"Go on home now," she said, backing up, backing away.

"He cut your fucking hand off," Rocky said. "Why do you want to be here?"

Darlene looked to Phil for support, but Phil had the same question.

"No, Rocky," she said, "You don't understand."

"I do understand. You've fallen in love with the bastard. It's the syndrome, don't you see it?" He turned to Lari. "See? Didn't I tell you?" She stared back at him with a horrified expression. "Didn't I?" He turned back to Darlene. "You're going to be here and be his fucking slave," he gestured at her leg, "his *toy* for God's sake, here, in this... this... this DUMP?"

"Rocky..." Darlene tried again, but Rocky had found his power and wasn't going to give it up.

"What's it going to take to wake you up, huh? What's it going to take to make you *see?*" He began to pace again, his gestures jerky, his eyes on the ground. "What if *I* tattooed you?" He stopped, looked at her. "What if I cut your *other* hand off? Would you come home with us then? Huh?" He strode to the kitchen cabinets, slammed open and shut some warped drawers until he found the cleaver, the cleaver that Patrick had used to cut up a stewing rabbit. Rocky held it up. "What about it, Mom? Would you be that loyal to me if *I* cut a few of your fingers off?"

Darlene looked to Phil for help, but Phil was immobilized.

"Rocky..." Lari said.

Rocky whirled at her, raising the cleaver higher. She backed away, cringing at the insane look in his eye.

Lari's cringing crystalized Rocky's power, his rage. He brandished the cleaver like a madman. "So *here* is the source of power in this sick fucking family," he said. "Maybe this is how I finally get some goddamned peace in life. I just hack you all to pieces and call the dog in to feast."

"That's enough, Rocky," Phil said, but his voice had turned weak and brittle. Rocky ignored him.

"What if I cut my *own* fingers off, Mom?" He seemed to like the sound of that. "Yeah. Hey, what if I cut my own fingers off? Then would you come home with us?" He pulled a chair away from the dining room table and sent it clattering across the room, then lay his hand on the wooden tabletop and brought the cleaver way up over his head for a good aim and a solid blow.

"C'mon, Rock," Lari said. "Don't be a jerk."

"Jerk?" he said, looking at her. "Jerk? Watch this."

"No!" Lari shoved him, changing the trajectory of the cleaver. He had never intended to cut his own hand, he intended to bury the cleaver in the wooden tabletop, but when Lari pushed him, the cleaver was already on its way down.

And it slammed down on his hand.

Lari screamed.

Rose closed her eyes and hung her head. She heard Lari and Phil rush past her to see to Rocky's hand, but all she felt was a pain in her heart so deep, she thought surely that cleaver had gone through it instead of through Rocky's hand. She stood silently, as the sounds and voices swirled around her, and she saw the pain in her heart. She saw its colors and heard its own sounds, and they were her sounds, not Rocky's sounds, not Phil's sounds, not Lari's sounds. Those people had become strangers. She knew her pain and she knew herself, and she knew that she no longer belonged to these people. She wanted to be with people who knew their own pain. She wanted to be with people who knew themselves.

Like Leathers.

Not these people.

When she opened her eyes, Phil was holding Rocky's hand up, wrapped in a blood-soaked kitchen towel. Rocky's face was white and disbelieving, and he looked at the bloody towel, then his eyes closed as he sank into Rose's captain's chair. The cleaver was embedded in the wooden table. Lari was talking to Phil and rummaging about for more cloths, but their voices were just sounds; they made no sense to Rose.

Rose looked at Rocky as if at a stranger, and as the last vestiges of the mother/son bond parted with an audible *snap*, Rocky's eyes opened and he and his mother regarded each other.

"Bottom drawer," Rose said to Lari without taking her eyes off Rocky.

Lari opened the bottom drawer, pulled out clean towels and bunched them around Rocky's hand. "I'm so sorry, Rock, oh my god, I'm so sorry."

Phil put an arm around him and got him up out of the chair and to the door. Lari followed. She held the screen door open for Phil and Rocky, then turned and looked at her mother.

Rose pulled the cleaver out of the table, and Rocky's four fingers lay in a row like little sausages. She pulled a plastic bag from a drawer, and dropped the fingers in it, one by one. Then she filled another plastic bag with ice cubes from the freezer and dropped the bag of fingers inside it. She held it out to Lari.

"You're really not coming?"

Rose saw tears on Lari's pale face. Lari's dark eyes looked large and red. Sunken. Haunted. Rose shook her head no, then jiggled the bag in a come-get-this gesture. Lari walked across the kitchen and took the bag, then set it on the table and wrapped her arms around her mother.

Snap. Rose hugged this grown woman who had been her

daughter, then kissed her cheek, the feeling of distance growing ever stronger.

"Please come?" Lari asked again. "We need you. I need you."

Rose shook her head. "I'm finished, Lari," Rose said. "It's my turn now." She picked up the bag of fingers and gave it to Lari, then crossed her arms over her chest and leaned against the counter.

"Okay," Lari said. "But you'll call? You'll come over? We'll see you, right?"

Rose smiled. Nodded.

Lari collected herself, picked up the plastic bag and her keys and walked outside. Rocky was sitting in Phil's car.

Lari walked over and leaned against Phil. He smoothed her hair. "She's not coming."

"I know."

"*I'm bleeding in here,*" Rocky whined.

Phil gave her a squeeze, took the bag of fingers, threw it into the front seat, followed it in, then stopped. "Be right back, Rock," he said.

"I need a fucking *hospital,*" Rocky said.

"I'll be back in a minute," Phil said, then pocketed the keys and walked back inside.

Darlene was mopping blood from the kitchen table.

"You're staying, then," he said. He wished he had something magical, something clever to say.

She looked up at him. He wasn't even attractive any more. His slick good looks had become cartoony. He was a total cliché.

"I don't know what to say, Darlene," he said, fumbling for words, "I wish things had been different. Lots of things. But, for whatever it's worth, I want you to know that Peaches..." Now it was his turn to choke on his emotions. He looked up at the stained ceiling and took a deep, open-mouthed breath and blinked back the tears. "Well, I'm going to try to do right by her. Maybe I won't be a total loss as a father."

Snap.

"Not that Lari is a failure... Hell, I don't even know what I'm saying."

Because you don't know yourself, Rose thought. *You've never, not even once, looked at your pain.*

Outside, the horn honked, startling hundreds of birds out of the canopy of trees.

"He's bleeding," Phil said.

Rose nodded.

"Well, bye. Keep in touch, okay?"

Rose nodded.

Phil stepped out onto the unstable porch and let the broken screen door slam behind him.

He got into his car, Rocky moaning and fogging up the window, Phil's guts churning over the stupid thing he had said to Darlene. *I'll do better next time. Sorry I fucked up your kids, I'll do better with Angela's.* Christ, what an ass he was.

He started the car. "I don't want to hear word one out of you," he said, "all the way to the hospital. If you start in, I'll make you walk. Understood?"

Rocky didn't answer.

"*Understood?*"

"Yes, yes! Jesus Christ, just drive!"

Phil started the car and backed up, then drove out through the blackberries.

Lari got into her own cold car, the early morning sunshine speckling the dew-covered windshield. She felt numb, and knew that she was just in shock. The pain would come, as surely as Rocky would soon feel pain in his finger-stumps.

She wanted to get home before the pain started. She wanted to get home, because once the pain began, she didn't know what she would do or how long it would last. She only knew that when the pain began, it would be bad, and she would be at its mercy.

Carolyn. Carolyn would fix it.

She followed her father's car out the hole in the blackberry hedge and wondered who in the hell was going to come back for Rocky's truck.

Rose leaned against the kitchen counter and listened to the sounds of cars driving away. Her family was leaving. She had sent them away. Severed the cords. A part of her wanted that hole in the blackberry hedge to heal closed behind them.

She closed her eyes, trying to define the feeling in her gut. It defied description. It was sadness. It was relief, and freedom. It was fear. It was excitement. It was calm. Divine calm. Ice-blue room calm.

She went back to mopping up Rocky's blood. She thought she ought to feel something deep and profound, cleaning her son's blood from the table, but she didn't. Rocky didn't belong to her; he never had.

The house did, and the animals, and she still had the kids, although their relationship would never be the same after this. Hell, *she* would never be the same after this. She wasn't even Darlene any more.

Someday, she would think about what to do with the house and the pets. She would think about getting a vehicle. Leathers would need to go back to the doctor fairly soon.

But not today, she thought, and smiled, because that's what Leathers would say. He was starting to rub off on her.

Rose rinsed off the last of the blood, threw the sponge into the garbage, washed her hand and sat heavily on the wrecked sofa. She closed her eyes and put her head back, relaxing.

She had decisions to make.

Didn't she?

Maybe not.

Darlene had always been the type of person who dealt with the situation at hand. She was never much for mapping out a plan of action and pursuing it. She went where the breeze blew her, and she

313

made the best of it.

What about Rose?

Rose was faced with two courses of action.

She could go home and begin a new life. She could lose weight, throw out the recliner, kill her TV, get a job, start dating.

It sounded good, but she knew she'd never do it.

Or, she could stay here and begin a new life. She could lose weight, there was no recliner or TV, this place had enough work to keep her busy and she wouldn't need to date, because she would have Leathers.

Leathers. A blessing and a curse.

But he was a sure thing. She wouldn't have to date, go through that horrible rejection ritual. And he had potential. She could help him over some of his weird obsessions. They could make a team, they really could.

She thought about the claustrophobic living room in Springfield, and she thought of the massive garden and peaceful solitude here in the woods.

Leathers, as he was, was better than nothing. She could turn him into something wonderful: a partner, a mate, a companion.

Decision made.

She went quietly into the bedroom. She pulled off the shorts and unbuttoned the shirt. She slid quietly into the warm bed next to her fiberglassed lover and warmed her good hand between her legs. As soon as she was bed temperature all over, she began to touch him, to feel him. His skin was so smooth, so velvety, so hot.

"I've been thinking," he said.

Rose didn't know he was awake. Had he heard her family drama in the kitchen? Of course he had. Had he heard the crackle of flames, smelled the acrid smoke as she calmly burned all her bridges?

Her fingers slid across his hip, his stomach, down to his penis, which remained limp and tender in her hand, as much a victim of his wounds as the rest of him. He would need time to heal. He would need lots of soup and love and time. She could love him, minister to him, tend him. She wanted to do that, she needed desperately to do that.

"Hmmm?" she said, continuing to explore his cast and his nakedness. She ran her unbandaged palm over the tops of his thighs, down over the tops of his knees. She scooted down under the covers and kissed his knees, then ran her hand lightly over the hairy shins, down to his feet. He smelled like the hospital. She rubbed the bottoms of his feet and felt his toes wiggle.

"Have you ever seen a black chicken in the sunlight?"

Rose smiled. "Not that I can recall," she said, her voice muffled by the covers.

"They're black and silver, but at the right angle, they flash green. The most beautiful green you've ever seen. Iridescent. Opalescent."

She nibbled on his little toe.

"A fabulous tattoo on your back. Three chickens. A white Leghorn, a Rhode Island red, and one of those black ones with the sun shining on it. Wondrous."

Maybe, she thought, thinking that the tattoo needle would feel good on her back. That contrast of the stinging needle and his soft hands as the two of them merged toward one purpose. Creating Larissa and Rocky took two people—probably all creative endeavors of value were brought forth by partnerships. Intimate partnerships. She liked the thought. She wanted to be a part of that.

But there needed to be boundaries. She will have to set boundaries for herself. For them. She wondered how he would take to that.

"The roses probably need to be weeded," he said.

"Um-hmm." She could do that. She loved working with the roses. She scratched her nails on the bottom of his feet, heard him gasp and he moved his feet as she tickled him.

"In a cage," he said. "The chickens will be in a cage. The brown one laying, the white one scratching, the black one crowing. Yeah, the black one will be a rooster, with long curved tailfeathers, and a wicked look in his eye."

She smiled and kept feeling him, kissing him as she went. She knew he needed sleep, he needed rest, but she needed to touch him, too. She needed to reassure herself of his presence, of the truth of him. And the more he talked, the more she could see the tattoo on her back as clearly as he could.

"The garden. The garden's been neglected."

She slid up and poked her face out of the covers, put her cheek next to his casted side. It was cold and hard, a studied contrast to his smooth, soft skin. "I'll take care of all of that," she said. "You just rest."

315

"I can't rest with you doing that to me."

Rose found that his parts were indeed waking up. "Yes, you can. Just relax. Visualize the sensations. See the chords of pleasure. Separate them. Concentrate on them." She scratched her nails lightly in his thick pubic hair.

"Patrick picked up my mail on Tuesday mornings," he said.

Rose burrowed under the covers and kissed his belly all along the edge of his cast. "I'll hijack a car," she said, then took his heavy penis in her hand and kissed it.

"Chickens," he said. "I love chickens. They'll be magnificent."

She smiled, picturing him visualizing his next creation.

His penis surged and for a moment, she thought it was because of her attentions.

"Oh, yes," he said. "And I'll use real chicken wire."

Rose paused in her ministrations. "Boundaries," she whispered, but she was the only one who heard.

About the Author

Elizabeth Engstrom is the author of sixteen books and many short stories, articles and essays. Her most recent novel is *Benediction Denied*, a Labyrinth of Souls novel, and her most recent nonfiction book is *How to Write a Sizzling Sex Scene*. Engstrom is an author, teacher, editor and former publisher who is a sought-after panelist, keynote speaker and instructor at writing conferences and conventions around the world. Her book *Candyland* was made into the feature film *Candiland*, starring Gary Busey, Chelah Horsdal, and James Clayton. Engstrom lives in the Pacific Northwest where she is always putting her pen to use for social justice, and working on the next book.

www.elizabethengstrom.com

IFD Publishing Paperbacks

Novels:

Of Thimble and Threat, by Alan M. Clark
Baggage Check, by Elizabeth Engstrom
Bull's Labyrinth, by Eric Witchey
The Surgeon's Mate: A Dismemoir, by Alan M. Clark
Siren Promised, by Jeremy Robert Johnson and Alan M. Clark
Say Anything but Your Prayers, by Alan M. Clark
Candyland, by Elizabeth Engstrom
Apologies to the Cat's Meat Man, by Alan M. Clark
Lizzie Borden, by Elizabeth Engstrom
A Parliament of Crows, by Alan M. Clark
Lizard Wine, by Elizabeth Engstrom
The Door that Faced West, by Alan M. Clark
The Northwoods Chronicles, by Elizabeth Engstrom
The Prostitute's Price, by Alan M. Clark
The Assassin's Coin, by John Linwood Grant
13 Miller's Court, by Alan M. Clark and John Linwood Grant
Guys Named Bob, by Elizabeth Engstrom

Collections:
Professor Witchey's Miracle Mood Cure, by Eric Witchey

Nonfiction:
How to Write a Sizzling Sex Scene, by Elizabeth Engstrom

IFD Publishing EBooks

(You can find the following titles at most distribution points for all ereading platforms.)

Novels:
Bull's Labyrinth, by Eric Witchey
The Surgeon's Mate: A Dismemoir, by Alan M. Clark
York's Moon, by Elizabeth Engstrom
Beyond the Serpent's Heart, by Eric Witchey

Lizzie Borden, by Elizabeth Engstrom
A Parliament of Crows, by Alan M. Clark
Lizard Wine, by Elizabeth Engstrom
Northwoods Chronicles, by Elizabeth Engstrom
Siren Promised, by Alan M. Clark and Jeremy Robert Johnson
To Kill a Common Loon, by Mitch Luckett
The Man in the Loon, by Mitch Luckett
Jack the Ripper Victim Series: Of Thimble and Threat by Alan M. Clark
Jack the Ripper Victim Series: The Double Event (includes two novels from the series: *Of Thimble and Threat* and *Say Anything But Your Prayers*) by Alan M. Clark
Candyland, by Elizabeth Engstrom
The Blood of Father Time: Book 1, The New Cut, by Alan M. Clark, Stephen C. Merritt & Lorelei Shannon
The Blood of Father Time: Book 2, The Mystic Clan's Grand Plot, by Alan M. Clark, Stephen C. Merritt & Lorelei Shannon
How I Met My Alien Bitch Lover: Book 1 from the Sunny World Inquisition Daily Letter Archives, by Eric Witchey
Baggage Check, by Elizabeth Engstrom
Death is a Star, by Christina Lay
D. D. Murphry, Secret Policeman, by Alan M. Clark and Elizabeth Massie
Black Leather, by Elizabeth Engstrom

Novelettes:
The Tao of Flynn, by Eric Witchey
To Build a Boat, Listen to Trees, by Eric Witchey

Children's Illustrated:
The Christmas Thingy, by F. Paul Wilson. Illustrated by Alan M. Clark

Collections:
Suspicions, by Elizabeth Engstrom
Professor Witchey's Miracle Mood Cure, by Eric Witchey

Short Fiction:
"Brittle Bones and Old Rope," by Alan M. Clark
"Crosley," by Elizabeth Engstrom
"The Apple Sniper," by Eric Witchey

Nonfiction:
How to Write a Sizzling Sex Scene, by Elizabeth Engstrom

IFD Publishing Audio Books

Novels:
The Door That Faced West by Alan M. Clark, read by Charles Hinckley
Jack the Ripper Victim Series: Of Thimble and Threat, by Alan M. Clark, read by Alicia Rose
Jack the Ripper Victim Series: Say Anything But Your Prayers, by Alan M. Clark, read by Alicia Rose
Jack the Ripper Victim Series: The Double Event by Alan M. Clark, read by Alicia Rose (includes two novels from the series: *Of Thimble and Threat* and *Say Anything But Your Prayers*)
A Parliament of Crows by Alan M. Clark, read by Laura Jennings
A Brutal Chill in August by Alan M. Clark, read by Alicia Rose
The Surgeon's Mate: A Dismemoir, by Alan M. Clark, read by Alan M. Clark
Apologies to the Cat's Meat Man, by Alan M. Clark, read by Alicia Rose
The Prostitute's Price, by Alan M. Clark, read by Alicia Rose